Striking of the Match

RENÉE ARONIS

DEDICATION

To my best friend, lover, and husband, Scott.
Thank you for being my rock, my sounding board, and my helper.
I love you!

Other books in this series:

Meet Your Match

CONTENTS

Part Two
The Other Side of the Pond

Chapter One

HOMEWARD BOUND

E rin March settled into her spacious, comfortable, first-class seat and tried to stay calm. Her emotions were being tugged in every direction as the events of the last five days swirled around in her mind. The heart-wrenching farewell only a few minutes earlier had been the most difficult to deal with.

She had been born with the Fertilis Defect, which caused unpredictable birth defects in only the female children whose parents had chosen to take the drug, Fertilis, to get pregnant. The symptoms always began at puberty when the girl started her first period.

In Erin, the disease inhibited the production of a surfactant usually found in the lungs; without it, her lungs would stick together, causing her to stop breathing for differing lengths of time. The 'episodes,' as they were called, happened every three to four weeks, though severe stress caused it to happen more frequently. The disease and its symptoms plagued her with extreme exhaustion and sucked her life away. Helplessness was a constant companion since, until recently, there had been no known treatments to give her any relief.

After twenty-seven years of suffering, at the age of thirty-nine, her doctor had informed her and her husband that the only treatment for her symptoms was sexual intercourse with a man, a stranger, with whom she was medically matched. It still seemed impossible to her that her match was David Elliott, the forty-five-year-old, tall, handsome, Scottish actor known for his role in her favorite TV program, *Future Explorations*. She had just spent the most amazing week with him in New Orleans, where they'd fallen head over heels for each other. Now, it was hard for her to fathom returning to her ordinary life in Green Bay, Wisconsin.

She stared at the wallet-sized photos of David and her, taken the night before. He had somehow managed to have them printed and then slipped them into her purse without her knowledge. She had found them moments earlier when she'd dropped the engraved gold locket her husband Todd had given her into it for safekeeping. Digging the necklace out again and putting it on crossed her mind, but her heart wasn't in it. Her heart was attached to the antique compass pendant from David she was wearing and taking it off was too difficult to imagine just then.

After the distressing morning she'd had, she wanted to sleep, but her mind was too anxious. *This is so hard! How am I going to deal with it and with… Todd?* The only thing she wanted to do was think about David making love to her, snuggling with her, talking about their lives, and walking around aimlessly together.

All she had to occupy her mind was the *Inflight* magazine and whatever was playing on the movie list. None of it interested her, so while looking out the window at the tiny landscape below her, she pulled up the silver chain around her neck and felt the cold, smooth compass in her hand. *David, I miss you!* she thought and then remembered she had planned on thinking about Todd instead.

The first leg of her flight made good time with no delays. After that, she had a two-hour layover in Atlanta, so she walked around for a bit and then sat in the VIP lounge that her first-class ticket afforded her. *Thank you, Tina!* she thought since it was David's assistant who had rescheduled her flight after the airport shooting, and then her episode had allowed them a few more days together. While waiting for her connecting flight, she half-heartedly flipped through a few uninteresting magazines while sipping a welcome glass of Moscato.

During the second leg of her journey, she watched David's newest movie, *Houlihan's Flat*, and enjoyed it a lot. She cried at the sad parts and laughed at the funny ones. Watching David on the screen in front of her was strange. She'd gotten to know him so well, but it was like he was a completely different person. There was a disconnect that allowed her to watch without distraction. She wondered if it was because she hadn't known him when he'd filmed it and if it would change for future films he'd be in.

It was 10:15 pm when she stepped through the sliding glass exit doors of Austin Straubel Airport and into the chilly night air. *Damn this midwestern weather!* she thought indignantly, as her jacket was in her luggage, and she was in short sleeves. Hoping to find a ride home quickly, she hurried toward the line of idling taxis and saw the driver who had brought her there the week before. Shivering, she waved and stepped up to the white minivan.

The older man smiled at her in the rearview mirror as she got into the back seat. "Hello there! You got a nice tan wherever you went," he said cheerfully.

"Hello again; am I that dark?" she asked as she got settled into the thankfully warm taxi. It was no luxury vehicle, but it suited her just fine. "I was in New Orleans; it was over eighty degrees there when I left."

He whistled and shook his head. Everyone longed for warm May weather in Wisconsin, though they rarely got it. "Back to where I picked you up from?" he asked as he pulled away from the terminal.

"You remember my address from a week ago? I'm impressed!" She was amazed he remembered *her*, let alone where she lived.

"Sure do; I've always liked the name Whistlers Way—I can't tell ya why, but it's a great name for a street, don't you think?"

Erin recalled David saying as much a few days earlier and smiled. "Yeah, I do." She opened her small, carry-on suitcase and had to suppress the urge to cry once more when she saw the neat stacks of clothing David had folded for her. *Thank you, David.* Trying not to disturb the contents, she took out her jacket, put it on, and zipped it up.

It wasn't long until the driver pulled up to the curb in front of her ranch-style, red brick house—the house where her husband of almost fifteen years would be waiting for her. She hadn't told him what time she'd be back and couldn't warn him since her cellphone had been stolen in a mugging while she'd been with David.

She fished her house key out of her purse and tucked the compass pendant back into her top. "I'm really sorry, but I have to run inside to pay you. My money was taken, so—" she said, feeling embarrassed.

"I can wait, no problem," he said with a smile.

She tried to psyche herself up for the frigid blast awaiting her when she opened the car door. It didn't work, and she shivered as she hurried to the side door and unlocked it with cold, shaking hands. When she'd left for New Orleans, she'd been glad to see how warm it was getting in Green Bay. That night, however, she cursed the winter, though it was already technically spring. The door finally opened, so she rushed through the small breezeway and into the kitchen. All the lights were out, except for the nightlight in the guest bathroom.

She opened the build-in desk drawer and snatched the grocery money. On her way back out, she grabbed Todd's jacket and hastily put it on, then she ran to the taxi. After thanking and tipping the driver, she sped back into the house, longing for the warm electric blanket on her bed where she could escape the chill she felt all over her body.

The door to their bedroom was ajar, and she could hear her husband, Todd, breathing as he slept. She didn't want to wake him but knew if she slept in the spare room, he'd be upset, so she tried to be as quiet as she could. The door opened silently, and she tiptoed to her side of the bed.

Erin placed her suitcase under the window next to her bedside table, seeing only by the moonlight streaming through the cheap, plastic mini blinds. Her compass necklace went into the pocket of her capris, and as she got undressed, she laid her clothing on the small, antique upholstered chair next to her dresser. She clicked on her side of the electric blanket and slid between her blue toile sheets. Though she tried not to disturb him, Todd woke right away.

"Erin?" he asked sleepily.

"Go back to sleep," she said, desperately wanting to avoid a long conversation. Instead, he sat up and clicked on the bedside lamp, causing her to squint and shield her eyes until she became accustomed to the brightness. "Why did you have to do that?"

"You've been gone for a week; I want to look at my wife," he said. "Wow, you must have spent a lot of time outdoors! You're as dark as—I don't know—" he said with a laugh, "something dark—toast, maybe?"

She had to laugh with him. "The taxi driver said the same thing. I used sunscreen every day, too," she said, wanting to look in a mirror yet wanting to be warm under the blankets more. "Lay down; it's cold in here." She was shaking with cold, so he turned off the lamp and snuggled up to her. His warm body felt good against her goosebump-peppered skin.

"I missed you so much," he said, wrapping his arm over her chest and his leg over hers.

She could feel him becoming aroused as he pressed himself against her. *Already?* she thought. *You can do this, Erin.* She relaxed and thought about David touching her, imagining it was him cupping her breast in his hand and kissing her shoulder. There was no feeling of electricity between them, so her body wasn't responding as it had with David, but as long as the light was off and he didn't say anything, it would be okay.

"I want you so bad!" he said, desperately.

She held her breath, trying to conjure David again, and allowed Todd to roll on top of her. *Just do it and get it over with.* She closed her eyes and waited as he kissed her and rubbed himself on her belly, which was his habit. At last, he entered her, and she gasped, not because it felt good but because she was sore from all the lovemaking of the previous week.

It was plain old sex, the same as it had been with him for the last fifteen years. She went through the motions, making the same noises she usually made, and then it was over. He got out of bed right away like he always did to clean off in the bathroom. She lay there, wanting sleep to take her back to New Orleans and the warmth of a bed with David Elliott in it. *This is gonna be much more difficult than I thought it would be.*

Chapter Two

DAVID ARRIVES IN LONDON

David Elliott made it through the flights and airline food well enough and was back in London before noon on Wednesday. He hired a car to pick him up and waited on a bench outside the terminal with his head down. Being a relatively well-known actor, he didn't want to be recognized. He ached to send Erin a message but wasn't sure how long it would take for her to replace her stolen phone and didn't want her husband to see it. *Bullocks! I should've given her some money tae pay for it,* he thought, still feeling a bit like the mugging was his fault.

A sleek, black BMW arrived for him, and as he got into the quiet darkness of the back seat, he could finally breathe again. He was relieved to no longer be on guard under the ever-watchful public eye. He stretched out his long, aching legs and waited until he was home again, having no idea what to expect when he arrived.

Nobody in his household knew when to expect him, so he hoped the house would be mostly empty, though it rarely was. There was always some hired person doing something somewhere; that is until his wife, Susannah, sacked them, then he had to learn new names and get used to unfamiliar people invading his privacy. There was no walking around the house naked as he had done with Erin in New Orleans. Just thinking about her brought him out of the London noise and traffic and into a peaceful state of mind. His breathing slowed, and he realized he was smiling.

The driver stopped a few doors away from his house, and David stepped out into the fog and gloom of a London day in May. Once the car was out of sight, he walked through the gate and up the five steps to his front door, then used his key to open it. Slowly, he entered the foyer, relieved to find that all was clear.

He didn't see or hear anyone nearby, so he climbed the stairs to find refuge in the small, dark, though mercifully private, spare bedroom. He'd transplanted himself there after agreeing to host a Fertilis Defect charity event, which had been the catalyst for him signing up for the Registry and led to being matched with Erin.

He touched the light switch, entered the room, and saw a pile of photographs on the bed. *Where did these come from?* he thought and closed the door before nervously picking them up. The very first one showed him kissing Champagne's hand. He grinned, remembering the drag queen they'd met on their first night together. Erin was sitting at the small table, smiling in his direction. *How did Susannah get these? So that's how she knew about us! I knew et; someone **was** followin' me!*

The second shot was of Erin telling him how much she wished she looked more like Champagne. The third was of him taking a knee in front of Erin on Bourbon Street. The fourth featured Erin yelling at the sodden bride-to-be, who'd caught him off guard when she unexpectedly copped a feel. The image showed him on his knees; he could barely make out the look on his face and grimaced at the memory of the pain.

The fifth photo was of their first kiss; he closed his eyes, remembering how much he'd longed to do it. If Susannah had thought to shame him by leaving the pictures there, it wasn't working. The sixth image was of a deeply passionate kiss in the empty, moonlit French Market. *Oh, God! I wish I were there with her right now!* he thought desperately.

The seventh image was of him and Erin in front of the silversmith's shop when she'd suggested eating at the Chartres House. The photographer had caught a real moment with his lens as they gazed at each other. He'd slipped out to buy her the compass pendant during their meal that day. There were a hundred feelings in that one picture, and he wanted to have it framed.

It was then that it dawned on him; someone he knew had paid to have him followed with photographs; someone who knew how to get them to Susannah, but whom? *I could make a fairly accurate guess! Ma Losh, At least I was careful not tae do anathin' terribly incriminating outside of the cottage—except for the one—time—*

The eighth shot made him stagger back and sit hard in the armchair next to the bed. *How'd they come by these?* There was Erin, laid out on his lap, robe opened, his hand on her beautiful ass; he could still remember the feel of her soft skin. It was a lovely picture to him, but he knew it would make a great cover photo for a tabloid as well.

He slid that one away, dreading what would come next, and rightfully so. There he was, standing behind Erin, his cock exposed to the world. In the heat of the moment, he had cared very little whether anyone saw them or not, though, evidently, someone did. Now he cared quite a lot as he held the 5x7 glossy print in his hand. The last two showed him with his hands on her hips, plainly having sex.

"Fuck!" *The look on ma face in the last one! This is horrible—sickening—If ma bairn were tae see these—Ma Losh! What've I done?* He put the photos in the nightstand drawer and paced the room, knowing Susannah, and most likely Martin, had seen them all. "FUCK!" he said again, quite loudly, not knowing what to do next.

David half expected Susannah to confront him, but she didn't. He hardly saw her for the first day, and when he did, she didn't stop to acknowledge him. On day two, he saw her in their bedroom and stepped in. "Susannah, we need to talk," he said, using his Received Pronunciation accent, as he knew she hated his native, Scottish one. She ignored him and entered her large, walk-in closet. "Don't walk away; it's important."

"Whatever do you mean, David? I'm busy, why don't you come back later?"

"Come back—I'm no' comin' back," he said, his accent returning with his aggravation. "We need tae discuss what's tae be done—"

"About what? If you want my opinion on what needs to change around here, then I think Kitty should be sacked and two others should take her place. We must also completely renovate the study; it's entirely too—"

"Are yeh takin' the piss? I'm talkin' about us. Yeh can't pretend everathin' is—"

"*Really*, David. If I came to you wanting to talk about each time—Well, never mind. I forgive you, now let's move on. Which do you prefer?" she asked, holding up two hangers with identical skirts on them.

"You… forgive me? I dinnae want yer forgiveness. I want a divorce!" he said.

"On the contrary, darling, you do *not* want that. You only believe you do because that big girl has taken your fancy. Eventually—"

"I want a divorce."

"Trust me, David, you do not. You would be quite sorry if you were to pursue that course of action, darling."

"Is that a threat? And what might you do, then? Show those pictures around? Go ahead, Susannah. I find them beautiful, and I dinnae care who else sees them."

"Is that so? Good, then I'll be sure to hold a family meeting as soon as the children arrive tomorrow. I'm sure they will be thrilled to see them," she said and began taking her clothes off. "Now, I must change. Are you going to stand there and watch, or would you prefer to help?"

David was seething; he couldn't think he was so angry. "I'm no' comin' anawhere near you, yeh—" he said, not finishing his thought. He left the room, frustrated and furious.

Chapter Three

ERIN'S FIRST MORNING AT HOME

In the morning, Erin woke feeling disoriented. She rolled over in bed and lay her hand where David would have been, only to find the space empty. She opened her eyes and saw her blue and white toile sheets; they smelled of Todd. His pillow still bore the indent of his head, though he was already up and getting ready for work. She rolled onto her back and then sat up on the edge of the mattress. There were her clothes, laid out on the chair, and her luggage, right where she left it.

She stood, lifted her suitcase onto the bed, and opened the top flap. When she'd thought she was leaving on Sunday, she'd thrown everything into it willy-nilly, figuring she'd take care of it all when she got home. It had been a surprise to learn in the taxi that David had folded everything for her as she recovered from her episode. She didn't want to disturb it; she wanted his touch to remain on everything. She even bent down to take a deep breath, hoping to find the lingering scent of him and New Orleans.

"What are you doing?" Todd said, making her jump.

"Todd! You scared me half to death! I didn't hear you," she said, breathing heavily as her heart raced.

"Obviously," he said, smiling, then he approached her, bent over, and sniffed. "Hmm, smells like dirty clothes to me."

"These are clean," she said dryly. "I was just going to—"

"Here, let me help." He unceremoniously grabbed one of her shirts off the top of the neatly folded pile.

"Stop!" she exclaimed, angry at his intrusion. "I'll do it." She took it out of his hand and laid it over the suitcase, hoping he'd get the message that she didn't want him to touch anything else.

"Sorry, just trying to help," he said and raised his hands in surrender. "I know you must be tired after your trip home."

"I'm fine. I'll put it away later; I was just getting my toothbrush." She was feeling irritated and couldn't hide it. She removed her toiletries bag and walked to the bathroom. He followed, lingering behind her as she stood in front of the sink, then he wrapped his arms around her middle and lay his chin on her shoulder. *Just go to work,* she thought.

He looked at their reflection in the mirror and smiled. It had come to the typical time when 'How was your trip?' might have been said, but neither of them wanted to get into that yet. She tried her best to smile back at him, but she wanted to be left alone and was getting frustrated.

She unzipped her small, black leather bag, extracting her toothbrush and toothpaste, hoping he'd stand back a little. Then, she went about brushing her teeth as if he weren't there, wanting things to be normal between them again but feeling smothered. He watched her through the whole routine, and it made her uncomfortable.

"I'm about to leave for work," he said at last and then hesitated, "…unless you want me to call in? I could—"

"No, it's okay, you go on to work. I have a lot to do today," she said, which was true.

"Is… everything alright, Erin?" he asked, frowning.

She was being short with him, but she didn't want to chat or have him hovering over her anymore, so she turned around and kissed his cheek. "Everything is fine. I need to readjust to my surroundings, that's all. As I said, I have stuff to take care of today, and my mind is preoccupied. Don't worry and have a good day. I'll see you when you get home."

He walked out of the bathroom and back to her suitcase, gently lifting her shirt again. She watched him, ready to get angry. He laid it on the bed and reached in, gingerly picking up her fancy bra by pinching one of the straps with two fingers as though it were dirty, and he didn't want to get the filth on his hands. His gaze betrayed the sadness and suspicion he was going through.

She took a deep breath, went to him, and took it out of his hand. "I brought it to wear with my dress," she said, and he looked at her like a wounded puppy. "Todd, I don't know what to say. There are things you're gonna have to adjust to. I can't give reasons for everything I do."

He sighed and kissed her cheek. "I know, just please be patient with me. My heart feels like raw meat right now. I'm sorry if I seem needy, but... I suppose I am," he said and walked out of the bedroom.

Relief washed over her when she heard the kitchen door slam behind him as he left. She should have felt contrite and sympathetic to his emotional state, but she simply couldn't. Her feelings would surely return, but it would take time, and she hoped he would be patient with her, too.

Her plan was to take a *quick* shower, but she missed David and longed for his touch on her body. As she spread the soap over her skin, she took her time, imagining it was him caressing her. *How am I going to make it for two weeks without him?*

She shaved her legs, rinsed off, and wrapped herself in one of their oversized bath towels, remembering the inadequate one she'd tried to cover herself with on the morning of the bikinied woman. She recalled the look of humor in David's eyes when he'd walked in and saw her. Then she'd gone and made a mess of everything by calling him 'honey.'

Why do you always ruin everything?

Not wanting to relive that horrible day, she shook her head, feeling like an idiot again. She got dressed and then slipped the beautiful, antique compass necklace over her head. Its cool, weighty metal felt soothing against her skin as she dropped it into the top of her blouse.

Her suitcase could wait till later, so she zipped it up and returned it to its temporary spot under the window. She walked out to the kitchen to pour herself a cup of the coffee Todd had made and noticed a note next to her favorite mug that read, *"I love you, and I'm so glad you're home. ~ Todd"*

Erin drove to her cellular phone provider, told them what had happened, and within half an hour, she had a new cell phone. Her hands trembled as she typed David's private mobile number into her contact list. The cash register receipt he'd written it on revealed his neat penmanship, and like a teenager, she pressed it to her heart, then typed:

E: *I'm home. I'm safe. I have a new
phone, and I miss you.*

She hit send but got an error, so she fumbled to find the International Dialing Code for Great Britain, and her heart pounded in her chest with the anticipation of talking to him again. That time the message went through, and she watched the screen, hoping to see the three dots dance at the bottom, telling her that he was replying. She waited much longer than she meant to, trying not to be discouraged or allow her fears to overtake her.

Did he also have sex with his wife last night? Is he coming to his senses now that he's home, and is he having second thoughts about his feelings for me? Is he looking back and cringing over the things we did and the words we said to each other?

When she got home, she brought the mail inside and sat on the living room sofa, looking through the thick stack of bills and ads. She leaned back and was about to close her eyes when she saw her collection of Pop Vinyl figures. She stood, went to the curio cabinet they were displayed in, and opened the door.

Right in front was her favorite one; the first Pop Vinyl she'd ever gotten and the one that meant the most to her. It was of David's character on *Future Explorations*, John Thomas Fife. She picked it up and looked closely at it, still not believing she'd met him or that they were—in love with each other.

Yeah, sure, her mind chimed in, *he loves you after knowing you for a week? You're kidding, right? Are you sure he wasn't just saying that because you said it first?*

But... I didn't say it first... did I? He did... didn't he?

*No, **you** did with your 'I think I'm starting to have... feelings that may turn into love for you,' or whatever stupid thing you said to him after the attack. **You*** *put it into his head, you idiot, and now that he's away from you, he'll regret saying it. Just you wait.*

At lunch, she finally got her reply and her heart leapt into her throat.

> D: *Hiya, beautiful. Your message has brightened my day. I miss you completely. I can't stop thinking of you. Nine days? Feels like forever!*

Her heart was thumping heavily in her chest as she read and re-read his words. She had to do a doubletake at first. For some reason, she'd imagined he'd text using his accent; however, on second thought, it made more sense that he didn't.

> E: *Oh, David! Thank you for replying! I was afraid you might not. I mean…I'm sure you're busy and I don't want to bother you or anything. I also don't want you to get in trouble with your wife.*

The dots rolled like an inchworm with his imminent reply.

> D: *Bother me? Never! And don't worry about her, though I did consider the same for Todd. Does he read your messages?*

> E: *No, I don't think so. I keep it with me all the time. I miss you even more than I realized now that I'm talking to you. Nine days is so far away!*

D: *How do you feel? Can you tell if it's working now? I admit to being worried you'll have an episode while we're apart, and I'll not be there to help you.*

E: *Don't worry about that. If, God forbid, it doesn't take, it'll be three weeks or so until I have another one. I feel amazing! I have energy, and it's been a long time since I could say that. I wish I could thank you in person.*

D: *And how would you do that?*

She gasped at the ideas that sprang to her mind.

E: *Well, I'd probably stand in front of you…on my toes. I might put my arms around your neck and then…*

She smiled, hoping a few seconds of waiting would increase his anticipation.

D: *And? Don't leave me hanging!*

E: *And…I'd lean in close…*

D: *And? You're driving me mad, woman.*

E: *And I'd put my mouth…*

D: …

E: *To your ear and whisper... Thank
you.*

There wasn't a quick reply that time. She waited, but the line of dots remained hidden.

E: *David?*

Silence.

While she waited, she opened Facebook and decided to share her selfies with the exquisite drag queen, Champagne, publicly. She longed to be back in the Big Easy with David—only a short walk away from her new friend and the remarkable French Quarter. Eventually, it became clear that he wasn't going to reply, so she scrolled for a while and then decided to take a nap.

That night, Todd was very touchy-feely with her. He kept putting his hands on her waist and kissing her shoulders as she made their supper. It didn't bother her too much, except she knew it would lead to him wanting more, and she was having a hard time with that.

"I want to make love to you, Erin," he said as she was setting the table.

"I know, honey, but... I'm pretty tired," she said, not wanting to say no, yet hoping to get out of it somehow.

"Please, don't push me away. It seems like—"

"I'm not," she lied, feeling guilty. "I'm just tired." The truth was that she was beginning to feel better than she had in a long time, but she hid it from him so he wouldn't ask her for sex. "I'm sorry, but it's harder than I thought it would be to go back to normal. Please, just give me more time." She hoped trying to be open would help.

"Okay," he said and left it at that.

During supper, her phone buzzed four times, making her heart jump and her stomach drop with each one. She ignored it, knowing that if she looked,

Todd would be upset. He'd know it was David, and she wouldn't be able to lie.

"You might as well look. You haven't heard anything I've said."

"Yes, I did; you said that Dennis has a conspiracy theory about climate change, and he wouldn't shut up about it at lunch today."

"Okay, you were listening, but the buzzing is driving me crazy," he said.

"Alright," she said, then stood and grabbed her phone off the counter. The first message made her laugh. Todd raised his eyebrows at her, so she read it out loud.

> Lily: *Hey you! Would you two like to come over for some games and a few laughs (very few if Nick is telling the jokes)?*

The next message was from Lily too.

> L: *Sorry. Hit send too soon. Lol Will next Sunday work for you? My mom will have Ariana, so we can act like we're in college and get hammered! LOL*

"Do you want to?" Erin asked hopefully, knowing how much fun they had with their best friends.

"Yeah, I'd like that."

Todd smiled at her, and she saw his eyes sparkle at her like they used to do before they learned about treatments and before she flew to New Orleans to meet the man who could give them to her. She typed a reply, thankful for the invitation.

> E: *We'd love to come! I'll let you know about the day, though, I may have a visitor. I have so many things to tell you. I'll call tomorrow.*

The next two messages were from David, but she would wait to read them.

After supper, Todd went to the basement to putter and Erin started washing the dishes. She found a streaming radio station called *Cajun Mardi Gras* and put her earbuds in to listen. During a commercial, she felt a sturdy arm wrap around her waist. One of the thugs had grabbed her in the exact same way when she and David had been attacked and mugged in New Orleans, and the flashback of it overwhelmed her.

She dropped the pan she was washing, splashing water all over her front and the floor. "No! Let go of me!" she screamed at the top of her voice. Startled, Todd let her go, and she ran, crying hysterically, to their bathroom, locking the door behind her.

"Wha—" he began.

She sat on the lid of the toilet, shaking and bawling, trying to get herself under control again. Images flashed through her mind of that warm, beautiful night, how it had started out so lovely and ended so badly. She could still smell the heavily spiced cologne of the man who'd held her. The deep pockmarks and rancid breath of the man who'd nearly assaulted her were still so vivid in her memory that she sprayed air freshener to try to cover it up. *David!* With trembling hands, she pulled her phone out of her back pocket and tried to unlock the screen with a swipe, but she was uncoordinated, and it took several tries.

"Erin? What was that about? I didn't mean to startle you. Come talk to me," Todd said through the door.

She heard him try the doorknob. "Just… leave me alone… for a while," she said, still trying to catch her breath, then her phone finally opened to the message list.

> D: *I'm sorry about earlier, the housekeeper needed my attention. I'd love for you to do that. I can almost*

feel your breath on my ear. You had me on the edge of my seat. If you're interested to know my reply, I'd say: You're welcome, my love, and then I'd kiss you until you begged me for another treatment.

D: *My heart is about to burst, Erin! I don't want to think about you at home with him. I know he's your husband, but I don't want you to have to...Maybe you won't, right? Maybe you'll be able to... I'm blathering now. Sorry, love. Only nine days, right?*

She couldn't tell him.

E: *Only nine days. I love you.*

Chapter Four

MISSING HER MATCH

E rin had a rough night; she didn't sleep well, having nightmares about the attack, and in the morning, Todd was moody with her. Once he was out of the house, she called her best friend, Lily, who was the only person she felt comfortable with enough to reveal the identity of her match. Her hands were clammy, and her face burned as the phone rang.

"Hey, you! So, tell me everything! Was he... normal?" Lily asked before Erin said a word. They had both wondered how any 'normal' married guy could sign up for the Registry.

"Actually, he was the farthest thing from normal you can get!"

"Oh no! Are you okay? That's hor—"

"I didn't say it was a bad thing, Lil," Erin interrupted with a light laugh.

"Oh? You need to come over for lunch! We'll have an hour or so before I have to get ready for my afternoon route."

"That depends on what you're serving, Chef Graves."

"Macaroni and cheese à la Oscar Mayer wiener."

"Yum! Be there soon," Erin said and grabbed her keys.

Erin was so nervous when she arrived at Lily's house that she knocked on the door, although it was her custom to just walk in. Lily answered it and didn't even scold her for making the dogs go crazy.

"Come in, already! Dang, you're as white as a ghost!" she exclaimed, which made Erin's face turn scarlet. "Woah! Come in and tell me everything!"

Erin felt a bit faint, but she managed to return the dogs' greeting and then sat on the bench seat at the kitchen island. She opened her mouth but didn't know where to start. "I… don't—"

"Go on, what was he like?" Lily said, stirring the macaroni and cheese on the stovetop while Erin took a seat at the tall work island.

"I think you should sit down first," she said. Lily turned to look at her, holding her spoon in the air. She didn't argue; she just turned the burner and oven off and sat on the high bench next to her. "You're not going to believe me!"

"Come on, spit it out!" Lily said as her friend stood and opened the window above the sink, allowing a fresh breeze into the warm room. Erin put her hand on her hips and began pacing, only it was in a circle, so she looked like a dog trying to find the best angle to lay down. Lily saw a tear fall down her face. "What's—"

"David… David freaking Elliott," Erin said and covered her face with her hands. She turned to face the open window and cried. Erin had never cried in front Lily before, not in all the years she'd known her.

"What? What… do you mean? Are you saying that he… David Elliott was—"

Erin nodded, not knowing why she was crying. She should be laughing and happy, excited to tell her friend all about it. "Yeah," she squeaked.

"No way! You're kidding—Really? But I don't understand? If David Elliott is your match, why are you crying? Was he an asshole or something?"

"No, he was perfect. He was everything I'd imagined—Everything I've dreamed he'd be like in person and… even better. Oh, Lil'! What am I going to do? Everything is all messed up now!"

"But why?"

"I… love him, Lily, and he loves me. See, everything is… totally fucked up!"

"Wait, slow down, what do you mean? I mean, I know you've loved him forever, we all do, but he loves you?"

The comment bit Erin's pride a little more than she wanted it to. "Don't sound so shocked, Lily—it's not impossible—" she began, feeling wounded.

"Woah! Hold on; you know I didn't mean it like that. Start at the beginning, and don't be angry, please?"

Erin's heart melted; if anyone could understand her fight with self-doubt and body image, it was Lily Graves. Both she and her husband, Nick, had been obese until they had gastric bypass surgery. "I'm sorry, I don't know why I'm crying. It's the most amazing, wonderful, fantastic thing in the world," she said and sat next to her friend.

"Okay, you tell me the whole story while I serve the gourmet meal."

She took a breath and told her everything, from falling on her ass, Champagne, the drunken bride-to-be, and the delicious kiss. "He wanted to kiss me, Lil'! And then later… he wanted to… well, you know." Lily sat with a chunk of hot dog at the end of her fork, listening with her mouth open. "Are you gonna eat that or sit there pointing your wiener at me?" Erin said with a laugh.

Lily waved her fork, "Go on," she said and then put it into her mouth.

Erin told her about the city, the food, and the music, but mainly about David. They both cried as she recounted the attack and again when she told her about having another episode. "He called Todd!" she said.

"No!" Lily said and put her fork on her plate. "Oh no!"

"Yes! He also talked to my doctor, at length, about… what we'd… done and how many times we'd… done it." She coughed and raised her eyebrows.

"What?"

"It seems that it's a thing. Other matched couples are feeling the same connection we felt. I can't imagine how hard it was for a Brit to talk about it like that!"

"Go on, this is amazing!"

"He bought me this," Erin said and pulled the silver chain out from under her top. The small charm flashed with reflected light as she took it off and handed it, warmed by her skin, to her best friend.

"A watch?"

"Compass. Said he saw it in a shop window, knew I'd love it, and managed to buy it without me knowing. He said it was '*So we can find our way back to each other.*'" Erin watched Lily examining it and sighed. It seemed so long ago.

"Wow, Erin, what an amazing story!"

Erin smiled broadly and said, "But wait, there's more!" She laughed at Lily's wide eyes. "He told me he loves me, Lil, and that he's never been able to be himself with anyone, not like he can be with me. He—" She closed her eyes, doubting her decision in hindsight.

"What?" Lily asked breathlessly.

"He asked me to run away with him." They heard the clack of dog claws on the tile floor and the tick of the clock on her wall. Their Boston terrier, Jax, came up and sniffed Erin's hand, wanting a scratch on his head, but she didn't move.

"I guess you said no, then?" Lily said and handed the necklace back to her.

Erin put the chain over her head once more. "How could I do that to Todd? Though what I'm doing now is probably worse! I thought I could have both, but I don't think it'll work that way." She stared at the small compass and tried not to cry.

"I'm sure you did what you had to, but I don't think I could turn down David Elliott!" Lily said, softly.

"I know," she said and then remembered their last morning together. "Oh, Lily! On the last day—there was this woman in a micro bikini… long story, but you know my history. I don't know if I can handle that! What if—I don't think I can… but I can't be without him now."

"Can't you still have both—"

"No, Lily, it's not what I thought it would be—simple treatments with David and love with Todd—It's more than a summer fling. I can't do both, and I don't know what to do now." She took her phone out of her pocket and opened her message app. She'd taken photos of the wallet-sized pictures he'd slipped into her purse, so she'd have them on her phone. David's face smiled at her, and she started crying again as she passed her phone to Lily.

"Oh my God, Erin! It sounds like a dream come true, but you're right, it *is* a big mess, isn't it?"

"I had to let Todd have sex with me. I didn't want to, but it would've been really bad if I'd said no; I just knew it would. I feel so guilty, and I don't know if I can tell David."

"Are you going to leave Todd?"

"I… don't know. Seems inevitable, doesn't it?"

"Oh no! It's already one-thirty! I have to get ready for work. I'm sorry, hon, I wish I had answers for you," Lily said as she and Erin cleared the plates.

"I'll figure it out. Thanks for listening."

"Of course! How many times have I sat here bawling my eyes out while you listened to me?"

"Thanks, Lil. Say hi to everyone at the terminal for me, okay?" Erin said.

"Okay. You should stop by and tell them the good news."

Erin's face blanched and then turned bright red again. "Are you crazy? I can't tell anyone, and you can't either, Lily! Promise that you won't tell a soul, not even Nick! Pinky promise!" she said, panic-ridden.

"I *meant* to tell them how things are looking up, silly, not who he is, but I promise," she said and held out her little finger for Erin to shake.

Todd woke with a start on Friday morning and looked at his alarm clock. Two-fourteen am. Erin had been home for two days and three nights and had woken him up every night with dreams which made her kick or move erratically. This time it was different though, she was flailing and talking. At first, he couldn't understand what she was saying, but then she said, "*NO! Please stop! That hurts!*" He was shocked and frightened, wondering what she could be dreaming about and didn't know what to do. He put his hand on her shoulder, and she stopped for a moment, seeming to relax.

"David!" she cried out. "David, help me!"

His stomach dropped, and he felt his heart start beating faster. Rage filled his mind as he elbowed her. "Wake up," he said, "You were dreaming about *him* again." All she did was groan and roll over, falling right back to sleep.

He wasn't stupid; he knew more than just a medical treatment had happened while she was gone. She was no longer interested in sex with him and would jump if he touched her unannounced. He was only trying to be spontaneous by hugging her from behind on Wednesday night, but her reaction had floored him. She'd acted like he was a stranger.

On Thursday morning, she'd rolled over, laying her arm across his chest, and made the little noise that meant she wanted him to make love to her. He was so excited, thinking she'd returned to him, not just in body but with her heart. He'd rolled over, embracing and kissing her, but then she woke up and nearly jumped out of the bed when she realized it was him and not her precious David. She made an excuse that she needed to use the toilet and didn't come back to bed.

His heart was raging and felt like an enormous block of granite in his chest, heavy and cold. It was no use trying to sleep next to her any longer, so he took his pillow and went to the spare room. In the morning, he left for work without saying goodbye. It was the second time that week and something he'd never done before she started treatments.

When he got home from work, her car was gone, and the house was silent. He walked into their bedroom to change and noticed that her small suitcase wasn't in the closet. He didn't know if she'd left him or if it was already time for her next treatment, so he rushed to the kitchen and scanned the calendar to find out. 'Girls Weekend' was written in her handwriting on that day's square with a line through the next two.

He sat on the smooth hardwood floor, breathing heavily as his body recovered from the panic. A few moments later, he realized he'd have the whole weekend to himself and felt that same old demon tug at his mind. After changing his clothes, he drove to the adult bookstore, vowing, as always, it would be the last time.

Chapter Five

GIRLS' WEEKEND

Erin and her girlfriends met at Marcia's cottage, which was a forty-five-minute drive, at least once a year for a weekend slumber party, to '*drink heavy and talk dirty*.' The house was an adorable two-bedroom summer home—nothing fancy, but it was comfortable and had everything they needed. A well-stocked liquor cabinet, a clean bathroom, several sets of bunk beds, and it was near a small lake where they went swimming if it was hot enough.

It was an anything-goes group of ladies; they talked about their husbands, sex life, issues, and heartaches. Sometimes they played games or watched movies, but no matter what, they laughed a lot, which was a much-needed release from the stress of life. The women were all similar sizes and shapes, and there was no judgment or fat-shaming between them. They could change in front of each other and get into swimming suits without feeling self-conscious, fat, or ugly. Erin needed them; they needed each other.

She drove to the cottage on Friday afternoon with a heavy heart. It was the second time she'd woken up long after Todd had already left for work. Why he stopped waking her every morning, she didn't know; nothing he did made sense to her anymore. She couldn't talk to him about it, or much of anything for that matter, either. Everything she said seemed to trigger his anger about the treatments. No subject was safe, so most often she said nothing. The atmosphere in their home was becoming more toxic every day, and she didn't have many people to confide in about it. When she'd talked to Lily, she hadn't gotten to the part about Todd's anger.

She pulled into the yard at the cottage and sent David a quick message:

Erin: *I really miss you, and I'll be thinking about you all weekend.*

She didn't expect a reply right away but saw the dots move as soon as she hit send.

David: *I was about to say the same to you just now. In my bed, wishing you were lying here with me. Longing for your smell, touch, taste. I miss your laughter and quick wit. No one here can compare to you, my love. How are you feeling? Still have that energy?*

E: *Oh, David! You know just how to make a girl feel desired and wanted! Thank you! My mind keeps trying to tell me that…well, that you'll change your mind, or that you didn't really mean what you said. It was real, wasn't it? I didn't imagine our connection, did I? Oh God, I don't really wanna be here! If I can't be with you, then I want to be somewhere where I can be alone and quiet so I can think about you! My energy level is dipping already. I need another treatment!*

D: *Your mind is wrong! I meant everything, and I do love you, Erin. It was the most real thing to happen to me, perhaps ever. Where are you that you'd rather not be? If I could, I'd hire a private jet and fly to you tonight! I'd wake you up with kisses and make love to you, wherever you are!*

Her heart beat faster in her chest at the thought.

E: *Oh, I wish you would! I'm sure the girls would be just as surprised as me to find you in the shared bedroom, having your way with me!*

D: *Ah, right, girls' weekend. Will you tell them about us?*

E: *No, I don't think so. It's too special, and it might spoil it a little bit WHEN we talk about you if they know. Also, they'll want to know what you're really like, and I don't want to make them upset by telling them all what a jerk you are. They think you're this really amazing guy. I just don't want to be that person.*

D: *The truth is hard to take, sometimes, I reckon. So, you WILL talk about me, then? Normally I wouldn't fancy that but with you, it rather turns me on.*

E: *Oh no! You're in your bed, turned on, and…next to your wife, I presume. That's not a very happy thought.*

D: *No, love, I've been turned out of the master bedroom and am alone in the guest room, where I may be as turned on by you as I wish…and I am.*

E: *Damn! Are you sure about that private jet? I could use a few of your kisses right about now! Are you, um, going to… help yourself out?*

D: *I hadn't planned to, but if you'll talk me through it I will. Would you? I'd like it if you did.*

E: *Wow, okay. I'll try. I've never sexted before. lol*

D: *And you imagine I have? I'm picturing you lying next to me…and that it's your hand on me, not mine.*

Erin saw the curtains move inside the house and knew there wasn't much time before someone came out to check on her.

E: *Yes, I'm stroking you, moving my hand up and down.*

D: *Yes, that's nice. Might you use your mouth?*

E: *If you begged me to, I would!*

D: *Ach, Erin, please, please!*

E: *Alright, but only for a little while, because afterward, I'm going to climb on top of you and make you…*

D: *Make me…I won't need much convincing! Oh, Erin, I'm so close!*

Erin felt strange—half excited and half left out.

E: *Good! I'll start rocking my hips as I ride you…*

There was quite a long pause.

E: *David?*

D: *Sorry, I…had to finish. That was brilliant, Erin, thank you. I hope you're able to…well, you know.*

E: *Yeah, I know. I'd better go in now. I'm glad I could help you. I can't wait till next weekend, and I'll be sure to talk about you all through this one! I love you!*

D: *I can't wait either. I love you, as well. x*

Erin had already told the ladies about the treatments and what they involved, including her match, but not who the man was. That night, she was the first to bring David's name up, just because she wanted to talk about him. "Did any of you see the new David Elliott movie, Houlihan's Flat? I saw it on the plane; it was so good!"

"Meh, he's not my type," Marcia weighed in as she usually did when his name was mentioned, "I'm more of a Dwayne Johnson kind-a girl; I wouldn't kick *him* out of bed for eating crackers!"

"What's it about again?" Carrie asked.

"It's about a married couple—David Elliott and Olivia Colman, living in a flat above Houlihan's Irish Pub. During renovations, they find a stack of WWII love letters from several different people. As they read them to each other, the stories come to life, played out for the audience. I really liked it," Erin said.

"I saw it," said 'Fucking Laura,' a name she got first because there were two Lauras and second because she liked to use the word 'fuck'—*a lot.* "It was good, but it would've fucking sucked without him in it! I'd let him feed me grapes on the veranda wearing a toga!" she said, making them all laugh. Fucking Laura always used food references for things.

"I just love him! I know I say it every time, but do you know how many times I've binged on *Future Explorations?*" 'New Laura' said enthusiastically. "His smile... and those big, luscious, deep brown eyes! God! I don't know about grapes, but I could nibble on other parts!" she said and then laughed. "But you know what? I'd settle for sitting in the same room as him—or on him!" Everyone groaned at her apparent afterthought.

'New Laura' received that name, again; because there were two of them, and she was the newest member of the group. She didn't drink much, but she was the one who would say anything, the dirtier the better, just to make people either laugh or groan. Her smug smile revealed that she was pleased with herself because it had worked again.

Colleen was already three sheets to the wind and started looking up photos of David on her phone. She was their drinks master; she knew all the trendy cocktails and brought the most amazing booze with her. "Oh! Look at these! They're new!" she said and handed the phone to New Laura.

"They must've been taken when he was in New Orleans. He's standing with a woman who looks like us; lucky her!" she said and handed the phone to Erin, who nearly screamed.

The photo was taken from a distance. Her face was turned just enough so you couldn't tell who it was, but it was, without a shred of doubt, David and her on the production set where he was a guest star on a television show. It was surreal and alarming to see herself online like that. "Yeah—lucky her," Erin said, feeling a bit light-headed.

"Wait," Marcia said, looking over Erin's shoulder, "you're wearing the same top!"

"Am I?" Erin said and blushed, "That's… crazy! She has good taste in clothing, I guess."

"It's probably one of the fucking actresses or something. Weren't you just in New Orleans for your *marvelous mystery man* treatment, Erin?" Fucking Laura said.

Erin thought her face would fall off. Between the embarrassment and the alcohol, she knew it must look bad. "Yeah, I was there. It was beautiful and warm—I didn't want to leave," she said truthfully.

"He's probably an asshole anyway," Colleen said, muttering to herself. "He was probably just trying to get that woman in the photo to go away. He can't be as amazing as he looks, right?"

"I think he is," Erin said under her breath.

"So… can I ask… what was your *mystery miracle macho man* like? Do you think the… *treatment* is working?" New Laura asked.

"I know… for a fact that he's going to be the next James… Bond. I also read that David Elliott has a mistress—Yes, and she's *not* skinny. Maybe that's her?" Carrie said, pausing often and slurring her speech. "App-arrrrently— someone on the set of whatever he was filming in New… Orleans saw her and… told one of the local papers… she was, uh— *'Not petite in any way,'* " she said with lazy air quotes. "I… say good for her! It's about time one of us gets someone… like him!" She put her head down on her arm and then lifted it again right away. "Weren't you just there, Erin? Did you see him? That would be a-mazing!"

"Good night nurse, Carrie, pay attention!" Erin said, laughing and successfully evading the question.

"Oh, he'd make an amazing James Bond!" Colleen said and closed her eyes, propping her head up with her hand, elbow on the table. "Can't you just see him in a shiny black tie and bow suit, sitting in a vintage Aston—Aston—

whatever… and smiling his smile!" Visions of martinis and long empty beaches swam in their imaginations.

"Shiny black tie and bow suit? You really *are* drunk, Colleen!" Erin teased.

"What if you'd bumped into him! Wouldn't that have been amazing?" Colleen sighed and put her head down on the table. "I'd like to be his mistress!"

"Me too!" Erin said and smiled, remembering what it was like to be with him. David told her that he wasn't on the shortlist to play 007, though he *had* gotten a mysterious call from his agent that same night. She didn't know for sure, but she doubted Carrie's sources were accurate. Even so, it was still nice to imagine him in the role. *Wow! I'm being called his mistress now?* she thought happily. She imagined a calling card, like the one Champagne had given her:

> *Erin G. March*
> *David Elliott's*
> *(not petite in any way)*
> *Mistress*

She was snapped out of her reverie by Carrie. "Isn't that where you had your… what are they calling it? Sex-medicine?" she said with a giggle.

"You weren't listening at all, were you? It's called a treatment, Carrie, and yes, I was just there," Erin rolled her eyes and laughed at her friend.

"By the way," Carrie continued, still not paying attention, "Steve and I are renewing… our vows in July. We're gonna have a reception, with food… and drinks. I hope you'll… all come?" she said, and they all said some form of 'I'll be there,' or 'Wouldn't miss it.'

The next day they were nursing serious hangovers with extra-strong coffee. Erin was daydreaming about David, imagining him sitting at the table with them, when she was startled back into reality by New Laura. "Let's go for a walk," she said. "It's stuffy in here, and I saw a hot guy doing yard work when I drove up yesterday. Let's see if he's back outside—maybe he'll be sunbathing!"

"A walk sounds nice, but I'm not going to ogle some poor guy, hot or not," Erin said, laughing at her friend when she rolled her eyes.

Marcia and Carrie didn't want to go, so the rest of them put on their windbreakers or sweaters and headed out to walk around the small 'L' shaped road that led to nowhere. It was something to do besides sit in the cottage.

Fucking Laura and Erin walked together, a little behind the rest. "We should go to a comic con this year! Wouldn't it be fucking amazing to meet some of the people we go all fangirl over?" Laura said.

Erin smiled at her friend. "Yeah, but they're just people like us. Can you imagine any of us sitting at a table and having people stand in line for hours wanting to get our autographs or to have their photo taken with us? It must be the same for them, don't you think?"

"I guess so, but people like David Elliott just seem so much more than us, don't they? I mean, who would want *my* photo?" Laura said and looked off into the distance.

Erin knew exactly what she meant. "I would, sweety!" She took her cell phone out of her pocket and took a selfie of them both, right there.

"Thanks, Erin; you're fucking amazing, you know?"

"*Someone* has to be, right?" she said and hugged her friend. They caught up with the rest of the ladies, walked the quarter mile or so around the neighborhood, then headed back to the cottage.

They were taking off their jackets when Marcia got Erin's attention. "How's Todd taking the whole 'treatment' thing?" she asked using air quotes, "I mean… now that you've had your first one."

Erin blushed, not really wanting to talk about Todd. "I don't know… he's not himself. I don't blame him, but *now* I can't mention *any* aspect of the disease, the treatments, or the first name of my match without—"

"Wait, he knows the name of your match?" Colleen said, perking up a bit. "I thought you said he didn't want to know."

"Yeah, it's a long story—"

They looked at each other. "We have a long weekend to hear it! Tell us!" New Laura said.

Careful not to use his name, Erin told them how her match had answered the phone on the second morning she was there. "Todd was beside himself, and I had to talk him down from a panic attack. Then, he called to tell us about the airport shooting on Sunday, the day I was supposed to leave." The women sat listening with their mouths open.

"But how did he find out what his name was?" Carrie asked.

"Oh, well, he answers the phone like this— 'This is Jim-Bob,' and no, I'm not gonna tell you his real name," Erin said and laughed. "Anyway… later that morning, I had a really bad episode, and he… my match, called the house and spoke to Todd because he didn't know what to do."

The girls sat in disbelief. "Umm, yeah, I can see why Todd would be upset! That would be really traumatic for him!" Marcia said.

"Yes, but I have to live every day not being able to say 'Fertilis Defect' without him getting upset. It's a bit of an overreaction if you ask me," Erin said.

"Yeah, I guess so. Seems like you're on a tightrope, girl, and you'd better not slip, or you're gonna fall hard!" Marcia continued.

Don't I know it, Erin thought. "Yeah, it's a real balancing act. Even the smallest slip-up is massive! It's *truly* like walking on eggshells—with bare feet—and it hurts!" She felt herself getting emotional and wanted to change the subject.

"Well, chicky, we're here for you if you need us!" Fucking Laura said.

Erin smiled at her group of friends; she was so glad she had them to lean on! She might never be able to tell them about David, but she knew they loved her, and that was everything. "Thanks, guys."

That night, Erin dreamed David was there with them in the small cottage. The women were pawing at him, to the point where it seemed like it would end in an orgy. At first, Erin was laughing and playing along, but then it got to be too much. She wanted it to stop, but no one would listen to her.

David also played along at first, but once it started to get more intense, he clearly wanted it to stop too. He was reaching for her and saying something she couldn't hear. When she looked again, there were more women—many more; dozens, then hundreds. David was being carried away, all the time reaching out for her. She woke up gasping and realized New Laura was standing over her.

"You were talking in your sleep," she whispered.

Erin had to use the bathroom anyway, so she sat up and got out of bed. When she came out of the bathroom, New Laura was sitting at the table, and Erin joined her. "What did I say?" she asked, praying it wasn't David's name.

"You said, '*Wait! No—stop—David!*' and you were reaching out to something or someone. Do you want to talk about it?"

The dream was still too vivid and not something she wanted to share. "Not really," she said. "It was a nightmare, so I'd rather not dwell on it. Thanks for asking though, I'm gonna go back to bed now, goodnight."

"Goodnight."

The weekend flew by, and on Sunday afternoon, after lots of hugs and goodbyes, Erin left. It was a nice drive home with time to think and dream, wishing David were with her and secretly imagining he was. She guessed that Todd hadn't thought of taking any meat out to thaw for supper, so she stopped at the grocery store.

Todd was in the garage, working on something interesting only to him, and came to the car when he saw her pull in and park. "How was your weekend?" he asked as he grabbed the food out of the passenger seat and then her suitcase out of the trunk. He kissed her cheek when they met near the garage door.

"Oh, it was fun. We did and said crazy things and drank crazy amounts of liquor, as usual. They all say hi, by the way," she said as they walked into the kitchen. Erin noticed he was in a good mood that evening as he washed his hands, getting ready to help with supper. She didn't want to rock the boat, so she was careful about what she said and did.

They worked together as they'd done for years, preparing a simple meal they made often. They had a comfortable supper, sitting across from each other at the table. Todd laughed at the stories she'd brought home with her about what her friends had done over the weekend, and she was relieved the tension had lifted off him. He'd been like a compressed spring, waiting to pop; she'd felt it every moment they were together, but that night, she finally felt like she could relax.

After they ate, they brought their dishes to the sink and Erin washed them while Todd went back to the garage. The weather was only pleasant for a few months of the year, so she didn't mind him wanting to be out there while he could. She was happy enough doing the dishes and humming the songs which kept rolling around in her mind from the special supper night in New Orleans.

———

That was nice, Todd thought as he walked to his workbench. *It felt like it used to—like things should be. Maybe it **will** get better.* He smiled hopefully and decided to get rid of the new Hustler and Magnum magazines he'd bought and hidden in the spidery attic, where he knew she wouldn't snoop.

<h1 style="text-align:center">Chapter Six</h1>

DAVID'S CONFRONTATION AND CONFESSION

On the Wednesday morning of their second week apart, David was in his office trying to avoid another fight with Susannah, especially whilst the children were home from school for the week. He had been daydreaming about Erin again, which he did quite often, and just as he was about to compose a message to her, he heard a light knock on the door.

It opened a crack, and an eye peeked inside. "Dad," Charlie said timidly. "May we come in?"

"Of course, you may. What's the matter?" he asked with the usual RP accent he used at home.

The door opened a bit further, and he saw Peter and Charlie, two of his boys, Peter being the older of the two. Charlie looked as though he might start to cry but was trying to be brave. They walked across the room and sat on the leather couch against the wall.

"Dad," Peter said, not making eye contact with him. Instead, his gaze stayed on Charlie as if for moral support. "We've just come from Mum… she was crying and—"

"And she suggested we ask you about it—" Charlie cut in.

"Oi, Charlie! Let me finish, would you?" Peter said, annoyed at being interrupted.

"Sorry, Peter, but she said, '*I suggest that you ask your father,*' so—"

"We asked her what was wrong, and she said to ask you. I didn't want to, but Charlie was quite upset." He paused, still not looking at him.

David wondered what she was up to; Susannah wasn't a crier. He pulled over an armchair and sat in front of them, wishing he knew what to say. "I'm not sure why your mum was crying, exactly—" he started, which was the truth. "Although I'm guessing it had to do with something 'Uncle' Martin tricked me into."

"Again?" both boys said in unison.

"Yes, it was a big deal this time, but it worked out alright in the end. Your mum is rather upset about the whole thing, though I can't say I blame her."

"But, Dad," Peter said, "why didn't you say no to Uncle Martin? Why did you do something that made Mum so upset?" He looked up at him then, his blue eyes flashing, and his mouth set in a frown, clearly not accepting his explanation that Martin was to blame.

"Mum said there was—" Charlie started, but Peter gave him another look of warning which made him stop.

This is too much; how could she burden these innocent young men with our personal business. I'm done with her games! "Boys, I wish I had an easy answer for you—"

"Are you having an affair, and are you going to divorce mummy?" Charlie blurted out and started crying, wrapping his arms around his brother. Peter looked at his father as if he were waiting for him to answer the question.

David's mouth was as dry as cotton wool. He could feel beads of sweat forming on his forehead and upper lip. *What should I say?* The last thing he wanted to do was lie to them, but they were only fifteen and ten; they wouldn't understand. It was complicated enough for *him* to wrap his head around. "Charlie, come here," he said, but the boy shook his head.

"Please answer the question, Dad," Peter said, very much like an adult.

David stood. He took the tissue box off his desk and handed it to Charlie, who took one and wiped his nose with it. How could he even start to explain? "Boys, you are growing up to be young men. You know how to gauge relationships and the way people interact around each other, correct?" The boys nodded, though clearly not satisfied with how the conversation was going. "Before I answer, tell me how you see your mother and me; how do we get along?"

Peter rolled his eyes, "You get along brilliantly, Dad," he said, but Charlie looked at him with questioning eyes.

"Brilliantly? Really, Peter?" Peter shot him another warning glance, but it didn't work that time. "You're the one who's forever goin' on about how you wish they'd split up already and have done with it."

David stared at Charlie, his eyes blinking; *They knew—this whole time? They figured out what took me over seventeen years to realize?* he thought and took a deep breath. "So, you've noticed we don't have the best of relationships. Believe it or not, I'm just now coming to that conclusion." He started pacing, not sure how to tell them about Erin, or even if he should. She'd know what to say. "Uncle Martin… he, well, secured ma involvement in a medical program involving… intimate relations… with someone whom I've been… paired with—" he began, but Peter interrupted him.

"Do you mean that disease; Fertility Defect, or what have you? You hosted a charity event for it, didn't you?"

David was amazed he knew anything about it. "Yes, that's the one. How—"

"I was made to watch part of it at school. Mrs. Evans thought it would be good for us to learn about the disease and about the new developments they've made. I was forced to sit and watch you make your plea for funds and hear you say the word… *intercourse* far too many times whilst the class mocked you and laughed at me," Peter said, blushing.

"I had no idea; I'm sorry you had to—"

"Dad! Please answer the question," he said. His eyes were starting to turn stormy and dark like his mother's when she was upset.

"It's not as simple as that, Peter, the treatment for the Fertilis Defect is—"

"But why didn't you say no?" cried Charlie.

"Your mum is precisely the reason I couldn't say no," he said, nearly losing his temper. If she was going to throw him under the bus and force him to tell them, then she wasn't going to come out smelling of roses. The boys looked up at him with enormous eyes as if he were lying. "Yes, that's the truth of it. She didn't want Martin going to the tabloids. I wouldn't have cared if he—"

"But he wouldn't do that—would he?" Charlie interrupted, and Peter bobbed his head in agreement.

"I'm afraid he was planning to do just that if I didn't go along with his scheme. I assure you—I didn't want to do it; you must believe me. Your mum thought it best to yield privately, as an alternative to everyone in the United Kingdom and around the world being privy to it."

"So, there *is* another woman then?" Peter said quietly.

David wished he knew what to say; how could he tell his young boys about her? In the end, he decided they were far more clever than he gave them credit for. Besides, they would find out eventually, so he'd better be truthful, as he needed them to trust him. "Yes," he said simply and sat again on the chair. Charlie looked at him as though he'd shot his dog, but Peter gave him a different sort of look, one that said now that he knew what had happened, he could at least look at him. "I didn't want to be unfaithful to your mum, but that's what the treatment involves, and… my match and I… we got on really well."

"Are you going to leave mum for her?" Peter asked softly.

"I… well… yes."

Charlie had calmed down and was listening to him intently. "Will you tell us about her?" he asked. Both Peter and David looked at him like he'd gone mad. The boy returned their stares and shrugged. "What? If Dad is with another woman, I want to know what she's like—and I don't care what you think!" He squinted his eyes at his older brother, then looked expectantly up at his father.

David was astonished; he had *not* expected that; then Peter looked at him, apparently thinking it was a good question. "Are you… sure you want to know?" David asked, silently begging for wisdom. They both nodded and sat back, getting comfortable on the couch. "Don't you think Rosie and Dan should have this news as well, before—" He heard a noise behind him and saw his other two children walk through the door. Rosie, the youngest of his children and the only girl, had red eyes, and Daniel, Charlie's fraternal twin, looked as if he had no idea what was happening; he just wanted to be in on it.

David stood, wishing he'd known they were hiding out there before he'd said anything. "Oh, darling," he said as Rosie ran to him and cried. He gathered her up in his arms and sat, cradling her while Dan sat next to his brothers on the couch. He stroked his daughter's hair and shushed her. *I should've known.*

"A'right then, I'm not getting out of this, am I, so what do you want to know?" David asked, hoping they would ask questions that were easy to answer. The last thing he wanted was to volunteer too much information. They all started asking questions at once so that he had to raise his voice to be heard. "One at a time, please! Charlie, you may go first."

Charlie looked at each of his siblings and, as if they could read each other's minds, they all nodded. "What's she like? Is she friendly? Is she—fond of children?" he asked without stopping for an answer.

"Charlie!" Rosie said, scolding him, "That's three questions!"

David couldn't help but smile; she was right, after all. "She is the friendliest person I know, and she is quite fond of children. She saw the pictures of you lot which I carry with me and later remembered your names. She wanted to learn about each one of you and was keen to know your personalities. Ach, she had you pegged, Dan."

The boy looked at him as if to say, 'What do you mean?' but the others just smiled.

"Perhaps she already knew about us, Dad. More likely, she's a mental fan—" Peter began.

David's laugh was good-humored, "No, Peter, she's not. Yes, she knew who I was, but she is a normal person, same as any of us."

His eldest son looked leery but let it go. "What's her name?" he asked.

"Her name is Erin." He couldn't help but smile when he said it.

They all mouthed her name as if trying it on to see if it fit.

"Daddy—" Rosie said, "Do you… love her more than Mummy?"

David's heart was ripped out and dropped on the floor at his feet. "You ask the most difficult questions," he said and kissed the top of her head. By the way they were looking at him, he knew they were keen to hear the answer, so he tried to be as gentle as he could. "I have strong feelings for her. I… do believe I love her, yes." He set Rosie standing again and stood, then he sat in the center of the sofa, two kids on either side of him.

"Where is she now?" Charlie asked.

"She lives in America."

At that, Daniel perked up. He was especially interested in the United States. He had learned the names of the states in school and could point out most of them on a map. "Which one? No, wait, which letter does it begin with?" Dan asked, excitedly.

Peter smiled at his father. "Leave it to Dan to make a game out of it," he said.

"I believe it starts with a W," David replied.

"Wyoming? West Virginia?" he rattled off, quick as a wink.

"Washington?" Charlie chimed in.

"West Carolina?" Rosie offered, and Dan rolled his eyes.

"There isn't a state called West Carolina, silly! That leaves Wisconsin!" he said triumphantly.

"Yes, well done, Dan," David said. The boy ran to his father's enormous atlas and brought it over, nearly dropping it on his way back. He found the page with a map of North America and ran his finger around the middle of the page until he found it. If he were being honest, David was curious as well, so he made out as though he were tolerating his son's antics, as usual.

Wisconsin was just northeast of the center of the country, west of a grouping of large lakes. He found a map showing only the United States and located the state, which was about a centimeter away from Canada. "In what city does she live, Dad?" Daniel said, keeping his finger on the state as though he thought he might lose it.

David wasn't sure he liked how excited his son was, considering it had to do with his lover, but he didn't think any harm would come from him knowing the city. "I believe she said Green Bay."

Daniel found Milwaukee and Madison, then pointed at the dot to the left of Lake Michigan that read Green Bay. They all stared at it for a few moments, but it didn't mean anything; it was only a yellow shape next to other colored shapes on the page.

Suddenly Rosie jumped up and snatched his mobile from off his desk. "Look it up, please, Daddy?" she said softly and handed it to him.

The situation was becoming a bit strange, but they were all too interested to stop at that point. David took his mobile from her, using his fingerprint to unlock the screen. Daniel then grabbed it out of his hand and waved it triumphantly toward his siblings before he could stop him. "Wait!" David said anxiously.

Rosie saw the screen first and gasped, shock filling her little eight-year-old face. "Is… that… her, Daddy?" she asked, making the others look at it, as well.

He'd forgotten that his wallpaper was now a photo of him and Erin on their last night together. "Oi! Give it to me!" David said, but it was too late; they had their heads together, looking over his mobile in Daniel's hand. *Shit!* He could see the reality of the situation come crashing down on them. They saw him and Erin smiling, obviously having a good time. "Yes, that's her—I wasn't going to—" he started to say, feeling completely out of control.

"She's—" Charlie began, and David prayed he wouldn't say fat, or big, or heavy. "… pretty," his young son said. He let out the breath he was holding and smiled.

"I think so as well. Now, what were we doing?" David said, trying to change the subject.

Daniel expertly located the maps application on the mobile, then he searched for Green Bay, Wisconsin and found it without difficulty. He chose the satellite image, then zoomed in and moved the map around. They saw Tower Drive Bridge and Lambeau Field. There it was—her city. David wished he could pinpoint her house and see it for himself, but it would have to wait for a better time.

"What's her address?" Daniel asked, looking expectantly at him. David shrugged, trying to put him off, but Dan saw through it. "Come on, Dad." When he still didn't get an answer, he rolled his eyes. "Fine," he said, and David hoped that meant he'd given up on the idea.

What happened next stunned him completely. Daniel was holding up his mobile to take a group selfie, and David was told to smile. They all smiled, and David caught a glimpse of the shot before Dan snatched the phone away again. The boy swiped and smiled, mischief playing on his bright, freckled face. "What are you up to—" David asked, but then the boy whooped, and it occurred to him that perhaps he had taken the selfie in order to send it to Erin. "Wait," he said, but it was too late.

"Sent," Daniel said victoriously, "Ha! I found it! Whistlers Way!"

David sat dumbfounded, concluding that Daniel had found Erin's profile through the messages app he'd neglected to close earlier and saw her address right there. *Damn!* he thought, *Why'd I allow any of this.* He tried to get the phone back from his son, but Dan jumped away too quickly. "Daniel!" he said in his angry father voice, "That is quite en—"

Dan turned the phone around so they all could see it. There was her house, 1324 Whistlers Way. It was a street view, and they could see two large maple trees in the front garden, as well as two cars parked in the drive. Erin and Todd had both been home when the image was taken. He didn't like the feeling that thought gave him. "Dan, hand it over now," he said, as sternly as he could. He wasn't any good at discipline, and it was showing. Daniel must have achieved his goal because he handed it back to him straight away.

"Will we get to meet her?" Rosie asked.

David knew things had gone way too far, and he needed to rein them all in. "I don't know, darling, but it's time to stop all this. Now, are there any more legitimate questions you need answered before—"

"Are you going to marry her?" she asked, gravely.

"He's still married to Mum, stupid," Daniel said.

"Now, Dan—" he scolded.

"Sorry, Dad, but honestly!" The boy rolled his eyes and Rosie stuck her tongue out at him.

"I don't know what will happen in the future, but you needn't worry about any of it now. Let's find something to do to get our minds off it, alright?" David said. *Aye and tae get my mind off it as well!* he thought.

They seemed disappointed as they got up off the sofa and filed out of the room, though Peter dropped back for a moment. "Thanks for telling us the truth, Dad," he said and hurried out the door.

David followed, and as he entered the hallway, he overheard Rosie and Charlie talking. "I hope we do meet her, don't you?" Rosie said.

David didn't hear his son's reply but thought he saw him nodding. "I'll meet you in the sunroom," he called out to them and then returned to his office. He unlocked his mobile again and found that Daniel *had* sent the selfie to Erin in a message. *How am I gonna explain this?* he thought. Hoping to keep her from becoming upset, he sent her a message under the picture.

> D: *I can explain this later. It was Daniel's doing. Sorry. X*

He hit send, hoping it would be good enough until he had more time to talk to her.

Chapter Seven

YOU TOLD THEM?

Erin didn't get David's message until the next morning since her phone was set to 'Do Not Disturb' after 8:30 every night. David's notification sound was the theme song from *Future Explorations*, and at 5:30 am, she heard it playing from her bedside table. Todd was in the bathroom getting ready for work, so he didn't hear it. *Thank goodness!* she thought as she swiped the screen and opened the new message, enjoying the butterflies that a text from *him* gave her.

She stared in disbelief at the image of David and his four beautiful children smiling at her. *What in the hell?* she thought. She read the message, sent nearly ten minutes after the picture had arrived, and was still confused. *Daniel's doing? How did Daniel manage to—Wait, what does that mean—he wouldn't have told them about us, would he?* She didn't like the idea of it and waited until Todd left for work before replying.

> E: *I'm confused. Are you saying Daniel*
> *sent this to me? How is that possible?*
> *Did you tell them about us?*

She hit send and then wished she'd called him instead. About an hour later, she heard the *F.E.* theme music and read:

> D: *It's quite a long story but put simply, I*
> *had to tell them. They came to me*

asking questions, and I couldn't lie.
I'll explain when I see you.

Erin was stunned. *What was he thinking? He told them without asking me first. Good night nurse, this isn't good.* She was just about to reply when another message popped up.

> D: *I miss you terribly, and I hate to do it, but I need to change our plans. I'm so sorry, but my children won't be returning to school until Sunday, and their mother is…well, I'd prefer to stay until they leave. Will you be alright if we move the date to Monday? X*

Truthfully, Monday was better for Erin, as well. Todd was home all day on the weekend, and it would be hard on him to sit around alone while she was off with David, especially since he was coming to Green Bay for the treatment that time.

> E: *I agree, Monday is better for me too, though I hate to admit it. I miss you! Please let me know when you'll arrive, and I'll pick you up.*

> D: *Will do. I love you, darling. x*

After supper that night, Todd helped by bringing the dishes to the sink for Erin to wash, then he headed to the sofa to watch the TV. She started singing like she always did while doing the dishes, not paying much attention to what she was doing.

"Would you shut up about feeling 'weak in the knees' already?" Todd barked, standing near the table. "I can't take it anymore! It's always the same songs, over and over, and I'm done hearing them!"

Erin stood, startled, and gaping at him. "I … didn't realize I was … singing. I'm … sorry," she said.

He'd never told her to *stop* singing before. He was always trying to get her to sing more often, telling her how much he loved her voice. He stormed out to the garage, this time slamming the kitchen door on purpose. She dried her hands and went after him, knowing she shouldn't. "Todd, what—" she began, but he turned to her, red in the face and she stopped.

"Do you think I'm stupid? Tell me, Erin, do you?" he yelled.

"What? No, I don't think you're stupid. Why are you yelling at me?"

"I know those songs have some special meaning to you—something you shared with *him*, right? You aren't hiding it very well, you know!"

"I was in New Orleans—there's music everywhere there. You know that when I hear a song, it gets stuck in my head. Quit being so sensitive! I can't do anything without you thinking it has something to do with *'him'*," she said, using air quotes and rolling her eyes. She couldn't tell him the truth about the CD or why those songs were special to her.

"Just—just stop singing them over and over! Are you—"

"Am I what, Todd?" she shouted, "What?"

"Are you in love with him?" he roared.

She should've known that's what he would say, but it caught her off guard. Her face instantly turned bright red as she stared wide-eyed at him. "I—"

"I see."

"Todd—I've only known—"

"Stop talking."

"But—"

"STOP! I don't want to hear those fucking songs anymore; do you hear me? Get something else stuck in your head! I'm—dying here, Erin. I can't take this!" he said and walked past her.

She followed him. "Who are you to talk about hiding anything?" she shot back at him, trembling with rage. What she wanted to say was, 'What are you currently hiding from me? Is it a Playboy this time, or something a bit more hardcore?' but she held her tongue. He entered the house and came back with his car keys. "Todd—"

"Don't wait up for me," he said, cutting her off, then he got into his car and started the engine.

The garage door started creaking and groaning as it began to open. Erin watched silently as he backed out and then drove away. She walked back into the house, forgetting about the dishes; her heart hurt so much. She wanted to talk to someone about it, but she knew what they'd say. 'Do you blame him?' or 'You just have to get past it, give it time.' Time was not going to help her marriage. It was falling apart in front of her eyes.

> E: *Are you busy? I know it's late over*
> *there, but I really need to talk.*

She typed into her phone, then hit 'send' and waited, hoping David would reply quickly.

It was still early for her, but she put on her pajamas and wrapped herself in a blanket on the sofa. She wished she had her stolen phone back. She'd taken some beautiful photos when she was in New Orleans, but she'd saved them to her SD card and not to Drive, so they were lost forever. She browsed Netflix and YouTube but didn't find anything she wanted to watch, so she turned off the television and went to bed. She happened to look at her phone and saw a message, though there'd been no noise.

> D: *I'm still awake, darling. What's*
> *wrong?*

She wanted to cry seeing his words to her. She was about to start typing but noticed that his message was nearly an hour old, so she went to bed early.

Chapter Eight

DOCTOR NAN CHECKUP

When Erin woke in the morning, she realized that Todd hadn't come to bed at all that night. She looked at her phone and saw a reminder for an appointment with Dr. Nanavala, the physician who treated her for the Fertilis Defect. Groaning, she got up, feeling tired and over-stressed. Stress made her symptoms worse, so she was supposed to avoid it, though it seemed determined to make its way into her life, like it or not. She started the water for a shower and got in, pondering the way time was dragging on; it seemed so long since she'd been with David.

She felt fairly good as she checked in at the doctor's office and waited, listening to the Muzak they had playing over the speakers. Doctor Nan's nurse called her in and took her weight then her vitals as usual. "Your heart rate and blood pressure are great, and it looks like you've lost a few pounds," the nurse said brightly. The two women smiled at each other, knowing the struggle.

"I did? Awesome!" Erin said. If anything, she thought she might have gained weight with all the rich foods she'd eaten in New Orleans.

As the nurse plugged the numbers into the computer, she asked, "Is there anything you'd like to mention? New symptoms or new medications?"

"Nope, nothing new."

"Okay then, Dr. Nanavala will be in soon," the nurse said and then left the room.

A few minutes later, Dr. Nan came in, smiling warmly at her. "Hello, Erin! It is good to see you. You look well, how do you feel?" he said in his friendly East Indian Accent.

Erin smiled, glad she could answer positively for once. "I felt great for the first week. I haven't had that much energy in years, but I'm starting to feel tired again."

"That is good news. We may have to space your treatments closer together. Please, sit on the table." He stood next to her and used his stethoscope to listen to her lungs. "Your lungs sound clear and healthy. Have you had another episode since you have been home?"

"Nope," she answered.

"Trouble breathing or any other symptoms?"

"Like I said, the first week was amazing, but now I'm losing steam—Oh, and I guess there's just the hint of a catch in my breathing every now and then."

"Alright, please let us know if it becomes worse. I see your next treatment is this weekend, which is good. How are things at home with Todd?" he asked.

She didn't want to discuss that. "Things have been better, to be honest. Todd is having a hard time, and I feel like I need to handle him with kid gloves all the time. I've tried to be careful of what I say and act like nothing is different, but if I mention anything close to the word treatment, or heaven forbid, the name David, even if I'm not referring to *that* David, he gets all moody and upset."

"It is understandable he would feel that way. Have you—had sex with him since you returned?"

"Yes, on the night I got back, but not again. He's so angry, and I don't want to make love to an angry man," she said and stared at the floor. The truth was that she didn't want to make love to Todd at all, and his anger was a good excuse to put him off.

"May I suggest that you try to get past the anger and put yourself out there? He must be feeling insecure and conflicted. I believe denying him will only fuel the anger," he said gently.

"I know, but things with David were so intense, and he could... well, please me like no one else has ever done before. It's hard to go back to something that's not as good, you know?" She had never spoken to him about sexual matters, and it was only because she knew he and David had discussed their sex life that she was able to be so open.

"I imagine it would be, but if you want your marriage to survive, you must give him some slack. Try to put yourself in his shoes, Erin."

"I know."

"Did David tell you we spoke on the telephone?"

"Yes."

"He was frightened, but I imagine he did a good job of helping you recover, correct?" he said with a smile.

"Yeah, he was great," she said. "What was it you were telling him about the other people involved in treatments?"

"Ah, yes. The newest data reveals that when a paired couple is a true match, they have a nearly instant, powerful connection. I asked David if he experienced the same phenomenon and he told me he had. Did you as well?"

Erin laughed and felt her cheeks get warm. "You have no idea. It was like… like we were two clouds on a hot summer night—exchanging heat lightning back and forth. It was amazing and exhilarating. I admit I long for more—all the time. Oh, and please excuse my bluntness, but if you can get a Brit to tell you about something so personal, I feel like I can open up too." Her cheeks and neck were radiating heat, so she took her sweatshirt off. "The sex was out of this world, Doctor Nan! Like nothing I'd ever had before." She closed her eyes and fanned her face with her hand, "I feel guilty about it, but it's like a drug or something."

Doctor Nanavala smiled at her. "I am glad you feel comfortable confiding in me. As for the amazing sex—my colleagues and I are being told the same thing from every patient who has started treatments. In fact, there have been some discoveries made over the last few weeks. I'll do my best to explain it to you, though before I begin, you must remember that this is not conclusive data. What I am going to share with you is the hypothesis of many scientists who are researching and exploring these and other possible venues of research.

"As you know, prostaglandin E2 causes infertility as well as varied known side effects. Chronic stress caused to the body through prolonged secretion of this hormone also causes many diverse problems in different people, including multisystem disorder in a few. After all, the body is an ecosystem, with limited resilience; if one function fails for a prolonged period, other systems will start collapsing eventually as well."

"Yes, I seem to remember being told that," she said.

"This hormone, PGE2, is only part of a bigger pathway in the endocrine system. Research is underway to elucidate the entire pathway and how it interacts with different endocrine pathways and body systems. So far, only bits of this complex pathway have been uncovered."

"Uh, elucidate?"

"Sorry, it means to make clear, interpret, or… perhaps unravel."

"Okay, go on."

"Due to multisystem disorder caused by stress and pathway interactions, no single targeted treatment approach has worked efficiently for everyone who has FD. Therefore, as you know firsthand, until recently, patients have only been offered symptomatic treatment, when available, to manage the disease, and a curative treatment is yet to be discovered."

"Yeah, an oxygen tent isn't much fun," Erin said.

"I believe you," he said with compassion. "But there is good news. There has been a breakthrough in the link between PGE2 and the fertility cycles of a woman. There seems to be a correlation between the beginning of the disease's symptoms at the start of the fertility cycle, puberty, menstruation, and the end of them, at menopause. Essentially, the disease may resolve itself at menopause. Seeing that FD is a relatively new disease, research is ongoing, and we learn more at each stage of our patient's lives. There are examples of women in early menopause whose symptoms have greatly decreased and one woman, whom I have met, who has been symptom-free for several months, without treatments."

"Wow! That's exciting, except it means we're dependent on the treatments until that happens. And for those who aren't willing to have them, they might not live long enough to get that relief," she said reflectively.

"Yes, although with this information, we may be able to use hysterectomy as a way to stop the symptoms. It is not the most ideal course of action, as it has its own set of issues, but it might be the only option for severe cases of FD."

"That's good to know, but what about the men? Have you found out why they get off scot-free, yet?"

Doctor Nan smiled at her. "We have continued studying the male FD children, with the logic that if FD affects female children, perhaps it has also impacted the male children, though in a more subtle manner, but to no avail. We had hoped to find a combination of molecules found only in the sperm of FD male children. However, that has, thus far, not been the case.

"On the other hand, the hypothesis for our current research is that it all boils down to genetics, not a connection with male FD children. The men born as a result of Fertilis make up only a small percentage of those with Registry matches. There are more men, born from natural conception, who are being matched. Those men have the perfect combination of the individualistic molecules to neutralize the harmful effect PGE2 is producing, naturally. The mixture, concentration, and healing effectiveness in the sperm of each male differs, depending on their genetics and lifestyle.

"When we tried creating a treatment using only the sperm of a man who should have been a match, it failed every time, and we were puzzled. There seemed to be a key—another phenomenon at play that allowed the molecules to do the job, and we believe we have figured it out. The other variable to consider is pheromones. Each human being emits its own unique cocktail of pheromones, and that cocktail can block the over-stimulation of PGE2 and can also block the pathway that causes chronic stress to the body. So, we have two separate functions that, hypothetically, treat the disease, but they cannot do it on their own. It is only when both the molecules in the matching male's sperm and pheromones are present with the right woman that it works, and there is an ideal match.

"Pheromones! Now it makes sense; David kept sniffing me, my hair, mostly, though I couldn't figure out why. I don't use anything special in it, but he seemed to be drawn to it like a June bug to the porch light," she said and laughed light-heartedly.

"That *is* interesting. Did you sense the same phenomenon with him?"

"Well, he's wealthy, so I assumed it was expensive cologne, but I was most definitely attracted to whatever the smell was. I could've lived in his neck," she said dreamily.

"I would conclude that you had the same experience then. Good," he said and was silent for a moment. She opened her eyes and saw him watching her. "Now, back to Todd; you are going to have to give him time—"

"Yeah, but my next treatment is in a few days. Even if he's started to come to grips with the first one, the next will steamroll him again. I'm not sure—I don't know what to do."

"Yes, it is complicated. All you can do is take it day by day." He stood and put his hand on her shoulder. "There are helplines for you and Todd to call if you need them. I will have my nurse give you the information. Also, please call the clinic if you have another episode, or any symptoms, no matter how minor. You should talk to David about decreasing the time between your treatments, as well, and I would like to see you again in six weeks," he said.

"Okay. Thank you, Dr. Nan."

Chapter Nine

COMPLICATED

On Friday afternoon, Erin received a message from David. Todd was home from work, but he'd gone straight to the garage to tinker while he was in his work clothes. Hearing David's ringtone was still exciting; her stomach felt fluttery, and her hand shook a bit as she unlocked her screen.

D: *Hello, Erin. I need to know the nearest airport to you so I can tell Tina which one you prefer. I'm excited to see you again!*

E: *I'm beside myself, longing to be with you! As for airports, there's one ten minutes away, but it's much less expensive to fly into Milwaukee or Chicago. I don't mind picking you up.*

D: *What? But there is one ten minutes from you?*

E: *Yes, Austin Straubel, but it'll cost less if you fly into Milwaukee or Chicago. It's usually over $500 more to fly into Green Bay.*

D: *Erin… I'm not bothered about the price. I need to see you, the sooner, the better.*

E: *Oh, yeah, I forgot. How awkward…talking to you about saving money? I mean…$500 is nothing to you, right? I'm sorry.*

D: *I wouldn't say it's nothing, but it's not going to stand in the way of me coming directly to you.*

E: *Okay.*

D: *I'm sorry, darling. I reckon that was insensitive of me. I'm just not used to considering costs.*

E: *It's okay, don't be sorry. I just don't know anything about NOT pinching pennies. It's completely foreign to me, and I'm embarrassed that I even brought that up.*

D: *I say we forget about being embarrassed and focus on seeing each other again in two days, okay? I've missed you!*

E: *I've moddrs ypu9*

(Five-minutes later)

D: *Erin?*

(Five more minutes later)

D: *Erin? What happened? Are you okay?*

(Ten min later)

D: *Well, I hope you're alright, darling. It's bedtime here, so I'll talk to you tomorrow. Sweet dreams.*

First thing in the morning, David looked at his phone and saw that Erin had finally replied.

E: *I'm so sorry! Todd came in from the garage, and I couldn't get back to my phone until now. I'm just about to go to bed. I wish you were here. I hope you weren't too worried. Xoxo*

When Erin woke in the morning, she saw a new message waiting for her on her lock screen, so she took her phone into the bathroom to read it.

D: *I was a bit anxious; I admit. I'm glad you're alright. I wish I were there as well...lying next to you...instead of him. I'm jealous he has your time and attention. My mind tries to conjure images of what you do...together. Usually, I can shut it down, but sometimes I can't, and it makes me feel ill and out of sorts.*

D: *Thank you for explaining what happened. I reckon I was more worried than I thought. Sweet dreams. x*

She hurried to reply before Todd became suspicious.

E: *I'm so sorry! I know what you mean about your mind trying to imagine THAT. Don't let your mind think like that! We don't do that anymore, so, please don't worry, okay? Two days is an eternity! I miss you.*

D: *What time is it there, 7:00 am? Good morning! Just after lunch here. I don't know what my mind believes is happening, but I'm glad you're not doing THAT. I'll let you know my arrival time for Monday as soon as Tina sends my itinerary, and yes, it's an eternity. X*

Erin heard Todd opening drawers in the bedroom and knew he'd want to take a shower, so she didn't reply. Instead, she brushed her teeth and put on her robe, which hung on a hook next to the door. She opened the door, hoping not to get groped, but Todd had other ideas.

He blocked the doorway and tried to kiss her, taking hold of her breast, then he pushed her gently into the bathroom again, pinning her against the sink. His anticipation of sex with her was apparent by the erection she could feel as he pressed himself against her. "I want you so bad!" he gasped as he tried to put his hand between her legs.

"It's... too early, Todd! I'm hardly awake," she said and tried to push him away, but he took hold of her waist and continued to press his hard-on against her.

"It's been two weeks, Erin. I want to make love to you! You told me nothing would change after—but you lied. Now let me—"

"Please stop, that hurts," she said, but he only pressed harder.

"Let me make love to you," he said more forcefully, which made her angry.

"I said no, Todd, now knock it off! Let me go!" she insisted and pushed him away. "God! I hate when you do stuff like that!"

He narrowed his eyes and stared at her as he took a step back. "You used to like it when I pretended to force you," he said.

"Not anymore." She knew he wasn't pretending that time.

"Obviously," he sneered and stormed out of the room.

She heard the kitchen door slam shut as she left the bathroom, breathing heavily, partly from anger and partly from the flashbacks she was having of the attack in New Orleans. She placed her hand on her heart; it was beating hard, then she lay her other arm against her tall dresser, resting her forehead on it while she tried to catch her breath. *This is getting far too complicated,* she thought and sat on the bed. She was startled when her breath caught as it did during lead-up symptoms. *Two weeks is too long between treatments.*

David's home life was becoming more complicated every day. Susannah was acting as though nothing was wrong and being more affectionate than she'd been in years. She tried to kiss him more than once and even crawled into bed with him one night, attempting to seduce him.

He'd been sound asleep when she snuggled up behind him and started fondling him. He'd rolled over, thinking it was Erin, but as soon as he felt her tiny frame, he jumped out of bed and told her to get out. He presumed that was why she'd been crying on the day their children had ambushed him in his office. Later, he had learned it was simply a cunning ploy to obtain information from them.

He was reading a script for a commercial in his office when there was a knock on the door. "Come in," he said, and Charlie stepped into the room.

"Hello—" was all he was able to get out before his son started talking a mile a minute.

"I don't know what to do, Dad! Mum is asking us questions… about what we learned other day—About the lady—Erin—" He ran his hand over his light-brown, wavy hair and scrunched up his face, showing just how uncomfortable he was. "I feel as though I'm betraying you—and now I feel as if I'm being disloyal to her!"

David patted the seat cushion on the sofa next to him, and the boy sat, elbows on his knees and head in his hands. "I don't feel betrayed, Charlie, and your Mum shouldn't be doing that to you. You aren't required to tell her anathing you don't wish to. If you're put on the spot again, be respectful, but kindly ask her to come to me."

He was tired of Susannah's games and wished he had someone to talk to. Merely texting Erin wasn't enough. He needed to see her, feel her, talk to her, to hear her voice. He felt he was going mad with it.

The young boy looked up at him gravely. "A'right, Dad. I'm sorry, but I told her—"

"Don't worry about it, mate, okay? There's no need to confess; I didn't tell you anathing that was a secret. I—wouldn't spread it around to your friends, mind, but you shouldn't feel guilty," he said and accepted the hug the boy gave him before running out of the room.

He knew he should confront Susannah about her behavior, but he didn't know how. He wasn't one for conflict and usually ended up steamrolled before he had a chance to make his full argument, anyway, so he left it alone. Thankfully, the children would be back in school soon and away from their mother's abuse.

Chapter Ten

ERIN HITS A HUMP

For the first few days back home, Erin had felt great. By day eleven, though, she could tell that the treatments had worn off. The energy she'd felt just a week before was gone, and it was hard to function again. After supper, she sat curled up on the sofa, trying to relax. She was starting to have difficulty breathing again and was tired most of the time. It wasn't quite as bad as it had been before starting the treatments, but it was enough that she just wanted to sleep.

"Erin?" Todd said as he came up from the basement, slamming the door.

"Mmm?" she said quietly.

"What is it *now*?" he asked, sounding exasperated. "I was going to ask you to—Oh, never mind. I can see that you'll just say you're too tired—again."

"Sorry," she mumbled, keeping her eyes closed. "I think the treatments have worn off already."

"Yeah, how convenient for you that the *treatment-s* aren't lasting the whole two weeks. Now you'll have to have them more often, won't you? That's what you want, isn't it?" he barked.

Erin opened her eyes and narrowed them at Todd. She'd known it was only a matter of time before there would be a confrontation. "I was the one who didn't want to do this," she reminded him. "But between you and Dr Nan, I gave in. I was right, it was a horrible idea, but I was also wrong. I hoped I'd be able to shut off my heart and come back to you as though nothing had happened. I couldn't, and now I can't pretend that things are going to be okay. They aren't, and all I'm doing is hurting you and you don't deserve it. I'm sorry—" She hadn't meant to blurt it out but couldn't take it back. It was true, so she wasn't going to regret it.

"No! Don't say that! We can make it work!"

"No, Todd, we can't, and I'm too tired to fight—" she began.

"Did it occur to you that maybe it has something to do with your weight? Maybe if you lost a few pounds—" he said

Her eyes widened, and she glared at him. "You know how hard I've tried to—No, I'm not doing this! You can just—If you want a smaller woman, go ahead and find one—"

"I only meant that—It might help—" He tried to backpedal, but it was too late.

They'd come to an agreement long ago that she wouldn't bring up how many times she'd found his stash of porn, and he wouldn't mention her losing weight. No holds were barred anymore. "Where are they hidden this time? Do you honestly believe that I don't know about the filthy magazines you buy while I'm at my girls' weekend? Are they in the attic? Oh, they are, aren't they? Maybe you should stop looking at *them* so you can last a bit longer with *me*! Did it occur to *you* that if you were a little bit less selfish in bed, I might want it more often? Perhaps, if you concentrated on *me* instead of pleasing only *yourself*—"

"Oh, you mean like your precious David does?" he spat.

Erin's eyes narrowed, and she stood laboriously. She walked right up to him and stood two inches from his face, out of breath and panting. "Exactly like my precious David has done *every time*, you selfish asshole. I'm going to bed; you can sleep in the spare room with your porn," she said and nearly fell as she stormed out of the living room and slammed the door to their bedroom.

She had never spoken to her dear husband like that before, and once she was in their room, she almost regretted it. The strain she'd put on herself was a huge regret, though, as she sat on the edge of the bed, wishing she had someone to undress her. She took her phone out of her pocket and climbed into bed, fully clothed, then she opened her message app and touched David's name.

E: *Oh, David, I can't stand it! We just
had a terrible fight, and I need you.
How many more days is it? I feel so
tired again. I think the treatments
have completely worn off already. I'm
sorry. I shouldn't burden you with my
problems, but I miss you so much, and
I need another treatment. More than
that, I need you to make love to me. I
miss you! XOXO*

The time on the alarm clock read 8:40 pm, which was only 2:40 am for
David, so she knew she'd have to wait to hear back from him. She took her
phone off *do not disturb* just in case and held it to her heart as she drifted off
into a restless sleep. An hour later, she was startled awake by Todd's message
alert.

T: *I deserved that. We had an agreement,
and I broke it. But how do you think
I feel? I'm just really frustrated. Please
forgive me.*

She didn't reply and fell back to sleep. Another hour later, she groaned as
she heard him open the hatch door to the attic, then she heard him close it,
and soon afterward, the spare room door closed. It was hard not to yell at him
and make him feel guilty, but she didn't care anymore. Just as she managed to
fall back to sleep again, she got a reply from David.

D: *I wish I were there to make love to
you right now. I dreamed that you
were in my arms last night and woke
to find it was just a dream. I'm sorry
you're feeling poorly again. I wish I
could help you. Also, you may lay your*

burdens on me whenever you need to,
darling. I'll gladly take them for you.

On Sunday morning, Erin woke feeling like she hadn't slept at all, though she could remember snippets of the odd dreams she'd had. She sat up on the edge of the bed, not wanting to change her clothes, and REALLY not wanting to deal with Todd. She looked at her phone and saw a new message from David which gave her a boost of adrenaline.

> D: *How are you this morning, darling? I hope you feel better. I've received my itinerary from Tina. I'll be arriving in Green Bay at 4:31 pm. Are you able to meet me there? I simply cannot wait to see you!*

She would pick him up at the airport, there was no doubt about that!

> E: *Honestly, I'm exhausted. I didn't sleep very well, but seeing your message makes me feel better! I'll pick you up! I wish I could use the time travel device to go forward in time, though it would probably take me ten years past where I want to be...lol*

> D: *Haha Yes, it probably would. A reliable time travel device would be brilliant now, wouldn't it? It's only 26 hours until we're together again! Oh, and I have a surprise for you!*

D: *I…hate to say this in a message, but I will be and am, even now, very ready for you. Please, darling, don't be late tomorrow!*

Erin gasped, feeling her body tingle in anticipation.

E: *Holy Moses, David! I'm ready for you too! I feel like I'm about to burst! The things I'd do if you were here right now! OH! I almost wish you hadn't said that! I can hardly stand the ache inside of me! Still, I'm so glad you did say it.*

Before she hit send, she heard the kitchen door slam, and then Todd's car started. She lifted the miniblinds and watched him pull out of the driveway, then she walked out to the kitchen and saw a note.

> *Erin,*
> *I'll be back in about an hour.*
> *Todd*

She went back into her room, shut the door, and finished her message to David.

Are you alone? Can you call me? Todd isn't here, and I want to hear your voice.

She hit send and waited. After a few minutes, her cell phone rang with David's ringtone, and she was suddenly nervous. "Hello?" she said as a question like she hadn't been expecting him to call her.

"Ach, darling, et's so good tae hear yer voice!" she heard the familiar accent say, and she wanted to cry from sheer joy.

"Oh, David!" she panted, wanting to reach through the phone and kiss him. All she could do was breathe heavily, though she wanted with all her heart to continue their conversation about what she'd do to him. "I'm sorry, but I just can't get the image out of my head of you being… ready for me, and it's making me crazy!"

"I am, Erin! I'm *so very* ready for yeh. I've never had phone sex before, but I'd like to with yeh now, is that a'right? Will you—"

"Yes, I want to so much," she interrupted, panting.

"I'm in ma study with the door locked, sittin' on ma desk chair. I'm gonna unfasten ma trousers now," he said, sounding like a pro.

The chair squeaked as he moved, then she heard him unzip his zipper, and she thought she'd have a heart attack. "I—I'm sitting on the edge of my bed. I'm naked and wish I could take hold of you. I want to—Holy Moses, this is difficult! I want to stroke you and take you into my mouth," she said and heard him moan.

"I'm holding maself in ma hand, imagining your tongue—Ach, Erin!" he said, and she could hear *him* panting, too.

"I am going to lay down and touch myself. I long to feel your tongue on me too," she said and put the phone on speaker as she did.

"Erin, I want tae enter you! I want tae slip maself into you, wet and wantin' me. I want tae feel you reach yer orgasm all around me!"

"I want that too, David! I… want you to fill me up and I want to… climax over and over again for you!" she said, increasing the effort she was giving to her task, but nothing was happening. It felt good, but it wasn't bringing her any closer to an orgasm. "David… I need to… I mean—Just one minute… please keep talking!"

She reached under her bed and found the lockbox where she kept her vibrator. She scrambled to find the small key she kept in her nightstand drawer and opened the lock with trembling hands. *Why do you lock it up, anyway? Who's gonna go looking through your stuff?*

"I want to touch yer breasts as I thrust into yeh! I want tae see them rock up and down as our bodies move together," he said quietly, but with so much intensity she gasped.

She finally got out her vibrator, but then she had to change the batteries. It was ruining the mood, and she was getting frustrated. "Damn," she whispered.

"Erin? What're yeh doin'?"

"I'm sorry. I—I'm embarrassed, but I need my... vibrator," she said near tears and wishing she'd thought about it earlier.

"Vibrator? Ma Losh!" he said.

She didn't know if that was a good exclamation or not. "I... it's just that I can't... get there without it—" she said, as all the blood that had been between her legs began filling her face, making it red and hot. "Does that... turn you off?"

"Ach, Erin—It doesn't turn me off. What... does et look like?"

"Oh—It's pink... and uh, sort of looks like a penis. It's soft and smooth and has, I think they call it a rabbit, but I don't usually use that part." She finally got the batteries in and laid back on the bed, then she turned it on and heard David moan again.

"Are yeh using it now?" he asked, his deep breaths shaking a bit. "Ach, I want to see you," he panted.

"Yes, I am, can't you hear it?" She began to run the tip of the long vibrator over her clitoris and labia, which felt good, but it wasn't the same as when she was with him in the flesh, and her frustration was quickly getting the better of her.

"Aye, I can hear et. How does it feel?"

"It feels good but... not like it feels when you touch me."

"Ach... Erin, I'm so close now; please tell me you are as well."

Her heart dropped; she knew it would take a lot longer for her to climax, a minimum of ten minutes, though probably a lot longer. She knew he'd never last that long, and she didn't have the stamina for it anyway, so she reverted to her old standby of faking it, though it made her feel horrible. "Ah, yes, I—I'm close," she said, building up her breathing. As she began to make quiet moaning sounds, he moaned again.

I'm—" he began and grunted, a sound she'd heard him make before, then he was silent for a few moments.

Erin made sounds simulating a small orgasm and waited for him to say something, feeling embarrassed in the aftermath. She heard his chair squeaking again and then the sound of tissues being pulled out of a box.

"Thank you, love," he said, still sounding out of breath. "I needed that. I hope it felt good for you, as well."

"Yeah, it was nice, thank you. I miss you so much," she said, as tears of frustration and anger at her inability to perform filled her eyes.

"Ach, dinnae cry, darling! Et's only a day before we'll be together again."

"Yeah, plus an extra six hours for me." She couldn't stop herself from crying and longed for David to hold her." Sorry, I'm just—Crap, Todd's home!" she said, hearing the garage door opening. "I've gotta go now. I love you, and I can't wait to see you again! Bye!" She ended the call and had just enough time to put her vibrator back in its box and push it under the bed before she heard Todd slam the kitchen door as he entered the house.

What in the hell are you doing, Erin? she thought as she tried to slow her breathing. *You're no better than Todd, sneaking behind his back and hiding your own version of porn from him. This isn't who you want to be, and you need to make a decision—soon!*

Erin dreaded the thought of telling Todd what time David would be arriving, but she managed to do it without starting a huge war. There was no way her husband would allow her to spend the night in the hotel; it was too close to home, so she was limited to the hours he was at work to be with David. However, as luck would have it, the support group meeting Todd attended was postponed to Monday night, which meant Erin would have more time to spend with him. She was planning to give him a tour of all her favorite places and hoped it would be warm, though there was no knowing what the weather would bring during the first week of June in Wisconsin. All she could do was hope it was on her side.

Chapter Eleven

GAMES & DIVERSIONS

On Sunday afternoon, Erin and Todd headed to Lily and Nick Graves's house for a game night, as planned. The two couples were good friends and often had dinner and/or games with each other. Erin knew Todd didn't want to hang out with anyone that night. Knowing she would be with David the next day had put him in a foul mood, but she'd managed to talk him into it. She knew he'd have fun, plus it had the added benefit of making time go faster for her.

They arrived on time, rang the doorbell, and as usual, their two dogs went wild. Things were undeniably strained between Todd and her, and it was difficult to hide as Nick opened the door and welcomed them inside. Lily showed up next and offered them drinks. "I'll have my usual, please," Erin said, having to raise her voice over the dogs.

Jax, a Boston Terrier-Labrador mix, was barking, sniffing, and pushing his way around them, while Khaleesi, a Pomeranian-Shih Tzu mix, was wagging her fluffy tail, yapping, and jumping up on their legs, wanting to be held. "Alright, you two, hush!" Lily said to the dogs and opened the back door so the pups would go outside, giving the humans a bit of peace. It was a bit too much peace and they could all feel the tension in the atmosphere. "A Bomb-Pop it is, then," Lily said brightly. "And what would you like, Todd? We have a few craft IPAs if you're interested?"

"Do you have a Miller Lite?" he asked, not being much of a drinker.

"I think I have a Bud Light in the downstairs fridge," Nick said and went to get it when Todd nodded his approval.

"Where's Ariana?" Erin asked, expecting to see their ten-year-old daughter.

"My mom's watching her tonight; it's nice to have a day off every now and then," Lily said.

"I imagine so," she replied.

They stood around the enormous island, making small talk, catching up, and getting drinks settled so they could get started gaming. The guys began talking about the Packers, so the ladies moved to the dining room to load the table with snacks. Since they were far enough away from the men, Erin could talk to Lily about her next treatment. "He's flying into Austin Straubel tomorrow afternoon," she said, softly. "I'm going to pick him up and I can't wait, Lily! I'm dying to be with him again, but I'm so torn!"

"I don't envy you—well, okay, maybe a little bit!" she admitted, and both women laughed. "Okay, maybe a lot, but I don't know how I'd choose between the two of them. I guess you'll just have to suffer through having both until... until something happens."

Erin didn't want anything to 'happen' in order to choose. "I guess," she said with a slight shrug.

"My stepdad made us watch this old movie called *Paint Your Wagon* with Clint Eastwood," Lily said as she filled a huge bowl with tortilla chips at one end of the table. "It was about a woman who ended up living out west with two men... as a trio... if you know what I mean?" She winked, and Erin smiled. "They reasoned that if Mormon men could have multiple wives, then women should be able to have multiple husbands. Maybe that's the route you should take?"

They laughed till their sides ached, trying to imagine something like that. "Good night nurse, Lil! Todd would NEVER go for it, and neither would David," *but wouldn't it be something!* "I wish you could meet him, Lil! He's wonderful, he really is!"

The two women grew quiet. They heard the men laughing about something in the other room, and the weight of Erin's dilemma settled around them like fog clouds. "I'm sorry for making it into a joke, Erin. I'm sure this is really hard for you. Even though the thought of being with David Elliott seems amazing, I wouldn't want the stress and heartache you're going through.

Erin was caught off guard by the sincerity of her friend's statement and felt hot tears pricking her eyes. She blew out a calming breath and smiled sadly. "Thanks for that. It's getting harder every day, but who knows, maybe something *will* 'happen' to help me decide. I just don't want anyone to get hurt more than they need to."

Lily hugged her, "I know," she said and then fanned her eyes, apparently fighting tears as well. "I think we need to get this party started, don't you?"

"Absolutely!"

"Hey, Nick!" Lily called out to him.

"Yes, dear?" he said, which was his usual reply.

"Why don't you reveal your surprise game now?"

"Okay."

"Ooh! A surprise?" Erin said since they'd been playing a Harry Potter-themed deck-building board game at least once a month for years.

"He said he found something we'll love, but he wouldn't tell me what it is!" Lily said.

Nick went back to their bedroom, and Todd entered the dining room. As soon as he saw Erin, the atmosphere in the room grew heavy. When Nick joined them, he was holding a small box she recognized as a card game called Fluxx.

"Oh! I love Fluxx!" she said, trying to ignore Todd's moodiness. "What version is it?" She knew there were quite a few themes, such as *Monty Python*, *Doctor Who*, and the *Wizard of Oz*, to name a few. He held it up, and the women gasped while Erin blushed ten shades of crimson.

"I know how much you both love *Future Explorations*, so when I saw this, I bought it," he said, sounding proud of himself.

"I… didn't know they'd… come out with a *Future Explorations* version," Erin said, trying to keep her cool. She and Lily exchanged looks of amazement and were laughing inwardly, though Erin's blush got darker when she saw Lily's knowing face.

Both men knew the ladies had at least minor crushes on David Elliott, the lead character in the show, so their behavior didn't seem to surprise them much. "Well, this ought to be interesting," Todd said, oblivious to the *true* reason they were so amused.

Erin usually drank a bit when they were over, and that night was no exception. She had taken a long nap that day and spoke to David, so she had a bit of energy, thus she had no qualms about having a large Bomb Pop, which contained Blue UV, lemonade, and grenadine. Todd and Lily had beer, while Nick had a hard apple cider.

They sat at the table, the men facing each other and the women doing the same, while Lily unwrapped the deck of cards. She made sure to set out the best ones for everyone to look at before shuffling them in. The images printed on the cards weren't actual pictures of the people and things from the show; they were artist renderings, which often didn't do them justice, or were downright ugly. The ones in that version, though, were fantastic.

The first card in the deck was of David as his character, John Thomas Fife. Erin wanted to stare at it all night but took Lily's gentle kick under the table as a cue to look at the next one. "I think I need another drink before we start," Erin said and gulped down her first one.

Lily went out to the kitchen and came back a few minutes later with another Bomb Pop. "Sorry," she said when Erin made a face with her first sip. "I think I used too much UV."

"No, it's good," Erin coughed out her reply.

They played several rounds of the game, and each time David's face would turn up, Erin blushed. It was annoying since she was already warm from the cocktail. She managed to hide the blushing pretty well because her face would get red and start burning, sometimes when she drank alcohol, anyway.

At one point, after three Bomb Pops, which was one more than usual, a card came up that read '*Le Potage!*' and Erin nearly spit out the mouthful she'd just sucked through her bendy straw. "Good night nurse! That's so funny! I just said that to Dav—"

The table went silent. Lily's eyes nearly popped out of their sockets, and Todd's face turned red. He stood and excused himself to use the bathroom. Nick looked at them in confusion. "What happened?" he asked.

"I'll tell you later," Lily whispered to her husband.

"Fuck!" Erin said and covered her mouth with her hands. She couldn't believe what she'd nearly said or that she'd said anything at all about David in front of Todd, even though he didn't know it was the same one.

After quite a long time, Todd finally came back to the table and sat in his chair, his face guarded and grim. "I'm sor—" Erin began, but Todd shook his head, so she stopped and looked down at the cards laid out in front of her on the table. She had ruined the evening, and she knew he'd want to leave.

"Want to play something else?" Nick offered.

Todd gave him a forced smile. "No, thanks," he said sullenly.

"I think we should go now," Erin said after a *very* long moment of awkwardness. "We had a lovely time! Thanks for having us over."

Nick still looked confused but went along with it. Lily got up with them as they gathered their things and made their way to the door. Todd left the house without saying anything, and Erin hugged Lily, feeling like an ass. "I'm sorry I ruined everything; we were having so much fun!" Erin said.

"It's okay—we'll just have to get together again sooner than usual next time. He'll be alright, won't he?" Lily asked, genuinely concerned.

"I hope so, but I'm getting tired of tiptoeing. I know I was out of line tonight, but it's getting worse and worse all the time." Erin was suddenly exhausted and just wanted to go home and go to sleep, though she predicted Todd wasn't going to let that happen.

As she stepped out into the crisp, late spring evening, she shivered. The days were much warmer, but the nights could still be a bit chilly. She shivered again, dreading the drive home. Todd had the radio on when she got into their car, which meant he wouldn't want to talk. That was okay with her, as it was better than their inevitable fight.

Todd bolted directly into the house as soon as they got home. Erin wanted nothing more than to get into the driver's seat and drive away. She knew it was because he was hurting, but she was too tired and intoxicated to deal with his pain through a fight just then. Wearily, she made her way inside, hanging her purse and jacket on the hook by the door. Then she slipped off her shoes and mechanically put them on the rack, one at a time.

When she entered their bedroom, she found him sitting naked on the edge of the bed, holding his pillow over his lap. She walked in and silently began taking off her clothes, not wanting to start anything. Once she was completely undressed, nightgown in hand, he stood and came up behind her. He wrapped his arms around hers, pinning them to her sides, then roughly took hold of her breasts with both hands while pressing himself against her backside.

She was frightened by how forceful he was being and tried to keep herself calm. "Oww, Todd! That hurts! What are you—" she began, but then he shifted one of his hands to cover her mouth, which caused her to start trembling. Next, he moved her, with some force, to the edge of the bed.

Erin had never experienced that side of her husband, and she was terrified. He let go of her and pushed her onto their Union Jack comforter. She flopped painfully onto her stomach and rolled to her side, dazed, and tried to back away, but he grabbed her ankle. There was a peculiar look in his eyes that made her want to escape.

"I'm going to fuck you now! You are my wife, goddammit, and you are going to let me do it," he said with a bone-chilling calmness that caused the hairs on the back of her neck to rise, then she felt goosebumps crawl up her arms and legs.

"You can… make love to me, but—" He put his finger to his lips to cut her off and then tried to drag her toward him. "You're scaring me! Please—"

"Be quiet, and lay down," he said, his voice relaxed and even.

Erin wanted to scream for help, but couldn't, just like when she'd been assaulted in New Orleans. She'd chosen not to tell Todd about that part of being mugged and regretted it once again. She had never, for one second, been afraid of her husband before, and until that moment, she'd trusted him with her life. Now, fear was gripping her, and she didn't know what to do. "I don't want to!" she said as calmly as she could. "Please stop this."

Todd crawled onto the bed, and with a move unlike anything he'd ever done before, or anything she had even imagined he *could* do, flipped her over. He wrangled her down onto her stomach, one hand pinned under her and the other one held to her side with his knee as he straddled her. She was in a full panic and was having a hard time catching her breath. *What's he going to do? Is he planning to rape me? This can't be happening!*

She wanted to call out for David, but that would be useless, plus it might even make him hit her, so she decided to go limp. There was no way she'd be able to fight him off, and the more she struggled, the more he was likely to hurt her, so she decided to play dead. "I know you're angry, but... you're scaring me, and... I don't want you to do this. That means... you'll be raping me if... you follow through," she panted, struggling for breath.

"I want you to be mine again," he hissed through clenched teeth. "I want to take you back from the man who so obviously has you under his spell. You were mine first, and I want what is mine!" He moved, allowing her arms to go free, and flipped her onto her back. She screamed and instinctively raised her arm to her face as though he was going to hit her.

Either he realized just how frightened she was, or he was appalled that she would think he might strike her; she didn't know the reason, but he froze. Seeming to return to his right mind, he retreated and resumed his position at the edge of the bed. "I'm going to sleep in the spare room tonight. I'm... sorry I scared you. I—Well—good night." He got up, taking his pillow with him, and left the room.

Once she heard the spare room door close, she was finally able to breathe normally again. She was shaking and felt hot tears running down her cheeks, though she didn't know when she'd started crying. She got up and locked the bedroom door, then she crawled back into bed, pulling the covers all the way up to her chin. *What in the hell? Please, don't let David's plane be delayed tomorrow!* she prayed, and cried herself to sleep.

Chapter Twelve

DAVID'S ARRIVAL

Erin woke an hour after Todd had left for work and then remembered the events of the night before. *What do I do now? I can't tell David, he'll go berserk!* she thought. She didn't know what to do, but she needed a cup of tea, so she put on her robe and headed into the kitchen. Memories of what Todd had done to her came back in waves of shivering and nausea that rolled over her like the tide coming in. Seeing the notepad sitting next to the landline telephone, she ripped off a piece of paper and wrote a note.

> *Todd,*
>
> *I don't understand what you were trying to do last night, but it scared the shit out of me. I will not be staying here tonight. I'm not sure when I'll be back.*
> *Erin*

She placed it under the flower arrangement on the kitchen table so it wouldn't blow away or somehow get lost.

Making tea took only fifteen minutes and getting dressed took five. Four o'clock seemed an eternity to wait, but now that there was some packing to do, she hoped it would seem to go a bit faster. Pulling up the chain around her neck, she retrieved her compass and held it, kissing its smooth glass top. Then she prayed for a safe journey for David.

Normally, she would have poured herself a bowl of cereal, but she was equally too upset about Todd and too excited about David to eat just then. Instead, she went back to her room and took a shower, listening to the CD she'd kept from their last night in New Orleans. At noon, she made herself eat half a sandwich with a bowl of tomato soup, which was all she could force down.

Her makeup turned out okay, doing it the way Champagne had taught her, but it wasn't nearly as nice as when the drag queen had done it for her. After that, all she had to do was wait. David's plane wasn't supposed to land until 4:31, but she wanted to be there early in case it arrived sooner than expected. She would make sure to leave before 3:50, which was when Todd usually got home, though it didn't take long to get to the airport.

A few minutes were used up washing the five dirty dishes and folding a load of laundry, then she tidied up a bit, just in case there was a reason for him to be invited into the house. She checked the toilets to make sure they were clean and made her bed, as well as the one in the spare room. When she was finished, it was just after 3:40, so she spritzed perfume under her top, grabbed her cell phone, keys, purse, and a book, though she doubted she'd be able to concentrate on it, and locked the door behind her.

Erin parked in the short-term lot at Austin Straubel airport. She walked under the sage-green covered walkway, entering the terminal through the sliding glass doors she'd gone through only two weeks earlier. The screen listing the arrivals showed that his flight was eight minutes ahead of schedule. The news made her so happy, she bounded halfway up the flight of stairs, only to run out of breath, thus forcing her to walk the rest of the way.

There was a long wait ahead of her, and as predicted, she couldn't concentrate on her book. Then, as the time of his plane's arrival grew nearer and nearer, she became more and more anxious. The thought of David Elliott being in Green Bay at all was thrilling, and knowing she'd get to spend that time with him—Well, honestly, it made her nervous. They'd been comfortable with each other two weeks earlier, but she was worried it wouldn't be the same as it was before.

As she gazed out the window, a small commuter plane landed and approached the terminal. It pulled up and stopped next to where she stood, and excitement bubbled up inside her, making her feel giddy. The tunnel connecting the plane to the building was attached, and soon passengers began to emerge.

She watched and waited until the steady stream of people stopped abruptly. The plane was tiny, and she started to panic when she didn't see David. *Did he change his mind?* she thought. She'd recently read a novel with a scenario like that, and fear gripped her heart.

After several minutes, one more person came out, followed by the pilot and two attendants, each pulling small rolling suitcases behind them. The last man was tall and thin and did look a bit like David, except he had grey hair and glasses, so she turned to find someone to speak with. She didn't know what she'd say, but she was growing more distraught every moment.

After searching for a few minutes, she couldn't find anyone to talk to about it. Feeling defeated, she sat on one of the padded chairs and typed a message to him with trembling hands and a hot, embarrassed face.

> E: *Where are you? Did you change your*
> *mind?*

She hit send and sat with her head in her hands until she heard a cellphone notification near her ear. It sounded like the one David used, but when she looked up, the only person nearby was the grey-haired man. He was watching her and didn't look away at her gaze. She looked away and checked her phone, again, for a reply from David.

The man walked right up to her, set his leather carry-on bag on the floor, and looked down, smiling at her, "Well, that's a fine way to greet a person," he said.

"Excuse me?" she said and then stood. He had taken his glasses off and was laughing at the look of bewilderment on her face. "David?" She looked at him closely, "Did you enter a time warp since I last saw you?" she asked, marveling at his transformation. "You look so different! Is it really you?"

He smiled, and his eyes twinkled at her, "A bit of bleach in ma hair and, *you* dinnae recognize me? Brilliant! I'll be able tae go anawhere with you, and no one will know who I am! I took a wee part in a television program in which I played an older man; what do yeh think?"

Erin laughed and stepped forward to kiss him, but he turned, acting cool toward her for the first time since they'd met. "What—" she began, but he was already walking toward the exit.

"Do you have a car here?" he asked a bit distantly.

"Um, yeah. What's wrong?"

"What's that? Nothing is wrong, Erin, I'd just like tae—"

"Right… okay," she interrupted, knowing he was lying. "I'm parked near the door." She braced herself and stood erect as she led him in a quick march out to the short-term parking lot. All her fears about things being different the next time they were together were coming true, and it was hard to take.

"Erin, slow down," he said as he hurried to keep up with her.

When she reached her car, she put her hand on the driver's side door handle and stopped, looking down at the blacktop. She didn't know whether to be angry, sad, disappointed, or a bit of everything. "Why?" she said softly.

David stood behind her and touched her shoulder. "Please, Erin, let's get into the—"

Her heart was breaking, so she nodded warily, not wanting to fight; she'd had enough of that with Todd. He had clearly gone home and made amends with his wife, so from now on, all she'd get from him was one treatment, that's it. "Alright." She opened the door, and David walked around to the passenger side.

He opened the back door first and placed his bag inside, then he got in and sat in the front seat. "Erin—" he began after putting his seatbelt on, but she was already backing out of the parking space. He saw tears falling down her cheek and put his hand on her thigh. "Please, pull over," he said, but they were at the kiosk to pay for parking. "Allow me." He handed her a twenty-dollar bill. She took it and gave it to the woman who'd taken her ticket.

"Thank you," Erin whispered as she waited for his change and then continued driving, not saying anything more.

"Stop, please—in there," he said and pointed to the Oneida Casino parking lot.

Erin did as he asked but couldn't look at him. "It's okay, I understand—"

"You dinnae understand anathin', now please get out," he said and opened his door. He stepped outside, walked to her side of the car, and then opened her door for her, but she didn't move. "Please, Erin."

She took his offered hand and looked at the ground. "What?"

"Look at me, please—Ach, never mind," he said and wrapped his arms around her, spinning her in a full circle. "Ach, Erin, I'm so sorry for that! I couldn't display any affection in the building. The pilot kent who I was, and I had tae be on ma guard, yeh ken? Please forgive me, and please, please allow me tae kiss you, darling."

Erin placed her cheek on his chest and began weeping, "I thought you'd changed your mind!" she said into his starched and ironed shirt—It smelled like him. "I thought you and Susannah had—" His heartbeat sang to her, and she knew she'd been wrong.

"Ach, no, darling. That will never happen; you have ma word. Dinnae be upset, ma love."

"Oh, David, I'm not... anymore." She raised her head and stood on her tiptoes to kiss him while running her fingers through his hair. *Oh, how I've missed his kisses.*

He pushed her away gently and smiled at her. "Ach, I've missed you!"

She stared into his soft brown eyes, his smile making his crow's feet more noticeable. The electricity was pulsing back and forth between them, and she felt weak. Her body craved him, and she didn't want to wait any longer. "I think the grey hair suits you very nicely! Where are you staying?" she asked, hoping it was close *and* where he wanted to go first.

"I'm at St. Brendan's Inn, do you know it?"

"Wow, I pegged you for a Lodge Kohler kind of guy."

"I looked at et, as well. Tina gave me a choice this time, but I wanted someplace less posh, where I could get a good pint and relax. The website mentioned a trail nearby that runs along a river; something about a fox, I believe? I thought mebbe we could take a stroll if the weather is fine."

Erin had been to St. Brendan's to eat several times but had never stayed there and had always wanted to see what their rooms were like. "That sounds lovely, David. Oh, I've missed you so much!" It had only been two weeks, but it felt like six months. She smiled at him and asked with feigned innocence, "Where do you want to go first?"

"Ye're a silly girl," he said, using his lovely Scottish accent. "Take me to ma room and be quick about et, lass!"

"As you wish," she said, wishing he *had* chosen Lodge Kohler, as it was much closer. "Get in, and I'll take you there, post-haste." It was nearly five 5:00 by the time they got back into the car, and Erin drove them east toward the Fox River.

The evening was perfect; they held hands and talked about his trip, oblivious to everything around them until she crossed the Hwy 172 bridge and took the first exit. "Is that a prison?" David asked as she rounded the cloverleaf that ended at Riverside Drive.

"Maximum security, I think. I've heard it's a really dangerous place."

"I don't believe I'd make et through time in prison. I don't have the proper constitution."

Erin laughed and smiled at him while they waited at the traffic lights. "That's good to know; I don't think I'd want to be with someone in prison. Seems like it would be difficult to form a healthy relationship."

"I reckon et's best to obey the law in that case."

"Probably a good idea," she said. The light turned green, and she turned right, toward downtown Green Bay.

"Erin," David said after a lull in their conversation. "Are we anawhere near the hotel? I—need you."

Her stomach did a somersault, then a cartwheel, and her breathing became heavy. She could feel her heart beating underneath her ribcage, and she nearly crossed the center line when he put his hand on her leg "Almost there," she breathed as she turned onto Porlier Street, then Adams Street, and finally onto Washington Street. David's hand had made its way up her thigh quite a distance when she signaled and then had to wait for a van before turning into the hotel parking lot.

Her legs were weak as she parked the car and walked into the building with David Elliott, the man of her dreams. The front desk was wrapped in darkly stained, beadboard wainscotting, while overhead hung two stained glass light fixtures. The two lovers stood, waiting for someone to help them, trying not to touch each other. Being intimate was far too risky; if someone recognized him, he could get into a lot of trouble, though it was difficult for them not to.

It was the beginning of the supper rush, and the lobby was starting to fill up, so Erin decided to ask the hostess for help. The woman walked up to the bartender, who came over to check them in. "So, it'll be a room for two then?" The man asked after checking David's reservation on the computer.

David was about to correct him, but Erin put her hand on his arm. "I'd like to stay here tonight if it's okay with you?"

He smiled at her and said, "Yes, a room for two, please." They covertly held hands as the man verified David's information, though he was using a fake name to ensure complete anonymity.

"Here you are, Mr. Everett," the man said and handed them each a key card. David grabbed his suitcase and they headed to the small elevator. He touched the 'up' button, and the tension rose as they waited. When the door opened, they walked calmly into the elevator, but as soon as the door closed, David hit the '3' button, let go of his bag, and pressed Erin up against the wall, kissing her passionately.

He had just buried his hands in her hair when the elevator stopped with a *ding*. It was difficult to collect themselves as the door opened to a burgundy-colored hallway with hand-painted, shiny gold numbers beside each room door. They found their number, down the hall and to the right just as the bartender had said, and David used his key card, with trembling hands, to open it.

The only thing either of them noticed about the room was the big bed in the center, and they headed straight for it. David first pressed her against the wall again, kissing her while trying to help her get undressed. "Maybe we should close the shade," Erin suggested and managed to get free from David's grasp.

She walked over to the window and pulled down the blinds. When she turned around, David was naked, standing only an inch or two away. He placed his hands on her face and neck and kissed her again. She wanted him to make love to her more than anything, but she suddenly felt a dread take hold of her, the same old fear of being seen naked.

He's seen you before, Erin, what's your problem? she thought, trying to push past the panic. She could feel a cold sweat break out on her forehead as he began tugging at her top, trying to get it above her head.

Just relax—what are you afraid of? She took a half step back and closed her eyes. Goosebumps sprang up over her arms and legs as a wave of anxiety loomed over her. She didn't want him to notice and tried to ignore it, pushing herself to go through the motions, but then he stopped.

"What's wrong, love?" he asked gently.

She was having a hard time breathing and wished she could crawl into a hole. "I... don't know. I can't... breathe and—" she started to say, shaking her head. He took her hand and led her to the bed. She sat on the edge and put her head down with her elbows on her knees. "Can we go a bit slower, please? I... I need to get used to you again—I'm afraid—"

"Afraid?" he said, visibly taken aback. She lifted her head, and he looked concerned. "Ye're sweating!" He knelt before her and took her hands in his. "My darling, take as much time as you need. What are you afraid of? Not me, I hope?"

"No! Not of you, but... and I know it's stupid—I know we've already been through this—but... I don't want you... to see me."

A mixture of relief and compassion lit up his face. He stood and pulled her up to stand before him. "A'right, darling, let me hold you. You ken I love yer body; I love yer curves and everathin' about you. I've been longin' tae see yeh and touch every part of you." He ran his hands down the front of her top and then put them under the fabric of her shirt, placing them on her waist. He looked into her eyes and smiled at her, then he slowly raised his hands until they were cupping her breasts over her new red satin and lace bra.

He slowly began to lift her shirt, waiting for her to tell him to stop. When she didn't, he pulled it over her head and threw it across the room; then, he looked down at her breasts. They were pushed up high, revealing acres of cleavage, and he gasped, "Ach, Erin!" as he lightly brushed the soft, pale skin with his first finger, staring at them with what looked like reverence.

He looked into her eyes again as his hands roamed over her body. They caressed her shoulders and arms, then made their way to her breasts and stomach. He knelt before her and unfastened her jeans, taking his time as he pulled them down, unveiling her matching red satin and lace panties. "Lovely," he whispered and then kissed the tiny ribbon bow at the center top. He ran his finger from the bow down to where her legs met and looked up at her. "Are yeh still afraid, love?" he asked.

She looked down at him and smiled. "No, I'm okay now," she said softly.

He stood and kissed her cleavage while reaching behind her to unfasten the hooks on her bra slowly, one at a time. The electricity coursed between them again as he gently pulled her bra off her arms and then gave it the same treatment as her top. She let out a moan as he wrapped his hands around her full, naked breasts.

"Let's continue on the bed, alright?" He gently pushed her against the mattress edge, causing her to sit and then lie back. Then, he knelt before her again and pulled her panties down, touching his lips to her dark wedge of pubic hair.

She allowed him to lift her legs over his shoulders and raised her arm over her head, grabbing the comforter as he buried his face into her folds, using his tongue to explore her. "Oh, David, you are so good at that," she panted, and her body responded with a delicious orgasm.

———

Placing his first two fingers inside her, he felt her body pulse and contract—experiencing a sense of pride almost at having the ability to make her do that. He removed his fingers and helped lift her further onto the bed, then he stood before her, looking at her body. There wasn't a curve, bulge, or imperfection he didn't love.

He needed her; he had to have her—to enter her before he went mad from waiting. He got into position and felt the firm pressure as his cock pushed against her. First, there was a slight resistance, and then came the moment when it yielded and enveloped him, "Oh, God, Erin!" he said as he thrust into her.

She looked into his eyes, and he smiled at her. "I missed you so much!" she whispered.

He saw a tear roll down her temple and disappear into her hairline. "Aye, and I've needed you and yer company every day! I've longed for yer touch and tae feel maself inside you every night," he said as he found the perfect rhythm.

"That's it—David! Right there!" she gasped, and he felt her body responding to him once again. Then—it was there again, the waves of her second climax.

He began to thrust a bit harder and used shorter faster strokes. "I'm—ready—" he said, and then reached his climax. While their bodies were still one, he kissed her mouth, then he watched her laying under him, breathing heavily with her eyes closed, and smiled at her. "Yer brilliant; did yeh ken that? Pure, bloody brilliant!"

"Thank you so much, David! I don't think I'll ever be able to live without you!"

"Aye, I ken I'll never be free of yer hold on me," he said and then laid on the bed facing her. "And I dinnae want tae be."

———

Erin wanted to ask him never to leave her again; it almost slipped out of her mouth, except she knew it couldn't happen, at least not yet. There wasn't any real reason for her not to leave Todd and she didn't know why she was hesitating.

It's too easy, that's why. You know how it feels to be left and deep down you don't want to do that to Todd.

I've also never left anyone before, and I don't know how to or what to say. I can't just walk into a room and say it's over and walk out. And what if it's just a fantasy and once I get there, David changes his mind and dumps me? Then what?

You're treading on thin ice, and starting to make a real mess of things, Erin, so you'd better make a decision soon!

Just then, her stomach growled at them. She realized she hadn't eaten since noon, and then it hadn't been much. The food in the restaurant below was calling her to the feast. "Sorry—"

"Perhaps we should go downstairs for a wee nibble," David said.

"Good night nurse! I feel like I'm always hungry when I'm with you, and not just for the amazing sex, either." She looked him in the eyes and ran her finger down the bridge of his perfect nose. "I wish we could do this every night," she said as he rolled onto his back, and they both stared at the ceiling.

"Say the word, ma darling, and I'll make et happen."

Erin rolled to her side and looked at him. "What do you mean?"

"I mean, I'm through with Susannah and her games. She's no' a good person, and I intend tae be rid of her as soon as possible. If you were tae come to me, I would take yeh in, and we could be together—whether et's in Britain or here. I'm yours, Erin, all of me."

She was speechless; he'd asked her to run away with him when they were in New Orleans, but it was different then. This time it seemed much more thought out. Dealing with Todd's emotional chaos was taxing and stressful, and she found herself wanting to say *yes* so badly. She'd ached to live in Great Britain for as long as she could remember. When she and Todd had traveled there a few years earlier, it had cemented the idea in her mind, and the thought of it actually happening was intoxicating.

"You're tempting me more than I can handle!" she said, still dreaming of her stone farmhouse and a flock of chickens and children. She could almost smell the jasmine flowers against the stone wall, basking in the summer sun. Her daydream was cut short by her stomach, once again having its say, which made them both laugh. "Someday, I'll tell you my fantasy about living over the pond, but for now, I think we'd better feed the beast before it eats me alive!"

"I look forward to it—The fantasy, I mean, no' yer bein' eaten alive— unless it's me doin' the eating," he said.

She rolled her eyes at him as she got out of bed, then tried to find where he'd thrown her clothing. She found her top and bra in the whirlpool tub; the rest was on the floor next to the bed.

Chapter Thirteen

SUPPER WITH DAVID, ERIN, AND TODD?

When David and Erin were dressed and ready, they made their way downstairs to the restaurant. Being nearly 6:30, it was busy, and they had to wait for a table. David seemed a bit agitated as they sat on the wooden pew-like bench across from the hotel check-in counter. "What's wrong," Erin asked softly.

He leaned over and whispered into her ear, "I forgot ma glasses; are yeh sure the hair is a sufficient disguise?"

She smiled to herself, having already forgotten how famous he was. "Dinnae fash, darling, no one is expecting to see a famous British person in Green Bay. I'm sure everyone will think you're an ordinary old guy and leave you alone."

"Humph, who are you calling ordinary?" he said and flashed his brilliant smile at her.

"Not you, but if you wanna remain incognito, I'd say to keep that smile under wraps," she said and put her finger to his lips.

Ten minutes later, they were seated in the dining room in front of one of the eight exquisite stained-glass windows. Each was adorned with colorful Celtic knots and the name of a city in Ireland; theirs was Wexford. The walls of the dining room were dark golden-yellow with Gaelic and English sayings hand-painted in gold in various places. "Look in the corner; there's a painting of St. Brendan. It says he's the patron saint of boatmen, mariners, travelers, elderly adventurers, and whales—oh, and also of portaging canoes," Erin said and laughed.

"Only the canoes?" David asked.

"That's what it says. There's a prayer, too. '*O King of glorious Heaven, shall I now go of my own choice to the Sea?*' Isn't that nice?"

"It's a bit short."

"That's the only line I can read without it looking like I'm staring at the family sitting next to it."

Their waiter came to the table; he was a diminutive man, probably in his mid to late thirties, with dark, nearly black hair. What Erin noticed were his eyes, they were brown with a ring of green around the edge, and they looked kind. "Welcome to St. Brendan's. My name is Matthew; what can I get you to drink?" David ordered a pint of Guinness, while Erin chose hard cider. A few minutes later, Matthew brought them their drinks, and then they ordered their food.

"Have you been here before?" David asked her.

"Yeah, a few times. Mainly for special occasions since it's a bit pricier than—" she began and blushed. "Um… yes, I have."

"Ye don't need tae be embarrassed, Erin. Et's no' a thing, a'right?" He took her hand and smiled at her.

"Okay," she said, though she was determined not to bring it up again.

Their food was brought out to them, steaming hot; it looked and smelled wonderful. Erin put her napkin on her lap, ready to dig in, but the waiter hesitated and looked over his shoulder. She smiled at him and then looked at David, wondering what was wrong. Matthew leaned in, speaking in a near whisper, as though he might get reprimanded for what he was about to say. "Has anyone ever told you that you look almost exactly like David Elliott… from *Future Explorations*? Are you related to him?" The poor waiter blushed and gave them a shy smile.

David forgot himself and gave him one of his breathtaking smiles. "I have been told that a time or two. Thank you for the compliment; he's a good-looking man!" he said with a very neutral accent, trying to sound a bit less like himself. "I believe we do share the same blood, actually."

"I'm sorry, but just had to say something. I'm a huge fan, and—I don't know what that has to do with you, but—I guess I hoped—Never mind," he said, obviously floundering, not knowing how to end the conversation.

"I'm sure Mister Elliott would be happy to know it," David said, graciously.

Erin loved him even more after that; he was such a kind-hearted man. "You know, now that you mention it, I can see the resemblance as well," she said. Matthew smiled, told them he'd be back to check on them shortly, and then walked away. "Did you know you're amazing?"

He shrugged and took a bite of his Guinness pot roast. "I thought I was ordinary and old?"

"Extraordinary and just old enough."

"... Peter was compelled tae do et, I reckon—" David was saying, when Erin, who was facing the entrance to the dining room, gasped and hid her face. Her eyes were wide, and she looked panicked. "What is et?" He looked around as if he might see the specter she'd spied.

"It's Todd!" she hissed in a hoarse whisper, "He just walked in, and... now he's sitting at the bar! How did he know we were here?"

"He's here—now? He couldn't have known; I only told you on the way here. Could it be a coincidence?" he said, eyes fixed on the group of men ordering their drinks.

"I don't recognize any of the men he came in with, so maybe his support group decided this was the place to go after their meeting," she said.

"Support group? It never occurred to me—We should stay here; I reckon they'll have a pint and leave, right?" David said.

"Yeah, you're probably right. He'd been attending meetings on how to cope with me having treatments."

"Which one is he?" he asked, and she gave him a look. "I may need tae know which bloke he is if I... see him comin' this way."

"Hmm, I think you're making an excuse, but he's the one in the middle, with the brown shirt."

"He needs a haircut—and a shave."

Erin didn't want to find out the reason he was there just then and to make matters worse, they were trapped. If they wanted to leave, they'd have to walk close enough to the bar that Todd might see them, and that would be bad. She kept her head down, but David's eyes were drawn to where Todd was sitting as though they were magnetized. "For goodness' sake, David, please stop looking at him. I know it's difficult, but someone is going to notice!" she hissed.

He reluctantly looked away, but his forehead was wrinkled up as though he were concentrating on something, and his mouth was set in a slight frown. "I'm sorry, love," he said, genuinely apologetic, "I just want tae look at the man who's allowed tae sleep with you every night and… wake up next tae you every mornin'."

"Well, you won't have to worry about that after last nigh—" She remembered too late that she'd decided not to tell him about the night before. *Shit!* David's eyes shot up to hers, and the fire behind them startled her.

"What did he do?" he growled and looked over at Todd sitting on his barstool, laughing.

It looked to her like David was about to launch himself from his chair and attack Todd. She didn't like that look; the last thing she needed was for him to go and make a scene, outing them sitting there and revealing who her match was. "Please, I beg you, don't make a scene. I'll tell you later, I promise," she whispered. She wanted to leave; too many things could go wrong. All she wanted was to be alone with David, away from watchful eyes.

They finished their meal in silence while Erin prayed that Todd would leave. *What time is it?* she thought, knowing he had to be at work early in the morning. She looked at her phone; it was only 7:20. *What can we do? He might be here all night.* Fifteen minutes later, Todd stood and lost his balance as he tried to get off his stool. When he recovered, he looked right at them but didn't register her at all before stumbling toward the bathrooms.

That was their chance! David took out a hundred-dollar bill and put it on the table, then they got up and told the hostess that the waiter should keep the change for such good service. They practically ran out the doors, down the concrete steps, and into the parking lot, feeling as though they were being chased. Finally, they stopped at her car, huffing and laughing. "I'm sorry about that! You're such a good sport—Thanks!" Erin panted as she tried to catch her breath.

"Ye're welcome. Et's always an adventure with you, isn't et?"

"I guess so." Erin quickly scanned the parking lot for Todd's car. She didn't see it, so either he'd walked, or someone had given him a ride.

"Is that the trail over there?" David asked and pointed toward the river.

Erin didn't need to look. "Yes, that's it."

"Fancy a stroll on the promenade? Mebbe he'll be gone when we return."

She smiled at him, knowing they'd be able to walk hand in hand and even kiss if they wanted to. He was in a great disguise, even without the glasses, and it would be plenty dark in a little while. "Ok, just let me grab a sweater from my suitcase. Good thing I left it in my car!" She hadn't bothered to lock it when they'd gone in earlier, thinking she'd be coming back out within a few minutes. It was still a bit too warm to put the sweater on, so she draped it over her arm and took David's hand.

They walked to the Fox River Trail and turned left, away from town, following the wide paved path past businesses and bars. With the warm weather, more people were choosing to sit outside. As they approached one bar, they heard a man who'd obviously had too much to drink, telling lame jokes very loudly. *What's the difference between you and an egg?'* he asked his friends.

"Oh, I know this one! *An egg gets laid,*" Erin shouted the answer toward the group of strangers. The man and his friends laughed and applauded her as they passed by.

"Ye're mad!" David said, "I can't believe yeh did that!"

"Expect the unexpected with me; that's what Todd—I mean, that's just how I am."

The sun was setting, and the huge orange ball was reflected in a million tiny waves along the river. They stopped to admire it, then David turned to her, putting his finger under her chin. "I love yeh, Erin," he said quietly and kissed her. She kissed him back, so happy he was there. She had spent the past two weeks imagining he was sharing her experiences, and he finally was.

An hour and a half later, they were walking back up the stairs into the hotel, laughing, sure Todd would no longer be there. Erin said she was about to burst, so she excused herself to use the lobby toilets before going to their room. She had just walked away when David saw Todd come around the corner on his way to the men's room. He was staggering drunk and looked up at David with his eyebrows knit together, getting up close to see him more clearly. David froze; he didn't know what to do and prayed Erin wouldn't come out before he was gone.

"Yoohoo look—like summwon I know—" Todd said. He lost his balance and fell into David so that he was forced to catch the man. He got him standing again and nearly pushed him into the men's room. "Wait! But—" Todd's voice echoed in the empty bathroom.

Come on, Erin! David thought as he paced the hallway and pushed the elevator button to make sure it was ready for them when she came out. Finally, she opened the door, and David took her by the damp, freshly washed hand, pulling her onto the elevator.

"What's going on?" she asked, completely confused. David was pushing the *door-close* button frantically. "I don't underst—" she said and then Todd's inebriated voice was heard, speaking far too loudly.

"I swahare—I saw somewone I know. I jus can't th-ink of his name… buhut I—saw him!"

Chapter Fourteen

NOW TELL ME

"**G**ood night nurse! That was—" Erin began and then saw David's unhappy face.

"Et was Todd; he got up in my face, said he knew me, and then proceeded tae fall onto me. I had tae lift him up and push him into the toilets." He closed his eyes and took a deep breath.

Erin was mortified and didn't know what to say. The elevator door opened, and they stepped out into the hallway then quietly walked back to their room. That's when they finally noticed what it looked like.

The front half, where the bed sat, was painted a nice, dark plum with matching carpet and wooden furniture. The other half, separated by a glass block wall, was painted white with black and white tile flooring and had four separate compartments. There was the whirlpool tub; the shower, which was floor to ceiling wall tiles and a rain shower head in the ceiling; the small toilet room, which had a door; and the sink area that also served as the place to make coffee in the morning.

"I can't believe he's still here! Holy Moses! I hope he doesn't try to drive home like that!" She looked over at David, who was seething; she could tell he was trying with all his might to act calmer than he was for her benefit.

"Now tell me what he did to you," David said between clenched teeth.

Erin knew that once she told him, he'd want to go back downstairs and kill her husband. "I… I don't want to tell you," she said, trying to stall, and went to the window at the end of the room between the shower and toilet room. She lifted the shade away from the window enough to look out on the nearly vacant parking lot. She watched as Todd stumbled out of the building and nearly fell down the tall flight of concrete steps.

One of the men he'd arrived with caught him and helped him the rest of the way down, followed by the others. Another man said something to him, and after a bit of persuading, Todd handed him his car keys. The men walked together to the sidewalk, crossed the street, and then continued down the road, out of sight. She figured their meeting must have been somewhere nearby.

"Please tell me," David said patiently.

She looked up from the deserted parking lot and faced him, knowing he was worried and that she'd have to tell him, though she also knew he'd be beside himself with rage about it. "Yesterday, we went to our friend's house for a game day," she started as she made her way back to the bed. "Lily is the only person who knows you're my match.

"Her husband, Nick, surprised us with a *Future Explorations* card game. Well, I had too much to drink, and when the '*le potage*' card came up, I started to tell an anecdote about saying it to you. I caught myself but not before I said your first name, and it was not taken well by Todd. We ended up leaving early because of it." Erin started pacing and wringing her hands, not wanting to continue.

"Go on, so far et doesn't sound that bad."

"Humph. Todd was really upset when we left. He's started getting irritated when I say anything to do with my disease, a treatment, or if he hears the name David, especially if I'm the one saying it. It sucks, but I can understand it. Last night though, he was acting oddly."

"Oddly?" David had been sitting on the edge of the bed, head down and eyes closed, listening to her story. However, at that word he looked up, a frown making the fine lines on his face stand out.

"When we got home… he was… rough with me. He pushed me onto our bed and started demanding that I—Well, he was scaring me, and I told him to stop, and he… ended up pinning me down… so I went limp because I didn't want to get hurt, and—"

David stood, his breathing heavy and his eyes wide. "If you tell me he raped yeh, Erin, I'm going tae go down there and kill him!"

Erin stopped pacing and wrapped her arms around his middle, laying her head on his chest. "He didn't rape me. I was afraid he would, but he didn't. I managed to talk him out of it somehow. He said he wanted to take me back—that I was his, and he was going to break the spell you had over me. Anyway, he slept in the spare room."

———

David was silent; a ribbon of rage began to wrap his heart and mind in knots of fury. He was scared to speak; afraid it would come out as a shout.

"That's why I didn't want to tell you. He's never behaved like that before. That's what scared me the most. He's never raised a hand to me or even yelled at me before. Hasn't Susannah done anything unusual because of this arrangement?"

"Humph, don't change the subject, Erin. Did he hurt you?" He held her away from him to look her in the eye. She looked away, so he quickly scanned what flesh he could see. He'd noticed a few small bruises on her arm and one on her leg earlier, but he hadn't thought anything of it at the time, now he lifted the sleeve of her sweater and looked closer at them. There were five fingertip-sized bruises on that arm plus four more on the other one, and he was furious. *How could he treat her that way; doesn't he know what he has in her?* "Did he do this to yeh?" he asked and kissed the little purple marks lightly.

"I don't wanna talk about it," she said and crossed her arms over her chest. He pulled her up to him again and held her tightly, trembling with rage. "So, what about Susannah?"

David relaxed his hold on her and sighed. "A'right, I'll tell you, but yeh dinnae want tae know. I'm warning yeh, you'll be upset."

———

Erin looked at him, trying to decide if her imagination would be worse than the truth or was ignorance bliss? "I think… you should tell me," she said finally.

He raised an eyebrow at her. "Okay, but I did warn you. First, she's been using and manipulating our children, or at least trying to, in order tae get information out of them about you. She played on their wee hearts by allowing them tae find her cryin' and told them tae ask me about et. That was the day Daniel sent the selfie. I ken I should set stricter boundaries, but I didn't want tae blow them off and send them away. I figured they would find out about you eventually anyway," he said.

Erin was taken aback. "They would? I mean—I guess they would, but wow, it's just so… it seems really soon to be thinking about that kind of thing. Don't get me wrong; I'm glad you feel that way… it's just unexpected." She couldn't believe he was already thinking about telling his children about them, or, more accurately, had already done so. "Keep going."

"I was suspicious because Susannah never cries, at least no' about things involving me. I found out about her plan from Charlie, poor wee boy. He was feelin' guilty because his mum was interrogating them tae learn what I'd told them about you. The poor lad felt as though he was betraying me. He's such a dear boy!"

"That's not right, and it pisses me off that she'd do something like that to her own children, but it's not something I'd get upset about, is it?" she said, wondering why he'd been so hesitant to tell her.

"Ach, there's more. Ever since I told her about Martin's plan and finding maself in his trap, I've been sleepin' in the guest bedroom. One night… she… came in and tried tae… seduce me."

Erin's breath caught in her throat, and she coughed several times, not believing what she'd heard. It was her turn to feel the rage and fury.

She's his wife, remember! You allowed Todd to make love to you, you can't be upset at this!

"She didn't succeed, Erin," he continued, looking her in the eye.

Erin closed her eyes, but the image of his beautiful wife lying next to him, naked and touching him, became as vivid in her mind as if she'd been in the room, watching. She shook her head, trying to get the mental image to go away.

"As soon as I realized it wasn't you, I got out of the bed and kicked her out of the room. I was furious!" David said while clenching his jaw. "The thing is, she didn't do et because she wanted me; she hasn't wanted me in years. Et's as if she were trying tae… trick me into being with her, being cunning and deceptive, and I can't stand it! I am also relatively sure she put something into ma glass of wine at supper one night. I saw her do it that time, so I didn't drink it." I dinnae trust her." He sat on the bed and put his head in his hands.

Erin could hear the disgust in his voice. She sat next to him again and lay her head on his arm. "You think she was trying to… drug you, or… kill… you? Oh God, David!"

"I know; I've gone through every scenario I can think of. She posed veiled threats tae me when I told her I want a divorce."

"Parts of this situation really suck, don't they?" she whispered.

"Especially the parts where ye're no' there," he said and squeezed her hand.

"Let's go to bed, my love. Things will be better tomorrow, right? They have to be," she said, longing for him to hold her through the night. They undressed, stripped most of the blankets off the bed, and crawled in. "Oh, shoot! I forgot my suitcase in the car!" Erin said, "Oh well, we can bring it up in the morning." The last thing she wanted to do was get dressed and go downstairs.

"Et's unlocked, though," David said as he got up and started putting his clothes back on. "I'll bring it up for yeh; where are yer keys?"

"He's gone now," Erin said, thinking he might be making an excuse to go downstairs to confront Todd.

"Aye, dinnae fash," he said and spotted her keys on the large desk at the end of the bed. He picked them up and went outside, wearing his jeans, shoes with no socks, and a plain white t-shirt. He looked like a grey-haired little boy, and she wanted to gobble him up.

She watched out the window, and when he got to the parking lot, he looked up at her. He waved, and she blew him kisses, then she watched him open the back door and pull her suitcase out by the handle. He didn't know that when she'd opened it to get her sweater, she hadn't zipped it back up. She covered her mouth and gasped when the bag opened, and most of her things fell out onto the blacktop. He looked up at her again, put his hand on his forehead, and then bent down to pick up what had fallen out.

After a few moments, he knocked on the door, having forgotten his key card in the room. "Thank you," she said and held him tightly. His t-shirt smelled like him, and his chest hair felt like a pillow, cushioning her head as she rested it on his chest. "I'm so glad you're here."

"And I'm glad yer staying with me tonight. Come, let me hold yeh, love," he said.

She smiled as she watched him undress again. They got back into the bed, and he wrapped himself around her as they spooned, falling asleep to the sound of their own breathing.

Chapter Fifteen

LILY AT THE MALL

In the morning, Erin rolled over in bed. She saw David lying next to her, sleeping, and stared at him. *God, he's beautiful!* She thought for the millionth time since they'd met; before that even, and then wrapped her arm over his chest. Not able to resist, she moved her hand slowly down his body to touch his morning wood.

He flinched, threw the covers off himself, and grabbed her hand, ready to jump out of bed, though when he saw her, he relaxed. "Thank God et's you!" he said, still breathing hard from the adrenalin rush.

"It's me," she said, glad he'd removed the blankets so she could see him. She began stroking him until he sat up and rolled on top of her, making her catch her breath.

"I want tae make love tae you more than once every day I'm here," he said as he entered her.

"Okay, I like that idea," she said and watched his face, studying him as he made love to her. What was he thinking and feeling when he was inside her? From the noises he made, she could tell it felt good.

He opened his eyes, and she didn't look away. Even as the feelings grew more and more intense with each stroke, they kept eye contact until they both reached their orgasms. They closed their eyes then, but Erin opened hers before he finished. She saw him at his most vulnerable—as unguarded as he most likely ever was, and it was beautiful.

He didn't rush to the bathroom to clean up like Todd always did; no, David stayed put and looked at her. He kissed her forehead, then her eyes, nose, cheeks, chin, temples, and finally her lips. She wrapped her arms around his neck and stretched. "That's a very nice way to wake up in the morning, isn't it?" she said.

He smiled and got up, doing his own stretching as he stood at the side of the bed. "Aye, it is, love, thank you," he said and then walked over to the tiny room with the toilet in it. Erin got out of bed and turned on the shower. She wasn't going to wash her hair, so she pinned it up and stepped under the huge shower head. When she was finished, she turned and saw him watching her. "Ach, ye're lovely," he said and stepped under the water with her.

"No, no, no, *you* are the lovely one," she contradicted and then laughed.

"What shall we do today, love?" he asked as she stepped out onto the bathmat and toweled off.

"I have to pick something up at the mall, but you don't have to come if you don't want to."

"Wherever you go, I will go; wherever you lodge, I will lodge; your people shall be my people... and so on, whilst I'm here," he said, quoting the Book of Ruth to her as he lathered up the washcloth.

"...Your God, my God. Where you die, I will die, and there will I be buried..." she finished the quote. You surprise me all the time, David."

"We can have lunch afterward," he said with an amused smile.

"I don't think Boaz said that, but it sounds good. You know it's rare for me to turn down lunch," she said and giggled.

Forty-five minutes later, they each grabbed a pastry in the lobby and left the hotel. Erin drove through town, making sure to go down Lombardi Avenue, with its green and gold painted fences, so David could see Lambeau Field. Then she turned down Oneida Street, which took them to the mall, where she parked the car.

They entered through the food court and walked past the various restaurants. She hadn't had any caffeine yet and felt a slight headache coming on, so she was determined to get a coffee at Gloria Jean's when they got that far.

"Fancy a coffee whilst we're here?" David asked as if reading her mind.

"Yes, please, thanks."

The smell of rich, freshly ground coffee greeted them as they entered the corner store. It was one of Erin's favorite smells in the world; that and fresh-baked bread. Well—and David, any part of David. They passed the displays of teapots with matching cups and the branded coffee mugs featuring everything from Batman to the Beatles and stepped up to the counter.

David ordered a chai latte, and she chose an iced cappuccino. He had just paid and stepped aside to get out of the way when Erin turned to say something to him and saw Lily walk in. "Lily!" she exclaimed! She went to her best friend, who was wide-eyed and looked like a frightened kitten who had just seen its first mouse.

"I swear I didn't know you'd be here!" Lily whispered, as though she thought Erin would think she was stalking her.

"Don't be silly; I'm so glad to see you! Where's Ariana?"

"She's still in school," Lily whispered. She looked over at David, who was by the counter, wearing less than attractive glasses. He started toward them, smiling, and carrying two cups. She took a step back and ran awkwardly into the condiment counter. As her face turned red, she looked at Erin, smiling bravely.

Erin took the drink David held out for her. "Thank you," she said. "David, this is my best friend, Lily. She's the one I told you about—the only one who knows you're my match."

"It's a pleasure to meet you, Lily. I'm glad Erin has you to confide in," he said, using his Received Pronunciation accent. Lily took his outstretched hand to shake, but he surprised her by kissing the back of hers. She stood with her mouth open, looking at Erin, who was laughing at the scene.

"Alright, enough of your gallantry, mister. Were you going to get something, Lily? We can wait for you at one of the tables while you order."

"Are you sure you're... not in a hurry... or something?" she said nervously.

"Nope, we have all day," Erin said. "Go ahead and order, we'll be right out here."

Being a weekday morning, the food court wasn't busy, so they found a table near the coffee shop and waited. The food court at Bay Park Square mall wasn't large by any means, but the high windowed ceilings made it seem more open. Originally it had been designed to look like a football stadium with grid lines tiled out on the floor. "Do you mind if I invite Lily to have lunch with us?" Erin asked.

"I dinnae mind at all. I fancy meeting the people you know. I'm also keen tae gain a bit of information about you from her!" He smiled his brilliant, perfect smile and chuckled.

"Har, har, har—I'm not worried. I'm a pretty boring person, and she can hardly speak louder than a whisper around you, so I doubt you'll get much out of her."

Erin saw Lily walk out of the store and waved her over, knowing she had a difficult choice to make. She could sit next to her, face to face with David Elliott, or sit next to him, shoulder to shoulder. She could see the conflict in her friend's eyes as she tried to decide which was worse, and she only had an instant to make up her mind.

David stood as she came to the table and smiled as Lily sat across from him. Erin was pleased he was acting so refined with her best friend; not every guy was that well-mannered. "So, what brings you here this morning?" Erin asked.

"I ordered a pair of shoes and got a call saying they were here," Lily said quietly.

Erin could tell Lily was nervous; she wouldn't look at David, choosing instead to gaze at her or the bright green and yellow table-top in front of them. "Really?" she said. "Same here! I just had to get my coffee fix first."

"Yeah, me too," Lily said, and they both laughed, touching their cups together in a mock toast, then each took a sip of their drink.

"*Slàinte mhath!*" Erin said, making David do a doubletake.

"Ah, Lily?" David said, still using his RP accent, "Would you care to join us for lunch when we've finished here?"

Lily finally managed to look at him and smiled, turning bright red again. Her coloring was just slightly lighter than Erin's, so it showed much brighter on her.

"Oh! Thank you! Are you sure I won't be a third wheel?" she said and looked at Erin.

"No, we'd love for you to join us," she said, while David nodded and smiled.

"Absolutely," he said.

Erin looked at her phone; it was 10:30. "Why don't we get going now so we can beat the rush?" She stood, and the others did likewise. "I'm gonna go to the lady's room; do you mind waiting for us?" she asked David, knowing Lily wouldn't be able to sit alone with him, plus, the two women needed to talk.

"I'm not going anywhere without you, remember?" he said.

"How could I forget," Erin said, wanting to kiss him as they walked away. The bathrooms were a good distance from where they were seated, but she imagined David could hear Lily's scream when they walked in. "Oh—My—God!" Lily exclaimed. "He's even more beautiful in person! I feel like a teenager and want to go all fangirl, but I'm resisting! And his hair! He looks good with gray hair! OH MY GOD!!! Eeeee!"

Erin laughed; she also felt like a teen, talking with her best friend after school.

"I know! I can't believe I'm with him and still don't know what *he* sees in *me*!" Erin stepped into a stall and kept talking. "He's so wonderful, Lily. Did you notice him stand up when you got to the table? I've never known a guy who acted that way without being prompted before! Guys are such numbskulls around here."

"Yeah, I can't even imagine Nick or Todd doing something so classy! Hey, thanks for inviting me for lunch. I was going to meet Nick, but I can do that anytime, plus how can anyone say no to that man?"

Erin flushed the toilet and opened the stall door. "No idea! I know I can't," she said and then washed her hands.

Lily leaned in closer. "What happened with Todd when you left? I was worried. He looked weird, like he was about to snap or something."

"Yeah, well, he did—in a way." She looked around to make sure they were alone. "He tried to—I mean... he was rough and tried to make me—" She spoke quietly, an odd feeling of shame coloring her cheeks, though she knew it wasn't her fault. "He said something about breaking the spell David has over me. I don't want to go back there, Lil."

Lily's mouth was open in shock. "I can't imagine him trying to hurt anyone; it doesn't sound like him at all! He must be totally messed up about all this!"

"I'd say he is. Oh, and we saw him last night at the hotel. He came to the bar after his support meeting. David and I were eating supper—"

Lily raised her eyebrows. "He didn't see you did he? That would've been awful!"

"I know! No, thank God; he eventually went to the bathroom, and we were able to escape. We walked along the Fox River Trail for over an hour. It was perfect, and I... really think I love him."

"God! Who wouldn't fall in love with *him*! I'm so jealous."

"I'd be jealous of me too. We'd better get back, or he'll think we've fallen in." They made their way back to the table, and again, David stood.

"Ladies," he said formally.

"You are just too wonderful," Erin said with a smile. She wanted with all her heart to hold his hand as they walked toward the shoe store, but too many people in town knew her to be able to do it safely.

They entered the store, told the salesman their names, and he found their orders quickly. The women sat together on a bench and laughed when the young man opened the boxes, revealing the same shoe, only in different colors and sizes. David offered to pay for them, but the man, who looked at him curiously, told him they were pre-paid.

On their way out, Erin spotted Hot Topic and suggested a quick look around. "Alright by me," David said, so they stepped inside the dark store. Death metal music was blasting over the speakers as she and Lily headed straight to the *Future Explorations* rack. It was what they did every time they went there.

———

David found himself surrounded by images of himself, young and in his prime. He felt old and marveled that Erin found him in any way attractive compared to his younger self. He stood back and watched as the ladies rounded the racks. After a while, they moved to the *Doctor Who* merchandise.

"I hope the next Doctor is attractive," he overheard Lily shout over the music.

"Me too, though I can't imagine a better-looking man than the one over there," he heard Erin respond, then she looked at him.

Lily looked his way then and said, "Agreed!"

They must not know I can hear them, he thought and smiled.

They didn't find anything extraordinary, so they left and Erin started laughing as they walked out the door. David looked down at her. "What's so funny?" he asked, not sure he wanted a truthful answer.

She's laughing at how old you look now, he thought.

"I was thinking that if anyone in there knew who had just walked in, they would shit themselves!"

Lily snorted as she laughed, and her eyes grew wide. She covered her mouth with her hand, and her face turned red again, which made all three of them laugh.

"Where should we eat?" Erin said. "I was thinking Margarita's? What do you think?" He couldn't resist and brushed his hand against hers. Energy shot through him, and he had to catch his breath.

"Oh, yeah, that would be great!" Lily said.

"You want margaritas for lunch? Isn't it a bit early?" he asked and then smiled, realizing he'd heard the same thing come from Erin when he'd ordered a pint of Guinness at lunch in New Orleans. She looked up at him and narrowed her eyes, so he raised his hands in surrender. "I know—it's never too early for a margarita."

He wanted to kiss her hair—to smell her and be intoxicated by her scent once more. He hadn't taken the time to savor it the night before, and that morning had been nice, but right then, he wanted to live in it.

"It's five o'clock somewhere!" she said and then tilted her head. "Actually, isn't it five o'clock in London right now?"

David looked at his watch; it was just after 11:00 am, so it *was* 5:00 in England. "Alright, you win." Without thinking, he put his arm around her shoulder, pulled her close to him, and kissed her temple. He immediately realized what he'd done and put his hand down, though not before getting a whiff of her. "Sorry," he said quietly, feeling a bit tipsy and hoping she wouldn't be annoyed at him.

"It's okay; I liked it. I wish we could be natural everywhere we went." She turned toward him, standing on her tiptoes, and for an instant, he thought she was going to kiss him. Instead, she whispered into his ear, "I love you. Oh, and thanks for being a good sport about the *Future Explorations* stuff. Truthfully, I think you're much more attractive now! You've only improved with age."

He was beaming and couldn't stop grinning. He wanted to lift her up and kiss her, right there, just outside the food court. She couldn't have said anything to make him feel better about himself. *How does she ken what I need tae hear? Dinnae fuck this up! Yeh need her!* he thought.

Chapter Sixteen

MARGARITA'S FOR LUNCH

Erin and David pulled into the parking lot of Margarita's Mexican restaurant, and David laughed. "Margarita's for lunch, eh? Well played."

"Thank you," she said with a smug smile. "The chips and salsa are complementary and the best anywhere; at least I think they are." They waited for Lily to arrive and then went in together, being seated immediately at a booth. Erin chose to sit next to David so she could hold his hand, needing his touch.

They ordered their drinks and food, then made small talk as they waited for it to arrive. "So, Lily," David said, with mischief in his eyes, "What can you tell me about Erin that I don't already know?"

"Hey! No fair! New rule—no ganging up on Erin!" she said, playfully nudging him in the ribs.

David and Lily smiled; they were now in cahoots, and Erin was afraid of what Lily might say. "Hmm, let me think," Lily said, "One thing I know for sure is that she *really* loves you!"

Erin sat speechless and blinking with her mouth open, completely gobsmacked. David sat with his eyebrows raised, looking stunned.

"Oh, fu-udge—I can't believe I said that! What I meant was… in *Future Explorations*; she loves it and—Oh my God! I'm so sorry," Lily said.

David squeezed Erin's hand as they recovered from their shock. "I'm glad to hear it," he said, the corners of his mouth twitching.

Erin knew he was trying, like her, to keep from laughing. He wouldn't want to embarrass Lily any more than she already seemed to be. She was struggling not to laugh herself, and put her head down, trying extra hard to regain control, but when she looked up at them with tears streaming down both her cheeks, their worried expressions were too much. Her body started to vibrate—a little at first, though soon it was a full tremor.

"Erin—are you—a'right?" David asked tenderly.

Lily looked mortified; Erin could almost read her friend's thoughts, and it went something like, '*I just made my best friend cry in front of the most beautiful man on the planet! She'll never forgive me!*' At last, she couldn't hold it in any longer and began to laugh. She snorted and guffawed—practically rolling on the seat next to David, which set him off. They both laughed until they were holding their sides and moaning in pain.

Once Erin could breathe enough to speak, she said, "*Le potage,* Lily! That was the best! I honestly can't believe you said that!"

"So you're not mad at me?" Lily said, watching the tears roll down their cheeks. "It was the only thing I could think of to say! My mind went blank! I searched all my 'Erin March Files,' and they were empty, then I felt like I was taking forever, so I blurted out the first thing that came to my mind."

———

Because the worst of the blunders were behind them, they were able to relax and enjoy the meal and each other's company. By the end of lunch, Lily was quite comfortable around David, and as Erin predicted, he was hooked on the salsa. They each had a box of leftover food to take with them when they headed out to the parking lot.

"It was nice to meet you… um—" Lily said when they got to her car.

"Call me David," he said and gave her a hug, which Erin could see in her eyes nearly killed her best friend right then and there. She rallied but just barely, staggering a little when he let her go.

"Wow! *That* just happened!" Lily managed to say then turned to Erin and hugged her. "I love you. Thanks for not being mad at me!"

"I love you, too. How can I be mad? I haven't laughed that hard in ages! It's all good," Erin said as Lily got into the driver's seat and started her car.

They waved as Lily drove away and then started laughing again when they looked at each other. "You could've knocked me over with a feather!" she said as they walked to her car and got in.

"I wasn't sure how tae react! It was so—I dinnae ken, unexpected," he said, holding his side as he laughed.

"I'm sure she did mean 'as an actor' like she said, but she's gonna be embarrassed about that one for a long time!"

"Aye, I imagine so."

"I'd like to put my leftovers in the fridge at my place and make sure everything is... in order... if you don't mind? Would you like to see my house?"

David looked askance at her. "Are yeh sure Todd won't be home? I *really* dinnae want tae run into him… again!"

"I'm one-hundred percent sure. He doesn't get home until about 3:50, so as long as we leave by 3:30, it'll be fine."

"A'right, then I *would* like tae see yer house. In fact, I've imagined what it was like many times."

"You have? I don't know why that surprises me."

"I'm sure there are many things that would surprise you about me, ma love."

Chapter Seventeen

ERIN'S HOUSE

Erin drove David through town and turned onto Whistlers Way without incident. She pulled into number 1324, a red brick ranch home with two large maple trees in the front yard. Much to his relief, he noticed that unlike what he'd seen on Google maps, there was only one car, the one they were in, sitting in the drive. She pushed the remote garage door opener and waited for the loud, slow-moving door to open before pulling in and then shutting the door behind them.

He followed her, carrying the boxes of food, through the breezeway into the kitchen, where they found what remained of Todd's breakfast. He'd made something with eggs and toast and left a nice big mess for her to clean up. She made an exasperated sound in her throat and then placed the dishes in the sink. "I'll do these later," she explained.

"This is nice," he said as he looked around the kitchen.

"Thanks," she said and took the black foam boxes out of his hands. "I'm just gonna put my leftovers in the basement fridge. Todd is less likely to look in there—Wait, how long will you be in town? Maybe I should freeze it."

"You may have mine as well. I dinnae ken when I'll leave; I reckon I'll go when yeh tell me to."

"Then you'll be here for a very long time." Erin smiled at him, kissed his cheek, and then set the bag of food on the kitchen counter. She filled two plastic storage containers with the leftovers and then threw the trash away. "I'm gonna take these to the basement; go ahead and make yourself at home.

The living room is right through there." She pointed toward the front of the house. "I'll be right back."

David watched her walk through the basement door and then made his way to the sitting room. It was a small room containing a comfortable-looking sofa, a much-used recliner that had seen better days, a rather large television, and a narrow curio cabinet in the corner. He stepped up to the cabinet and looked inside, laughing out loud at what he saw. Instead of the usual vases or ceramic figurines, this one was filled with Pop Vinyl figures. There were several from *Doctor Who*, a few from *Outlander* and *Star Wars*, but the most prominent ones were of him in *Future Explorations*.

"Doesn't look much like me," he said out loud and opened the cabinet door to get a closer look.

"I disagree," Erin said, startling him. He dropped his hands as though he'd been caught snooping. She walked up to the cabinet and opened the door a bit wider. Taking the small vinyl John Thomas Fife off the shelf, she held it up to his face. She tilted her head as if concentrating on finding the similarities between the two. "I don't know how to pinpoint it, but they've captured something about you; it just says John Thomas to me. I've had this one for at least three years; it was the first one I got."

Her cheeks went pink after saying that, and he smiled. "Yeh never went on about the program. Et's generally the first thing people mention when— You're a proper fan, aren't you?"

"I guess I am—I don't know why I didn't bring it up, I mean, I love the show, and—you in it."

"As Lily pointed out so brilliantly," he said with a smile. "So, when yeh saw me through the bedroom door on the day we met in New Orleans, you must've been—"

"I was beside myself. It was like an out-of-body experience or a dream where you're watching yourself do something from a different vantage point. I was also utterly terrified."

"Terrified? What of—me?"

"I should say I was terrified until you helped me up. As soon as you touched me, I felt... safe; out of my mind, but safe."

He took the figure of himself out of her hand, placed it back on the shelf, and closed the cabinet door. "Et was the same for me, hen. I was—apprehensive as well, but as soon as I touched you and smelled yer perfume, I felt less nervous. That is, until I turned 'round and nearly ran you down; that was the end of all comfort for the night."

"Oh! That was insane—and wonderful! My insides were already doing flips, but when your body was only an inch away from mine—I could hardly contain myself." She closed her eyes, "I never want to forget how that felt; it was—magical."

He stood in front of her, just like he'd done two weeks earlier. When she opened her eyes, he lifted her hand, placed her palm on his chest, and kissed her. The room was suddenly filled with their energy, making his knees weak. "That's what I wanted tae do that night; I couldn't get it out of ma head. I had tae tell maself again and again tae slow down—that it was too soon." He laughed, remembering the turmoil he'd gone through the whole night—until he'd finally found the courage to pull her into a secluded driveway and kissed her. "It was bliss—" he said, closing his eyes.

"Telling yourself to stop was blissful?" she said.

"What? Oh, no, our first kiss. Sorry, my mind ran away a bit there."

The memories had them excited and they were both breathing heavily. Finally, David placed his hand on her ass and pulled her up against him. "Erin," he said with urgency, "I..." He wanted to ask if he could make love to her, to give her something tae remember when she was watchin' the telly with Todd—whilst he was far away in London, but he knew it was wrong.

"You?"

"Ach, never mind, love. It was inappropriate."

———

"Oh, David! If it's what I think you mean, I want that too, but you're right, that would be very wrong. I already feel like I'm becoming the 'bad guy,' and I don't wanna make it worse. *I just wish I knew how to end it and what to say to Todd.* Do you want a tour, instead?" she asked.

"I'd like that."

She led him by the hand back through the kitchen to the short hallway, then into the spare bedroom. It was a simple room, nothing special about it. She then led him through the short hallway into her bedroom. The covers were everywhere, and her pillow was lying long ways in the middle of the bed. It appeared as though Todd had held it to him while he slept the night before.

"Do you think of me whilst ye're tryin' tae fall asleep in here?" David asked her quietly.

"Yes, every night. I lay here and wish you were with me, making love to me." She leaned against his arm as they stood, looking at her bed, each having their own private thoughts about it and in what way Todd was involved. "Would you do something for me?" she asked. "Would you lay next to me and spoon with me in my bed? Nothing more; I just want to feel you here when I close my eyes."

"Of course," he said simply.

Erin slipped off her shoes and climbed in on her side, replacing her pillow where it should be, and waited for him to get in behind her. David held her while she tried to soak up the feeling of him, hoping she'd be able to recall every detail; the pressure of his arm resting on her side, the sound of his breath, slow and measured, down to the smell of his soap or cologne.

Between Erin's exhaustion and David's change in time zone, they ended up falling asleep. The next thing she knew, she was startled awake, having heard a noise. She jumped out of bed and looked at the clock—3:45. Todd would be home any minute—if he wasn't already there. She had no idea what had woken her up, so she stood still and listened. She didn't hear anything, so she motioned for David to get up, placing her finger to her lips, asking him to be silent.

They put their shoes back on, and Erin whispered, "If you hear me talking to someone… well, I'm sorry, my love, but you'll have to climb out the window." They both smiled at the ridiculousness of that idea, but there wasn't anything else they could do unless they wanted Todd to know who David was *and* start an enormous fight.

Erin tiptoed out of the room while David stood near the window, ready to open it and crawl out. After a few moments, she returned to tell him the coast was clear, but they'd better hurry because he could pull into the driveway at any moment. At the last second, she saw her pillow lying where it should be and thought to put it back where it had been when they'd entered the room.

They rushed through the kitchen and out to the garage, making a mad dash to get into the car. Erin hit the remote door opener and waited for the wide heavy door to open, which took far too long. As soon as she could, she backed out and turned around in the driveway, hitting the remote again to close the door. She turned right and looked in the rearview mirror. Her heart skipped a beat when she saw Todd turn onto Whistlers Way behind them.

Chapter Eighteen

PANIC ATTACK

Erin turned right onto the next street and drove a block before she had to pull over. She got out of the car and laid her arm against the door frame, resting her forehead on it. She thought she might throw up and needed to get some fresh air.

David got out and walked around the car to see what was wrong. "Are yeh a'right, love? Ye're as white as a ghost," he said and put his hand on her back.

She turned so that her back was against the door, then she bent over double, placing her hands on her knees. She felt utterly sick and thought she might even faint. Her chest hurt, and she was moments away from bursting into tears. She was scared—of what exactly, she didn't know, but fear was gripping her chest, and she prayed it wasn't the start of another episode. Willing herself to stand upright again, she looked at David. "I don't know, I feel sick—My heart… it's—I don't know, it hurts, like a heart attack."

"A'right. darling, let's get you off the street." He took her gently by the arm and led her to the curb, "Why don't we sit for a moment; do you think it's an episode? Shall I ring for an ambulance?"

"No, it's not like that at all." He wrapped his arm around her shoulders, and she laid her head on his chest, praying the pain would go away. He kissed her head and petted her hair until she calmed down a bit. After a few minutes, she felt her breathing slow, and her muscles began to relax.

It occurred to her that she might be having a panic attack. All the symptoms were there, and once she realized that's what it was, she was able to calm down. "Thank you," she said and gave him a sideways hug. "You were perfect. Your calmness helped me so much. I think it was a panic attack. I can't believe we fell asleep! I saw him—Todd, turn the corner just as we left the driveway."

"Aye, that would've been an unpleasant confrontation. What say we return tae the hotel? We can have a proper kip, a'right?" he said gently.

"Yeah, if kip means nap, that would be nice. Do you think you could drive us there?"

"I reckon I could manage et. Ye'll have tae point me in the right direction though; I won't remember."

"I can do that," she said, thankful she could breathe again.

They stood, and David opened and closed the passenger door for her. Then, he went to the driver's side and got in, though he had to fold himself up to fit because the seat was too far forward for his long legs. Erin laughed at the sight of him like that. He pulled the adjustment lever, and it rolled back so *he* could breathe again. "Has anaone ever told you ye're far too short?" he said and laughed with her.

"I prefer altitudinally disinclined or vertically challenged, thank you," she said.

Todd sat in his car, watching the scene unfold in front of him. He'd seen Erin pull out of the driveway and decided to follow her. He wanted to know if the vague memory of the man he'd seen the night before was, first, who he thought it was and second, if he was with her.

He'd woken up that morning in a fog of headache and suddenly remembered the tall man who had pushed him into the men's room at St. Brendan's. It had been on his mind all day, then, on his way home, he'd finally figured out who he looked like. If it hadn't been for the grey hair, he would have sworn it was David Elliott, though he reasoned it couldn't be him, since he wasn't that old.

He also knew that David Elliott was married to a smoking hot model, and he couldn't fathom the idea of signing up for the registry with a wife like her. *I shouldn't have gotten rid of that swimsuit edition she was in!* he thought, recalling vividly the photos of the sand on her flat stomach and the foamy wave churning between her legs. *What must that feel like?*

She had only driven a short distance when he watched her pull to the side of the road and get out of her car, obviously in distress. He wanted to help her, but before he could even open his door, the man he'd seen in the pub got out of the passenger seat and went to her. He wanted to storm over there and confront him, beating him to a pulp for ruining his marriage and stealing his wife's affection from him. He nearly got out twice but lost his courage. They sat on the curb for a while, and then he watched as they pulled away, the man driving. He couldn't help himself and continued following from a good distance away.

David managed to drive them back to St. Brendan's as Erin directed him. She was so tired that it was a chore getting up the steps into the building, and she was thankful for the elevator that brought them quickly upstairs. They entered the room and hurried to take their clothes off before falling onto the bed. David spooned her as he'd done at her house, and they were sound asleep in a few minutes. An hour later, they woke up feeling much better.

"Thank you, my love, for being exactly what I need," Erin said as they lay together on the bed. "I'm sorry you had to go through all of that today."

"I'm glad I was there for you, darling, and it's over now, so let's hope for better times from here on out, a'right?"

"Aright, now what was it you said about making love to me more than once every day? How about more than twice?" she asked and rolled over to kiss him.

Chapter Nineteen

CONFRONTATION

"I think we should get out of town; this place knows me too well. There are too many opportunities for us to run into people I know here, especially Todd," Erin said as they got dressed again.

"Aye, I agree. Do yeh have a destination in mind?" David asked.

"I was born about an hour and a half south of here in Port Washington. It's a small, picturesque lakeside town, which, more importantly, I haven't lived in for over twenty years, so no one knows me anymore. I'd like to show you where I grew up. What do you say?"

He smiled at her and watched as she put her bra back on. "I'd like that. I can't think of anywhere I'd like to see more, actually," he said.

"Yay! How about we leave in the morning?"

"Alright, I'll call Tina and—"

"What do you say we play it by ear instead? There are a couple of small towns nearby that I'd love to show you, too. I thought that maybe once we get down there, we could find a place to stay that looks nice."

"I reckon we can live on the wild side," he said as he tied his shoes.

Erin laughed, feeling excited about going on an adventure with him. "Good, now, what do you say to a nice long walk on the trail? There are restaurants along the way, and we can stop at one that tickles our fancy, okay?" she said.

"A'right, I'd like that."

"Yay, now don't forget the room key."

They made their way down to the main floor and headed toward the door, looking forward to a good meal; however, Erin stopped dead in her tracks when she heard her husband's voice behind them.

"No *fucking* way—it *is* you! I thought you looked familiar last night!" Todd was standing in front of David, trembling, with his fists balled up at his sides. "How many times did I have to sit through that *ridiculous* show while Erin drooled over you? Now, here you are, fucking her? No way!"

Erin opened her mouth to say something, but Todd was too quick. She saw, as if it were in slow motion, her husband raise his fist and punch David in the face. There was a loud *pop* sound and blood started gushing from his nose. "What in the—Todd! What are you doing? Stop it!" Erin yelled while trying to intervene.

"Arrrhhh!" Todd bellowed as he swung at him. "I should've known! I should've *fucking* known. Who else could it be but your fucking David Elliott! Aaaarrrrhhhh!" he roared again, as another swing of his fist hit its target.

———

Todd managed to punch him a few times in the ribs and once in the gut. They weren't overly hard blows, but they stung. David couldn't get close enough to do anything except try to shield his face. Erin almost got ahold of Todd's arm, but he swung his elbow back and knocked her to the ground, which set David off. He hadn't planned on fighting back; he was a good four or five inches taller than him, and he didn't want to hurt the man.

Although he was pretty sure his nose was broken, David was much more calm and rational than Todd, who didn't even notice he'd knocked his wife to the floor. He needed to be stopped before anyone else got hurt, so before Todd could bring his fist around for another swing, David pushed him hard into the check-in desk. Todd lost his balance and fell to the floor.

Hardly able to breathe at that point, David still managed to pin him down with his arm behind his back. "Yeh need-tae leave, undless you want-tae wait for da p'lice tae arrive," he said menacingly in Todd's ear, blood dripping from his nose. His face throbbing and his vision blurry, he just wanted to sit and take stock of the damage he'd sustained.

It was suddenly quiet after the brawl, and over his shoulder, he heard Erin's gentle voice say, "David, please let him go now." He was happy to comply, tired of the man and of holding him down.

———

Once released, Todd lay motionless, his cheek flat on the dark green carpet and his hand clutching his side where he'd slammed into the countertop. He was shaking with sobs, and Erin crouched beside him, offering to help him up.

He ignored her at first, but after a few seconds, he took her hand. As soon as he was standing, he let go and narrowed his eyes at her, tears and snot running down his face. He was breathing with shallow gasps and continued to hold his side, grimacing with every breath. "I loved you, Erin," he wheezed and wiped his face with his sleeve.

Two large men came out from the kitchen to break up the fight, one of them brandishing a shillelagh. When Todd saw them, he turned to go. "Todd!" Erin said, not knowing what to do. He looked back at her and then staggered out the door.

She wouldn't go after him, but it hurt horribly. There walked away fifteen years of her life. Good, happy years. She turned and sitting against the wall in front of her, his hand covering his nose, was the last three weeks of her life. There was no telling how far into the future they would go together.

"David! Are you alright? Holy Moses! Oh, no!" He was holding his nose gingerly, his chin and shirt front soaked in blood.

"I tink 'ee broke ma doze," he said.

One of the big kitchen guys ran to get a bar towel while the other tried to clear the crowd of curious onlookers. "Okay, I'll take you to the emergency room," Erin said, not able to think. Her mind kept replaying what had just happened on a loop. She felt like she was running in circles, like a dog chasing its tail, until David took her hand, silently asking for help standing.

"Ah'll need a spe-shlist," he said, but with his nose broken, it was hard to understand him, "Ma unsurance enformashon es in the room, in ma houdawll."

"A what? Oh, a specialist, yes, you do. I'll go up and get your papers; then we can go." She ran up the stairs to their room, adrenalin making her heart pound.

She found his holdall in the closet and set it on the bed. The bag was soft and supple and smelled like fine leather. She was hesitant about going through his things, but she had to, so she unzipped it and looked inside, not seeing anything. Then she remembered that after they'd been attacked and mugged in New Orleans, he'd unzipped a hidden pocket that held some extra cash and credit cards.

She felt along the seam, located the small brass zipper, and unzipped it. Inside was his passport, money clip, a credit card, and some other important-looking paperwork. The sight of his small accordion photo holder and the photographs of them from their last night in New Orleans made her smile.

She left the cash and photos then zipped it up again and hurried down the stairs. David had a bar towel covering his nose and she asked one of the bouncers to help her get him to the car.

Chapter Twenty

ER—A&E

Erin drove to the emergency room valet area and an older man came out to park the car for her. She and David got out and walked through the sliding glass doors into the patient registration and waiting room. They had to stand in line for twenty minutes before checking in with the receptionist.

She offered to stay in the waiting room while he told the woman his personal information, but he insisted she stay with him. She did her best to translate the words that were just too hard to pronounce or understand with a broken nose *and* a Scottish accent; RP was simply out of the question. The young woman put an identification bracelet around his wrist and told them to have a seat. They sat in a quiet corner of the waiting area, and David rested his head in his hands, looking miserable.

"David, I'm so sorry—" she began, but he put his hand up.

"You shou'n't ab-ologise for 'im, Er'n."

"I know, but I *am* sorry you had to deal with him tonight and that he did this to you. I'm not trying to excuse his behavior but please, David—" She took his hand in hers, "Please, my love, try to see his side. He's been living a nightmare for the last two months."

"Aye—"

"I don't understand how he knew about us, though."

"I dink he re-called our encounter las' nigh' and sussed it out."

"Oh yeah, I forgot that he saw you."

"I dinnae blame himb for h'idting me; I only wish he'd no' broken ma doze."

A nurse opened the door that led to the exam rooms and called out, "David?" Three men stood, looked at each other and then at the nurse. "David Hansen?" That David walked forward, and the other two sat down.

Thirty minutes later, Erin could tell he was in a lot of pain since he started answering her small questions and comments with 'no' or 'aye' and sometimes only a slight nod. She held his hand, grateful no one in the room recognized him or knew her. Eventually, the other David was called in, and then, after another twenty minutes, it was their turn.

They were led into a small room with an exam table and a computer screen, keyboard, and mouse, along with all the usual ER gadgets and whizbangs hanging on the walls. David sat on the only chair, and Erin stood next to him. The nurse took his vitals and then asked him what had happened.

"A drunken man pundched me," he said.

"How long ago did that happen?" she asked.

"An hour or so," Erin replied for him.

After quite a few questions, the nurse said, "Alright, Mr. Elliott, the doctor will be in soon."

"Thank you, Nurse," Erin said as the woman closed the fabric curtain and then left the room, sliding the glass door shut behind her.

David smiled; she saw him and knitted her brows together. "What?"

"I lobe who you are. Ye're *always* nice."

She laughed at the way he said it and kissed his temple. "Good night nurse, your hair smells really good. I just want to stand here and bury my face in it." He leaned against her side, and she lay her cheek against his head. She was getting tired and knew he must be exhausted, especially since he never really had a chance to recover from any jet lag he might have.

There was a knock on the glass sliding door and a middle-aged man came in. He held out his hand for David and then Erin to shake. "Hello, I'm Dr. LeClair. So, you ran into a bit of fisticuffs, I see?" he said good-naturedly.

"I beliebe the fisticubffs ran d'into me—'At would be more acc-urate," David said and smiled.

"Fair enough. So, what would you like to do about your nose, Mr. Elliott—Wait; you're not THE David Elliott from—" He looked at Erin, who was nodding her head.

"He is—one and the same," she said. "So, you can see how important it is for him to have his nose fixed as perfectly as possible, right?"

"I see. Yes, well, it's a good thing you've come in here tonight. We have one of the region's best facial reconstruction surgeons on call, so let me take a look."

David lowered the towel, which was saturated with blood, both fresh and dried, revealing that his face was a mess. Erin gasped when she saw it, and David looked worried. "Sorry, it's just that there's a lot of blood," she fibbed. There *was* a lot of blood, but it was the swelling and sizeable nodule protruding out of the bridge of his nose that made her gasp.

"Alright now," the doctor said as he examined David's nose. "It's not so bad; I don't think it will take much to correct the damage. We'll call the surgeon and get everything set up for the procedure. I'll try to find you a private room to wait in Mrs. Elliott."

Erin was about to correct him but changed her mind. David didn't say anything either.

"My nurse will return in a few minutes and show you where to go; we will get this fixed in no time." He stood and shook Erin's hand.

"Thank you so much, Doctor!" She smiled genuinely at him.

"It's my pleasure," he said, smiling back.

David was grinning at her when she turned back to him, and she rolled her eyes. "What now?" she said, with mock exasperation. "You're so d'nice, *Mrs. Elliott*," he said, and Erin blushed deeply. "I'm glad yeh din't correct him. I like tae hear yeh called tha'."

"I didn't want to get ushered out or something once they found out I wasn't your wife."

"Would they?" he said, wide-eyed.

"I don't know, but I wouldn't be given as much liberty as I will be if they think I am."

Forty minutes later, the nurse came back in, and Erin was led to a private room to wait until David's procedure was done. They were able to do it in the room he was in with local anesthesia, and she was told it wouldn't take long. He would have to wear a cast for a week, and it would be tender for a while afterward. Both were assured that it should look just as it did before Todd behaved like a Neanderthal.

What am I gonna do about Todd? Erin thought while scrolling on Facebook. *I know he was drunk, but I'm pretty sure he would have done it dead sober too.* "Say the word, ma darling, and I'll make et happen... If you were tae come to me, I would take yeh in, and we could be together—whether et's in Britain or here. I'm yours, Erin, all of me," she could still hear David's lilting Scottish accent say to her, and there was nothing she wanted more. She also liked being called Mrs. Elliott; it made her feel a rush of joy.

Damn, Erin, you're thinking a little far ahead, aren't you? You hardly know each other and you're already trying on his last name? Next, you'll be writing it out in your diary! Grow up already!

When the procedure was complete, David was brought up to the room to recoup and for the local anesthesia to wear off. His nose was covered with bandages and capped with a white plastic cast that made him look like Rudolph's less colorful cousin. On the other hand, it would make a terrific disguise, combined with the grey hair. It meant they'd be able to go anywhere and do anything without anyone recognizing him.

"So, when we spring you from this prison, I think we should go back to the hotel, pack our things and leave bright and early tomorrow morning," Erin suggested.

He was groggy from the pain and sedation medication, but he answered, "A'right," and then winced. "Da an-ess-tee-ssia is wearin' off. Et prickles when I talk."

"Oh, David, don't talk then. I'll ask you questions you can answer with your fist. Up and down means yes, side to side means no, okay?"

He waved his fist up and down and smiled at her.

"I think we should spend the day in Port Washington and then go visit a few other small towns if you're okay with that?"

He nodded his fist. "What's there tae do in—"

"In Port Washington? Nothing; not much, anyway," she laughed. "That's why most young people leave and why all of the rich yuppies have moved in. They build their high-rise condos and ruin the lovely charm of the town. I haven't been there in years, so I'm sure there are new things to see and do. Anyway, I'll give you the nickel tour that's only worth two pence."

David smiled and bobbed his fist a few times, but his eyes were droopy. It was getting late, and they still hadn't eaten supper. Again, like clockwork, her stomach sounded the alarm saying it was officially time to eat. That time, *his* belly replied in kind, and they both laughed.

"I can run down to the cafeteria and get us something to eat if you want me to?" she offered, but he shook his fist. "Okay, I'm sure we can find some food when we get back to the hotel. Maybe soup or something easy to eat?"

He nodded his fist and closed his eyes. She yearned to crawl up next to him on the bed they'd wheeled him in on, but it was too narrow, and he needed to rest. Half an hour later, the nurse came in and asked how he was feeling. Erin could see by his expression when he answered her that he thought they were making too much of a fuss over the whole thing.

"I donb't bean tae be rude, but may I go dow?"

The nurse smiled at him compassionately. "Not quite yet. Dr. Lee will need to talk to you first, and then we'll get you out of here."

When the nurse was gone, Erin went to him and held his hand. "How do you feel?"

"No' tae combplain, but I just wan'tae sleep. Ma head is throbbin' again, now the meds have worn off, and whatever they've put on ma nose is itchin' like mad! I hope they prescribe somebthin' good for the pain."

"Oh, hon—I mean, David, I hope they do too."

It was past ten o'clock when the doctor finally came in. David and Erin were both asleep. She woke David, which in turn, woke Erin. "Hello, Mrs. Elliott, I'm Doctor Amy Lee," she said and shook Erin's hand.

Erin blushed. "Nice to meet you."

They sat, only half awake, listening to Doctor Lee tell them what to expect, then she handed them some paperwork, explaining everything she'd said in writing. Instead of a prescription, she said he should take ibuprofen and acetaminophen for the pain, then she wrote down the doses and how far apart to take them.

They were weary to the bone as they walked back to the ER entrance and gave the valet the neon coil bracelet she'd been given when they'd arrived. Erin thanked the older man who brought her car back and then drove off, glad to see the place in her rear-view mirror. It was difficult, but she stayed awake and alert until they parked at the hotel.

She could have slept in the car and been happy at that point, but then David was outside her door. He opened it for her, so she roused herself enough to take his hand and get out. They made it back to their room and dropped everything on the desk, then once they were undressed, David took his pain relievers, and they fell into bed.

Chapter Twenty-One

CHANGE OF PLAN

Sometime during the night, Erin had a dream that made her feel sick; something about hospitals. She must have been partly awake because she could remember thinking she wanted to wake up, hoping she'd feel better. Later, when David got out of bed and headed to the toilet, she finally woke and sat up, still feeling sick.

The clock at the end of the bed read 9:14. *Good night nurse!* she thought and swiveled to the edge of the bed. Afraid she might need to throw up, it was a relief when she heard the toilet flush. She felt like she'd been hit by a truck; she couldn't imagine how David must feel.

The door opened, and the man who exited the tiny room looked like he'd not only been hit by the same truck but also dragged fifty yards down the road with it. There were purple bruises under his eyes, and the middle part of his face was puffy. The white plastic splint just made it all the more glaring, and he looked utterly miserable. "Oh, my darling! Oh, let me get you your meds." She stood and then sat back down, willing the bile to stay in her stomach.

"Whadt's the madder, dove?" David asked.

"I… had a dream about… hospitals—Oh crap—" She launched herself off the bed to the toilet, retching into the bowl. After a few minutes, she returned to the bed, feeling a bit better. "I've never had a dream make me sick before; I *don't* like it! Is there anything like crackers or a cookie or something in here to settle my stomach?"

"I dinnae ken. I dond't dink so. Ledt's get dressed and go down tae breakfast." He read the printout from the hospital to confirm the correct dose of the painkillers, then he downed all the pills at one time and sat on the bed.

"Maybe we should wait till tomorrow to go out of town?" Erin said, seeing how much pain he was in and not feeling much like traveling, herself.

David nodded slowly, then both their stomachs started yelling at them simultaneously, which made them smile. "I dink I was right; we need tae eat somebthin'," he said, just above a whisper.

She sat next to him on the bed and held his hand. "I know I said it before, and I remember what you said, but I really am *so* sorry about all this," she said and laid her head on his arm.

They got dressed and were downstairs in ten minutes. As they entered the dining room, people looked at them and winced when they saw David's face. They hurried to their table, trying to ignore everyone around them. "Et's odd tae see people pull a face when day see be," he said once they were seated.

"I bet! You're used to everyone swooning as they gaze on your tremendous beauty," Erin teased.

"Har, har, har, fundy."

The waitress brought them good, strong coffee, and they ordered their food, hoping for one peaceful meal while they were there. They were seated at a small, two-person booth along the wall that separated the dining room from the bar. It was cozy, and Erin held David's hand while they sipped their coffee and waited for breakfast.

After the meal, Erin felt much better, so they went for a stroll on the trail, heading in the opposite direction from the night before. They held hands while Erin did most of the talking. Walkers, bikers, and inline skaters passed them, and many of them waved or said, 'Good morning.' One man, who looked to be in his late seventies, walked with them for a few minutes. "Beautiful day, en so?" he said.

"Finally! Right?" Erin replied.

"Yeah, but it's worth the wait. Broke my nose in a flag football game over fifty years ago," he said and touched his nose. There was a definite curve to it. "Didn't get it fixed—couldn't afford it. Plus, I thought it gave me some much-needed character." He laughed and then flinched. "Can still feel the 'crack' when I think about it."

"I bet it's not something you think about very often, then," Erin said.

"I try not to. Anyway, enjoy the weather; I hear it's supposed to be cold and rainy next week," he said and jogged ahead of them.

"I loved that," she said. "Hearing a tiny excerpt from a person's life before they vanish; it makes me want to know more."

"I rarely get thadt opportunditdy. When I meedt people in public, they udsually load me with complimendts or ask for things. No one stops tae simply talk—as dhat man did, et was nice. Ye're so nadtural with everaone yeh meedt; I should spend more time wid'th you."

Erin laughed at the way he was speaking and put her head on his arm. "I agree, you should." She felt her phone vibrate in her pocket and then heard the ringtone she'd set for Lily's number. Loud and clear, they heard, "*The future is never far away!*" spoken by David as John Thomas Fife.

"Nice," he said.

She laughed and looked at the message.

> Lily: *Hey, would you and David like to come over for supper tonight? I know it's last minute, but I thought it would be nice if you could. LOL Is he still here? Let me know.*

The answer could wait, so she put the phone back in her pocket, not sure what would be happening in the next few days. She decided to see what David wanted to do before she replied. "David," she said hesitantly.

"Aye?"

"How long can you stay?" she asked.

"Undtil Friday; Sadurday would be cudtin' it close. I've a meedtin' on Monday, so need I tae be well prepared and rested. Hopefully, this dambed plaster will be off by then. I'd stay longer If I could—I dinnae like the thoughdt of you returnin' tae Todd."

Erin didn't like the idea either but didn't want him to worry. "It'll be fine, and if it's not, I'll stay with Lily or something. Speaking of Lily, that message was her asking if we'd join them for supper tonight. I wanted to talk to you about it first, though I completely understand if you'd rather chill at the hotel."

David looked at her and grinned, "We can *chill* at Lil-y's. I'd like dat."

"Good, she'll be thrilled, and her husband will freak out. Oh, wait, they are Todd's friends too. Wouldn't it be bad to do that to him?" She took her phone out of her pocket and replied.

> Erin: *We'd love to have supper with you and Nick tonight but I don't want to hurt Todd by infiltrating his friends, you know?*

> L: *Oh, I didn't think about it that way. I just thought it would neat for Nick to meet him too. If he finds out that I did and he didn't get a chance to…that might upset him more. IDK…Couldn't you two lovebirds just cool it on the lovey-dovey stuff for one night?*

Erin read the text to David "I reckon I'd be able to do that, but only for one night," he said with a smile.

> E: *When should we arrive?*

She hit 'send' and knew Lily would 'squee!' when she saw it. A moment later, she got a reply.

L: *Eeee! That's so cool! How about 5:00?*
Or is that too early? I don't know...I
didn't think that far ahead. Oh shit!
Is he vegan or something?

Erin laughed out loud as she stared at her phone and then showed David the messages. He laughed too and said, "She should ken I'm no' a vedgetarian; I ordered a steak burridto at the resdtaurant."

"She's just excited. Is five good for you?"

"Aye," he said, so Erin replied again.

E: *5:00 is great! Should we bring*
anything?

The reply was almost instant.

L: *Nope, just your awesome selves. See ya*
then...EEE!!!! Nick is gonna flip out!
LOL

She showed him the messages, and they laughed again, then Erin stopped suddenly. "Good night nurse! I just realized—there's something wrong!" she said.

He turned and looked anxiously at her. "Whadt is et, hen?"

She smiled at him and closed her eyes. "You haven't kissed me once today!"

———

David chuckled and looked at her with her eyes closed and her face upturned; her lips were pursed, waiting for him to fix the problem. He loved the woman, no doubt about it. He never knew what she would do next, which was precisely what he needed in his life. Tilting his head so as not to bump his tender nose, he pressed his lips to hers.

She breathed in sharply and kissed him back, standing on her tiptoes and wrapped her arms around his neck. They were at Hagemeister Park, a restaurant with a boardwalk in the back that met up with the trail. They stood kissing for quite a long time and got a few whistles and whoops from passersby. They didn't care; the weather was warm, the river sailed past them, rushing up to the bay of Lake Michigan, and they were together, in each other's arms.

When they were finally kissed out, Erin hugged him, "Thank you, that was lovely!" she said, and he smiled down at her.

"Aye, it was. Ye're quidte welcombe."

They sat on the large wooden bench built into the boardwalk, and Erin leaned against him with her hand on his chest. He looked out on the river with his arm around her shoulder. "Whadt's in thadt buildin'?" He pointed across the river to a two-story, brown brick building.

"That's the Neville Museum. There are some interesting things in it, I guess."

"Would yeh fancy goin' there?"

"To the museum—with you?" she said.

"Aye."

"Okay—I'll go anywhere with you," she said, then laughed and looked up at him.

"Good tae know. Next timbe I'm headed tae Siberia…" He laughed, and she playfully slapped his hand, which was inching closer and closer to the top of her breast.

"Why don't we go after lunch. There is a farmer's market over there; I think it starts at three. We can go to the museum at around two, hit the farmer's market, and get Lily a bouquet of fresh flowers."

"A'right, and whadt shall we do undtil then?"

"I have a few ideas. Let's go back to the hotel, and I'll tell you all about them."

Chapter Twenty-Two

FUTURE EXPLORATIONS

At 12:45, after some fooling around and a nice nap, David and Erin walked to Hagemeister Park for lunch. She wasn't against the whole museum idea, though she thought it might be unexciting compared to what Britain has to offer. On the flip side, it meant spending time with David, and as long as they were together, it didn't matter what they did.

While they ate, she told him how the Hmong women sold beautiful flower bouquets at the farmer's market. She'd never had a reason to buy one before, considering Todd was allergic to pollen and would get a migraine if she brought real flowers into the house. "Lily will love it," she said.

It was only one thirty when they finished their meal, so they decided to go early and take their time. They crossed the bridge and then headed to the building. David held the door for her and paid the entrance fee; then, they set off toward the permanent exhibit. The first section led them through a tunnel made to look like an Ice Age glacier, followed by a leisurely voyage through time from the Neanderthal peoples all the way through the twentieth century, learning about local history. "Huh, we're on a future exploration together, aren't we?" Erin said, laughing.

"Aye, I reckon so," David said.

They wandered through the displays and eventually found themselves at the temporary exhibit called, *The Darker Side*, which focused on things unknown and unseen. The description on one of the main displays read: *In times of trauma, can human emotions or energy become attached to everyday objects? Can those objects bring their energy into the present day? Can that energy be seen, felt, or communicated? The Darker Side will introduce you to artifacts of personal tragedy and terror in an intimate setting.*

David noticed a sign near the room's entrance displaying times when there would be special guests, speakers, and events. They cost a bit extra but were more personalized. The guest that day was a seer or fortune teller, and for ten dollars per person, they could have their fortune read while a museum employee recorded their reading on a phone or camera. "Yeh mendtioned a fudture exploration—whadt do you think; fandcy a go with me?" he asked.

Erin was skeptical of supernatural stuff, but David seemed eager to do it, so she agreed. "It's a waste of money, but I guess it won't hurt to hear whatever nonsense they come up with. We should pay and go in separately, though, then they won't know we're together."

"A'right, good idea," David said.

She fished a ten-dollar bill from her purse, then stepped up to the table where the tickets were being sold and got one for herself. David bought his, and they walked into a smaller, darker room. Erin entered first, followed by a small woman wearing a black, sleeveless Harley Davidson t-shirt who smelled strongly of cigarette smoke. After her, a very short, burly man stepped in, wearing a bright blue t-shirt and black knit shorts. His shoes were nearly falling apart, and he smelled like pickles, which wasn't pleasant in the confined room.

David entered after him and acted as though he were alone. Erin heard the man in blue asked if his nose hurt and then snicker. "A bit," David said politely, though she could almost read his mind, knowing he'd want to reply with something like, 'Not as much as yours will in a minute,' and then pop him one. She was glad he held his tongue.

When it was her turn, Erin opened her phone to the camera app and handed it to a man standing to the side of the seer, then she stepped up to the table. As soon as she was a foot away from her, the woman stood, took Erin's hand, and looked directly at David. She looked back at Erin and said, "Soon, you shall visit the doctor who shall provide for your child—or—it might be children, it is unclear to me at this time, but you need not worry about the future. Also, you will finally explore your dearest dream in the future, and if you choose it, you will have it."

———

David had goosebumps from head to toe. The woman and man in between him and Erin stared at him. The last thing he wanted was to be close to the seer, but as soon as she finished speaking, she kept hold of Erin's hand, walked around the table she'd been sitting at, and brought her over to stand next to him.

"And you," she said, making him shudder. She took his hand, and he felt something like lightning flow through it. It was much different than the energy he shared with Erin, and he wanted to pull away, but she had a firm grip on him. "I see that you have already tried to explore your future, and it has looked dim and fruitless to you. You have many things, but there is something that you have desired for a very long time. That thing shall come to you; all you must do is ask, but you must wait for the right time, and DO NOT trust the birds! Do not trust the birds, or they will peck your eyes out! Also, I'm not sure what this means, but the mother means no harm; forgive her." She smiled at the two of them and joined their hands together, then she walked back to her chair behind the table and resumed her fortune-telling with the rest of the people in line.

Erin and David stood there holding hands, speechless. Finally, Erin went back up to the employee who had recorded it all on her phone. She took it from him, thanked him, and they walked out of the room, feeling dumbfounded and completely stunned.

"What in the hell? My child will be provided for by some doctor; what does that even mean? I can't have children! That was just cruel, unless… some doctor will help me get pregnant, but why on earth would *they* be providing for its future? And what she said to you—forgive the mother, don't trust the bird? It makes no sense!"

David was still feeling spooked; parts of it made some sense to him, but he couldn't say anything about it yet. He desperately wanted to tell her, but he couldn't. *Does that mean we're gonna have a child, or that she'll have a child, whether et's mine or not?*

"David? What is it? Did any of that make sense to you?" she asked, gazing up at his face.

"I dinnae ken, but it was intendse—thadt's all I can say. Did… yeh feel anathin' when she touched you?"

"No, did you? I was just going to say that it was all, to quote Hagrid, 'Codswallop,' but you seem genuinely alarmed."

He looked at her, not sure if he wanted to admit it, though he didn't know why not. "I… thoughdt I did. Maybe it was just nerves."

"I have to admit it was really creepy how she looked right at you when it was my turn and then walked over to you like that. I mean, how did she know we were together? Unless someone told her, but how would they have been able to?"

"I dinnae ken how they could've," he said, glad to be out of there. He was still freaked out and wanted to watch the recording a few times to see if he missed anything.

They left the museum feeling unnerved; the weather was beautiful, but they both felt a bit chilled. When they got to the farmer's market, they began to feel things thaw out gradually, and by the time they were in front of the vendor with the flowers Erin liked best, it was almost as though nothing had happened. The museum had taken longer than Erin thought it would, so by the time they finished wandering around, it was nearly four.

David needed to take another dose of painkillers, so they made their way back to their room at St. Brendan's. "Erin, may I see the video from the fortune teller, pleadse?" David asked her tentatively.

"Sure, I wanted to watch it again anyway." She took her phone out of her pocket, swiped the screen, and then opened the video. She tapped 'play' and winced when she saw herself. "Ugg! I'm so fat!" she said and then turned up the volume so they could hear the woman's voice.

"Soon, you shall visit the doctor who shall provide for your child—or—it might be children, it is unclear to me at this time, but you need not worry about the future…"

Erin paused it there. "At least I don't have to worry about the future! Right?" she mocked.

David smiled, "No' if I'm around, anaway," he said.

"Oh, I didn't think about it like that." She started to pay closer attention to what the woman said after that.

"You will finally explore your dearest dream in the future, and if you choose it, you will have it."

"That's nice, isn't it?" she said.

"Whadt's yer dearest dream? Do yeh ken whadt she meant?" he asked.

"It's kinda silly, but I've always dreamed of living in England… or Scotland. Somewhere with a few acres to grow things; maybe a farm where I can raise chickens… and, well, lots of children." She said 'children' very quietly. She'd accepted long ago that children weren't in the future for her, but the woman had said *your* child or children. *David has children; maybe that's what it means.*

"I dinnae think et's silly. Sounds delightful, adctually," David said and rubbed her back.

Erin held the phone back up and pressed 'play' again.

"And you …"

Erin noticed him flinch when the lady touched him. "Is that when you felt something?" she asked.

David took the phone, slid the play bar back a few seconds, and watched it again. "There—I feldt somedthin' flow through ma hand—similar tae stadtic electridcity, except it didn't hurt," he said and hit the play button again.

"I see that you have already tried to explore your future, and it has looked dim and fruitless to you …"

"Okay," Erin said. "Do you think she knew who you were? I mean she kept saying the words 'future' and 'explore' in both our fortunes."

"I dinnae ken; am I recogdnisable with this blasted thing on ma doze?"

"I don't think so, but how—Wait, do you agree with her? That your future has seemed dim and fruitless?"

———

David didn't like to talk about what he saw in his future. It seemed to him as though it were a never-ending parade—a boring, repetitive one. Susannah was the leader—waving her baton and marching in time with the beat of trends, fashion, and status. "Et didn't look verra happy undtil I met you."

"Oh, David," she said. He gave her a shrug and touched 'play' again.

"You have many things, but there is something that you have desired for a very long time. That thing shall come to you; all you must do is ask, but you must wait for the right time ... "

"I can tell yeh righdt now what that is. Et's real love and I know she's talkin' aboudt you."

Erin turned and kissed him, long and slow, then she put her hand on his cheek and looked him in his eyes, "I love you, David Elliott, and nothing will ever cause me to stop!"

He smiled at her. "Good, I feel exactdly the same, darling. There's one tick on the seer's checklidst." He held the phone up and listened to the last part.

"... and DO NOT trust the birds! Do not trust the birds, or they will peck your eyes out!"

Erin looked at him and raised her eyebrows.

"No clue—I mean we sometimbes call women birds, but did yeh notice she was looking at you when she said it? Do yeh ken anathin' aboudt a bird?"

"No, I don't. I guess it'll remain a mystery." They watched the very last bit, spoken almost as an afterthought.

"Also, I'm not sure what this means, but the mother means no harm; forgive her."

"This one is just strange," Erin said.

"I agree—whose mother?" David said and handed the phone back to her.

"Right?" she said and then noticed the time. "Shit! It's late; we need to go!" She opened the messaging app. "I'll send a quick note to Lily, telling her we're running a bit late."

He grabbed the bouquet, Erin took her purse, and they headed out the door.

Chapter Twenty-Three

DINNER WITH NICK AND LILY

Twenty minutes later and ten minutes late, Erin and David pulled into Nick and Lily's driveway. She was excited to be there with David and hoped Nick would be okay with it. She knew he would be delighted to meet David, but she didn't want him to feel like he was betraying Todd's friendship.

They rang the doorbell, and the dogs went nuts, as always. Nick opened the door. "Come in," he said and walked away. The house smelled amazing, and he came back a few seconds later. "Sorry, I had to turn the oven temperature down before I forgot."

He hugged Erin, and then Lily appeared in the entryway. "Welcome to our, uh, humble home," she said awkwardly to David and then turned to hug Erin, which left Nick face to face with David.

"What? Who—" Nick began, clearly confused at seeing someone other than Todd standing in his kitchen.

"Sorry, Nick, this is my friend, David," Erin interrupted. She didn't know if she wanted him to know it was David Elliott right away or have him figure it out, though she wasn't given the chance to draw it out.

"David Elliott; It's a true plea-sure to mee-t you," David said, using his RP accent when he shook Nick's hand. "And, hello again, Lily." He leaned in to air-kiss her cheek and then noticed the look on Nick's face. "I me-t Lily at the mall wi-th Erin, yesterday, so we don't need introductions."

Erin could tell David was trying hard to enunciate everything he said as clearly as he could. "Awww, David, I was going to see if he figured it out. Now you've gone and ruined it," Erin said, laughing at Nick, who stood frozen with his mouth open in complete shock, staring at David, then at his wife. "You didn't tell him, Lil?"

David handed Lily the flower bouquet, and she thanked him, blushing furiously. "I… wanted to surprise him," she said and then left to find a vase while they continued their greetings.

Finally, Nick snapped out of it and said, "It's, uh, nice to meet you… David… Elliott. Why don't you come in. Would you like something to drink?" He was awkward and seemed lost in his own kitchen.

"Might you have a Guinness, by chance?" David asked a bit too formally, Erin thought.

"We do, actually," Lily said, having reentered the room.

"The usual, please," said Erin. They sat at the large square island in the center of the kitchen while Lily gathered things to make Erin's drink. Everyone watched as Nick went to the refrigerator, looked around, and then closed the door, only to go back a few seconds later and do the same thing. "Nick, can I help you find something?" Erin said.

He looked at her and frowned. "I keep going over there to get a cider and Guinness, but when I open the door, I forget what I was looking for," he admitted quietly to her.

"Here, allow me," she said and laughed. She stood, went to the fridge, and pulled out a bottle of hard cider for him. She even twisted off the cap using the hem of her shirt to help grip it. Then, she took a bottle of Guinness out for David. "Relax, he doesn't bite," she whispered as she used the magnet bottle opener. She placed the dark brown bottle in front of David. "Would you like a glass?"

"No, thanks," David said and smiled at her.

She then stood next to Lily, who was just finishing up her drink. "How can we break the ice with them?" she whispered. They watched Nick look over at David and give him a strained smile. Erin began to wonder if he was starstruck or if he was having a problem with her bringing someone other than Todd to their house.

"I don't know! You know him better than me," Lily said.

"Didn't you tell him I wasn't bringing Todd tonight? He seems genuinely shocked," Erin whispered to her friend as she helped put the lemonade back in the fridge.

"I kinda forgot that part. I was so busy planning what to make and cleaning, it slipped my mind," Lily said, looking guilty.

"We'll have to think of something," she said quietly, then spoke up, "Where's Ariana? I'd like for her to meet David too." She took a sip and set her drink next to David. Mmm, this is so good, Lily, thanks!"

"Yes, thank you!" David echoed.

"Ariana is watching a movie right now. I'll bring her out here in a few minutes," Nick said and took a drink of his cider. After a long, awkward silence, he put his cider down, "I'll… get Ariana now," he said and walked out of the kitchen.

"Oh, David, you're gonna love her. She's so sweet!" Erin said.

A few minutes later, Lily and Nick's ten-year-old daughter, Ariana, was wheeled into the room. She had been born with an undiagnosed disease that had her bound in a wheelchair. A rare blood disease caused her to have low immunity to infection, and she had multiple seizures every day, although you couldn't tell because of the medication she was on. She didn't talk much, but her smile could light up a room.

She'd been conceived during a previous relationship, but Nick had adopted her. Erin thought they were an amazing family, full of love and lots of patience. She felt a bond with Ariana, seeing they both had diseases without a cure and suffered because of it.

Ariana smiled when she saw Erin and reached out for a hug. After that, she began looking around as if searching for something, and Erin realized that it was Todd. "Todd isn't here tonight, sweety, but I have a friend I'd like you to meet," Erin said and brushed a black ringlet off the girl's face.

The young girl looked up at the tall man with the white thing on his nose. David crouched down to her level and gently took her hand in a makeshift handshake. "Hello, Ariana," he said, doing his best to enunciate. "It's a pleadsure to meet you."

She knit her brows and said something that only her parents could understand. Lily laughed, and Nick shook his head. "Apparently, she knows who you are and wants you to talk like you're supposed to," Lily said.

David didn't miss a beat, "Ach, ah'm sae sorry, lassie! Ah didnae want tae condfuse yer Mum and Da' wi' ma full accent, yeh ken? Ah shouldae kent *ye'd* understand me," David said, using his John Thomas Fife accent and playing the part brilliantly for her. She smiled then, showing all her teeth and pulled his hand, which she was still holding, closer to her. David looked up at Nick, not knowing what she wanted.

"She wants a hug," he said with a smile.

"Ach, aye. And ah'm happy tae give yeh one, as well," he said and leaned in.

Erin was beside herself, and Lily looked as if she'd cry. Ariana then reached up, trying to grab David's nose splint, but Erin caught her arm just in time. "Sorry, hun, but that doesn't come off—at least not yet," Erin said. She could tell Ariana wasn't too happy about it, but she didn't try to do it again. David spoke with her for several more minutes and then had to stand, as his feet were beginning to go numb.

"Well, it's time for bed, isn't it?" Lily said and then mouthed, 'thank you,' to David.

"Isn't it a bit early for bed?" Erin asked Nick as Lily rolled Ariana to her room.

"Oh, she's not going there to sleep. She ate already, so we're going to put her in her bedroom and start a movie. We'll bring her back out after supper," he said and then excused himself to help Lily.

"That was one of the sweetest things I've ever witnessed in my life, David," Erin said when the family was gone.

"Ach, it was nothin'," he said, and Erin hugged him.

"It's not nothing; you were so easy and comfortable with her. Lily was near tears."

"I love children, whadt can I say?" he said.

After about five minutes, Nick and Lily returned to the kitchen. "That was incredible! Thank you so much!" Lily said, "I didn't know she was paying attention to the show when we watched it."

"She knows good television when she sees it!" Erin said, and Lily raised her eyebrows, nodding her agreement.

"So, I need to finish setting the table; why don't you two get to know each other a bit while we go into the dining room?" Lily said awkwardly, not being good at segues but wanting to talk privately with Erin.

"I... uh... guess I don't need to tell you that we really like *Future Explorations* after that, do I?" Erin heard Nick say to David. "We watch it all the time actually."

"I'm glad you like it; it was fun to make, but let's not talk about thadt. Whadt do *you* do for a living?" David asked Nick. They started to talk, and after a while, Nick seemed to relax.

Erin joined Lily in the dining room, and as soon as they were out of earshot of the men, Lily exclaimed, "What happened to his nose? Wait—let me guess, Todd?" she said.

Erin told her about stopping at the house, falling asleep, and waking up with only a few minutes to spare before Todd got home. "I saw him turn onto our street; I guess he saw us and followed us to the hotel. He sat at the bar, drinking, and waited for us to come back down—for an hour! I've never seen him like that, Lily; he was raging—hitting and punching poor David!"

"That's horrible, Erin! I mean, I can see how he would be upset and all, but to hit him? I've known you both for a long time, and I just can't see Todd acting like that! He must be really messed up! I hope David's nose will look the same as it did before," Lily said, then she glanced into the kitchen where Nick and David were laughing.

"We got him to the hospital right away, so the doctor said it should be fine."

"Good thing! It would be horrible if it changed the way he looked!" Lily took down a few more serving dishes from the china cabinet against the wall and handed them to Erin to put onto the table. "I think Nick had a slight internal meltdown when David introduced himself.

"I wish David wouldn't have said his last name right away. I would've liked to see how things went down without him knowing." Just then, they heard the two men laughing loudly. The ladies looked at each other and smiled.

During the meal, as they sat around the table making small talk, David watched Erin. She was lively and animated, laughing easily, and seemed to be carefree. Occasionally she'd looked at him, smiling her beautiful smile, and he wanted to stop everything to kiss her lovely mouth. She was somehow able to lessen the awkwardness in the room, and everyone seemed to be having a good time.

He wasn't sure how things were going with Nick. He could tell that he'd been quite taken aback by him being in his house. Eventually, they found something to talk about, and presently everything seemed to be fine. He liked Lily; she was a lot of fun. She and Erin seemed to play off each other, making conversations funny and engaging. He was glad Erin had a mate like her and wished it were like that with Martin, his oldest and, besides Erin, only mate. *Martin isn't anathin' like these people—open and real. He's closed and selfish, jealous of things other people have, yet he isn't willin' tae apply himself to earn it.*

It was because of Martin's jealousy that David was in the company of such good people. He was the one who'd tricked him into signing up for the Fertilis Defect Registry in the first place. At the time, David had been upset, though it turned out to be one of the best things that could've ever happened in his life.

When supper was finished, David helped the women clear the table while Nick went to bring Ariana back in from her room. "I like your kit-chen very mu-ch," he said to Lily, "I wish the one in my home looked like it," he said, trying his best to speak clearly.

"What does *yours* look like? I imagined it would be beautiful since, well, since you… aren't, uh, poor," Erin said, feeling like an ass as she set her plate in the sink.

"One would think tha-t, wouldn't one?" he said, laughing, "But, alas, you'd be mis-taken. My wife… designed it, and I reckon it fits her personality—dull, concrete, and lifeless." He hadn't meant to bring Susannah into the conversation and now felt awkward about it.

"I guess money doesn't buy happiness, huh?" Erin said quietly.

"Aye," he said, wishing she knew just how miserable his life had become. "So, I've been told you endjoy games. I've been known to dabble in the odd game myself. Would you care to have a go?" David said, trying to divert the subject, having seen Erin and Lily exchange a look.

They then heard Ariana making noises as she was wheeled into the dining room. "Yes, he's still here. Everyone will come back in, I promise," Nick was heard, assuring his daughter.

Lily, Erin, and David went back to the dining room and agreed that a game would be great. They discussed their options and settled on a Harry Potter deck-building game since they all loved it and David had never played it before. David spoke with Ariana while the others began setting up the game.

"You were wat-chin' *Tangled* in yer bedroom just now, were yeh no'?" he asked, and the girl smiled brightly at him. "I've seen the film with ma wee daughter. Her name is Rosie, and she's eight—No, wait, she's only just turned nine years old. Dinnae tell anaone, but ma favorite scene is the one with the lanterns; I cannae help but sing along. Do yeh like tae sing, Ariana?"

"Ahhh!" is what it sounded like the young girl said, and Lily smiled.

"Go on and sing, Ariana!" she said, so she repeated herself.

"Ahhh! Ahhh!"

"Echo, play, "I See the Light," from *Tangled*," Lily said and took out her phone, ready to record whatever happened next. "Sorry, it's too irresistible."

"Playing "I See the Light' from the film *Tangled*," their Echo said.

"Your Alexa has a British accent!" David observed, but Ariana was singing, so no one replied. When it was time for Flynn Rider to sing, David looked around the table at all the waiting faces. Ariana held her hand out to him; he took it and began to sing along.

Ariana was spellbound and sang, "Ahh, ahh, ahh," along with him.

Erin looked at Lily and Nick, hardly able to keep her composure. Then, when David began to lead her forward and backward in her chair as though they were dancing, both women lost it. Nick had to get the box of tissues from the living room.

When the song was over, Ariana pulled David close for a hug and said something he didn't understand, though it didn't matter. He lifted her hand and kissed it, then he turned, saw the crying women plus a stunned Nick, and blushed.

"She said, 'Thank you,' by the way," Nick said softly.

"Ach, lassie, et was ma pleadsure, indeed," he said and then turned to Lily. "She makes me miss my Rosie. How old is she?"

"She just turned ten," she said in a near whisper.

He heard Erin take a shaky breath next to him and looked at her. She had her head down with a tissue pressed to her eyes. "Erin? Are you a'right?" he asked. She shook her head, then stood and rushed out of the room. David looked at his hosts, not sure what to do.

"I'll go," Lily said and followed her friend.

Erin was sitting on the edge of the bathtub sobbing when she heard a light knock on the door. "Erin? What's wrong? Can I come in?" Lily said so Erin opened the door. "Oh, Erin! What is it?"

It took a long time for her to calm down enough to talk. "I'm sorry. It… it's just… that was the purest, most unselfish, and loving thing, Lily, and… I don't know." She stood and began pacing the floor of the tiny room, trying to understand what she was so upset about.

"I think I'm… jealous. I want a child, Lily. I guess I understand why my parents resorted to Fertilis; the need for a baby is so strong! I know that caring for Ariana is challenging at the best of times, but I see how much she loves you and how you and Nick would die for her. I want that too.

"It's a long story, but David and I saw a fortune teller today. She had the nerve to tell me I'm going to have a child—or children; she wasn't sure. Can you believe that? It's just… wrong of her to say things like that! David has four children. Did you know that? Three boys and a girl. He has what I want more than anything with a woman who—well, who isn't me and from what *he* says doesn't love him, *and* she manipulates him and their beautiful children.

She doesn't deserve them, Lily! Why does she get everything—kids, a perfect body, *and* a perfect husband—"

"I'm no' perfect, Erin," they heard David say through the crack in the door. "May I come in, please?"

Lily looked at Erin, who nodded and grabbed a wad of toilet paper to cover her red, leaking face. She opened the door and smiled at him as he entered the room, then she left.

"Yer spot on, though, she doesn't deserve our children. You, Erin, would be a brilliant Mum, and I wish with all ma heart you could have that. I'm sorry I made you upset, darling, I didn't—"

"I love you, David. What you did just now with Ariana was… beautiful. I'm jealous and selfish, and—I don't know, needy. I just had to let it out, and I already feel better. Please hold me for a few minutes, alright?" She smiled at him as she stood, and one last tear slid down her face.

"Aye, ma love, come here." David held her close, not speaking. Their breathing soon became in sync, and eventually he felt her relax. He thought about his children and longed to hold them as well, wanting more than ever to take them out of the boarding school.

He longed to have them meet Erin, knowing they would love her and that she'd love them. *She'll be a far better mother than Susannah will ever be.* He made up his mind then and there that someday, if they both became free, he would ask her to marry him—properly, on one knee. *If she says yes, I'll never give her cause tae leave us.* "Come, darling, let's return to our hosts, a'right?"

"Alright," she said and looked up at him. He kissed her again and then opened the door.

The game was already set up when they returned, and David was taught how to play. He revealed that he'd actually been in *Harry Potter and the Prisoner of Azkaban*, uncredited, as one of the moving portraits. His part had only gotten two seconds on screen, but it was his two seconds.

Everyone wanted to know where, so he took out his mobile and searched in his photo gallery to find a still shot he kept handy for just that reason. He showed them the picture, pointing to a man in an ornate frame near the far corner of the image. You could only see one eye, an ear, and his cheek, but once pointed out to them, they could tell it was him.

"That's so cool!" Lily said, "Now I have a reason to love the movie even more!"

"Me too," Erin agreed, and he felt her touch his ankle with her foot.

Ariana sat at the end of the table with her own deck of Disney princess cards and proceeded to throw them on the floor. Nick picked pick them up, and she did it again several times throughout the game. By then, everyone was relatively comfortable with one another, so after losing three times to Voldemort and then giving up, Nick looked at David and Erin, obviously wanting to say something.

"What is it, Nick?" Erin asked.

"So, I'm not sure I understand how you two know each other?" he said, just after Lily left to bring in dessert.

"David's my match—for treating the Fertilis Defect. I assumed you'd figured that out."

Nick still looked confused. "I'm sorry, but I still don't understand. What does that mean? How does he treat your disease?"

Lily came back into the room just as he said the last part and turned bright red. "Nick! I'll explain it later," she interjected.

"But—I told you all about it, didn't I?" Erin said.

Nick looked ashamed. "Yeah, you probably did. I guess I wasn't really listening. I'm sorry, but Todd was distracting me, so I didn't hear what the treatments were, exactly, or—at all."

David watched Erin exchanged a look with Lily. "I'll fill him in after you leave," Lily said as she set one dessert in front of everyone, blushing furiously. She had made an individual Eton Mess for everyone in long-stemmed wine glasses, like little trifles. Each one contained two layers of broken meringue, real whipped cream, and sliced strawberries. It was a showstopper, and Nick's question was forgotten for the moment.

"Oh, Lily, they're beautiful! Eton Mess is my second favorite dessert, next to crème brûlée," Erin exclaimed and then took a bite, "Good night nurse, this tastes just like the one I had at the Bridport Arms, in Dorset!"

David gave her an astonished look. "I've been there several times," he said. "It's in West Bay, I believe. My gran lived in Dorset, and we spendt our summers there when I was a child."

Erin smiled. "Really? That's just weird! I guess it's meant to be," she said and took hold of his hand, which made Nick clear his throat and get up from the table. "Oops, sorry."

"Ah, I agree, Lily, the… ah, Eton mess is brilliant; well done, indeed!" David said as they watched Nick walking away.

"Thank you, and don't worry, he just needs to… get used to… you two," Lily said and followed her husband. They returned a few minutes later, but Nick was acting awkward again.

After dessert, it was time for Ariana to go to bed, so everyone said goodnight, and her parents wheeled her to her room. David decided to take the dishes out to the kitchen, and Erin helped. Once they'd set them on the counter, David pulled her up to him and held her.

"What's that for?" she asked, slightly out of breath at the suddenness of it.

"I'm just chuffed tae be here width you. I like yer mates, and I've had a brilliant evening, though et's so far removed from what I've become accustomed. I'm no' used tae genuinely frien-dly people like them. Su-sannah will only associate width posh, rich snobs who've no fun left in them—if they *ever* had any."

"They *are* pretty awesome, aren't they?" she said, as they listened to Nick and Lily singing, "One-two, buckle my shoe" from Ariana's room. It was clearly a long-standing routine for them.

David was suddenly overwhelmed with love and admiration for who Erin was as a person and how she could be herself with so many people. She was the only one with whom he could truly be himself. He had his chin propped up on the top of her head and her arms were wrapped tightly around his middle. "Erin, I—" he began but was interrupted by Nick clearing his throat when he and Lily entered the kitchen and saw them.

Erin let go of him and took a step back. "I think it's time for us to go," she said. "We're heading out of town in the morning, so we should be getting to sleep soon. I'm so glad you thought to invite us over; I had a fantastic time!" She hugged Lily and then Nick.

"I've had a lovely time, as well. I don't of-ten have a chance to, what did you call it, Erin, chill, with such good people. I honest-ly hope we can do it again," David said, then hugged Lily and shook Nick's hand. "Give Ariana a-nother hug for me in the morning, please."

"I will, and, uh, it was… great to meet you, David," Nick said awkwardly as they were shaking hands.

"You too, mate!" David said.

They stepped out the door and held hands as they walked down the path that led to the driveway. "How of-ten do yeh visit them like this?" he asked when they got into the car.

"About once a month; I really look forward to it."

"I can see why," David said.

Chapter Twenty-Four

WHAT MATTERS & WHAT DOESN'T

On the way back to the hotel, Erin's phone started ringing, and she ignored it. David assumed it was Todd since it was a little girl singing, *The Cuppycake Song*. It was completely adorable and something he knew she would pick for someone she loved. Then, her phone *pinged* twice in a row. He presumed they were messages and desperately wanted to know what Todd would be texting to her at that hour.

She pulled into the hotel parking lot, and as they got out of the car and walked toward the building, he noticed she didn't even look at her mobile. Finally, his curiosity got the better of him, so he asked, "Did you hear your mobile alert?"

Erin smiled at him. "It can wait. It was Todd, and I don't want to know what he has to say," she said.

"I can't believe I'm saying this, but it might be important."

She eyed him up. "You want to know what he said, don't you? You can read it if you want to." She sat on the top step of the concrete stairs by the hotel entrance and swiped the screen, then she opened the messaging app and handed him her phone.

He was about to hand it back when another one came through, so he reluctantly read them out loud.

Todd: *Erin, honey, I'm sorry, but what*
    do you expect me to do when faced

*with your lover? I was just jealous.
Can you honestly blame me?*

T: *I would never do anything to hurt
you…you know that! I'm sorry I hit
him, but if you weren't staying with
him, none of this would've happened!
I miss you, and I promise never to do
anything like that again.*

Then he read the next message,

T: *Erin, please answer me. Can we talk?
I need to know that you're ok. You
said I was your favorite, remember?
This isn't like you, Erin! You don't do
this kind of thing! I would NEVER
do this to you! I said I was sorry I hit
him. What more can I say? Please
don't hate me. I love you.*

David felt for him but could see he was using classic manipulation. He
desperately hoped she wouldn't fall for it.

Erin took her phone back. "I don't care—If he does it once, he'll do it
again. I honestly can't believe he did it at all, but he's come unhinged. I don't
think he'll be able to get past it now. I'll reply, though, just so he stops.

Erin: *Thank you for the apology, but I'm
not the one you punched in the face!
The face that is the way he earns his
living! I already told you that it's over
and you said you didn't think so, but
it is and we can talk about it later. I
am busy now, and I don't want to
talk to you. I am fine, just don't*

message me again until I come home.
I don't know when that will be.

She hit send and showed it to David. He couldn't believe how open she was being. She didn't try to hide it or keep it her business, which it was, completely. To him, it showed she honestly felt for him the same way he did for her. "Yeh didn't have tae show me thadt," he said, then stood and held out his hand to help her up.

She took his hand and stood. "Why shouldn't I? You are part of my life now, one of the most important parts of it, actually, and I'm not going to take that for granted. I don't want you to worry that a stupid text from Todd is gonna change that. I'm an open book, David."

"Erin, you surprise me at every turn."

"Well," she said as they went inside and walked to the elevator, "I hope you like surprises!"

In the morning, David and Erin packed and headed downstairs. They stepped out of the elevator and saw Matthew, the waiter, step from the dining room into the kitchen. David asked Erin to excuse him for a moment and stuck his head through the door he'd disappeared behind.

"I would like a word with Mat-thew if it is at all poss-ible?" he said, carefully enunciating his words to the cook who was preparing for the lunch crowd.

"Matt! Someone wants to talk to you—get out here!" the cook yelled. Matthew came around the corner from behind the cooler and stopped short, his eyes wide. David waved him over, so Matthew followed him out into the hallway, blushing.

"I—I have the rest of the money you left on the table… sir," he said anxiously."

"What? Oh, no, no, I left tha-t for you. Tha-t's not why I asked to speak with you," David said, and Matthew looked confused.

"But… the whole bill was only about fifty dollars. Your tip was way too much! Are you sure you really meant to—"

David was touched by the man's honesty and smiled; even more glad he'd done it. "I'm quite sure. I'd like to ap-ologize for leaving so suddenly— You see, we saw some-one we wanted to avoid—An-away, I do hope you understand?"

"Um, sure, I understand," he said, looking completely befuddled.

———

Erin couldn't resist giving the timid man a clue to his identity, "David, we really should be going—"

Matthew's eyes widened; David put his finger to his lips, then put his left hand on the man's shoulder. "I like you, Matthew, so I'll let you in on our secret. I know it's hard to tell under this cast, but I *am* David Elliott, and you should know I *do* appreciate how much you enjoy *Fu-ture Explorations*. Thank you for being a fan." He held out his right hand and shook Matthew's, which was trembling.

Matthew opened his mouth and shut it again several times before he recovered enough to speak. "That's… I mean… thank you! I mean, thanks for finding me like this; it's really nice of you!"

"Are you looking for your phone? Erin asked, noticing he was patting his pockets. "I think we can wait a few minutes if you'd like a selfie."

Matthew smiled brightly. "Yes, please! I'll be right back," he said and ran into the kitchen, the door swinging behind him.

Erin looked at David. "You're a great guy, did you know that?"

"Ye make me want tae be nicer."

Matthew was soon back with his phone; it had a protective case over it embellished with the *Future Explorations* logo. Erin offered to take a photo of them as they stood side by side. David, at six-foot-two-inches tall, made Matthew look even smaller, but the smile on his face made up for any lack of height. Erin kept his phone and went to the front desk; she asked for a permanent marker and then handed it to David. "I think this case needs one more thing to make it look its best, don't you agree, Matthew?"

The anxious man looked confused. "What—"

"Ah, yes, what a good idea," David said, signed his name on it, and handed it back to a speechless Matthew. "Now, all I ask is tha-t you don't share those pictures for about a week. I don't wan-t anaone looking for me like this. It's a great disguise!" He smiled and nudged him.

"I won't! You have my word. Thanks again, Mr. Elliott. You have made my day, sir," he said as his gaze went back and forth from his phone case to David. He looked so happy his face was beaming.

Erin smiled at the scene, glad she'd been a part of it, and as they stepped outside, she took David's hand. When they got to the car, she kissed him. "The more time we spend together, the more I fall in love with you," she said.

Chapter Twenty-Five

PORT WASHINGTON

E rin drove David an hour and a half south on Highway 43 to Port Washington. She took the first exit and made her way downtown past the familiar buildings she'd passed countless times as a teenager. They descended the high, steep hill where St. Mary's Roman Catholic Church had stood for over 135 years. It had kept watch over the town, just as its lighthouse neighbor had kept watch over the water.

She was glad to get out of the car when she finally parked on the street, near the marina. The old familiar scent of dead fish greeted her as she stretched and took David's hand. "I love that smell," she said. "Reminds me of my childhood."

"Hmm, smelly childhood, huh?"

"Yup! That's the very best kind to have."

They walked hand-in-hand to the Harborview Holiday Inn to ask if there were any rooms available.

"Sorry, but we're booked solid for this weekend," said the young African American man, whose nametag said 'Isaiah.' He actually seemed sincerely sorry that they couldn't accommodate them.

"We'll have to try somewhere else then. Thanks, anyway," Erin said, and they walked out. She took out her phone and called every place listed in Port Washington, including the Bed and Breakfast, but there wasn't a vacancy anywhere. "We have two options, we can keep playing it by ear, or we can… stay at my parent's house. What do think?"

"Your... parendts? Really? I—I don't think they'll appreciate you bringing me to—"

"Don't be silly. I'll explain who you are to me, and it'll be fine."

"I... reckon we should ask your parendts if they'll have me first, don't you?" he said, still convinced they wouldn't allow it.

"They'll have *me*, and you come with me, so—"

"A'right, then—if you're so sure."

"I'm sure!"

They ate lunch and then headed toward the lake. She was amazed to see how much was different; she didn't like change, but even she had to admit a lot had been improved.

She led him to what was once a narrow, overgrown metal walkway. It had been transformed into a spacious, tidy, concrete walk with new benches. "My dad used to bring me here; it's part of my earliest memories and one of my favorite places."

Taking hold of David's hand, they began their journey to the Pierhead light. After about a hundred and fifty feet, the railed walkway transitioned into a concrete and stone breakwater. The marina was to their right and the lake to their left. The path was scalloped there, making it look, from above, like someone had taken a long, straight, wide path and pinched it every thirty feet, like sausage links. White and grey gulls flew overhead looking for anything they could eat, crying to Lake Michigan to give up its bounty.

The day was hot for early June, and the lake breeze felt delicious, making the blazing sun on their faces less fierce. Erin recounted stories of Independence Day fireworks; the breakwater was the best place to view them, hands down. Also, she spoke of more fireworks, and eating fish and chips on Fish Days, a local celebration of the lake's harvest.

As they progressed, Erin saw a red sign on a metal bar blocking the way and read out loud, "Closed due to dangerous conditions. Oh no! It used to be open to the public and you could walk all the way out to the lighthouse."

"This is nice and... privadte," David said, pressing her against the concrete wall.

"Ha! Not private enough," she said, seeing a woman walking toward them. "Back up and take a selfie with me," she whispered, trying to make it look less obvious that he'd just been grinding against her. She took out her phone, and they posed for a selfie with the lighthouse behind them. The woman noticed them and offered to take a photo, so they stood with the town as their background.

As they thanked the kind stranger, she cocked her head to the side and looked at David more closely. "Wait, you aren't David Elliott, are you? It's hard to tell with your nose covered up like that."

David smiled, and Erin took a step back to allow the lady to have a few moments with him, but David took her hand. "Where do you think ye're goin'?" he said in her ear. "Yes, I am," he said to the lady and shook her hand.

"I'm a huge fan! I've seen everything you've done, and I'm thrilled to meet you! Uh, if… you don't mind, may I have… a selfie with you?" she asked.

"You may, on the con-dition you dond't share it on social media for a week or so. I'd rather stay as anonymous as I can; I'm sure you can understand."

"Mum's the word," she said, so Erin took the photo of them together.

"David," Erin said, pointing to a couple who were getting closer, "we should go now."

Erin led David north, past the Veteran's Memorial Park and bandshell. They walked the path leading up to the Bluff, as the locals called it, although its official name was Lake Park. They sat on a bench looking out on the lake, and Erin told him how she'd lost her first tooth at a church picnic there, while eating a cob of roasted corn. "Just up there," she said and turned, pointing at a group of buildings and structures that looked to be fairly new. They started walking in that direction and saw that it was a beer garden with a picnic bench shelter and what looked to be a small bandshell next to a much older building.

"I lodst *my* first tooth when Mardtin hit me width his cricket bat. I'd just helped tae win the madtch. He was jealous, so he hit me width et. Good thing we were small, and the bat was too heavy for him tae swing hard, or he mighdt've done some real damage. As it was, he only knocked out one of ma frondt teeth and loosened the other. I prefer yer story," David said and pulled her close.

They had just walked up to the pretty old brick building which housed the toilets. It looked to have been built sometime in the 1930s; it was small and solid, with flower boxes and wooden shutters around the glass block windows. As they rounded the back of the building, he suddenly grabbed her and pushed her against the cream-colored bricks under the shade of a crabapple tree. He began kissing her and grinding himself hard against her. She responded by putting her hand between his legs, and when she let go, he pressed himself even more firmly against her.

"Ma Losh, I feel like a teenadger. I can't get enough of you," David said as he lifted her leg by the knee and rubbed himself against her again, this time, making her moan.

"I want you so badly!" she gasped, "My insides are going crazy right now, but we need to stop, or—or I don't know what I'll do." He continued kissing her neck until she finally pushed him away. "I mean it. I can't take anymore without making love to you, and I'm not going to do it here! It's the middle of the day; people could see us!" He reluctantly stepped away, putting his hands up in surrender.

"What about inside—" He walked around to one of the beautifully crafted wooden bathroom doors and pulled the handle. "Buggar, it's locked!"

She could see his erection bulging from the front of his jeans and longed to unzip his fly to gratify him right there, but it was impossible. Feeling weak, she sat on one of the nearby picnic benches, bent over, her elbows on her knees and her head in her hands. She was panting, and her private parts were pulsing with the rhythm of her heartbeat. She needed to recalibrate.

"Are yeh a'right, hen?" he asked, sounding a bit worried as he sat next to her.

She held up her finger to ask for a moment. "Yeah, I'm fine. That was just so intense!" Her body was aching for him and the release it knew he could give her. *If he'd just move away for a minute, maybe it wouldn't be so strong,* she thought. "I'm gonna take a short walk; please stay here. She scanned the area, trying to find a location to walk to. "I'll just—go to that garbage can and back." She stood, willing her body to calm down, but two steps later, her head filled with a *whooshing* noise. Tiny spots began to fill her vision, but she was too far away to sit back down. The next thing she knew, she was lying on the ground with David kneeling over her.

"Erin! Can yeh hear me? Erin?" he was saying.

She opened her eyes and saw the worry on his face. "What happened? Did I just… faint? What the hell?" she said as he helped her to sit upright. "I've never fainted before in my life, except during an episode."

"How do you feel now?" he asked.

"I feel fine. I think it was just that all the blood rushed to… well, it rushed away from my head, and—"

"We should get back to yer car now, don't you agree?" he said cautiously.

"Yeah." She slowly got to her feet again with his help. Her head still felt foggy, but she wasn't going to faint again. *What the hell is wrong with you, Erin?* she thought, trying not to worry about it. She let David take her by the arm to steady her as they walked down the sidewalk, descending the steep, tree-covered hill

They made it back to her car, which was extremely hot on the inside. David had said nothing the whole way there. She started the engine, opened the windows and the moon roof to let some of the heat escape, then turned the air conditioning on to max. They sat gingerly on the seats with the doors open, allowing the cool lake breeze to flow through it. "Is something wrong?" she asked, a bit puzzled by his silence.

He flinched at her voice. "What? Somebthing wrong? No—Why would you think that?"

"Well, you haven't said much since we left the Bluff. What are you thinking about?"

He looked away from her and stared at the floormat. "I'm worried about you and why yeh fainted. I feel as though et's ma fault. I didn't want tae stop snoggin' you up there, and—" he began.

Erin put her hand on his knee. "Oh, David, I'm sure it's not your fault; I didn't want you to stop either. I just stood too quickly; it happens sometimes. Granted, I've never actually fainted because of it, but I've had the same feeling before now," she said, trying to ease his mind.

"All the same, et makes me nervous that… there's something wrong," he said.

"I *really* don't think—Listen, my body is still processing our treatments. I'm sure there will be adjustments I'll have to go through before I'm fully in remission, or whatever they're calling it. I will tell you if I genuinely think there's something to worry about, okay?"

He smiled at her and placed his hand over hers. "A'right. Reckon I'll just have tae trust yer judgmendt, then."

"Thank you." She bit her lower lip and turned her body to face him. "Speaking of trusting my judgement, there's somewhere else I'd like to take you. It's about twenty minutes away and will involve a lot of walking around, but it's so beautiful, and I'd really like you to see it. I promise I'm fine—What do you say?" she asked, hopefully.

He looked at her with worry in his eyes. "Are you sure? I mean, I wouldn't wandt you tae overdo et."

"I'm not a child or an invalid, and I'm not going to have an episode if that's what you're worried about. I am sure fainting had nothing to do with that at all. My blood pressure just dropped for a second; it's alright." She started thinking about what might cause something like that to happen. "I bet it has something to do with my cycle—I'm just about to start it. That can mess with your hormones and cause your body to do weird things. I'm sure I just needed to reboot with all the excitement."

He frowned but then held his hands up in surrender. "If ye're sure ye're a'right, then I reckon et's okay."

As they headed through downtown, Erin pointed at several of the old buildings, telling him what they used to be. "This was what we referred to as the Dime Store, but its real name was Ben Franklin's; they sold crafts and stuff. That one used to be Leider's Drug Store." She told him how it was the only place she'd ever shoplifted in her life. "I was about five and wanted a small stuffed owl, but my mom said no, so I stuffed it into the front of my dress. When we got home and my mother saw what I'd done, I was given a spanking and then had to go back and hand it to the woman behind the counter. The lady said, '*People who steal things go to jail,*' but I remember, even at such a young age, thinking, 'How would you know it was me if my parents hadn't brought me back?' But I never stole anything again."

"You were a clever lass, and I'm glad yeh like owls. Whadt did you look like then?" he asked.

"I had long, dark-brown, wavy hair, which my mother would braid, one on either side of my head. I was a tomboy, always riding my bike and scraping my knees. I loved climbing trees and roller-skating, too. What about you? What were you like back then?"

"I'd have been around ten when you were five; ledt me think. I had a bowl cut and wore thick, black-framed glasses. No' because I needed them, mind, the lenses had been removed, but they'd been ma father's, and I fancied them. I had a pair of brown corduroy trousers which I tried tae wear evera day, though Millie, she was ma nanny, usually caughdt me and forced me tae change into somebthin' clean."

"Nanny, huh?" Erin said, raising her eyebrows and shaking her head.

"Aye," he said and gave her a sideways glance.

"How long did you have a nanny? I mean, how old were you?"

"Ach, well, when I didn't need a nanny any longer, she was kept on as our housekeeper. She's still employed by ma Mum. She cooks and cleands and is amazin'. I hope ye'll meedt her... somebday," he said.

"Meet the woman who raised you? Sounds intimidating."

"Ach, she'll love yeh and so will ma mum, I judst know et."

Me? Meeting David Elliott's mother and nanny? That'll be the day! I can't even imagine it! she thought. "I... hope you're right."

Chapter Twenty-Six

CEDARBURG

Twenty minutes later, Erin parked her car on Washington Avenue in Cedarburg. It was an old city, at least in American terms. She and David got out of the car and started walking past shops and eateries. At an overpriced boutique, David bought her a dress she'd made the mistake of admiring out loud. He'd made her try it on, and when it looked good on her, he bought it, not allowing her to protest. She knew he was a wealthy man, and she didn't want him to buy things for her all the time, so she decided from then on, not to mention the things she liked.

They wandered into antique stores and interesting shops, enjoying the atmosphere and each other's company. Erin saw a beautiful display in the window of a jewelry store named Nouveau and decided to go inside. The place sold mostly vintage and antique pieces, each one more spectacular than the other, so she forced herself to bite her tongue, trying not to ooh and ahh over everything she saw. She was doing well until she came to the case with the window display artist's work.

The jewelry looked as though they were from the Art Nouveau period of the early twentieth century, though it was all new. She couldn't help herself and gasped at each piece she saw. There were earring and necklace sets that were whimsical and delightful, of bleeding hearts, ginkgo leaves, and lovely little pea pods with tiny seed pearls posing as the peas. She was enchanted, swept off her feet, and reluctantly allowed David to buy her a set of delicate, blue forget-me-nots.

A few doors down, they stepped into a French bakery. Erin told him what she wanted, and he ordered. "*Bonsoir, mademoiselle. Deux pains au chocolat, s'il vous plaît,*" he said with a perfect French accent.

"You speak French?" she said and almost swooned.

"*Oui,* but only enough tae get by," he admitted with a smile.

"I don't speak French either," the tall, red-haired woman behind the counter said when she handed them a paper bag with two chocolate-filled pastries, "but you make me want to learn."

"Me too! Uh, *merci beaucoup,*" Erin said as they were leaving. Once outside, she opened the bag, handed one to David, then bit into hers. "Oh! That's yummy!"

They ate their treat as they walked, and when they came to an intersection decided to cross the street. As they waited for the light to change, she saw the old-fashioned sign on the Rivoli movie theater and had a flashback. She was in high school watching her boyfriend, Doug Gable, standing in line with her best friend's little sister, Betsy. It was so vivid she had to turn away, trying to act like nothing was wrong.

David took the bag from her and threw it away; then, he touched her cheek tenderly with the back of his hand. "Whadt is et, hen?" he asked.

"Nothing, really. I just had a stupid flashback of a bad memory. It's funny; I've been past this place dozens of times and never thought about it. Today, for some reason, it's crystal-clear in my mind."

"Do you want tae share the bad memory with me?" David asked, so sweetly, that Erin found herself telling him all about Doug and Betsy, as well as more details about the other guys who had dumped her for prettier girls.

David listened as they ambled past more touristy shops and began to better understand her insecurities about beautiful women and why she thought of herself as unattractive. When she was done talking, he stopped and kissed her. "I'm glad you told me, hen. Now I wandt tae find evera-one of the bawbags, and give them a piece of ma mind," he said passionately.

She laughed and laid her head on his arm. "I'm sure they don't even remember me, but thanks."

David and Erin continued walking until they got to Fiddleheads Coffee shop. "Let's get a coffee and head to my parent's house. I'm sure my mom is getting supper ready now, and we can surprise her," Erin said.

"Aye, a coffee sounds good."

They entered the cozy building and stepped up to the counter to place their order. It was a bit crowded, so they kept their heads down, not paying much attention to the people around them. They were standing by the baked goods display, waiting for their drinks to be finished, when a girl who was no more than ten stepped up to David. She had dark hair that was in French braids on either side of her head and brown eyes. She touched him on the arm to get his attention and politely asked for his autograph in the paperback book she held out to him.

David gave her his winning smile and crouched down to her level, looking at the front of the battered, well-worn book. "Of course, and wha-t is it I'm signing?" He read the title out loud, trying extra hard to enunciate. "'*Fu-ture Explorations #28: John Thomas Finds Him-self In a Pickle; A Grade Four book series.*' I wasn't aware they made things like this. To whom shall I sign it, then?"

The girl smiled, revealing two perfect little dimples, one on each cheek. "My name is Kayla, and this is my favorite book of all of them. I've read them all, and there's, like, a hundred and ten of them. They're my older sister's books, but she won't mind you signing it."

Erin asked the barista for a pen and handed it to David, who signed:

> *'To Kayla, I'm so glad to have met you. I*
> *hope your sister...'*

"What's your sister's name, then?" he asked.

"Ruby," she said, and he continued,

> *'...I hope your sister, Ruby, isn't upset with*
> *me for writing in her book! Keep reading and*
> *pay attention—the future is closer than you*
> *think. David Elliott x'*

"Would you like a picture with him?" Erin offered.

"Oh! Yeah!" Kayla said and ran to the table by the window seat where two women, who Erin thought were probably her mother and aunt were seated. The girl said something to one of them and came back with an iPhone, the camera open. Erin took a few shots and then handed the phone back. "Thank you," she said and started to walk away, grinning from ear to ear, but David stopped her.

"Ex-cuse me, Kayla?" he said, and she turned around. "I'm curious; how'd you know it was me?"

"Oh, I'd know you anywhere! You're my favorite actor, and I just knew I'd get to meet you someday, so I've been watching people, and I saw you right away!"

"Well, you've got a keen eye, or my disguise isn't so good. Have a brilliant day, Kayla, and say hello to Ruby for me, alright?"

The girl smiled as she rushed back over to give him a big hug, which nearly knocked him off balance. He returned her hug, and she ran off to show the two women her book and the photos on the iPhone. Erin offered her hand to help him stand, and he groaned as he reached his full height. "Ach, I feel old somedtimes."

"Compared to your little fan there, you *are* old," she teased. "I grabbed your coffee for you." She handed him the paper cup, and they made their way to the door. Before they could leave, they heard a quiet voice behind them.

"Excuse me?"

When they turned around, one of the women from Kayla's table was standing a few feet away. She was wringing her hands and chewing her bottom lip. Erin thought she looked to be about twenty-five, with dark, almost black hair cut in a medium-length bob. She had porcelain white skin and looked like the china doll Erin's mother had bought her when she was a girl. "Hello," David said and smiled, closing the door he had been holding for Erin.

"Umm, I'm Ruby. I just wanted to thank you for what you did for my sister—"

"You're Ruby?" he exclaimed, "Oh, I'm sorry. I'd assumed you were Kayla's aunt." He smiled again, and the girl blushed deeply.

"I get that a lot," she said with a slight shrug. "Umm, anyway, I grew up watching *Future Explorations*. I just think… well… that you are amazing… and after the way you were with Kayla… I think you're even more amazing! I had to catch you before you left to say thank you—So… well… thank you." She smiled, and they both laughed.

"You are qui-te welcome, Ruby. I'm glad Kayla sto-pped to say hello today; it tru-ly was a plea-sure to mee-t you both."

She stood awkwardly for a few seconds, and it seemed she wanted to say something more. Erin noticed and decided to rescue her, "Would—you like a photo, too, Ruby?" she asked, and the young woman's eyes grew large.

"Oh! Only if—" She looked at David to make sure it would be okay with him.

"It would be my plea-sure, Ruby," he said with a smile.

She gave Erin her phone, then stood next to David, looking happy but nervous as they posed, then Kayla hurried over, so Erin took another photo of the three of them together. The girls said 'goodbye' and 'thanks' several times, then he and Erin left.

"Thadt was verra nice, wasn't et?" David said as they walked to Erin's car. "I'd no idea books like that were published in America. Also, what a mad coincidence she was at *thadt* coffee house at the same time we were. What are the odds?"

"I'd say very slim, but a girl with a dream is hard to stop. She knew in her heart of hearts she would get to meet you, so there you go."

"Did you know in yer 'heart of hearts' ye'd meet me?" he asked with a smile as they opened the car doors to let some of the heat dissipate.

Erin smiled back at him as she turned the key in the ignition and hit the MAX AC button. "I'm not sure—I might have, but I never let myself dream that big. I like that kind of fan encounter; it was fun, though I imagine they aren't usually like that, are they? They're usually more like the ladies on Bourbon Street, right?"

"I reckon it depends on where I am and whadt's going on around me. I'd say et's usually somewhere in between the two." They got in, and Erin drove them north toward Saukville, where her parents lived.

Chapter Twenty-Seven

ERIN'S PARENTS

Twelve minutes later, Erin turned onto the long gravel driveway at her parent's house. They lived in an old log cabin that had been added to, remodeled, and covered over so many times you'd never have known it. It wasn't until they'd done some work of their own on the place that they uncovered log walls with white chinking still in between them. They had a bit of land with several old outbuildings, including a summer kitchen used for storage. Most of the other buildings had become piles of stone, wooden beams, and rusty old farm machinery covered by their caved-in roofs.

"This is where you grew up?" David asked, looking at the picturesque cream and white-sided house.

"We moved here when I was thirteen; I grew up about a mile and a half from here. If we get a chance, I'll take you past it if you want to."

"Aye, I'd like that verra much."

She parked the car in front of the barn and got out. The sun was shining, and there was a lovely breeze blowing through the trees near the road that her dad had planted a few years after they'd moved in. The tiny, spindly things had grown tall and blocked much of the noise from the busy highway. Erin closed her eyes, facing the breeze; she heard a dog barking and a lawnmower somewhere far off and was glad to be home.

"How are you feeling?" she asked, touching her nose to signify what she meant. It had been nearly forty-eight hours since Todd had broken his nose, but Erin still found herself cringing at the dark bruises under his eyes and the red, puffy bits of his nose she could see under the cast.

"Ach, I reckon I'll live," he said, still with the slightest speech impediment.

She walked around the car, took his hand, and led him up the old concrete path, past the mock orange tree and the old red water pump to the side door. They ascended the short set of rickety steps and entered an enclosed porch that contained an enormous chest freezer. "You could fit a full-grown horse in there!" David said, pointing to it.

"Yes, of course, good horse meat is hard to come by," she teased and then knocked on the door.

The door opened, and a woman who looked to be around seventy, with silver-grey hair streaked with brown leftover from her youth, threw her hands up in the air, "Oh, Erin!" she exclaimed, "You didn't say you were coming, did you? You're positively glowing!"

"Thanks, Mom, I feel good, and no, I didn't tell you I was coming," Erin said as she and David stepped into the large kitchen. "I wanted to surprise you. Surprise!"

The kitchen was painted white and had hardwood floors. There was a big wooden table in the center of the room, while the sink, stove, and refrigerator were in the corner. "And who is this?" her mother asked and flinched when she saw the cast over his nose.

"This is David; he's visiting me from London." She wanted to tell her mom who he was but thought it would be more fun to wait and see if she'd figure it out. Her mother was also a fan of David Elliott, and Erin watched as her mom studied him, knowing he must look familiar, though the grey hair and nose cast succeeded in throwing her off.

David held out his hand for a handshake, but when her mother took it, he gingerly, so as not to bump his nose, kissed the back of hers. "It's a pleasure to mee-t you, Mrs. Wallace," David said formally, using his RP accent.

Erin was surprised he'd remembered her maiden name. He'd probably only ever read it in the tiny bit of information she'd put into his phone when they were in New Orleans.

"Well, aren't you charming? You can call me Liz. I imagine there's an interesting story behind that nose?"

David looked at Erin, not wanting to out their son-in-law, so she intervened. "Yes, Mom, a story for another time. Can we stay the night? I called all over the place and everything is booked up. Where's Dad?"

"Of course, you can stay. Your father is puttering in his workroom; why don't you go down and say hello."

Erin walked over to the basement stairs and called out, "Dad, it's me! I'm coming down—put the romance novel away!"

"Come and make me!" Came a man's voice in reply.

Erin smiled at David, then led the way down the steep, narrow steps into the dank, old basement. David had to duck under the joist, and his head nearly touched the ceiling as he stood next to her.

Her dad grabbed her and hugged her tightly. "You look amazing! What's got you all lit up like that?" he said.

"Daddy, stop it! It's too tight, and you're embarrassing me in front of my friend."

Her dad looked over her shoulder, not letting her go. "Doesn't look like he minds too much—he's smiling, at least. Where's Todd? I have something I want to show him."

"Dad!"

He let her go, not waiting for her answer about Todd, and laughed, sticking out his hand to shake David's. "Frank Wallace, and you are?"

———

David smiled at the man who had to be nearing seventy-five, with a full head of white hair. He wanted to say, 'Completely in love with your beautiful daughter,' but he settled for the more traditional, "David Elliott, nice to mee-t you."

Frank shot a glance at Erin as if she'd be able to translate the foreign language he was sure he'd misunderstood.

"Yeah, Dad, you heard him right. It's *THAT* David Elliott."

He hadn't yet let go of David's hand and started shaking it more fervently. "Well, isn't this an honor? It's nice to meet you, uh, Mr.—"

"Pleadse, call me David." He was tired of sounding like he had a head cold. It was improving but not fast enough for him. He'd started speaking more slowly and trying to enunciate a bit better than he usually did, but it was exhausting after a while. "Erin, could you poin-t me to the water closet?" he asked.

"Sure, I'll show you. It's just upstairs—"

"No, I'll go up and ask your mum. You stay here; I'll only be a tick." He ascended the stairs, careful not to bang his head on the beam, and reentered the kitchen.

Liz Wallace was sitting at the table, peeling potatoes and carrots, preparing to make a stew for supper. When she saw him, she stood and wiped her hands on the towel she had next to her. "How can I help you, David?" she asked politely.

"May I use your toiledt, please?" he asked, sounding like a little boy asking permission from an adult.

"Of course, it's right over there." She pointed to a door in the corner of the room. "You'll need to jiggle the handle when you're done or it'll run all day."

"A'right, thank you," he said, not knowing what she meant, having never been asked to jiggle anything in the loo before. He'd ask Erin later and hope it wasn't anything serious.

When he was done, he flushed and washed his hands, looking at his reflection in the mirror, embarrassed at the state of himself. *These people must think I'm trouble, or perhaps clumsy.* He looked around for a handle to jiggle, and it occurred to him to shake the handle on the toilet, being the only thing he imagined might run, other than the taps, but they weren't leaking. Sure enough, as soon as he did, the tank stopped filling, and he felt rather clever. When he came out, Erin was standing in the kitchen with both her parents.

She looked at him and smiled, "Hope everything came out all right," she said and laughed. Her mother rolled her eyes and her dad seemed proud of his daughter's wit.

David could see the family resemblance; Erin had her mother's smile and eyes and her father's chin, nose, and cheekbones. "Judst fine, thanks for asking." He saw the pile of vegetables still needing to be peeled and asked, "Would you like some help, Liz?"

Both Erin and her mother sighed while it was her dad's turn to roll his eyes. "Now you're just trying to get brownie points!" Frank said. "I can't blame you, though; it'll probably work." They sat at the table while Erin got a knife for him. "So, David, what brings a famous actor like you to this neck of the woods?"

David shifted in his seat; he wasn't sure what to say, but Erin came to the rescue again. "Now, Dad, don't start quizzing him; we just got here. I'll explain it all later."

"Famous actor?" her mother said, looking more closely at David to figure out who he was under the nose cast and bruises.

"Yes, dear, did you know our daughter had any famous friends? This is none other than—"

"Dad! Wait…" Erin tried to stop him from spilling the beans, but it was too late.

"David Elliott, in the flesh."

"David—Elliott?" her mother said as she fumbled the carrot in her hand and her cheeks bloomed deep pink. "I thought your voice sounded familiar." She put her head down and continued peeling her carrot in earnest.

"Now you've ruined it, Dad." Erin rolled her eyes at her father, then set a knife and towel on the table in front of David. "Have you ever actually peeled a potato?" she asked him.

He shot her a look that imitated being hurt and offended but then smiled. "Of course, I have, silly girl. Grandted, I reckon it's been thir-ty years." They all laughed. "I used to help my grandmother whil-st on holiday in Dorset when I was a child." He started in on a nice large spud, and Erin laughed, holding up one of the peels, showing him how much potato he'd taken with the skin.

"You might wanna try peeling it a bit thinner if you want anything to eat later. Here—" She went back to the drawer she'd taken the knife from, extracted a potato peeler, and handed it to him.

"You know I've never been a patient man, daughter, so tell us," Frank said, "The suspense is killing me!"

David pretended to be intent on peeling his potato but eventually looked up. She was staring at him, so he gave her a little shrug. "Where do I start?"

she said. I don't know what you know about the newest treatment for the Fertilis Defect?"

"I'm sorry, honey, we just haven't kept up with it," Liz said and set her paring knife on the table.

David saw a sadness wash over her face. He remembered what Erin had said happened when they found out it was the drug, Fertilis, that had caused their daughter so much suffering. Erin smiled and put her hand on her mom's shoulder. She took the abandoned knife, sat across from David, and continued peeling. He noticed she was peeling hers so thin he could practically see through the flaky brown skin; not only that, but she was flying through them, at least two to his one potato.

"Well, it turns out… the only way to have a remission from my symptoms is… uh—I can't believe I'm saying this to my parents. Umm—" She glanced at David, and he looked at her, raising his eyebrows. "David and I were matched up through the Registry. You see, it… well, it's sex. The-only-remedy-is-to-have-intercourse-with-someone-who-matches-my-profile. I-can't-explain-it-all. I-don't-know-how-it-works, only-it—does," she said, all in one breath, with most of the words strung together.

Liz and Frank looked at each other, then at Erin and David. He made sure to keep his head down, concentrating on the brown and white orb in his hand. Erin stopped peeling and stood, taking the bowl of peeled veggies to the sink. She stood there with her eyes closed. The room was silent as she rinsed off her knife, laid it on the counter, and walked over to David. He was almost finished with his last potato, but he handed it and the peeler to her when she held out her hand.

He didn't want to make eye contact with the lovely people who had just learned he was their only daughter's—what, sex partner… lover? *What is my role? What should I be referred to as?* he thought.

"Well," her father said, at last. "What can we say to that? I imagine Todd isn't thrilled about it."

Liz looked at David's nose. "Todd did that to you, didn't he?" she asked.

David looked up at Erin, not sure what she wanted him to say. She shrugged and waved her hand as if to say, 'go ahead.' "Ah, yes, he did. I reckon I don't blame him, though."

———

Erin's mother looked at Frank, who was shaking his head. "And he—agreed to you doing this?" he asked his daughter.

She could see the thoughts running through her dad's mind on his face, plain as day. He was thinking that he'd never let her mother go off and do that. She knew he was also wondering if it was actually working or not. "There wasn't a choice, Dad," she said, knowing he wouldn't accept that answer. He looked at her skeptically. "Really, Dad, my episodes were getting worse and more frequent; the last one was what, well over a minute, right?" She looked at David, and he nodded.

"You were with him when it happened? So then, it isn't working," Frank said.

"It's too soon to know if it is or not. We've only—it's only been a month since we started the treatments. I haven't had another one since, and I don't feel one coming on. Actually, I don't remember the last time I've felt this good and healthy."

"So, to bring up the elephant in the room, where is Todd now, and why is David *here* with you?" her dad continued, "There's something missing in all this; I mean, he's here to give you a type of medical treatment, correct? Please forgive me talking as though you're not here, David," he said.

———

"A'right," David said, not knowing what else to say.

"Well, wouldn't he have already done—that? Shouldn't he be, I don't know, going back home? There must be more to this than just sex treatments, right?"

David saw Erin blush and felt his forehead break out in beads of sweat, making him glad he'd put on antiperspirant that morning. He looked at Erin; she had her hands on her hips like a teenager trying to come up with a story to tell her parents about why she'd been out past curfew. "I'm in love with your daughter," he blurted out.

He was furious that 'love' came out sounding like 'lubb', and he didn't know what had possessed him to do it, except that it was the truth. He wanted to break the tension; he didn't expect it to intensify. Erin stood with her mouth agape, exactly the same as her mother's at that moment. He could see her focusing on her breathing and remaining calm.

"David," she whispered and closed her eyes. "Okay, fine—Yes, we are in love with each other. Todd doesn't know that part. Actually, there are only five people who know, and four of them are in this room." She was biting her lower lip and kept her eyes closed. Her lip started to tremble, and a single tear rolled down her cheek. David stood and went to her. "Erin, darling, I'm sorry. I shouldn't have said anathing, but—Well, I shouldn't' have said anathing."

She wrapped her arms around his waist. "It's okay. *I* wouldn't have come out with it quite like that, but it's alright. I'm just… overwhelmed. You told my parents you're in love with me. It's a big deal—in a good way."

Liz and Frank sat at the table, watching them hold one another. Finally, Frank spoke up, "So, you say you are in love with my daughter, and you've known each other for how long? A whole month? Are you crazy, Erin?"

"Dad!"

"You're going to throw away fifteen years in a happy marriage because someone you've known for a month says he loves you? What's got into you, girl?" Frank continued and stood.

"Dad! Stop!"

David went back to his chair and put his head down. "I know it sounds mental, like a childish infatuation, but et's real," he said softly, his discomfort causing his natural accent to reveal itself.

"You don't understand, Dad," Erin said and started pacing. "I was the one who wasn't going to do it, but Todd convinced me it was my only chance at freedom from the disease. He thought he'd be able to handle it, but it turns out he can't. He's become aggressive and controlling… and… he even got, well, physically rough with me. You can see he's leaning toward violence by David's face." She stood up tall and looked her father in the eye."

"Wait," her father said, turning his attention back to David, "Aren't you married to that supermodel—What's her name—Susan, or something?"

"Susannah, and yes, but our marriage is over. Listen, neither of us expected this tae happen but it has and…"

"And that's how it is," Erin finished for him. "Please, I know it's a shock, and you probably have a million more questions, but I've been driving most of the day, and I'm tired. We can talk about it later if you need to, but I'd like to take a nap now." She took David's hand, and he stood. They were about to leave the room when she turned and looked pleadingly at her father. "Please, Daddy, don't call Todd. He needs to cool off, and telling him we're here will only make things worse, alright?"

Frank looked guilty, like a kid with his hand in the cookie jar. He seemed to say, 'who me' with his eyes, then he shrugged. "Okay, okay. I won't call anyone about anything."

"Pinky promise?" She held out her hand with her pinky extended. He looked at her and sighed dramatically, linking his pinky with hers.

"Frank, please don't cause her any more stress, you know stress can trigger… well, it might—Even so, just don't," Liz said.

"I said I wouldn't." He gave his wife an injured look, then crossed his arms over his chest like a petulant child who'd just been scolded.

"You'll have to put sheets on your bed; you know where they are," Liz said to Erin. "Go on upstairs, and I'll finish supper." She went to her daughter and kissed her cheek. "I love you, baby girl."

"I love you too, Mom, thanks," Erin whispered and hugged her.

"They're staying—"

"Frank, shush …." they heard her parents say as they made their way up the stairs holding hands. Erin led David down the hallway to her room, which was at the front of the house. It had a row of four picture windows that looked out onto the driveway and barn. There were still posters of Christian Slater and Michael Jackson on the walls and looked very much like a teenage girl's bedroom.

Erin walked out of the room and came back a few moments later with a set of sheets. "Come help me with these," she said and shook out the fitted sheet, putting the rest on the floor next to her. They managed to cover the bed with the fresh linens and pillowcases, then Erin closed the door and stood in front of him.

"I'm sorry for the drama, Erin. I—" he started to say.

"It would've come out eventually; don't worry about it. The shock will wear off soon."

"Do you honestdly think yer dad would call Todd?"

"It wouldn't surprise me. They're friends now, and I think my dad would consider it disloyal if he didn't at least call to make sure he's okay. I just don't want Todd to know we're here."

David walked to the windows and looked out on the trees at the end of the long driveway. He liked the place; it was quiet and had lots of space without houses crowded one on top of another. He smiled, and Erin came up behind him. She wrapped her arms around his middle and lay her head against his back.

"Penny for your thoughts?" she asked.

"I was imadginin' ma children here—Watchin' them play in the frondt garden. I know… et's a wee bit premature of me, but I like it here, and I hope tae come back again… width them."

"I hope so too. It's good for children to run and play outside without fences and gates. I never thought of exploring this place when I was a teenager; I guess I had other things on my mind, but we could do it now, as adults, right? Put on our wellies and long sleeves to go rambling through the wilds of the land?"

"Yeh ken judst how tae get a man excited, don't you?" He turned around to face her and kissed her tenderly until the tenderness turned to passion and then into desire.

Erin broke free from his kisses, panting. "Not here! Not now—you know my parent's Spidey sense is turned up to eleven, right? If they even think we are having sex up here in the middle of the day—Well, I don't know what they'd do, but I don't want to find out.

"A'righdt, fair enough," he said and pulled her up against him, pressing their bodies together so she could feel his excitement.

———

"Good night nurse! I want you so badly! But please, let's wait till tonight, when everyone is asleep on the other side of the house, okay?" She kissed him he held himself against her until finally, she pushed him away.

David was breathing hard as he leaned against the window sash to steady himself. "Ma Losh! What you do tae me, woman! I wandt yeh all the time! Even after I've just had yeh, I wandt yeh again. Et's drivin' me mad, and I dinnae wandt it tae stop!" He stood at the end of the bed, willing his now uncomfortable erection to subside, but it was obstinate; it wanted what it wanted and didn't want to give up so easily. He had to find something to distract him from the desire to touch her full, soft, round breasts.

Losh, David! Just shut et down! he thought.

Looking for a distraction, he scanned the room and saw a painting on the wall of a house in winter, decorated for Christmas. It wasn't painted professionally, but it was quite good. "Did you paindt this?" he asked and pointed to it.

"Yeah, I did it in my high school art class. I copied it from a Christmas card. I think I still have it around here somewhere." She went over to a corkboard with lots of papers and pictures pinned to it and took down a greeting card. She handed it to him, and he held it up to compare.

"Et's brilliandt, Erin! Well done!"

"Thanks, it's one of my favorite assignments. I got an A on it," she said proudly. "Listen, I really would like to take a nap. You can join me if you want to, but no fooling around. Otherwise, you can… I don't know… you can go sit with my parents?" She laughed at the look on his face.

"Not likely."

"Or you can take a bath or shower?"

"Are yeh tryin' tae tell me somebthin'? Do I need one?" He played at smelling his armpit.

"No, silly, I don't care what you do. I'm just trying to think of things to keep you busy, that's all."

What he wanted to do was make love to her, but that wasn't going to happen, and he knew lying next to her and trying to sleep would be torture. On the other hand, going back downstairs alone, where her parents were waiting to grill him some more, wasn't something he wanted to do either. *Maybe a bath would be nice.* "A badth it is, I reckon."

———

The idea of David laying naked in a tub of hot soapy water just next door to her was shockingly exciting. Her mind filled with thoughts of coming in after he'd gotten comfortable and feeling him up under the water. It was making her hot. "Good," she said, her voice cracking and pitched a bit too high.

They walked into the bathroom, and she showed him the linen closet behind the door. She got out a towel, washcloth, and a bathmat, then she quickly checked behind the shower curtain to make sure the tub was clean, which of course, it was. She then showed him how to work the tap and drain plug, which was a bit tricky.

She didn't want to leave him, she wanted to watch him get undressed as the water filled the tub, but she really didn't want her parents to catch them. She knew she was an adult, but it still seemed wrong to have sex with her sort of lover in her parent's house, at least while they were awake. "I'll… leave you to it then." She kissed him and turned to leave, but he took her hand and pulled her to him.

"You could stay and bathe me… or… join me even?"

She smiled and regretfully pushed him away. "I am so tempted, but I need to sleep for a bit. If you are still in here when I wake up, I'll join you; otherwise, just go downstairs and charm my parents for a while. I don't want to sleep for long, maybe half an hour—no more than an hour," she said and walked out of the room.

Chapter Twenty-Eight

BATH TIME INTERRUPTED

David turned on the taps, making sure the temperature was right as the water filled the bathtub. He found a disposable razor and some shaving cream in the linen closet and, seeing he hadn't shaved since Todd had broken his nose, he filled the sink with hot water and started to clean away the stubble, revealing his bare face again. He let the water in the sink drain and rinsed the hairs off with his hands, then he looked closely at his face reflected back at him.

He had laugh lines, crow's feet, and deep lines etched into his forehead. Also, much of the stubble he'd rinsed from the sink basin was grey, and although he knew it was the bruises from the broken nose, it looked as though he had enormous bags under his eyes. He was getting old, and it was only a matter of time before he would start getting offered grandfather roles.

He thought about the last part he'd been offered. Only him, his agent, and the people involved with the project knew about it, and it was huge. They still hadn't had the meeting he'd told Erin about when they were in New Orleans, but it was coming up soon. He just needed to decide if he wanted to do it or not. It would mean less time with Erin and his kids, but he could make it work, and it could potentially change his life.

The tub was full, so he shut off the tap and got undressed. He hung his clothes on the hook behind the door and got into his bath. The water was at the perfect temperature, and it felt nice to soak and unwind. He was a lot taller than the manufacturer of the bathtub had taken into consideration, so his knees were still dry while the rest of him was submerged.

He closed the curtain against the glare of the room, wanting the dark retreat it offered so he could relax. A few bruises remained on his torso from Todd's assault, and his muscles were still tender, though he would never tell Erin that. Shrouded in water vapor, he laid hidden in a private retreat, thinking about her sleeping in the other room.

He thought about her face, so peaceful, and how her eyes darted back and forth under her eyelids as she dreamed. After the episode in New Orleans, he'd had plenty of time to watch her. Todd could beat on him all he wanted, as long as Erin was safe, healthy, and with him.

After a while, he used the washcloth to clean himself with the bar of white Dove soap sitting in a small dish in the corner. He started from the top, worked his way down, and had just finished rinsing off when he heard the door open and close, then the *click* of the lock. It hadn't been a long nap, but he thought maybe Erin couldn't sleep, thinking about him there in the tub. Whatever the reason, he was getting quite excited to see her.

A female hand reached in, turned on the tap, and then flipped a lever up to start the shower. Freezing cold water rained down on him. "Oh, fuck!" he said and jumped out of the tub, standing stark naked and fully erect in front of Erin's mother. She stood there, before him, holding her bathrobe shut at the neck, her face flushed bright red.

Time seemed to stop as they stared at each other. David tried to cover himself with his hand, but that was useless, and he couldn't remember where Erin had set the towel. Then he saw it, just past Liz on the toilet seat, mocking him because he couldn't reach it without her moving first, and she seemed frozen in place.

"Could I please—" he said, pointing to the towel and wishing a hole would form in the floor for him to fall into. She looked slowly at the towel, picked it up, and handed it to him in slow motion as if she weren't sure where she was or what she was doing. A second later, after he'd wrapped the towel around his waist, she snapped out of it.

"Oh… Oh, my God! I'm… Oh my God, I'm so sorry!" she stammered. "Erin! Oh no! She can't find out about this or… she'll be upset! Oh, God… please, please don't tell her!" She put her hand up to her mouth, forgetting about the neck of her robe, looked him in the eyes, and then bolted for the door.

The next thing David knew, he was alone again, not sure what to do next. He turned off the shower and let the water out of the tub, watching as it slowly receded, forming a small whirlpool as it went down the drain. His mind was racing; the look on Liz's face was unsettling, to say the least. What had she been thinking while she stood there like a statue, gaping at him? He sat on the edge of the tub and tried to make sense of it.

Liz Wallace hadn't known what to do as she stood there, staring at David Elliott in the flesh—in *only* his flesh. She'd wanted to run but couldn't move! A naked man was nothing new, but it was *that* naked man and with an erection like—like the one he'd had. It made no difference that she was over seventy; she was still breathing, and it was such a surprise.

She had just wanted to take a quick shower—how was she to know he would be in there—in that state? And now, the feelings were overwhelming her. She just knew everyone would be able to see the evil thoughts all over her face. It was too much like a soap opera; the mother guilty of lustful thoughts involving her daughter's movie star lover!

She was a mess and needed to find a private place to process what had just happened. She ran down the hall and up the small flight of stairs to her bedroom above the kitchen. She closed the door behind her, locked it, and then leaned against it, worried someone might come barging in and see the guilt on her face. *How will I ever be able to look at him or Erin ever again!*

You old fool! That's what you get for being so wicked. "Your sins will find you out, Elizabeth." Her mother's words haunted her. *Mother was right!*

She didn't have an extensive fantasy life, but the few she'd had about David Elliott were enough to paralyze her after their unexpected encounter. She was taught as a young woman that lustful thoughts were sinful and that God punished girls who didn't control themselves. Thus, she limited them, hoping her sins wouldn't bite her in the ass. *This is the worst punishment that could have ever happened! What am I going to do?*

David dried himself off and got dressed, reckoning it must have been over thirty minutes by then, so he left the bathroom and quietly entered Erin's bedroom. He walked up to the bed and bent down to kiss her shoulder, that being the safest place he could reach without bumping his nose. It was difficult not to blurt out everything that had happened right then and there, but Liz had asked him not to.

Erin stirred and rolled over, smiling up at him. "I was dreaming you were in the tub, and I was coming up from the drain. I was going to—"

"What? Whadt were you goin' tae do?" he asked, smiling.

"No clue, you woke me up just as I was about to decide. Wait, what happened; you look stressed?"

"Ach… nothing really—just a slighdt run-in with yer mum."

"What? What did she say? Was it rude or something?"

"Well, no. It was nothing. If et ends up being an issue, I'll tell you all aboudt it, alright darling?"

Erin eyed him suspiciously and got out of bed. She had only taken her capris off for her nap, and as she reached for them, he picked them up and handed them to her without any comments and without trying to get her to keep them off. *Something big happened, and he's trying to hide it,* she thought. She put her capris on while David stood at the row of windows, looking out at the growing darkness. The sun was setting, turning the sky into an amber, pink, and orange showstopper. "Oh, that's pretty!" she said.

It was only then David seemed to notice the dazzling show before him, "Oh, aye… it is."

Erin touched his shoulder, and he turned to look at her wearing a frown, his forehead full of lines and his mouth turned down. He tried to fake a smile, but it was too late. "David, you're worrying me. If it's something I need to know, please tell me."

"No, hen, et's a'right. I'm just distracted; dinnae fash."

She didn't believe him but knew she wouldn't get anything more out of him then. "Let's go downstairs and see when supper will be ready, okay?"

"Okay," he said, though it seemed like he didn't really want to.

Liz was standing in front of the stove stirring something in a large pot when they entered the kitchen. Her back was to them, and she didn't turn around when Erin asked her if they could help with anything. "No, honey, you just relax. I've got it all under control," she said.

Erin could tell right away that nothing was under control with her mother just then. *She won't turn around, but why? Did she have a fight with David or say something offensive and is now embarrassed? There is definitely something wrong in the Wallace household!* "Mom, what's up? I know something happened, now out with it."

Liz hung her head and took a deep breath. She slowly turned around, revealing her bright red face. "Erin, I—" she started to confess.

"No, Liz, I'll tell her," David interrupted her.

She turned back to face the stove, and it was Erin's turn to frown. "Holy Moses, it must be serious!"

"I just can't believe I… did that," Liz whispered.

Erin was getting upset, "Will someone tell me? This is getting ridiculous! God, Mom, what?" She looked to David, pleading with her eyes for him to tell her.

"Et was ma fault, really—I… left the door unlocked, thinkin' you might wandt tae join me and… well, yer mum came in. The curtain was shut, and I reezin it was you, and well… I was ah, anticipatin' what ye'd do—And she started the shower, which was bloody reezing' and… reflexes… I jumped out of the tub, and—"

"Good night nurse! Mom!" Her mother put a towel up to her face and walked out of the kitchen. Erin looked at David, who was blushing furiously and frowning. She didn't know what to do or say; the last thing she wanted to do was talk to her mom, but she knew her mother would beat herself up if she didn't.

Reluctantly, she went to the living room, where her mom was standing at the deep-set, leaded glass windows, watching the squirrels running around the yard in the twilight. David followed but stayed far back. "Mom, it's alright, don't worry about it. It was just a silly mistake; it's not like you've never seen a naked man before." She said it to lighten the mood, but it seemed to make everything heavier and even more uncomfortable.

Erin looked desperately at David as if to say, 'help me here,' but he shook his head, so she rolled her eyes and continued, "I'm sure David isn't upset about it, Mom—he's European, they like nudity, right?" She looked at him to back her up, but now *his* eyes were huge. *Shit, I said something wrong again.* She motioned with her head for him to say or do something.

———

"Right—I'm not upset, Liz." *Extremely uncomfortable and embarrassed, but not upset.* "Et was an accident—et's not as though you knew I was in there and… just wanted tae see… me—" He realized then that, in fact, he didn't know if that were true or not. *Mebbe she did go in there on purpose—*

David! Yeh bloody idiot! Why would she do that? Ye're off yer block!

They watched as her mom stood with her head down, wrapping the end of the towel around her finger. "Mom, what is it? Is there something else? Tell me, please," Erin said softly.

Liz shook her head, "Please—leave me alone."

"Okay, Mom. When do you think supper will be ready?"

"In about an hour or so," Liz said, under her breath.

Erin and David went outside and wandered down the long driveway. "That must've been embarrassing," Erin said after a long silence.

"Aye," he said and told her everything that had happened.

They came back, taking their time, winding their way through the trees, and then sat on the low stone wall separating the front yard from the driveway. "It was an accident, that's all. I'm sure she's just completely and utterly embarrassed about the whole thing… unless—"

David looked at her grimly, "I dinnae like the sound of that."

"No—No way!" she said.

"Just say it, Erin."

"But it's so—dreadful!" He gave her an 'I'm waiting,' look, and she continued. "Several Christmases ago, she gave me one of the *Future Explorations* figures you saw in my living room, the one of you shielding your eyes."

"Aye, continue."

"We had a laugh together… as two grown women, well… admiring you. It's not like we thought we'd ever meet you… and so… for her to walk in on you… like that—"

"Holy Modses!" he said, borrowing one of Erin's catchphrases, "*That* doesn't make things wordse a'tall!" He put his head in his hands, being careful not to bump his tender nose. "Now whadt? I don't believe I've ever been *this* uncomfortable before in ma life! Whadt am I meant tae say to her?"

"I think—maybe the best thing to do is ignore it. She's already making a big deal of it, so we need to diffuse the situation as much as possible. And anyway, that might not even be what she's so upset about, right?"

David looked at her and raised an eyebrow. "I have an uneasy feeling thadt it is. Bloody hell! I just wandt to be able tae meet people as maself—not as a, I dinnae ken, drooled-over piece of meat—" Erin started shaking, so he looked at her to see what was going on.

"A drooled-over piece of meat, huh?" She was laughing hard and holding her side. "You poor baby, with all the good looks and talent! I feel really sorry for you." She smiled and wiped the tears from her eyes. "I love you. Do you mind if *I* drool over you?"

He reluctantly smiled back at her. "I reckon *you* can, but yer mum? Ugh!"

Erin leaned against him, and he wrapped his arm around her shoulders, then she got up and stood in front of him. He put his hand up to touch one of her breasts, and she inhaled sharply. Then, she bent over, placing one hand on his thigh and the other between his legs, which made *him* catch *his* breath.

He put his hand over hers, pressing it down more firmly as his excitement rose, then he gently pushed her back, stood, and held her, pressing his erection against her. "I need you," he whispered.

"Erin? David? Supper's ready," They heard Frank call out from the porch steps.

"We'll be right there!" Erin shouted back to him. "Do you need a minute to… collect yourself?" she asked.

"Mmm, aye." He did NOT want to go into the house in his present state of excitement, so he tried to think about rugby or football—cricket? None of that worked, but then an image of Liz in her yellow robe, staring at him, returned to his memory, back far too soon from the dark recesses of his mind where he'd tried to bury it. That worked instantly. He shuddered and walked up to the house with Erin, at least slightly less uncomfortable.

When they got to the steps, Frank said, "Your mother is in a state. I have no clue what it's about, so best be on your toes, okay?"

"Thanks, Dad, but we already know about it. Don't worry; it has nothing to do with you," Erin said.

He looked relieved and allowed them to enter the house first, lagging behind.

Chapter Twenty-Nine

AWKWARD EVENING

"That smells fantastic, Liz," David offered, hoping to brighten the mood. She had somehow found the time to bake dinner rolls, and the kitchen smelled of delicious stew and fresh-baked bread. Because of that, much of David's stress seemed to melt away with the aroma, and his mouth started watering. "May I help set the table or anathing?" he asked, noticing the kitchen table was unmade.

"We're eating in the dining room tonight," Frank said and pointed through the short, narrow hallway, which transitioned the newer kitchen into the log cabin.

They walked through the living room to the dining room, and Erin squeezed David's hand. "That's their best wedding china," she whispered. "They even have the lead crystal wine glasses out, which means this is a big deal."

The dining room was old-fashioned, with leaded glass windows and an etched, rose-colored glass light shade, which hung over the dark wooden table in the center. The room wasn't large but could fit plenty of people for Christmas dinner and was more than ample for their foursome that evening.

"Honey, everything looks delicious!" Frank said as his wife set the last of the serving dishes on the table.

"Thank you, Frank," was her simple, quiet reply.

Silence filled the room as they sat around the table. David wondered what everyone was waiting for and hoped his stomach wouldn't start speaking for him. Then it dawned on him; the only person not in-the-know about earlier events was Frank, and he felt bad. Even though Erin had told her dad that it had nothing to do with him, he imagined Frank didn't believe her.

"Dad, please start," Erin said softly and took Frank's hand, then she held her mother's, which left David holding hands with Frank and Liz. He felt extremely awkward. Liz sat like a statue; her hand was moist and trembled a bit.

"For this food which we are about to eat, let us be truly grateful. Amen," Frank prayed, and they each echoed 'Amen.'

David was glad to let go of Liz's hand and get on with dinner. "That's the same prayer my mother says before each meal," he remarked.

The room was weighed down by each person's discomfort so there was very little chit-chat as they ate. After a while, Frank rose and lifted his glass. "I need to apologize to David and Erin. I was rude and insensitive earlier, and I'm sorry. It's just that she's my little girl, and… I don't want her to make a mistake." He cleared his throat, "To Erin and David and… uh… to being symptom-free."

Erin smiled at David and then at her dad as the three Wallaces said "Slàinte mhath (Slan-ja-vah)," which is the Scots Gaelic for 'Good health,' while David said, "Cheers," which made them all laugh. Even Liz laughed at the irony of the only person in the room having been born in Scotland using the English toast.

Things seemed to lighten up after that, and when they had all eaten their fill, Liz and Erin got up to clear the dishes while the men were allowed to stay seated and talk. David would have preferred to help with the clean-up, not knowing what to say to Frank. "Are you a game player, David?" Frank asked as they watched Erin, busy as a bee, flitting around the table, in and out of the kitchen, smiling and laughing with her mother.

"What do you mean by that?" he asked, not sure if it was a trick question.

"Games—like Monopoly, Trivial Pursuit, Cribbage."

David was relieved he didn't mean 'with women's hearts.' "Aye, I do, adctually—" He watched Erin whispering something into her mother's ear and then laughing and running away as Liz tried to swat her with the towel she was holding. "Sorry, whadt were you—Oh, right, games."

"You really do care for Erin, don't you?" Frank said as he watched the two women acting like young girls.

"Very much. I… didn't know I wasn't in love with Susannah. I thought marriage was somebtimes like that after a while—no feelings and no joy; that people grew apart and yeh had to dig in and deal with et. I never once felt anathin' even remodtely like this for her. Erin is a spark of light in ma bleak and lonely world," he said and then knit his eyebrows together. "Ach, that sounds like an exaggeration and remarkably ungrateful, I reckon, but I was the only one trying. Susannah stopped caring a long time ago, and I didn't realize it until I met your daughter."

"How long were you married?"

"It's been seventeen years."

At least it's not like he didn't try, I guess. "Do you have kids?"

"Aye, I have four children."

"Four? Well, *you've* been busy, then, haven't you?"

David studied him for a moment, wondering what he was trying to say. Was that some form of insult? "I've been—blessed," he said simply. "I… need a wee; please excuse me." He stood and walked out of the room, wanting to get away from Frank. He couldn't tell if he was joking or judging, and it was tiring trying to work it out without Erin in the room to help.

He entered the kitchen and smiled as he saw the two women standing side by side, washing and drying the dishes together. Erin spotted him and smiled; he loved her smile! She scooped up a hand full of soap suds, kissed the air, and then blew the suds at him. *She* is *glowing—that's what Liz said when we arrived earlier isn't it? Glowing is just the word for it.* He pretended to catch the kiss but missed the suds as they fell to the floor and started to pop, leaving a wet mark on the wooden floor.

He stepped into the bathroom and made sure to lock the door. When he finished, he remembered to jiggle the handle and then washed his hands. He looked in the mirror, tired of seeing the unsightly white plaster over his nose, though he did notice that it had become much easier to talk over the last hour, which was something.

When he stepped into the kitchen, he saw that the ladies were done with the dishes and found them in the dining room, setting up what looked like a card game. He took his seat, wishing they were leaving for a hotel room where he could finally make love to Erin.

"This is the game I mentioned to you the other day, David. It's called Fluxx, the *Future Explorations* edition. I guess everyone's got one but me!" Erin said and laughed.

"Great," David said unenthusiastically. It was difficult to be excited about it when some of the merch with his face on it was horrendous. He hadn't heard of the game before she mentioned it, but if she fancied it, he'd at least give it a go.

Erin held up a card to her dad and started laughing. He smiled and said, "That's not bad actually."

Liz had come back from getting another bottle of wine and blushed when she saw it. "Not bad," she said and took a large drink of her wine.

"A'right, et's obviously me, so let's see et," David said, not really wanting to look, but his curiosity was peaked. Erin turned the card around, and there he was, as his character, John Thomas Fife. It was a drawing, not a photograph, and it resembled him enough that he didn't hate it, at least.

The game was easy to play, and he got the hang of it right away. They played quite a few hands; he won three, and Erin won two. At one point, she decided to place her foot on the chair between his legs; that was a round she won. All he wanted to do after that was make their excuses and go to bed, but he had to endure four more games before she finally spoke up.

"Well, I think it's time for bed," she said, then pressed her foot a bit harder against him. He coughed and gathered his cards quickly, adding them to the pile while Frank put them back into their box. Liz stood and seemed quite tipsy. "Mom! Are you okay?"

"Yess, I'm f-ine. I jusst didn't realize how mu-uch I'd drunk—or is it drank?" Liz slurred.

"Alright, off to bed with you too!" Erin scolded and stood, ready to help her mom, since it was clear she wouldn't make it far in her state of drunkenness. Liz saluted her and took great care to set her leaded crystal glass onto the table, away from the edge. "David, will you help me, please?"

He couldn't believe she'd just asked *him* to help her with her drunken mother, after what happened earlier? "Me?"

"Yess, Daavid, please help me to my—bed," Liz said and laughed, staggering forward.

David looked at Erin, hoping she'd change her mind and ask Frank; however, she glared at him instead, having a hard time holding her up. *Ma Losh, this isn't gonna be good at all!* He walked over and lifted her arm around his shoulder, but he was too tall, so she wrapped her arm around his waist and put her head on his arm.

"You smell really, really good!" Liz said.

"I've never seen her like this before," Erin whispered, sounding worried.

The stairs were too narrow for all three of them to fit side by side, and Erin couldn't help her mom alone, so David had to help Liz up the stairs. She looked up at him adoringly the whole time. *Can this night get any worse?* He knew it could, but he didn't want to think of anything like that. *Frank should be doin' this!*

Erin followed behind them, and when they got to the top of the stairs, she walked into the bedroom after them. As soon as David set her mother down on the bed, Liz started to take her shirt off, and he jumped back. "Bloody hell!" he said and walked out the door.

"Don't go," Liz said disappointedly.

He went straight to Erin's room and shut the door. He paced back and forth, shaking his hands at his sides as if trying to shake off the feeling of her beside him. "Arrrgh!" he said in exasperation and annoyance just as Erin opened the door, looking worried and startled. "I'm sorry, but I can't… I just can't," he said.

"No, I'm sorry," she said, "I should've asked my dad to help me. I didn't think it through. I've never seen her drunk before, ever. This isn't like her at all! I don't understand it! We can leave right away in the morning, okay?"

David took a deep breath; he was safe with Erin in her room. He wouldn't have to worry about her mom trying anything or getting too close, so he felt like he could relax. Erin turned the bedside lamp on, and he turned off the light in the center of the room, then he walked around the bed and stood in front of her. As she kissed him, his anxiety melted away. He took off his shirt and realized there were no covers for the windows. There wasn't anyone to see them, but it was unnerving, nonetheless.

Erin saw his hesitancy and flicked the switch on the lamp, throwing them into darkness. Only the yard light over the outbuilding her dad used as a garage, the moon, and a small gash of light under her door gave them anything to see by. He wanted her so badly as he lifted her shirt and unfastened her bra, letting them both fall to the floor. Then he took her breast in his hand and felt her nipple rise.

She unbuckled the belt on his trousers, then she unbuttoned the fly and unzipped the zipper, allowing them to fall to the floor as well. She knelt in front of him and pulled his underpants down to his ankles, releasing his erection, which lightly touched her face. "David, I want to—"

She took his cock in her hand, and he nearly let out an exclamation but held it in until she took him into her mouth. "Ma Losh! Erin!" he said under his breath and pushed himself in deeper. He wasn't going to last like that, already wanting to explode into her warm, wet mouth. Even more, he wanted to be inside of her. "Erin, stop! Wait—" It was too late; he couldn't hold it in any longer and released into her mouth.

She crawled over to her nightstand, took some tissues from the box, and spit it out into them. "Sorry, but I can't swallow," she said and smiled as he helped her get to her feet.

"Et's... a'right, but... why'd yeh do that? I have nothing for *you* now?"

"We have all night—I'm not in a hurry," she said. "You can play with me while you recharge."

I can't believe this woman; she's incredible. I never know what she'll come up with next. He helped her undress and got into bed with her. Then, he gingerly kissed her breasts, being careful of his nose, longing to use his fingers to explore between her legs. There were so many parts to play with down there, and he enjoyed each one.

Slowly, he slid his hand down her chest, stopping at her belly button. He liked how he could make her moan or squirm with his hands. As he expected, the anticipation of where he was heading made her wiggle and move, trying to keep his hand moving, but it wasn't going to work. He wanted to draw it out so he'd be ready again when he finished examining her.

He continued kissing her, discovering her, and he brought her over the edge once. She moaned quietly, and he felt, with his fingers inside her, as the spasms of her release made her contract. He was about to bury his face in her folds when he realized he couldn't do it!

He couldn't get the cast wet and wouldn't be able to wash it off afterward either. All he could do was use the tip of his tongue on her very erect clitoris, which seemed to do the job nicely enough. He drew large circles, round and round, as she flexed and panted.

"Yes, just like that!" she whispered, and again, he felt the contracting muscles as she was able to release from his touch once again.

He felt powerful, in a way, being able to do that to her, and that feeling made him rock hard again. Waiting until she was still once more, he entered her, and she moaned more loudly than she meant to. As he covered her mouth with his hand, he felt more power and thrust into her, making her cry out, muffled by his palm.

It was taking longer than usual, being the second go, and he was enjoying the control he had. He thrust and thrust, taking his time, building up as she arched her back and clawed at his arms. He wanted it to last all night, but he could feel himself getting closer. When he felt her clenching again, it was his turn, and as he released with a deep groan, there was a knock at the door.

"I… heard noisess—It sounded like somewone-wass hurt… in there," Liz said through the door.

"Mom! Go away! I'm fine," Erin shouted. Then they heard the doorknob rattle as though she were about to open it. David was up and had the sheet wrapped around him as Erin flung herself to the door, sitting up against it, lest her mother succeed in opening it. "This isn't happening! My mother is possessed! I can't believe it!"

David sat on the long low radiator under the row of windows. The old metal heater was bumpy and not comfortable to sit on while naked, so he stood again and quickly got dressed. "I can't stay here any longer. We have tae go now," he hissed.

"I know," she said and got up off the floor. As she stepped away from the door, they watched it, afraid her mother would come crashing in. When she didn't, they got dressed and made sure they had all their belongings packed up before Erin slowly opened her bedroom door.

Seeing no sign of her mother, they quietly walked out of her room, down the stairs, through the living room, and into the kitchen. Erin lifted her keys off the hook next to the door that still read in faded blue ink, 'Erin's Keys.' "I can't leave without saying goodbye to my dad," she said, and David followed her to the top of the basement stairs. "Dad—are you down there?" she said, only just louder than a whisper. "Dad?" There was no answer. "I'm just going to go down and check. I'll be right back."

David didn't like the idea of standing there alone, but he agreed. He stood, listening for voices to tell him whether or not she'd found him, and then felt something touch his shoulder. He jumped a foot in the air and heard Frank's voice, "Whatcha doin', David?"

"Bloody hell! Erin, he's up here. I'm goin' to the car." He pushed past Frank and headed straight for the door. Once outside, he stopped and took a deep breath. The night was warm, and he was thankful to be out of that circus. *How did Erin turn out so normal?*

It was dark, and the yard light didn't quite make it as far as the porch, which had its own light, though it wasn't on at the moment. He slowly walked down the path leading to the driveway, past the mock orange tree and the red water pump. When he made it to Erin's car, he touched the top to get his balance and felt something move near his hand.

He let out a short scream that would have made any horror film proud and then heard purring and a faint *meow. A bloody cat? Fuck!* He opened the car door and got in, locking it behind him. It took a long time for Erin to come out, and by then, he'd fallen asleep. He woke up when she finally got in beside him. "What took you so long?" he asked.

"I talked to my dad about what happened with Mom. He said she had an overly strict, religious upbringing, so a lot of her issues get internalized. He thinks that somehow having you here brought a few deep-seated demons to the surface, and the alcohol flipped a switch. He saw her drink most of the first bottle of wine with dinner; then she drank almost all the second one herself too. She's never drunk that much wine in all her life, and she had a meltdown or a crisis of some sort."

David *had* noticed she was drinking a lot at supper and suspected that she'd started before then, even. "A'right, I can understand that. I just need tae get away from here. I won't hold a grudge or anathin' if we ever come back, but I can't enter that house again tonight."

"I understand completely. I'm freaked out too! Wait!" she said, "What did the fortune teller say? 'Forgive the mother…' or something?"

David stared at her, the dome light in the car being the only means to see her by. He instantly got goosebumps and shivered. "Okay, now I'm utterly flummoxed. How'd she—" he said, rubbing his arm, trying to get his hairs to lay back down.

"She couldn't—" Erin said, and he saw her shiver. She put the key into the ignition and started the car, but she didn't back up. "What do you think it means, David?"

"I've no clue, but we need tae get out of here."

"Yeah, I guess you're right. If my mom was mortified today, she'll be humiliated tomorrow."

Chapter Thirty

ROOM AT THE INN

Erin drove down the long driveway again, gravel crunching under the tires. She turned onto Highway 33, headed east. "There's a cheap motel in Saukville that I didn't bother trying earlier; I think it's our best chance of finding a room for the night," she said. Seven minutes later, she pulled into a parking space at the Seventh Haven motel.

"If et's full up, I say we sleep in the car," David said.

She groaned; "I can't sleep in a car. If it comes to that, you'll be driving us home."

Home… I'd like us to have a home together, David thought as they headed to the entrance door.

The hotel lobby smelled like disinfectant with a musty undertone. The furniture, wallpaper, and carpeting were old and dingy. It was like stepping back at least thirty years, with a few new things thrown in to 'freshen it up' ten years later. They stood at the check-in counter, where a large, faded painting of a meadow in pink and cream hung on the wall.

Not seeing anyone, Erin rang the bell. A man of about sixty poked his head out from a back room. "Oh! Welcome," he said and stepped out from behind the wall. "How can I help you?"

David thought it was a stupid question, seeing it was a motel. "We need a room for the night," he said.

"I'm pretty sure we're booked solid, but I can check the computer." He smiled but didn't move.

"Yes, please," he said, biting his tongue to keep from saying something snotty.

"Actually, we're kinda desperate, so any size room will be okay if that, I don't know, helps your search?" Erin said.

He turned and clicked the power button on a desktop computer, most likely original to the building. "It will just take a minute to warm up," he said. After a while, he started typing on his keyboard while David and Erin waited. "Good news! We have one room; it used to be a smoking room, and it's only got one double bed. We mostly use it for employees—if they need a place to crash since it hasn't been refurbished since the smoking bans, ya know? Will that work for you?"

"We'll take it," Erin said, "Thanks so much for looking!"

There she goes, being nice again. It's the man's job and she thanks him as if he's done us an enormous favor. David took her hand; "I'll retrieve our bags from the boot. May I have the keys?"

Erin gave him an odd smile and took her keys out of her pocket. She dangled them in front of him but moved her hand as he tried to take them. "Only if you say that again," she said.

"Say what, exactly? That I'll get the bags from the car boot?" he said, utterly confused.

She giggled and kissed his cheek, handing him the keys. "Yes, that's it. Thanks."

He shook his head as he walked out to the car. Erin waited by the desk for their room information and key cards. It didn't take long, and when he re-entered the lobby, he saw her hand the man her debit card. "Wait, I'll take care of that." He took the card from the man, gave it back to her, and then handed him his credit card.

They found their room on the second floor. It smelled of stale tobacco and had stains on the walls and carpets. "Hmmm—I didn't think places like this still existed," David said. He put his holdall on the luggage rack he'd just unfolded, not trusting the cleanliness of the carpets.

"Yeah, this place is just below where I'm usually willing to stay, and my standards are much lower than yours, but I'm too tired to care right now,"

Erin said. Once undressed, they both got into the narrow bed and fell asleep quickly.

In the morning, Erin again woke from a disturbing dream which left her feeling sick, and she was starting to worry. It had been less than three weeks since they'd been together in New Orleans. *Could I be pregnant? Is it normal to have morning sickness so early if I am?* She tried to remember the first day of her last period. It was written on her calendar at home, but that wasn't much help.

How could you be pregnant? Even if the treatments could reverse your infertility, you had an episode after you started the treatments last time, remember? It clearly takes a while to start working, so it's just impossible! Or—highly unlikely, at least.

There was too much stress happening all at once again; she knew David would be leaving that day and didn't want him to go. *I'm sure that's what it is,* she thought. *It's a combination of stress and dreading being away from him, that's all.*

"Soon, you shall visit the doctor who shall provide for your child—or—it might be children, it is unclear to me at this time," she heard the seer's voice say in her head. Knowing it would bother her until she checked, she decided to make an excuse to stop at her house to look at her calendar. She rolled over to try to find a position to ease her nausea, but it didn't help, and she had to rush to the toilet. Feeling slightly better, she found her toothbrush, brushed the acidic taste out of her mouth, and crawled back into the cozy little bed after opening the curtains a bit. The room was unimproved by the light of day.

"Are you a'right?" David asked as she snuggled up behind him.

"Yeah, I think it's just stress. I'm… going to miss you so much."

David rolled over and gave her a puzzled look. "Ach, right, et's Friday already."

Erin nodded; she suddenly had a lump in her throat and knew if she said anything, she'd start crying.

"Why don't we talk about our next treatment adventure?" he said with a smile. "Depending on what happens at the meeting on Monday, I may not be able tae come here again for a while, but I'd like it if you came tae me. Are you willin' tae do that?"

"Oh, David, yes! I'd love to!" She got up and took her phone out of her purse, then she grabbed his mobile, which he'd set on the low dresser that doubled as a TV stand. He sat up with his back against the headboard, and she handed it to him. She sat facing him with her shoulder against the headboard as they both opened their calendars and compared schedules.

"I've a few jobs lined up next week and an interview the week after that," David said, and she closed her eyes. "What is et, love?"

"I just remembered that next Monday is my… fifteenth anniversary with Todd. He wants to take me for an overnight getaway." She could have cried; the last thing she wanted to do was go somewhere romantic with Todd. *What are you doing? Why is this even an issue?* she thought.

David frowned. "Technically, our next official treatment time *should* be for the seventeenth. We could plan for you tae be with me so you won't have tae go with him—I mean if… you dinnae want to."

She felt disheartened as she explained, "Our anniversary is on the seventeenth. I'm sure I don't have to tell you that I *don't* want to go."

Then don't go! Go with David! Just cut the cord and go live your dream… What are you so afraid of?

"He has it planned for the night of the fourteenth to the fifteenth. I might be able to—"

"We can push it to the twenty-first since we've had more than one treatment this week," he interrupted, then he set his phone down and took her hand. "Erin, come early… if… yeh want to, I mean. I can have Tina set you up in a lovely suite in London if ye'd like that? If I have appointments, I'll come tae see you before and after them. I'll leave yeh some spending money, and you can go shopping tae yer heart's content. Then, at the weekend, I'll drive you to ma cottage in Scotland—"

"You have a cottage in Scotland? Of course, you do, why wouldn't you?"

"Aye, and I think ye'll like et. I can write to ma children, as well. Perhaps… we can visit them. Their school isn't far from there… and I can … ask if they'd like tae meet you if ye're up for that… mebbe?"

He smiled in a way that made her sure he wanted nothing more than for his kids to meet her, though she wasn't sure it was a good idea. "Maybe they won't want to meet me," she said, trying to delay her answer.

"Bah, I ken Charlie will, but let's wait and see what they say. How about we plan for the sixteenth, and if ye'd like tae come earlier, let me know, and I'll arrange everathin'? Well, I'll have Tina arrange everathin'."

"But we won't be able to be together… in public."

Is that what you're afraid of? Being seen with him in public and then being judged?

I don't know! I'm afraid of everything!

"Ach, mebbe no' as we can here but I know a few places where we'll be left to ourselves."

His excitement was infectious, and Erin perked up, setting her phone down on the bed. She got onto her knees and straddled him, putting one hand on either side of his face. She kissed him, and he responded by grabbing both of her cheeks, though not the ones on her face. They made love, Erin sitting on top, with no worries about anyone opening the door or being interrupted. It made no difference how crappy the room was; they were alone and together. That's what mattered.

As they were getting dressed, David's phone made a noise that meant he had a message. "That'll be Tina asking about ma flight home. I… could… tell her tae book two tickets?" he said and looked at her hopefully.

She was overwhelmed at the idea of just up and going overseas at the last minute. "David… I—"

"Shh, never mind, love; it was a silly idea." He went to her and kissed her forehead. "I shouldn't have said anathin'."

She relaxed into his hug. "Go ahead and make your plans. I'll go downstairs and see if they have any doughnuts or coffee or something," she said, then took her keycard off the TV stand and left the room.

David sighed, *Yeh eegit! Why'd yeh have tae open yer gob!* He picked up his phone, opened the screen with his fingerprint, and read the message. He wasn't sure how far from Green Bay they were, so he had her book an evening flight. There was one at 7:17 pm, so he told Tina to book it. He also asked her to look into flights for Erin on or around the sixteenth and to make it a one-way or open-ended ticket.

Erin came back to the room empty-handed, "Nothing looked good at all. Let's eat at the restaurant across the parking lot. I haven't eaten there in a long time, but it can't be worse than the stuff they have downstairs."

"A'right, that sounds good. By the way, ma flight leaves Green Bay at quarter past seven tonight."

———

"Okay," Erin said softly as she approached him. She wrapped her arms around his middle and rested her head against his chest. His heart sang to her without words; *thump-thump, lalala, thump-thump, lalala*. She swallowed the lump in her throat and managed to keep the tears locked away for the time being.

You're gonna have to make up your mind and you need to tell him what's been buzzing around in your brain for the last few days! her mind warned her.

I know, all of that! I just need time to think!

He'd already put his trousers on, but his chest was bare. She kissed his sternum and nuzzled her face into his chest hair, smelling the last remnants of his cologne. She wanted to pitch a tent right there and live in that spot, never being more than an inch away from his skin at all times.

He's not gonna wait forever, you know. Just go! her mind continued its nagging.

After a few moments, she stepped away and went about gathering the things they had taken out of their luggage.

"Erin," he said and placed his hand on her shoulder, turning her toward him. "I wish we never had tae say goodbye. When I went home last time, I was beside maself for the want of yer company. I've never felt so alone. I tried tae keep maself busy, but it was never enough. I need for you tae know that my greatest desire is tae be with you forever. Tae someday make you Mrs. Erin Elliott, and tae live with you as ma wife until the day I die."

The lock broke, the dam was breached, and tears streamed down her face. She wished for some kind of instant replay button for life so she could hear that speech from him over and over again. "You say the most beautiful things to me, David. Sometimes, it seems like you've managed to read my heart and tell me what's inside, only from your perspective. You say what I need to hear. Please love me forever."

"A'right, I will," he said quietly and kissed her hair.

They packed up their things and checked out, putting their bags in Erin's car, then they walked to the restaurant. The meal was good, the coffee, not so much, but it didn't matter; they could get coffee somewhere else. When they left the restaurant, Erin got nervous.

Talk to him about it!

"I was—" she began but changed her mind. *I better make sure before I go and say something stupid.*

David looked at her, waiting for her to continue, so she thought fast, "Uh... wondering... what you'd like to do today?"

"I'd really like tae get this bloody thing off ma nose, but I reckon I'll have tae wait until I'm home. I hope they let me back in; I dinnae look much like ma passport photo."

"I'd like to see your passport photo," she said and laughed, relieved she had averted the fumbled question.

"I'll show yeh before I leave. Et's not so bad."

"I'm sure it's amazing—how could you look bad in anything?"

He tilted his head and pointed to his nose. "How about in this?"

She laughed and took his hand in hers, "Nope, still gorgeous! Did you want me to drive past the house where I grew up? It's only a tiny bit out of the way, and then we can take the more scenic way back to Green Bay."

"Ach, aye, I'd forgotten all about et; I'd love that."

Chapter Thirty-One

STINKING PAPIST

Erin and David got back onto Hwy 33 and headed west. After three and a half miles, they passed Erin's parent's house, and in another half mile, she turned onto Lakeland Road. On the corner was a large farm with a white farmhouse. "That was the Krause farm. They raised pigs and pumpkins. You could smell the place for miles on a hot summer day!" she said and laughed.

It was an old country road, with houses and stone quarries dotted amongst the fallow fields. Many years had passed since she'd driven it, but she knew it by heart. It was nearly a mile to the small house her parents had rented so long ago. She pulled to the side of the road and was shocked at the transformation. "Oh, David, it's so different! The house is the same, but all the land around it is—derelict! That makes me sad." She got out of the car and leaned her back against it. David got out and stood next to her. "I wonder what it looks like on the inside now," she pondered.

"There's one way tae find out," he said.

"I couldn't knock on their door unannounced! I mean—No, it doesn't matter. I'll just be disappointed, I'm sure. If the state of the grounds is any indication of the state of the interior, it's better to stay away." She pointed to the large tree in the front yard she used to climb and the huge mulberry tree in the backyard that yielded an abundance of huge, plump, dark purple berries every year. "What I wouldn't give for a few of them right now," she said, leaning her head on his arm.

The day was fine and warm, with big white clouds that shielded them on and off from the sun's menacing rays. There was also a slight breeze that made the leaves sing. "It was a great childhood. I'm glad I grew up here," she said and took one more look before they got back into the car and she drove down the hill, pointing out the house of her childhood friends, Mindy, and her little sister, Betsy.

"Betsy—the one you saw with yer boyfriend—"

"Doug, yeah, that's the one. I have half a mind to pull in and catch up with her mother to find out whatever happened to her." She smiled and passed the driveway, turning left onto Shady Lane and then right onto St. Finbar's. She pulled over at the tiny cemetery bearing the same name and turned off the ignition.

They got out of the car and climbed the old concrete steps up to where about two hundred old headstones sat, wearing away to sand in the weather. The plots were well-tended, and trees surrounded it all. At the center of the cemetery stood an enormous, life-size crucifix with Jesus hanging on it, forever dead and sad. Erin had never liked it; she was taught that He had been taken down, buried, and rose again. Seeing Him like that made it seem like a sad story without a happy ending.

"It's sad—" David started to say; "Oh, sorry… are yeh Catholic?"

"Nope, I'm not a 'stinking papist'," she quoted from one of her favorite books, *Voyager* and the *Outlander* television series. Then she laughed, sure he wouldn't get the reference.

David smiled at her, "Aye, neither am I, Sassenach," he said, and Erin did a doubletake.

"Did you just quote *Outlander* to me? Good night nurse, I love you!"

"Aye, I've read the first two books and am halfway through the third. I had tae find somethin' tae keep me occupied for those lonesome ten, well, thirteen days," he said with a grin. "I've watched season one of the television program as well. I asked so as not tae offend you. Et's sad, to me, anaway, tae keep Him up on the cross like that. The cross should be empty, do yeh no' agree?" He gazed at the figure above his head introspectively and then looked down into her eyes.

Erin stared at him, her mouth open. "You won't believe me, but I was thinking the exact same thing. How is it we think so much alike? It's uncanny!" she said.

"I agree, I mean, as far as I ken, most Scots of ma age are Catholic, or dinnae give a—Well, they dinnae care," he said.

"It's the same here, yet, neither of us is Catholic. How'd that happen?"

"Well, I'm glad of et; less fighting about religion," he said and took her hand. They walked around the cemetery, trying to read the long-forgotten names, but most of them were unreadable. "There's an old Scottish sayin'— 'Ye're a long time deid.' It means tae enjoy yer life whilst yeh have it because once ye're deid, ye're deid a long time. These people lived near here, aye? They loved, fought, and had wee bairns—but now they're forgotten; their names washed away, though their bones remain under our feet," he said, contemplatively.

Erin looked up at him; he looked sad, so she put her arm around his waist. "Feeling your immortality?" she asked with a smile.

"Aye. I want tae live a good long time so I can watch ma children grow up and have children of their own. So that I can be with you for a verra long time and so that someday, we can look back and remember how, long ago, we stood in this wee cemetery on a hill and contemplated eternity when our love was still young."

"Wow, David, that's so beautiful. I want that too." They stood together in silence, looking at the decaying stones, each lost in thoughts of where life would take them before they, too, ended up six feet under. Soon they made their way back down the steps and got back into the car. They didn't speak; they just existed together for a long time.

"Thank you for taking me there," he said at last. "I dinnae ken what inspired yeh, but it was extraordinary." A serenity had settled between them, and they chose not to break it with idle words. He took her hand and held it as she drove them through the old, winding country roads, all the way back to Green Bay.

Chapter Thirty-Two

MAKING AN ASS OF YOU AND ME

As David and Erin got back into town, the nagging feeling was too much, and she knew she couldn't put it off any longer. She had to do it—to find out—she had to do it right away. "I need to stop by my house for a minute… to… check on something. Is that okay with you?" she asked David, her heart palpitating wildly in her chest.

"Aye, as long as ye're certain Todd won't be there," he said cautiously.

"No, he'll be at work, don't worry." They drove to her house, and she parked in the driveway. "I'll just be a minute," she said and jumped out of the car, leaving him there.

She ran into the house and looked at the calendar. June—*what day is it? June seventh—Oh Holy Moses! Five. Days. Late!* Her eyes stung with tears that threatened to come pouring down, but she held them in. *How could I be? Could it just be my hormones acting up because of the treatments? But the morning sickness—What am I going to do?* she thought.

Be calm. You need to take a pregnancy test to be sure. Don't panic until you've done that. Dazed, she walked soberly back out the door and got into her car, feeling like a zombie.

"What's wrong? Yeh look as if you've seen a ghost," David said.

"Hmm? A ghost? Oh, no, not a ghost—Ah, David… I—" She saw his concerned face looking back at her.

No melodrama, Erin, just tell him.

She knew she might start to cry, but she had to do it immediately. "I'm… five days late," she said and took a deep breath, letting it out slowly.

"Ye're… you mean—" he said and took her hand. His face changed from concern to confusion, to surprise, and then finally, to delight.

Erin was relieved until his face changed once more, this time to a look she couldn't read. *Good night nurse, he doesn't want it,* she thought.

"How… do *you* feel about et?" he asked tentatively.

She could tell he was choosing his words carefully, and she pulled her hand away. "How do *I* feel? I'm terrified." She angrily jammed the car into reverse and pulled out of the driveway. "I'm especially afraid of the look you're giving me right now. I can't tell what you're thinking at all." She'd hoped he'd be excited or at least *pretend* to be happy about it. "I'm going to Walmart and get a test."

"Erin," David said, but she shook her head.

I can manage without him if he doesn't want it to ruin his other family. I'm a big girl, she thought, knowing she was lying to herself. She couldn't manage without him; she needed him. She bit her lip to try to stop the tears, but it didn't work, and they started rolling down her face, clouding her vision. She had to pull her car over so she could try to calm down.

"Erin, I'm—I'm afraid tae tell you how I… truly feel," he said, sounding worried.

"Afraid? What could you be afraid of, unless… you don't… want it? For a minute there, you seemed to be happy, but then something changed your mind, I could see it in your face. What is it? Is it your family back home? Is it the thought of supporting me? Do you feel you have too many children already and don't want more? What is it, Todd?" She gasped and put her hands over her mouth "Oh! Shit! Oh, I'm… I'm so sorry, David! I can't believe I said that. Please, please forgive me," she said as panic filled her whole being.

She saw him recoil at being called Todd. He looked out the windshield and closed his eyes. "Actually, it was none of those things," he said quietly. "I only wanted tae know how you felt before I told yeh how happy it would make me. I didn't want yeh tae feel as though you had tae keep it… if you didn't want et."

Erin put the car in park, got out, and walked to the passenger side. She opened his door and took his hand to pull him out. His eyes were still closed, but he reluctantly got out and stood next to the car. "David, I'm so sorry." She stood in front of him and wrapped her arms around his waist. He was very upset; she could feel it in how he held her, or more accurately, *didn't* hold her.

Fuck! Now you've done it.

"Please forgive me. I was just so scared, and then your face changed, and I was even more afraid you didn't want it… I—I need you. I need you so much, and I was… afraid this might… push you away or… something."

"Push me away?" he said passionately, "Have I no' made it clear tae you that I'm in this—all the way, no matter what? Yeh ken how much I love ma children—what would make you think I'd not love ours? Ours—" he said again and suddenly held her tightly. "Erin! We're gonna have a bairn! A wee bairn, created by the two of us! Wait… but I thought you couldn't—"

"I couldn't. I don't know how it happened; it must be the treatments."

He looked down at her and smiled, his face shining. There were little puddles of tears threatening to fall from his lower eyelids. "I'll have another chance tae get things right as a father. Oh, Erin, I couldn't be more excited! You said yeh wanted tae go tae Walmart?" he said, sounding as giddy as a child.

"Oh yeah, to get a pregnancy test. I'm so scared, David. I'm afraid for it to be positive and for it to be negative. I'm really torn."

"Dinnae fash, ma love, I'll be with you. Now let's get that test!"

He was beaming. Erin thought that if all the lights in the world, including the sun, went out at that moment, he'd be glowing.

They got back into the car, and she drove them to Walmart. They walked hand-in-hand to the health and beauty section, near the condoms and K-Y jelly. She read the backs of all the boxes and found out you were supposed to wait till morning to use most of them. Neither of them wanted to wait that long, so they decided to buy an early pregnancy test that said they didn't have to wait. David purchased it and then waited outside the toilets while Erin went in to take the test.

Chapter Thirty-Three

RESULTS

bout five minutes later, Erin emerged from the lady's room in Walmart, holding the pregnancy test in her hand. Her eyes were huge and red, but she was smiling. She handed it to David, explaining that a minus sign meant not pregnant and a plus sign meant pregnant. He looked her in the eyes and then at the test. There was a very definite plus sign in the center of the test strip.

David let out a *whoop*, which Erin thought was very un-British of him, and lifted her up in a hug, spinning her around. When the people around looked at their display, he proudly informed them that he was going to be a father. He earned many handshakes and 'congratulations' from the people of Walmart that day.

They practically floated back to the car, and as they got in, he said, "Ach, ye're making it unbearably difficult tae leave yeh! I'm meant tae be at the airport in only a few hours, and here I am, not wantin' tae leave. I know I've said this already, and you weren't keen tae do it, but would you consider coming back with me?"

"I need to think for a few minutes." Erin wanted nothing more than to go to the UK with him and to stay there for the rest of her life. *"A bairn, our bairn,"* he'd said. She looked at him; it was such a huge decision, and what about Todd?

Oh, no! What about Todd?

Her face must have changed expressions drastically because David looked suddenly anxious. "What is et, hen?

"I—I need to go back to my house—it's really important."

Erin rushed home, and as soon as the car was at a full stop, she jumped out and ran into the house, leaving every door open as she went. David came in behind her, closing the doors and wondering what on earth was happening. "Erin?" She was standing at her calendar with her phone in her hand. "What are yeh doin'?" Looking up at him, she seemed terrified. Her expression was similar yet much worse than the one he'd seen on her face the day they'd met. "Ma Losh! What's wrong? You look as though ye're scared tae death!"

"But—" she was breathing heavily and he caught her when she leaned into him.

Erin woke up lying on the kitchen floor with her head on David's lap. It took her a moment to remember what had happened. "Oh, David! I was supposed to get my period on the third, which means I was… ovulating on May twentieth. I know that my egg can live for twelve to twenty-four hours— I mean the chances are very, very slim—like three percent, maybe—I mean it depends on when my egg actually dropped, but if it lived for twenty-four hours, then—"

"Then?" He looked utterly confused at her apparent babbling.

"It could be Todd's baby," she whispered and felt a ripple of shock shoot through David.

"It—"

"I didn't want to—I had to!"

He closed his eyes once more, obviously trying to order his thoughts. "What does that mean… for us? If it's his, will you—" He didn't get to finish his question. They heard the door open, and Todd walked in, looking disgusted to find them on the floor together.

"Erin! What is going on?" Todd said and blushed as if he were ashamed when he saw the white plastic splint on David's nose. Erin figured that would be the only reason he wasn't lashing out at him.

"I fainted, and David was keeping my head off the floor," she said.

"You… fainted? I've never known you to faint. What's the matter? Are you sick?" he asked.

Erin knew in those crucial moments that it didn't matter if the baby was David's or Todd's; she wanted to be with David. No matter how unfair it was to Todd, she didn't want to be with him anymore. "I'm not… sick, Todd, I'm—" she took a deep breath, "I'm pregnant."

Todd dropped to his knees and took her hand. All three of them were now on the floor in the middle of the kitchen. "But… the doctor said we couldn't—" Todd said, excitement and joy taking the place of his suspicion and anger.

"The doctor was wrong, or… the treatments have reversed—" Erin began.

Realization washed over Todd's face, and he let go of her hand. "Oh, I see, so it's not mine then. Isn't that just… perfect," he spat and stood to his feet again. A frightening look came over his face then, that startled them.

"Now, calm down—" David began.

"No, it's not yours," she interrupted, which made David stare at her. "I'm going to London with David tonight, and I need to pack."

I don't care! We'll do a DNA test when it's born, and if it's Todd's, I'll deal with it then, she thought. *Until then, it's David's baby! Maybe I can't get pregnant with someone who isn't my match! Maybe the egg wouldn't accept that man's sperm. Good night nurse, please let that be true!* she thought desperately.

David helped her stand. She set off toward her room to pack her things without so much as a tear—determined to shut off her heart and emotions. However, when she opened the door, a flood of memories rose up inside her and tried to drown her.

You are a real idiot; do you know that? You had better know what you're doing!

She felt a hand on her shoulder and jumped. She slowly turned to find her best friend of the last fifteen years, the man she'd laughed with and loved dearly, standing behind her. "I'm sorry, Todd," she said and buried her face into his work shirt. He wrapped his arms around her and held her. "You've been a wonderful husband, and I'm a selfish, ungrateful woman. I'm sorry I've hurt you; you deserve better than me. I know that's cliché, but it's true. I'm going... to miss you, but I can't go back and forth. This isn't an easy decision—"

"You sure are making it look easy," he said bitterly, "Is it the money, Erin, or his looks, or the fame? What does he have other than that?"

She let go of him and sat on the end of the bed. "Do you really think it has anything to do with that stuff? I thought you knew me better."

"I thought I did, too. I thought that you *really* loved me, but I'm just not enough for you."

"Oh yeah, and *I* wasn't enough for *you,* so you had to go off and buy those filthy magazines," she spat and then put her head down. "I don't want to fight. I did really love you, and you were enough. I thought it would work out... when I came back. I wanted to keep things good between us while I tried to figure out what to do, but you've been so angry. I felt like I was being closed up in a little box of what I could and couldn't say, think, and feel. I didn't handle things right, I know that, but then... you were so rough with me that night—"

Todd bowed his head. "I know, I'm sorry about that. I don't know what came over me," he said gently.

"Then, when you hit him—I'm not sure what you thought that would do for our relationship, but if you thought it would make me come running back into your arms or something, it did the opposite."

"Yeah, that was stupid. I pushed you away, I know, I just couldn't handle the thought of him—" He shuddered and shook his head as if trying to clear it of the imaginations he'd formed.

"I pushed you away too. I'm not blaming you, Todd; we were doomed from the start of the treatment option being offered to me. I was naive to think I could come back and everything would be like it had been. Wishful thinking, I guess," Erin said and looked at the clock next to her side of the bed. It was 4:32. She didn't know if she'd be able to go on the same plane as David, last minute as it was, but she knew she should be packing.

Remembering her large suitcase was in the spare room, she stood and started walking out of the room.

"Erin," Todd said. She turned to face him and saw the tears on his cheeks. "I'm sorry this is happening… and I don't want you to go. I will always love you, and if you ever change your mind, I won't turn you away." He walked up to her and kissed her forehead, then walked out of the room.

She heard him close the basement door, so she made her way to the spare bedroom. David wasn't in the kitchen anymore, so she figured he'd gone outside, not wanting to hear their conversation. Opening the closet door, she pulled out her large suitcase and wheeled it to her room.

She lifted it onto the bed, unzipped the top, and started to fill it quickly, feeling like a tornado, causing destruction and upheaval as she went. She emptied drawers, pulled clothing off their hangers, and threw in as many of her good-fitting shoes as she could. *Am I doing the right thing?* she thought as she rolled up her jeans and tops, stuffing them inside, too.

Her compass necklace stuck to her sweaty skin, and when she gathered what little jewelry she had, she didn't bother to pack the silver locket Todd had given her. She was emptying her nightstand drawer when she noticed her wedding band and stopped. Ten days short of fifteen years.

It wasn't fair.

It wasn't something she'd planned to do, but she slowly slipped the ring off her finger. She kissed it tenderly and placed it on her bedside table, knowing things could never be the same with Todd again, and giving up David wasn't an option.

That room held too many memories, and she had to say goodbye, so she zipped up her suitcase and locked the tiny padlock. She slid it off the bed and wheeled it out to her car. David was sitting in the passenger seat, waiting patiently for her. When she saw her, he got out and helped her get the suitcase into the trunk.

"Do yeh have everathin' hen, ah… I mean… yer passport?"

"Oh! My passport! I'll go get it," she said and went back in, remembering it was in the safe that was in the basement. She knocked on the door and descended the stairs into the cool darkness. Todd was sitting at his workbench, holding something small in his hand. He looked up at her as she went to the safe and started turning the dial to unlock it. It snapped open, and she took out her passport, plus a copy of her birth certificate, just in case she'd need it.

When she turned around, Todd was standing before her. He kissed her mouth before she could stop him, but she didn't struggle. Then he held her tightly and cried; she could feel his tears on her neck as he sobbed. "What am I going to do without you?" he said.

She laid her head on his shoulder and thought the same thing but then gently pushed him away and kissed his cheek. "You'll be okay. I have to go now, but I'll come back to get my stuff and… to get things settled… between us. Please take care of yourself and if you need help, call my dad; he'll help you." He nodded and wiped his face with his sleeve. "Please, don't do anything to hurt yourself—" she said and looked him in the eye.

"I won't," he whispered and turned away, heading back to his workbench. "I love you, Erin," he said with his back to her.

"I… love you too, Todd. Goodbye."

She was crying as she walked up the stairs and went back out to the car. She slumped into the driver's seat and closed the door, then she laid her head on her arms over the steering wheel and cried, bawling like a baby.

Chapter Thirty-Four

SAYING GOODBYE

David called Tina while Erin was in the house, glad to find her still in her office, working late. He explained that he would now require two tickets home. She found a flight leaving five minutes later, with a short layover in Chicago and a slightly longer one in Istanbul.

He had just gotten off the phone with her when Erin came out the first time with her suitcase. Now that she was back in the car again, he looked at her, sobbing and muttering to herself, and it made him feel a bit like the villain in the story. She had been happy with Todd, and here he was sweeping her off her feet. He sat still and quiet, letting her get it out and feeling terrible that things had to end for her like that. He wished he could comfort her, though he knew it was better to stay silent just then.

Finally, she sat up and reached over to the glove box to get a napkin. Her face was red and puffy, and she didn't look at him. She blew her nose and stared out the windshield. "I should probably leave the car here. Maybe we should get a taxi to take us to the airport?" she said softly.

David put his hand on her leg, but she didn't seem to notice. "I'll order an Uber," he said and took out his phone. He opened his app and used the information Erin had put into her profile while in New Orleans to fill in her address. A confirmation text told him a car would be there in under twenty minutes. He was afraid she was partly upset with him for all of it, so he didn't say anything as he got out and leaned on the passenger door, waiting for their ride to arrive.

———

Erin reopened the glove box and other various compartments, taking out the things of hers that had been stashed in them. She took out her spare pair of sunglasses, a CD of Eartha Kitt, and one of Abbey Road, which had been a Christmas present from her mother-in-law. Then, she got out of the car and opened the trunk, allowing David to remove the large suitcase while she grabbed the smaller one out of the back seat. Next, she made sure she had everything she might want, including what they had brought back from their trip out of town, and stuffed it all into her luggage. The trunk lid closed with an emphatic *thud*.

It was all so final—her home, her car, and her husband, all gone in what seemed like only a few minutes. She felt impossibly sad and didn't want to talk, glad David wasn't trying to make her feel better. She knew she'd get through it, and she'd be alright again, eventually, but standing in her driveway like that, waiting to leave, was almost more than she could take. She was leaving her security. Everything she knew and loved would be gone—too far away to see or visit—

Lily!

She had to call her best friend and say goodbye! Crying again, she searched for her phone and fumbled it out of her pocket, nearly dropping it. Her eyes were blurred with tears, so she had a tough time trying to find Lily's number, but she managed and tapped the call icon.

The phone rang, and then Lily's voice, so happy and friendly, said, "Hi, Erin, what's up?"

"Lil, I'm going to London with David. I don't know when I'll be back." She broke down, sobbing, not wanting to be saying that to her best friend, not on the phone, anyway.

"What happened? Are you okay?" Lily asked.

Erin tried to talk, to tell her she would be fine, but all she could do was cry. The more she tried, the harder she cried until the Uber arrived, and David had to take the phone from her.

———

"Hi, Lily, I'll make sure Erin rings you once she's calmed down; she's having a hard time saying goodbye."

"Okay, David, please give her a hug from me and tell her I'll miss her." Now Lily was crying.

"I will. Thank you for understanding," he said.

"Um, safe travels!" she cried.

David now had two bawling women to deal with and the driver to speak to. "I'm sorry, but I have to go now, Lily, goodbye." He touched the hang-up symbol and told the driver they were going to the airport.

———

As the black sedan rolled away from the curb, Erin watched her former life fade into the distance behind her. She buried her head in David's arm and continued to sob until they reached the drop-off at Austin Straubel Airport. Her head ached, and she just wanted to sleep, but she had to roll her luggage into the building and stand in line at the check-in counter.

David did all the talking until they got to security, where she was tagged, randomly, for a more thorough search. She had to stand to the side while a woman TSA officer took a metal detector rod and dragged it over her body. Then, the lady gave her a physical pat-down, just to be sure. She was okayed to proceed and didn't say anything as they walked to the departures gate, then sat next to each other.

Erin was emotionally exhausted and didn't want to deal with anything more. She also felt bad for David, having to put up with her, probably unsure what to do with the grown baby sitting next to him. "I'm sorry for the dramatics," she said softly. "I just need some time."

———

David took Erin's hand and kissed her temple, thankful she wasn't upset at him, at least. "Dinnae fash, ma love. Let me know if yeh want to talk. Otherwise, take as long as yeh need. I love you," he said. She closed her eyes and leaned her head against his arm. He took out his phone and started writing a text to Tina, asking her to set up a room for Erin in London. He was glad she was coming with him, but it was bittersweet seeing her in so much pain.

He thought about saying goodbye to Susannah and knew it would play out nothing at all like that. Any tears on her part would be for show, not from the heart. They would probably have to sell the house, but he didn't care. He could buy a place Erin would love, and they could build a new life together. He could feel that she was sleeping, so he tried to keep still to let her rest. He was nodding off himself when their flight was called for boarding.

Part Two

THE OTHER SIDE OF THE POND

Chapter Thirty-Five

AIRPLANE TO LONDON

"Erin, my love, wake up, et's time tae board the plane," David said as he smoothed her hair. She sat up and rubbed her eyes like a child.

"Okay, thanks for letting me sleep," she said softly.

He kissed her hand, and they got in line. Being business class, they were allowed to board before those in economy class. They found their seats in the small commuter jet and arrived at Chicago O'Hare without any problems, having an hour and twenty-minute layover before their next flight.

———

David hadn't gotten a chance to tell Erin where their second layover would be. It wasn't until they had settled in on the next flight and the pilot made his initial announcement that Erin paid attention to any flight information. "Istanbul! Oh wow! How exciting!" she said, finally having a bit more animation.

"We can relax in the lounge."

Erin smiled at him and discreetly held his hand. "Thank you for understanding and putting up with—with me today. You seem to know what I need even when I don't. Today, I needed silence and a chance to work things out in my own time, and you gave me that."

"Ye're welcome, but a lot of it was me bein' terrified I'd say the wrong thing and make everathin' worse. I've learned that in situations such as these, silent is best."

"You're a wise man, Mr. Elliott."

The flight was remarkable; the staff were friendly and courteous, and the food was like something from a magazine. There was plenty of room, and the seats folded down flat. It was an overnight flight, so much of their time was spent sleeping, but Erin had never had a better flying experience.

They landed at the Istanbul Airport at 4:15 pm Turkish time, which felt like 8:15 am Wisconsin time. Erin hadn't thought about jet lag; it was hard on her, so she hoped that once they got to London, they would go right to wherever they were staying. That way, she could rest and try to get past it as soon as possible.

They had a two-hour and twenty-minute layover in Turkey, so they headed straight to the Business class lounge. "I've never been in a VIP lounge before; it's nice," Erin said, trying not to look like a tourist and failing miserably. David was relaxed and natural, revealing to her that he was a world traveler.

"Are you thirsty?" he asked, "They have drinks over there."

"I'm gonna be fighting a nasty bout of jet lag soon, so I think I'll skip the alcohol. I should probably warn you now that it may include panic attacks and lots of tears."

"I don't believe they serve alcohol here, so find a comfortable place to sit, and I'll be back in a tick."

———

David wanted to kiss her, but they were no longer allowed to display their affection. It was too easy to be photographed without ever knowing about it. Instead, he smiled at her and made his way to the long row of coolers that held soda, juice, and water.

He chose a bottle of Coke, and while waiting for someone to move away from the cooler with bottled water, he watched Erin sit at a small table. She looked around, taking everything in, and he was glad Tina had found that flight. He took her drink from the cooler and turned around just as a beautiful, elegantly dressed woman approached him.

"Hello," she said.

"Hi," he said and turned away.

"I've a six-hour layover and thought perhaps... we might spend that time—together?"

I can't believe et! Even the nose splint doesn't deter them! "No, thank you," he said, not wanting to be seen with her any longer than necessary, and walked away. "Is this seat taken?" he asked Erin with impeccable manners as he approached her.

She smiled. "I was waiting for my friend, but I suppose you could keep his seat warm for him."

David handed her the plastic bottle. "I hope water is a'right? I've heard being hydrated can help with jet lag."

She took a sip and smiled. "Ah, a nice dry vintage; I like my water quite dry."

"Ach, fantastic, because it cost a small fortune!" he said and laughed.

"Good thing you have a fortune then, hmm?"

———

She took another sip and watched as businessmen and women entered the lounge looking so sharp, clean, and put together perfectly. It made her feel like a plus-sized Walmart mannequin dressed by a ten-year-old boy.

She picked at the label on her bottle, screwing up her courage. "David?" she said at last, "Is there any way we could maybe... if it's alright to ask... I mean—"

"Spit it out, woman!" he said and laughed.

"I need... better clothes. I feel like a lump. Could we, maybe... I have some money... I can chip in—" she stammered and blushed, wishing she didn't have to ask.

———

David looked at what she was wearing. He hadn't paid much attention to it before, but he could see how she didn't fit in with the people around her. "Say no more, ma love; we will purchase some nice things for yeh. I know just the place in London. I'm glad you asked; I wouldn't have thought tae offer anathin' like that. Promise me ye'll always ask if you need anathin', even if you think it's insignificant or too expensive."

"Okay… though I… I don't want you to feel like I expect you to buy me things. It feels weird asking you for stuff, but I'll try—I mean, if the tables were turned; if I was the wealthy one and you were… well… poor, in comparison, would you want to ask me to buy you things?"

"I would not. I ken what ye're saying, but I want tae give yeh what you need, and I ken ye'd want tae do the same." He knit his brows and sat back for a moment rubbing his chin. Then he leaned in close to her. "A'right, we need tae come to an understanding. I am in a position tae offer you… essentially, the world. You have come here with me, spur of the moment, with nothin' but what you have in yer suitcases. It would be wrong of me no' tae offer to cover your needs when I'm the one who invited you, correct?" *No' tae mention everathin' I have is yers now, anaway. I wish yeh knew that.*

"I guess so. But you have to promise that if I ask for too much, you'll say no, or tell me. I—"

"I promise. There, now, what do you want?" he said, dying to kiss her.

"There is one thing I do need right now," she said, with a playful smile, making him wonder.

"Name et."

"I need more water! Please?" she said, sweetly.

He laughed and stood. "As you wish; they also have food over there if ye're in need of a nibble." He pointed to several stations where there were platters piled high with delicious-looking food.

"I'll wait till you come back. I feel… really self-conscious right now."

He looked at her thoughtfully. "We have two hours here; I believe our time would be well spent in finding something that makes you feel more comfortable. Would you fancy that?"

Erin smiled at him. "I'd appreciate it so much, thank you."

David took her hand to help her up; it was the only way he'd get to hold it, so he took the opportunity. They walked out of the lounge and found the area with the designer label stores. Erin was about to walk into the first one when he took her by the arm. "You must promise me one thing," he said, looking serious.

"Of course, what is it?"

"Yeh mustn't look at the tags. I know you; you would take one look at the prices and run away screaming, but I won't, so trust me—you can have whatever you fancy in here, or in any store we enter, a'right?"

———

Erin was stunned. '…*whatever you fancy…*' She wasn't born yesterday; she knew designer fashion was expensive, but for him to take her aside like that made her question the wisdom of asking.

You should've just waited! Why are you so impatient?

"Erin? You must promise; I can see the wheels turning in yer brain, probably wantin' tae change yer mind about askin' me, but et's too late now. Please, let me do this for yeh, darling." He smiled his million-dollar smile and led her into the store.

Erin was a size in between U.S. women's and plus-size clothing, which most of the places at the airport didn't stock. She was becoming discouraged, but after a few misses, they found a store with plenty to offer her. The salesman was flamboyantly gay, flirting openly with David, and treated Erin like a queen. He was honest when something wasn't flattering and encouraged her to experiment with styles and colors she would never have tried on her own. "How do I look?" she asked David as she stepped out of the changing room.

"Pure braw! Yeh clean up nicely—" He stopped, embarrassment clouding his eyes.

"What is it? What just happened there? David?" She knit her brows and looked him in the eyes.

He smiled sheepishly. "Ach, I was just about tae call you Mrs. March but changed ma mind, no' wantin' tae bring that up again."

Erin smiled. "I've been Mrs. March for a long time now. I don't think it would bother me, but I understand what you mean. Why don't you use Ms. March instead?" She reached out her left hand to him, wanting him to hold it.

Lifting her fingers toward his mouth, he was about to kiss it when his eyebrows furrowed, and he studied the back of her hand for several moments. He ran his thumb gently over her bare ring finger and then gazed into her eyes, surprise unmistakable on his face. "Erin—"

She felt her cheeks grow warm. "I left it on my bedside table. I don't think I'll be needing it anymore."

David kissed the indent where her wedding ring had rested for so long. "I don't know what to say. Words aren't enough to tell you how deeply I feel about this right now."

She didn't know what to say, but she didn't need to worry because the clerk returned, waving a silk scarf toward them speaking excitedly in a thick accent.

After over an hour of shopping, they walked back to the lounge with several bags of clothing. Erin had changed and was now wearing a comfortable yet elegant pantsuit in black, a simple white top, and shoes with a slight heel. She was sure they alone cost more than two month's mortgage payments, but she felt lovely. She felt like she belonged in the company of the others around her and *almost* presentable enough to be in the same room as David Elliott.

"This is so much better! Thank you, David!" she said. "Now, where is the food you were telling me about?" They walked up to a kiosk, and each took a tiny plate. She wanted to try everything but only took three dainty portions that looked like desserts, not wanting to look greedy. Each of them was delicious; one was made with figs, one was filled with goat cheese, and one was rolled in sesame seeds, but she couldn't have guessed what was inside of it.

She would have liked to go back and try more, but their flight was called, and they had to go. Erin felt like a million bucks as business-class was called and they got onto the plane. "How long is this flight?" she asked him as they got comfortable in their seats while everyone was still boarding.

"About four hours, why?"

"No reason, I'm just excited to get to London. Honestly, I didn't like it when I was there last time, but I'm sure I'll have a much better experience with you." She looked at him and smiled brightly. Then she remembered that he wouldn't be able to explore with her, and she'd probably be stuck in a stupid hotel room while he was out doing the things he did, like interviews and glamourous, famous person things.

"I hope so."

"Did you say you have a few acting jobs this week? Oh, and you have the big meeting on Monday, don't you?"

"Aye, I have the meetin' on Monday, which I'm quite anxious about! I wish I could share it with you, but et's completely secret; no one is tae know about it yet. I moved a magazine interview to next week Wednesday, with the photoshoot for it the following Thursday morning. I'm no' lookin' forward tae that!"

"But why? I would think it would be fun, 'make love to the camera,' and 'give me a pouty look,' and all that," she said, using a silly, vaguely European accent, and laughed at the thought of a photographer saying that to him.

"Ach, no! They are quite awkward, in fact! Perhaps et's fun for women, but et's embarrassin' for me."

"*Perhaps...* we can have a photoshoot of our own at the hotel?" she said wickedly.

David laughed. "Mebbe, but we'll need to make certain tae close the drapes tightly. I wouldn't want a paparazzo with a telephoto lens climbing a tree and havin' *his* own photoshoot!"

"I can see the wisdom in that. So, where will we be staying?" she asked.

He shined his smile in her direction; his eyes were twinkling, and he leaned in, "I'm no' gonna tell yeh; et's a surprise," he whispered and sat back up. When she glared at him, he laughed again. "Trust me, ye'll like it well enough, I expect."

"I'm sure I will. By the way, if you haven't already, you should make an appointment to have the splint removed. The paperwork said it should stay on for a week to ten days."

He gently touched the white plastic splint. "I'd forgotten about having to get it removed; what a nuisance. I'll text Tina tae make an appointment; thanks for the reminder."

They watched a movie together and then looked through the *SkyMall* catalog, marveling that they could sell all that stuff from a plane. "Oh, look, a

Nap Anywhere Pillow! Might be useful, and it's only £37.99! Do you think they'd let me try it before I buy it?" Erin laughed.

"Highly unlikely, though I'd prefer the solar survival backpack. One never knows with you where one will end up. It would set ma mind at rest tae ken I'd survive in the wilds of London should I run out of battery in ma mobile. Ach, unfortunately, it works strictly on solar power, and London doesn't have any of that."

They continued their scrutiny of the items until a waiter with a cart came out for a light meal. Erin was so impressed she took a photo of the food and place setting and sent it to Lily. She also sent a message apologizing for the dramatic phone call and promised she would call once they were settled at the hotel.

An hour after the meal, the pilot made an announcement informing them that they were approaching Heathrow airport and gave them the local time and a simple weather report. Erin was excited and took David's hand. "I'm glad I'm here with you," she said.

He lifted her hand to his mouth and kissed it. "I am as well, darling." He smiled at her, making her melt in her seat.

The plane touched down at 8:42 pm, which felt like 2:42 pm for Erin. They were allowed to disembark just after first-class, and as they walked through the sky bridge into the terminal David ordered a car to pick them up. They made their way to baggage claim and were glad to see Erin's luggage was some of the first to come around the belt.

David helped her grab her things, and they moved quickly, hoping not to be noticed. They made it to the immigration line, and Erin stepped up to an immigration officer's booth. The angry-looking woman with a nametag that read 'Venetia' compared her to her passport photo. "Why are you visiting the United Kingdom?" she asked.

"I'm visiting a friend," Erin replied.

"And where does your friend live?"

"London."

"How long will you be staying?"

"How long am I allowed to stay?"

"Six months."

"Six months, then."

"And what's your friend's name?"

"My friend's name? His name is... David," Erin said, hoping she wouldn't have to give her his surname.

"David... what?" she asked impatiently.

Erin was flustered. "David... Elliott," she said quietly.

The woman holding her passport looked up at her and raised her eyebrow skeptically. "And what does your friend David Elliott *do* for a living, then?" she asked.

"Uh, he's... an actor," Erin said.

"An actor? Are you taking the piss? You expect me to believe that *you* know David Elliott? And that you've been invited to stay with him as his guest?" The woman laughed at her.

Erin's face burned with embarrassment and anger. She wanted to go off on the snotty woman, but she also wanted to be allowed into the country, so she decided to stay calm. Just as she was about to answer, David, who had already gotten through, approached them. "Is there a problem?" he asked.

The woman froze, and her face changed from mockery to utter disbelief. "Ah, no, sir, no problem." She looked at Erin again, but this time she was the one red in the face. She stamped a random page in her passport while Erin smiled and took it from her, standing next to David Elliott, knowing that the bitch would never be so lucky.

"Oh, David! She was so rude! She asked me who my friend was, and I didn't want to lie, not that I'd have a random name to give her anyway, but when I said your name, she looked at me like I was crazy. Thank you for saving me. The only thing that kept me from giving her a piece of my mind was that I wanted to be let in," Erin said as they walked toward the main terminal.

"That was probably wise of you." He stopped and looked around them, then he got a bit antsy. "I'm sorry, hen, but from now on, we can't be seen as together. There may be photographers in the next bit of the terminal, so prepare yerself, and don't show any signs of affection, a'right?" He allowed a couple to pass by before he kissed her forehead. "I love you," he whispered in her ear.

"I agree," she said with a smile, then they each took a deep breath, readying themselves for the barrage.

They stepped through the doorway into the arrivals terminal, and nothing happened. There were no greedy photographers stepping over each other to get the best picture—nothing. "You seem tae be good luck," he said as they walked unbothered through the terminal and out to the waiting car. The driver got out and put their luggage into the trunk while David opened the door for Erin. He got in next to her and stole a kiss before the driver came back.

Erin's stomach did a somersault, and she longed for more, but she knew she'd have to wait. "You… are evil!" she said to him, closing her eyes and trying to control her breathing. She took his hand and squeezed it, really wanting to get to the hotel!

The driver pulled away from the pavement. "Take the M4, please," David said to the driver.

"A'right," the driver said.

"Is it really nine-thirty? It's still so light outside," Erin commented.

"In midsummer, we don't actually have full darkness, or what we do have is very short. In Scotland it can be nearly midnight, and et's still not fully dark outside."

"We'll have to stay up so I can witness that, then."

"Aye, I'd like that." David identified landmarks as they got into the city; he pointed out the Victoria and Albert Museum, with its elaborate Italian renaissance architecture, which Erin had always wanted to visit. Then he pointed out Harrods, with its grand, Edwardian facade. Erin had been there once and loved it, though she remembered that the prices were completely crazy! He pointed out the Wellington arch, standing strong at the corner of Hyde Park, dwarfing the pedestrians who walked through it, past its tall stone pillars and intricately carved stonework.

When they got to the corner of Piccadilly and Berkeley Street, Erin gasped.

"Oh, David! There's the Ritz! They filmed part of *Notting Hill* there!"

"Yes, I remember," he said and smiled at her as she craned her head, trying to get a better look. They passed it by, turning right onto St. James's Street, and then again onto Bennett Street, and finally right onto Arlington. They had gone around the block to end up at the entrance to The Ritz.

Chapter Thirty-Six

PUTTING ON THE RITZ

Davi d and Erin's Driver pulled up to the main entrance of The Ritz, London. A man in a perfectly tailored uniform opened the car door. "Good evening, and welcome to the Ritz," he said.

Erin was absolutely stunned. Things were going on all around her; people were talking, a man was carrying her luggage, and then they were entering through the door, stepping into something out of her dreams. She looked at David, unable to speak. He smiled at her and spoke quietly in her ear, "Please remember we can't be seen as together, a'right?" She nodded and tried to look like she was by herself, following about three feet behind him.

While David stood at the check-in counter, she sat in the circular lobby, looking up through the opening the stairs that hugged the outer walls created. When she saw him head for the elevator, she waited a moment then followed him. She stepped into the elevator car after the bellboy, not saying anything, too afraid it *was* a dream and that she'd wake up if she tried to speak.

She followed as David and the bellboy got off on the same floor. David fell back behind the young boy carrying their luggage, and she was thankful the hallway was empty of people so they could walk together. Suddenly, Erin thought it looked familiar, then she saw the gold lettering on the door. "David! The Trafalgar Suite?" she said and had to stop herself from hugging him.

The bellboy opened the door, and they walked into the most luxurious room she had ever seen, except in movies. It felt like she was halfway between this world and a dream-like state, where her senses were either muffled or overly clear and brilliant. David was thanking and tipping the bellboy, and all Erin could think of was Hugh Grant, sitting in that very room, speaking to the red-headed actor about bringing flowers for his grandmother in *Notting Hill.*

As soon as the bellboy left and the door closed, she burst into tears. David went to her and held her, stroking her hair. "I… just can't believe it! How? I… just can't believe it." She looked up at him; he was grinning like a cat, having just brought his 'person' a nice, fresh mouse, all proud of himself.

He took her by the hand and led her into the opulent bedroom with its luxurious draperies and gold accented walls and doors. "I reckon I dinnae need tae ask if you like et, then?" He bent his head down and kissed her. She dropped her purse onto the beautifully ornamented carpet and stood on her tiptoes. She held his head in her hands while he unbuttoned her slacks, which then fell to the floor. She simply stepped out of her shoes, leaving everything in a puddle next to her as they continued undressing each other.

David threw the decorative pillows off the bed and pulled down the covers. "I've wanted you so badly all day! Not bein' able tae touch you has me longing to more than ever; come here!" He pulled her to him and turned her so that the backs of her legs were against the mattress; then, he knelt in front of her naked body.

She thought she knew what to expect as he touched her breasts and smiled up at her, but then he looked at her belly and kissed it. He put his ear against her navel and whispered, "Hello, ma wee one. This is the first chance I've gotten tae speak tae yeh. I want yeh tae know that I love you and yer mummy, and I can't wait tae meet you." He kissed her belly again and stood, hugging her tightly. When he let go, she saw they both had been crying.

"I love you, David! That was beautiful," she said.

He wiped the tears off her face with his thumbs and said, "I wish I could ask you tae marry me right now. If I did, what would yeh say?"

Erin smiled. "Are yeh daft?" she said and stood on her toes to kiss him. She continued kissing him for a very long time. Finally, she let go and said, "Of course I would David. I—I really think we're meant to be—together; I mean, it's crazy how fast everything has been, and yet I feel like I've known you forever. What's more, I want to know you forever, from this point on."

David pressed himself against her, pushing her up against the bed frame. He then pushed her gently backward until she was sitting on the edge of the mattress. The sheets were soft and crisp against her skin as he helped her move to the center of the bed, and she lay on her back.

She watched as he crawled on top of her, lifted her leg over his forearm, and entered her. "You feel so good inside me!" she said.

He kissed her, starting with her lips; he moved to her neck and then her breasts, suckling them as he doubled his efforts. She cried out, over and over, until he felt her body contract and then release, enveloping him in a pulsing sheath that made him shudder as he climaxed inside of her.

After their long day of emotions and exertion, they were exhausted, so they rolled over and held each other. Erin was almost asleep when David started to get out of bed. She watched him, thinking he needed to use the bathroom, but when he started getting dressed, she sat up, not understanding.

He saw the look on her face and sighed. "I'm sorry, love, and I'm gutted about et, but I can't stay here," he said sadly. "Please believe I dinnae want tae go, but et's vital for me tae return to ma house tonight. I can't be seen in town and then stay here all night. I guarantee someone saw me or took photos on their mobile, so I have tae make out as though all is well at home. I'm so verra sorry."

She wasn't expecting that and moved to the edge of the bed, feeling stunned and began to panic. She wanted to beg him to stay, yet knew she had to bite her tongue and suck it up. "I… don't know how to respond. I… hadn't thought about—I didn't know you wouldn't be staying. God, I… know I should just accept it, but it feels like shit. I… feel like… a prostitute. Maybe not that, but your kept woman, hidden away in a room, just waiting for your return," she said, knowing she wasn't going to deal with it well, she could feel it, but she took a deep breath. "I'm sorry, I know that's not fair, and I'm not trying to make you feel guilty; I just needed to voice it, you know?"

"Et's not fair to you, and you have every right tae be upset. You are so much more tae me than what this must feel like for yeh, and I ken that's no' enough right now. I ken et's gotta sting, but I can't change it yet. Give me some time, and I swear I'll make it up to you, a'right?" he said, sounding miserable.

Erin didn't want to be in that enormous room all alone, especially with jet lag setting in. She already felt the frenzy and heart palpitations and needed him to know what to expect. "David," she said, sensing herself losing control of her emotions. Closing her eyes, she tried to steady her breathing, but it wasn't working. "I'm not—I'm not trying to get you to stay by saying this, but I can feel the jet lag starting to make me panic. I might say things I don't mean, and I'll be okay tomorrow, but I'm gonna lose it really soon. It's just how I react, so… please… please… wait until I'm over… most of it or I'll be dealing with it all alone, and I really—I really don't want—"

"A'right, et's a'right; I willnae leave just yet. Shh," he said and sat on the edge of the bed next to her.

She suddenly felt the weight of the events from the last twenty-four hours land on her like a boulder, covering her with fear and anxiety. "Oh, God! What did I do?" she said, her eyes wide and frantic. "What am I doing here? How could I be so evil to Todd? He's been so good to me, and now I'm gonna be stuck in this room for God knows how long, just waiting for you to come and go. I'm such an idiot!" she said and then stood, picking her things up off the floor. I need to leave! I need to go home! I'm sorry, David, but you have to send me back!" she begged him. She was crying and breathing heavily.

———

David sat her on the bed and held her tightly, trying to soothe her. He said things like, 'A'right; okay; dinnae worry, darling; whatever you want, ma love,' and the like. She rocked back and forth, crying and saying she needed to go home, over and over. He held her until she was drained and fell asleep in his arms, then he laid her on the bed and covered her up, kissing her forehead. He was also exhausted, and wished with all his heart he could stay and hold her until morning. Instead, he left her a note on the small desk next to the marble fireplace.

Erin-
    I'm sorry I had to leave. I hope you sleep well. I will return tomorrow morning, as early as I can manage it.
I love you, my darling,
David xx

He felt bleak, wanting only to go home and sleep so he could come back and be with Erin again. He took one of the key cards from the small table in the sitting room where the bellman had left them, then picked up the phone and asked the concierge to order him a car. When he hung up, he looked around the ornate room, feeling melancholy about the whole thing.

When he got down to the lobby, he was utterly exhausted. The concierge greeted him and led him to the car already waiting for him. It was very late, so traffic wasn't bad, and fifteen minutes later, he was dropped off a few doors away from his house. He remembered a night, eight weeks earlier, when he'd come stumbling up to his front door, drunk and not wanting to tell his wife he'd agreeing to sign up for the Registry. *How things have changed,* he thought.

Using his key to unlock the door, he stepped into his house. Nothing had changed; it was still too tidy and sterile. He didn't know what time it was, but he guessed it was after midnight as he took off his shoes and carried them up to the spare bedroom. His watch read six twenty-eight, he noticed as he took it off, then dutifully wiped it down and set it atop his dresser, *the time in Green Bay.* Maybe it was his own form of jet lag, but he desperately wanted to be back there, where he could walk around freely and do whatever he wanted with the woman he loved.

He undressed and put on his boxer shorts, then pulled down the duvet and got into bed, thankful for clean sheets and a chance to finally sleep. Unfortunately, sleep wouldn't be coming to him any time soon. He heard a knock on the door, and before he had a chance to say anything, it opened. Susannah stood in the doorway with her arms crossed in her robe and house slippers. She looked angry, which did not surprise him. "I'm knackered; can we talk in the mornin'?" he asked, not wanting to deal with her.

"I don't think so, David," she said with icy resolution. "You haven't been home for a week! Where have you been, and whatever happened to your nose?" She looked disgusted at the sight of the obtrusive white plastic splint marring his face.

He sat up, and she came into the room, standing next to him with her arms still folded in front of her. He looked into her sallow, sunken-in face, noticing the dark circles under her eyes. "Honestly, do yeh truly care,

Susannah? What difference does it make tae you what goes on in ma life or whether I'm here or no'?" he asked, getting impatient with her intrusion.

She took a step back and let her light silk robe fall to the floor, revealing her naked body, looking more bony and gaunt than he remembered it ever looking in the past. He fixed his gaze on her face and scowled. "I'm no' interested, now please let me sleep," he said, then laid back down and rolled away from her.

She wasn't deterred and started to get into bed with him, running her hand across his back, but he sat bolt upright.

"I told you no!" he said, raising his voice in anger. "Yeh had all the chances you could want two months ago, but yeh didnae want me then. Now I dinnae want you. Go back tae your own bed and leave me be. Also, yeh need tae eat somethin' you look sick."

She made an offended noise and backed away. "Ah, yes," she said, obviously angry and embarrassed at being turned away by her husband. "I'd forgotten you now prefer obese women!" She turned on her heel, leaving her robe on the floor, and stormed out, slamming the door, which caused all the wall hangings to tremble in her wake.

"And good riddance," he added to the empty room.

Chapter Thirty-Seven

MISSING FEMALE

In the morning, David awoke feeling hungover. His head pounded as he rose to start his morning routine. About halfway into his shower, he finally woke completely and remembered he would get to see Erin and that she was only fifteen minutes away. *Well, at this time of day, et's more like forty-five,* he thought, but it wasn't six hours anymore. His energy level skyrocketed, and he rushed to finish up.

Once he was dressed and ready to go, he picked up his mobile and sent Erin a message:

> D: *Good morning, my love. I hope you feel better. I'll be leaving soon, that is if I don't have any confrontations on my way out the door. I've missed you.*
> *xx*

There wasn't a quick reply, so he carried his shoes downstairs, hoping to make it out the door without seeing anyone. He was sitting on the small chair next to the hall tree, putting on his shoes, when their housekeeper, Kitty, walked into the foyer and saw him.

"Aww, Mr. Elliott, sir! I'm chuffed ta see ya! I were beginnin' ta fink ya might not be comin' back!" she said and smiled warmly at him. She noticed his nose, then, and winced. "Aww, 'at looks painful! Would ya like for me ta fetch ya a cold compress?" she asked kindly.

Touched by her thoughtfulness, David thought she looked sincerely happy as she turned, ready to hurry to the kitchen and find something to help him. "Wait, Kitty," he said, and she turned to face him again. "Thank you, but I won't be needing anything. Do you know if Mrs. Elliott has any plans in the next few days?" he asked.

Her face made a sort of frown as she thought for a moment. "I fink 'er women's luncheon is on Tuesday, sir. I can check with 'er if you'd—" she began to say, but David stood, interrupting her.

"No—No, Kitty, it's quite alright. I will talk to her about it… later," he lied. "Oh, and Kitty, what do you do whilst Mrs. Elliott is at her luncheon?"

"Aww, I go 'ome ta visit me mum and sometimes me auntie—Why sir, did ya need me ta do somfin' for ya?" she asked, looking so eager to please he was sorry she would soon be out of a job, at least in that house.

"Ach… er, I mean, no, I'm glad you get a day off," he said. "I… presume Francie goes out as well?" he asked, knowing he was pushing his luck with his questions. Any other person would've figured out he was up to something, but he knew Kitty wasn't as bright as some folks.

"Francie does the shoppin' on Tuesday, sir, but I can ask 'er ta stay—"

"No, please don't, Kitty." She was beginning to frown as though she wasn't sure why he was asking, so he decided to close the subject. "I was hoping to be alone is all… to… work on a project in peace. I'll plan to do it then," he said, hoping she'd buy into his lie.

"A'right, sir," she said, looking satisfied with his explanation.

"Oh, and Kitty, I'll be gone all day today, so it's best not to mention anything to anyone, alright?" he said, realizing too late that it made him sound as though he were hiding something.

"Yes, sir. I'm glad you're 'ome," she said, then she bobbed her head formally and walked away, humming a song.

He used his mobile to order a car, and when it arrived, he hurried to get in, glad to be headed away from that place. Erin still hadn't replied to his message, and he was beginning to worry. *Did she wake in the middle of the night and decide to leave? Ma Losh!* The thought filled him with dread, so when the car was only a few blocks away from the hotel, with traffic at a standstill, he got out and walked the rest of the way.

He tried to appear as though he weren't in a hurry or upset, but he was and made a beeline for the elevator. When he got to the room, he called out for her, but she didn't answer. He walked into the bathroom; she wasn't in the shower. He entered the bedroom, and she wasn't in there, either, though her clothes were still there, which helped to calm him down.

He searched for a note or some clue as to where she was, but all he found was her mobile sitting on the bedside table, turned off. *Now, what do I do?* He thought, not wanting to panic. *Where could she have gone?* He thought for a moment about where to look and then saw a light blinking on the landline telephone. He picked up the handset, and when the operator came on, he asked for his messages. He was connected to the room's voicemail and heard Erin's sweet voice.

"Hello, David, I was famished when I woke up, so I went downstairs for breakfast. My phone doesn't seem to be working, so I turned it off. Please come join me if I don't see you first."

Overjoyed to know she was safe and sound and still in Great Britain, he hurried to the Louis XIV-styled dining room in search of her. He saw her immediately, sitting alone at a small table at the edge of the room. She was wearing the clothing he'd bought her in Istanbul. Her hair was up in a messy twist which looked lovely on her, and she had done her makeup perfectly. She looked up from her robin's egg blue dinnerware and smiled at him, waving her hand in greeting.

"Good morning!" she said brightly as he approached her table. "I'm glad you found me."

She's glad! he thought. "So am I." He sat in the mauve upholstered chair opposite her, wanting to kiss her so badly. "Tae tell the truth; I was more than a wee bit worried when you didn't answer ma message, thinkin' maybe ye'd found a way tae fly home, I mean after what you were sayin' last night."

"About that, I'm so sorry—" she said, looking embarrassed.

"Yeh dinnae need tae apologize; you warned me, and et's a'right. I'm just glad ye're still here," he said and smiled sheepishly at her. She offered him a bite of her omelet, but he declined, only because that would be the time someone would take a photo. He hated having to think that way. He'd spoiled himself in America, running around free when, in reality, he was a caged animal.

"Isn't this the most beautiful dining room you've—Well, maybe you've seen prettier ones, but I haven't. It's like something out of a dream! I've had to control myself and not stare at the walls. Now I can stare at you, though. Would you mind if I used your phone to send a photo to Lily… oh, and can I call her too?" she asked. "I didn't get a chance to last night."

David laughed, lightly. "Of course, I dinnae mind, but et's only half two in the mornin' in Green Bay, love. I dinnae imagine she would appreciate you callin' her that early," he said with a smile.

"I think you're probably right," she said and laughed. "Uh, may I… take a discreet photo or two with it?"

"Of course, here," he said and unlocked his mobile for her.

Chapter Thirty-Eight

RITZY BREAKFAST

A waiter approached the table and asked if David would like to order something, which he did, so he and Erin sat together eating their breakfast. No one could fault him for dining with a professional-looking woman, and Erin certainly was that morning. As far as anyone knew, she could be his accountant, a consultant, or even a reporter. "We should buy you some more clothing; yeh can't very well wear that every day," he said out of the blue.

"Okay, where did that come from?" she asked, seemingly puzzled at his train of thought.

"I was thinkin' about—Well, never mind. I think we need tae go clothes shopping again," he said, ashamed to admit that the reason was so she'd look more like a businesswoman around him and less like his mistress.

"What—now? Today? Hmm, let me look at my schedule—" she said and looked at the palm of her hand, pretending to flip imaginary pages. She gazed up at him and smiled. "You're in luck, I just had a cancellation, so I'm free all day!"

"You do the silliest things sometimes, hen! I think I'll keep yeh," he said and smiled, shaking his head at her. He wanted to take her hand but instead took a drink of his coffee.

"Wait, don't you have a huge meeting tomorrow?" she asked. "Shouldn't you be getting prepared for that?"

"Aye, I reckon so," David said. "But—there's something I need to tell yeh when we get back—before I can even start to prepare for it."

"Should I be worried or intrigued!" she asked.

"I'd reckon intrigued would fit best," he assured her.

"Good, I would prefer that," she said as they finished their breakfast. David told the waiter to charge it to the room, and then they headed for the lobby, where David asked the concierge to order a car.

They were taken to Harrods first, where they found a few things Erin liked, that is until she made the mistake of looking at a price tag while she was in the fitting room. The skirt's price made her turn tail immediately and end that part of the shopping spree. She was tactful and allowed David to buy the few things she had already decided on, but she was not going to spend that much money on clothing; she just couldn't. They went to a few other upscale shops, where she allowed him to buy her some more lovely things, but she was feeling drained by noon and told David she'd like to be done if it was alright with him.

"If you're sure, hen. What's wrong?" he asked.

"Nothing," she lied. He gave her a look that told her he knew it, so she confessed. "I just can't allow anyone to spend so much on clothes. I accidentally saw the price tag on something at Harrods, and it was just insane. I wouldn't care if you had… ten million dolla—I mean, pounds. I… can't."

David smiled playfully. "And what if I told you I *did* have ten million pounds?" he said and raised his eyebrows at her.

Erin peered at him, expecting to see something in his face that told her he was teasing her, but he looked serious. "You—Oh—" she said wide-eyed, "Well, I still wouldn't pay those prices for any of it. I mean, I don't need to shop at Wal—I mean Asda, but there has to be something in the middle," she said, knowing what he'd say and wanting to explain how she felt. "David, that Victoria Beckham skirt was a *thousand pounds*! Do you understand how… impossible that is to me?"

"Aye, I do," he said gently. "A'right, love, let's head back to the room then."

"Ten—Million?" she said and swallowed hard.

"Et may only be nine and a half. I haven't checked lately," he said and laughed, kissing her hair. Then he sent for a car to take them back.

They arrived at the Ritz at half-past twelve and had to act like they were strangers again. On the way through the lobby, a short man with black hair and Cuban heels, who seemed to know him, stopped David, wanting to talk. Erin kept walking as if she were by herself. She saw David look back as she ascended the elegant, carpeted, spiral staircase that led to the room alone, carrying quite a few shopping bags.

Twenty-five minutes later, David returned to the room, looking ashamed and guilty. "Why the long face?" Erin asked him. She was smiling and happily hanging up her new clothing.

He went to her and wrapped his arms around her waist. "Erin March, I love yeh! That man went on endlessly about the market and stocks and things I have no knowledge of, but he wanted tae know my opinion. I've no clue why. I tried tae get away several times, but he wouldn't take the hint. I'm sorry you had tae—"

Erin put her finger up to his mouth. "Dinnae fash, *mo ghràidh* (mo gry), I'm fine," she said, using some of the Scottish Gaelic she'd learned from *Outlander*.

"*Mo ghràidh*? Well, I wish I knew what *that* meant," he said, sounding impressed.

"It means, 'my love,'" she said proudly.

David's eyes widened a bit, then he smiled and knelt before her. He lifted her blouse and spoke to her belly. "How are yeh this afternoon, *mo ghràidh*?" he said, then put his ear to her belly button and listened. He said things like, "Aye? Yeh dinnae say?" and "Mummy loves you just as much!"

"And what did you hear?" she asked, laughing.

"Ach, *that* is between me and the bairn," he said. He pulled her blouse back down and stood, then he kissed her and took her hand. "Come, sit with me."

She allowed herself to be led into the sitting room and sat next to him on the sofa. "What is it?" she asked. "Oh, right, you wanted to tell me something. Well, go on, I'm all ears."

Chapter Thirty-Nine

BIG DEAL

David took a deep breath and stood. He started pacing in front of the coffee table, so Erin got herself comfortable in the corner of the couch and waited for him to figure out what to say. "A'right," he said apprehensively, "I very much want tae tell you somethin', but yeh cannot tell another soul under any circumstance whatsoever."

She was a bit startled by how serious he'd suddenly become. "Ooo-kay?" she said.

"Yeh must promise, Erin," he said, looking nervous and very serious.

She wasn't sure she wanted to hear it after all, but she could tell he needed to get it out. "Then I solemnly swear I won't tell anyone, ever!" she said. "Well, unless you've killed someone, and in that case, I'm going straight to Scotland Yard to file a complaint!" She laughed, and David smiled.

"No, et's nothin' like that," he said. "I… want tae tell you about tomorrow's meeting and the part I've been offered—but only if I can trust yeh won't tell anaone, and yeh may have tae keep the secret for a verra long time."

"Oh, David, really? You want to tell *me?*" He nodded and started biting his fingernails, which was something she hadn't seen him do before. "I don't have anyone to tell, but I pinky promise, which everyone knows is the most powerfully binding promise next to the Unbreakable Vow," she said and held out her hand with her pinky extended. He smiled and played along, wrapping his pinky around hers and shook it. "Alright, it's sealed; now tell me! I'm dying to know!"

"I hope I'm doing the right thing, but I simply must examine the pros and cons with someone, and you are the best someone I know," he said and closed his eyes. "I've been offered… the role of… The Doctor," he said and stood breathless, awaiting her reaction.

Erin's eyes and mouth grew wider and wider as she opened them in shock and surprise. "The… Doctor? For real? Oh, David! Good night nurse, you'd be perfect as the Doctor!" she said, making a squealing noise. She stood, expecting to hug and congratulate him, but he didn't look all that excited, so she resumed her seat. "You… don't seem very happy about it; what am I not getting?"

"Oh, I'm happy, chuffed, even, but… et's an enormous decision. I'll be recognized all over the world, much more often than I am now. There will be interviews, public speaking, conventions—" he said. "Can we deal with that?"

He said 'we'! We are a 'we' now! "I didn't think of that," she said thoughtfully. "You would forever be The Doctor, and—Wow, no wonder you can't decide."

"I'm of two minds about the whole thing, Erin," he said, his true emotions transparent on his unsure and pained face.

She looked at him with compassion and was about to discuss his options when she suddenly started. "Wait!" she said as goosebumps lifted the hairs on her arms. She took her phone off the table and turned it on. It took a long time to boot up. "Come on," she said to it. As soon as she could, she began scrolling through her files until she found what she was looking for. "That woman—the seer—didn't she say—" She pressed play on the video.

"Soon, you shall visit the doctor who shall provide for your child—or—it might be children, it is unclear to me at this time…" The fortune teller's voice said through her phone.

Erin was frightened at first then her emotions quickly changed from discomposure to disbelief. "So, you understood what she meant this whole time and didn't tell me?" she said.

David smiled sheepishly. "Aye, I did, but only that part; I *couldn't* tell yeh!" he reasoned, but she raised an eyebrow. "A'right, I wasn't supposed tae tell yeh, but I need yer help with this decision. After all, at the end of the day, other than me, ye're the one who will be affected the most by et."

She hated to bring it up, except it was valid. "What about—Susannah and your kids? It would affect them too, right?" she said.

He sat next to her. "Ye're right, of course, although I'm determined Susannah will no' be involved in our lives for much longer," he said with resolve, but Erin knew better.

"She's the mother of your children, David. I'm afraid she'll be involved in some parts of your life forever," she said and watched him. He was really struggling with the decision and wasn't thinking straight. "I wish you'd told me sooner, so we'd have had more time to figure it out."

Aye, I ken it well enough now." He laid his head on her lap, looking at the ceiling and drumming his fingers on the back of his other hand.

"Okay, this is going to sound crazy, but the seer said, '…you will soon visit the doctor who will take care of your child…' right? She spoke as though you were already that character. Do you think she might have said that for us both—to help you make up your mind?" she theorized.

He sat up and stared at her. "Good night nurse!" he said, which made Erin laugh. "That *is* what she said, after all—See there, a perfect example as tae why I need you! You catch the things I miss."

"Well, we all know The Doctor's lost without his companion," she said and smiled at him.

He leaned over and kissed her, then he stood and took her hand to help her up. "Thank you, Erin, you've helped me enormously!" he said, then he pulled her close and held her.

"That's what your companion is there for."

"Aye! I only hope I won't have tae wipe yer memory after yeh meld with me."

"On the other hand," she said, "I could get your half-human—sort of twin, all to myself."

David seemed startled by the comment and held her away from him for a few seconds. "Ach, Losh, dinnae say that!" he said and then shuddered visibly.

"Well, that was a bit over-dramatic," she said, confused at his reaction.

He let her go and turned away. "So then, that's that, sorted. What shall we do now?" he asked brightly, but Erin wasn't so easily distracted.

"I'm going to find out what your odd reaction was about, but I'm starving, so let's go find something to nibble. Holy Moses, I'm dating the Doctor! This is exciting! Hey—now you'll be able to go *back* in time as well as forward," she observed.

"Aye, I won't know what tae do with maself! Oh, one more thing; dinnae make any plans for Tuesday. I want tae show yeh somethin'."

They ate lunch at a fancy restaurant that David suggested; the food was amazing, though the atmosphere was stuffy and sterile. After the meal, they decided to walk around town for a while. As they passed a Boots, with its blue and white sign looking down on them, they heard a notification on his mobile. When he looked at it, he groaned.

Erin looked up at him. "What is it?" she asked.

"Martin," was all he said.

She gazed at him with compassion; she knew how Martin had always been a thorn in David's side and wished he'd leave him alone already. *Hasn't he done enough to try and ruin his life? He already got him to go along with his Fertilis Defect plan, which thankfully backfired, but what's next, framing him for murder?* She shuddered at that thought and put it out of her mind. "What does *he* want?" she asked, predicting it was money.

He opened the message and read it out loud.

> M: *Hallo, David. I heard you were back*
> *in town. I need to speak with you in*
> *person. When might you be available?*

"In person usually means he wants something and thinks I'll cave in if I see his pathetic face," he said and then laughed. "Tae be honest, it *has* worked—up until now anaway."

She smiled at him; he was so generous and kind, some would say to a fault. "I could come with you?" she offered.

He looked at her with a sly smile. "That gives me an idea. It's risky and has the potential to backfire, but it could prove whether Martin is simply a jokester or an enemy. How'd you like tae expose his true colors along with me?" he said.

"Ooh, I'd love to! What's your plan?" she asked.

They discussed several ways to get him to show his cards and decided on one, then David sent him a message, hoping he'd take the bait.

D: *Today is ideal, actually. What do you
say to tea at the Savoy…4:00?*

Chapter Forty

TEA AT THE SAVOY

Martin was always glad to get something from David without even asking, and tea at the Savoy was one of his favorite things. He knew David craved being the savior and that he'd do almost anything to feel needed, so he made sure to feed that in him. That's how he knew David would follow through on the Fertilis Defect Registry scheme. Helping some poor, sick female was right up his alley, no matter how much he denied it.

At 4:09, Martin walked across the black and white checkered floors of the Savoy Hotel lobby. Heading straight to the Thames Foyer, he heard music from its grand piano drifting out from the familiar Victorian gazebo positioned underneath the stained-glass dome. He asked to be seated with Mr. Elliott and was led to a table where a grey-haired man, and a woman who looked strangely familiar, were seated. It was only when the man turned his head that he realized it was David. "Going for the walloped grandfather look now, are we?" he said, using an overly posh RP accent. He pointed to the splint on David's nose and then shook his hand.

"Aye, and truth be told, it's come in quite handy. Don't bother asking about the nose; it was an accident. Martin, I'd like you to meet my friend, Erin March. Erin, this is Martin Green."

Martin shook her hand and then took a seat. *Well, well, the whore from New Orleans.* "Pleased to meet you Mrs. March," he said.

"Same here. David's told me all about you. It's nice to finally put a face with the name," she said, politely.

———

Erin had seen him come in and knew immediately it was Martin. He was average in every way, except he had obviously dyed black hair, cut and styled perfectly to hide the balding, and was dressed impeccably. If David looked like a million bucks, Martin looked like half a million.

When he came closer, she could smell a pleasant cologne, though he'd used way too much. As he spoke to them, she noticed his teeth had been whitened, yet she could smell smoke on him. He was trying too hard, and everyone knew it except him.

The waiter came and placed a three-tiered platter of delicious looking confections and a rectangular plate of finger sandwiches onto the starched white tablecloth, then he poured the tea. "So, where have you been, mate?" Martin asked David. "People have been looking for you."

David raised his eyebrows at him. "People? Do you mean *you* have been looking for me?" he asked, and Martin chuckled light-heartedly.

"Well, yes, Susannah and I have wondered where you were hiding," he said.

"You and Susannah, hmm? So now you're in an alliance with my wife, are you?" David said with mock accusation.

"Now, now, I didn't say that!" he said. "Don't soil your knickers."

"I'm not worried," David said blandly. "So, you wanted to talk to me?" Just then, David's phone started to ring. "Oh, it's Becky; I must take this. Martin, hold down the fort, and—be nice!"

Martin waved his hand as if to say—'go ahead, I've got this,' so David stood and walked out of the room.

"So, David tells me you've been friends since school?" Erin said. She smiled and took a sip of her tea. She'd changed into one of the expensive outfits they'd chosen earlier in the day, and she looked quite good.

———

Even Martin noticed how different she appeared now compared to the photographs he'd seen her in. "Ah, yes, well, we go way back, David and me. He's always gotten the pretty girls, and I've always covered for him," he said with a wink. "Oh, and don't worry, I'll do the same for you, as well, of course;

I'm used to it by now." He placed one of the finger sandwiches on his plate and then took a sip of his tea.

"What do you mean? Was he a player in his youth?" she asked, smiling.

Martin pretended to choke on his tea and coughed. "Was he? You mean *is* he," he corrected her. "He likes women, as I'm sure you know. Look at you, a beautiful woman, having tea at the Savoy with David Elliott! He knows how to make a woman feel special," he said poisonously.

"I don't understand," she said. "He told me he doesn't—"

"What?" Martin interrupted her. "He doesn't do things like this, and he's been completely faithful to his wife all these long, lonely years?" He smiled and looked at her with pity. "He's a man, a handsome man who has needs, just like every one of us, but you needn't worry, my dear, your secret is safe with me!" he said. Erin looked upset, so he put his hand on hers, which she had on the handle of her teacup, and said, "Oh, dear, I see I've upset you. I shouldn't have said anything. I'm so sorry, but... I thought you knew about him."

After rewarding him with a fake smile, he took his hand off hers. "No, I didn't, silly me," she said and sat, looking slightly deflated as David returned and apologized for his lengthy absence.

He seemed to notice something was amiss with her, so he placed his hand on hers. "Erin, what's the matter? What did I miss? You seem upset."

Erin sat up, her back rigid, and her mouth set in a very fake, plastered-on smile. "I'm fine, David, I'm going to go powder my nose. Please excuse me," she said, then stood and walked away from the table.

Both men pushed their chairs out to stand, but only David got to his feet. Martin pulled his chair up to the table just as soon as she'd taken a step away from them. "What did you say to her, Martin?" David said.

He was angry; Martin could see it all over him. He also noticed David wanted to go after her, but he knew he couldn't without causing a scene, and he wouldn't do that. "I didn't say anything," he lied. "I told her your secret is safe with me, that's all."

"What secret?" David said, still looking in the direction Erin had gone.

"Come now, David, I know what you're up to with that woman. She's clearly infatuated with you; it's written all over her face. I can also see she's enjoying your money with the way she's dressed," he said. "But we can discuss that later; I must speak with you whilst she's away."

"What is it this time?" David asked.

"You see, I've a debt with the bookies. Had to rob Peter to pay Paul a few times and thought I'd make it back on the races. Well, I lost big time, and they are not happy with me. They are going to repossess things shortly," he said, looking desperate and worried.

"How much?" David asked and could feel his wallet shrinking, even as they spoke.

"Well, now, I'd say three thousand quid ought to cover it and a little extra to keep me quiet about your affair with *Mrs.* March," he said, not batting an eyelid.

David looked at him and narrowed his eyes. "So, if I give you four thousand quid, you'll keep quiet about her and me, then?" he asked, leaning in closer to him. Martin nodded, and they shook hands again. "The problem is, I don't have that kind of money on me. I'll have to get it to you," he said.

"Fine, only don't take too long, or I'll end up serving Her Majesty's pleasure!" he said, ungratefully. "Well, then, I must be off; it's been lovely to catch up. Do tell *Mrs.* March goodbye for me," he said. David stood, and so did Martin, who took a teacake with him and rushed out as he saw Erin coming back to the table. He didn't want to be involved in the fight he expected would ensue at any moment.

Chapter Forty-One

I LOVE IT WHEN A PLAN COMES TOGETHER

Erin returned to find Martin gone. She sat in front of David and poured herself another cup of tea. When she looked up at him, he had an odd expression on his face. She smiled, and they both started laughing. It was difficult not to make a scene. "You-were-pure-brilliant, hen!" he said, clearly impressed by how she'd pulled it off so well. "Ye'll be wantin' an agent soon; you're a natural!"

She smiled. Honestly, it wasn't that difficult; she was just herself, and it worked.

"What did he say whilst I was away?" he asked.

"What didn't he say is more like it. He told me that our secret is safe with him, and he has been covering for your many women over the years. That you're a handsome man who has needs, and I'm just one in a string of women he's helped you keep under wraps. God, that sounds just like all of my fears tied up in one tidy little package!" she said, starting to feel a bit shaken and unnerved after saying it out loud.

"He said all that? Really?" he asked.

"If we hadn't already talked about it, I would have been out the door and on a plane by now," she said, meaning it. "What did he want from you?"

"Humph! He wanted three thousand pounds to pay a debt and another grand for hush money," he said. "I told him I didn't have it on me, and he'd have tae wait, so I've bought us some time."

"He asked you for *four thousand pounds*? I can barely ask you to spend thirty pounds on me! Are you going to give it to him?" she asked, astonished at the nerve of his so-called mate.

"I've done so in the past, so he'll expect it of me this time, and when I continue puttin' him off, he shouldn't be suspicious. Perhaps I won't give it to him; no' all of et, at least," he said with a shrug. "I can't believe he'd try tae throw me under the bus with you straight away like that! He doesn't even know you!"

"I know! And it was right off the bat too. He didn't even try to feel me out or see if I had an agenda; he just started in with being the one to keep your secrets. How did he know I was your—mistress, anyway? Holy Moses am I that obvious?" she said with a sigh. "Maybe he's pegged me as the insecure type and is playing that angle first? It was unnerving, the way he said things— the ploys he used. It was almost like he read my mind or heard some of our conversations. He even said something to the effect of '...*and I bet he told you that he's always been faithful to his wife...*' I mean, things you've—said to me," she said and lowered her chin.

Erin! Don't! You're not going to start believing this con artist! she tried to tell herself.

David took her hand, but only for the briefest time possible. "Erin? You aren't beginnin' tae believe what he's said, are you?" he asked.

She tried to smile and took a deep breath. She didn't want to answer until he'd heard exactly what Martin said. "I have a confession to make," she said, and David raised an eyebrow.

"Go on."

"While you and Martin were greeting each other, I quickly put my phone on record, so I have the whole conversation on it—Well, I hope I do, anyway."

David smiled his best smile at her. "Ach, you are a sly one!" he said. "A'right, let's go back tae the room and have a listen."

"Okay," she said, feeling off-balance.

David ordered a car on his mobile, and they returned to the hotel. They went up to the room and sat on the sofa.

When Erin took her American phone out of her pocket, David knit his brows. "Yeh said it wasn't working—"

"Not for calls, but some of the apps still work," she said and found the voice recording, not really wanting to hear it all again, but she tapped play and listened with him.

"*… People? Do you mean you have been looking for me?*" his voice said.

"I'll forward it a bit," she said.

"*…hold down the fort, and—be nice!*"

"*So, David tells me you've been friends since school?*"

"*Ah, yes, well, we go way back, David and me. He's always gotten the pretty girls, and I've always covered for him. Oh, and don't worry, I'll do the same for you. I'm used to it by now.*"

"*What do you mean? Was he a player in his youth?*"

"*Was he? You mean is he. He likes women, as I'm sure you know. Look at you, a beautiful woman, having tea at the Savoy with David Elliott! He knows how to make a woman feel special.*"

"*I don't understand. He told me he doesn't—*"

"*What? He doesn't do things like this, and he's been completely faithful to his wife all these long, lonely years? He's a man, a handsome man who has needs, just like every one of us, but you needn't worry, my dear, your secret is safe with me! Oh, dear, I see I've upset you. I shouldn't have said anything. I'm so sorry, but… I thought you knew about him.*"

"*No, I didn't, silly me.*"

"Pause it here, please," David said.

Erin stopped the recording feeling like she wanted to cry. *How was he able to get me to doubt?* She looked at the phone in her hand, not saying anything for fear of breaking down into tears.

David took the phone out of her hand and set it on the coffee table. "Ma love, I dinnae ken why he chose tae say what he did, but I swear tae you he's lying," he said. "Erin, please look at me."

She lifted her head and looked into his soft brown eyes; eyes desperate for her to believe him. She wanted to, with all her heart, only Martin had managed to plant a tiny seed of doubt, and she didn't know how to uproot it. "I don't know why I'm feeling this way," she said. "I don't want to doubt you. I believe you in my heart, but what he said was so perfectly what I was—am afraid of, it's—well, it's messed me up."

"I love you, Erin. I'm a one-woman man. I know it doesn't look that way right now, as I'm still married, but... I truly have never even thought of cheatin' on Susannah. No' once in the whole seventeen years we've been married. Well, not until I met you, my darling, and you are so much more tae me than she ever was. Yeh must believe that I've never cheated on her and will never cheat on you, no matter what Martin would have you believe," he said, sounding desperate for her trust. "I'm afraid his scheme is startin' tae work on you; please tell me it won't."

She leaned over to lay her head against his arm. "No, it won't work," she said, hoping she was right. "I love you too, but you need to know that now my radar will be set to high, and I don't have a lot of control over what my brain will be trying to show me. Just be prepared for me to be suspicious and question things a little—okay, maybe a lot more for a while."

"Whatever it takes, ma love," he said.

"I also remembered to leave my phone on the table when I went to the bathroom, so I should have the whole thing," she said as she lifted it again and tapped play.

"Erin, what's the matter? What did I miss? You seem upset."

"I'm fine, I'm going to go powder my nose. Please excuse me."

They could hear the chairs scraping against the floor as the men stood for her.

"What did you say to her, Martin?"

"I didn't say anything. I told her your secret is safe with me. That's all."

"What secret?"

"Come now, David, I know what you're up to with that woman. She's clearly infatuated with you; it's written all over her face. I can also see she's enjoying your money with the way she's dressed, but we can discuss that later; I must speak with you whilst she's away."

"Please pause it again," he said, and Erin tapped the pause button.

"So, I'm a gold digger, *and* being used by you, what an asshole!" she said. David looked at her as though he were searching for something in her face. "What? What are you looking at?" she asked, feeling like she was under a microscope.

"He said yer infatuation with me is written all over yer face. I was just checking," he said and laughed.

She playfully punched his arm. "That's no secret! I'm all-out obsessed!" she said and tapped play again.

"What is it this time?" David's voice said.

"You see, I've a debt with the bookies. Had to rob Peter to pay Paul a few times and thought I'd make it back on the races. Well, I lost big time, and they are not happy with me. They are going to repossess things shortly."

"How much?"

"Well now, I'd say three thousand quid ought to cover it and a little extra to keep me quiet about your affair with Mrs. March."

"So, if I give you four thousand quid, you'll keep quiet about her and me then? The thing is, I don't have that kind of money on me, I'll have to get it to you."

"Fine, only don't take too long, or I'll end up serving Her Majesty's pleasure! Well, then, I must be off; it's been lovely to catch up. Tell Mrs. March goodbye for me."

David and Erin sat quietly for a few seconds after the recording stopped. "I'm sincerely and thoroughly mystified. I've granted him *every*-single-thing requested of me. Why would he abuse me in this way?" David said.

"Did you notice he always referred to me as *Mrs.* March? Don't you think that's odd? You never said I was married, and I'm not wearing my ring. What do you think it means?"

"I think it means he's been up tae no good. I think he knows more than he's lettin' on, and I mean tae get to the bottom of et, though for now, I'll keep ma distance and make certain you do the same. He's shown that he is no' tae be trusted."

Chapter Forty-Two

NOT TO BE TRUSTED

A thought occurred to Erin as she sat next to David on the floral sofa in her suite at the Ritz, and she didn't like it. She opened the video of the fortune teller on her phone and forwarded it to the last few seconds. They heard the woman's voice say:

"DO NOT trust the birds! Do not trust the birds, or they will peck your eyes out!"

David looked up at her, tilting his head like a confused dog.

"Okay, now I'm starting to get really scared. A Purple Martin is a bird, right?" Erin said. David stood. She could see the hairs on his arms rise, and he shivered.

"But… that's impossible. How much of what she's said has already come tae pass? Perhaps we should start putting more stock in et."

They listened to her words again. That time, Erin wrote them down and then read them out:

I will visit the Doctor who will take care of my child—or children.

"Ye're here, visitin' me, and I *shall be* the Doctor who will take care of yer, no—*our* child… or children," David said softly.

I don't need to worry about the future.

"If ye're here with me, you need no' worry about the future, aye?"

I will explore my dearest dreams in the future, and if I choose it, I will have it.

"You said yer dearest dream was tae have a home here with children, in the country. I can provide that. She says all yeh must do is choose et," he said with a grin.

"Okay, I choose it then," she said quietly, and he kissed the top of her head. "Now for you."

You've tried to explore your future, but it's looked dim and fruitless.

"Ma future has looked dim and fruitless until now."

You have many things, but there is something that you have desired for a very long time. That thing shall come to you; all you must do is ask, but you must wait for the right time.

"I do have many things, but I finally have what I've always wanted in you; you and our bairn," he said. "I wonder if asking at the right time referred tae how I asked you to come with me, but you said no. Then you changed yer mind when yeh learned about the bairn, and I asked again?"

"Oh, I didn't think about that; maybe so."

Don't trust the birds, or they will peck your eyes out.

"The birds—birds, she used the plural form of the word. Do yeh reckon that was on purpose? Who else do we know who has a bird's name?" he asked.

"No clue; we'll have to keep our eyes peeled."

The mother means no harm; forgive her.

"And we already ken who the mother is, now don't we?" he said, finally able to laugh about it.

"Good night nurse! Don't remind me!" she said with a groan. She had a sense of humor about it, but it was just too soon. "I guess all we need to worry about now are the birds."

"We've figured one of them out already, which is good," David said.

Erin was starting to feel the pull to take on bits of David's speech. She had resisted it up till then, but she loved accents and dialects. It was in her nature to fall into those she found herself around for extended periods. In some cases, as with a southern American accent, she would start as soon as she heard it. Being surrounded by so many of them in London, it was only a matter of time before she gave in.

She could feel herself losing the battle every day she was with him, though she knew the dangers of getting carried away with it. Years earlier, when she and Todd were there, she found herself using a cross between the 'Queen's English' and something that probably sounded like Bert from *Mary Poppins*. Looking back, it made her cringe. "Aye, Martin is most definitely one of the birds," she said.

David smiled at her. "Et's funny when you do that."

Erin rolled her eyes at him. "What did I do now?"

"You said 'aye' instead of 'yes.' Didn't yeh notice et?"

She blushed and covered her mouth with her hand. "Oops. I forgot to tell you—" (She wanted to say 'yeh,') "I tend to do that," she said and explained her tendency to him. "I don't always know I'm doing it, so I'm sorry," she said, feeling stupid, and embarrassed.

David took her into his arms and kissed her. "Dinnae fash, love. Look at me; I stopped using ma natural accent long ago. I think they started teachin' it out of me at boardin' school," he said. "Et's only since I've met you that I'm usin' it again.

"For what it's worth, I love the way you speak, whichever accent you use. I should make you read Dickens or Shakespeare's sonnets to me; that would be lovely!"

"Ach, I can do that for yeh now!" he said. He sat up tall and took a full breath. His voice came out, clear and perfect as he quoted:

> *"Let me not to the marriage of true minds*
> *Admit impediments. Love is not love*
> *Which alters when it alteration finds,*
> *Or bends with the remover to remove.*
> *O no! it is an ever-fixed mark*
> *That looks on tempests and is never shaken;*
> *It is the star to every wand'ring bark,*
> *Whose worth's unknown, although his height be taken.*
> *Love's not Time's fool, though rosy lips and cheeks*
> *Within his bending sickle's compass come;*
> *Love alters not with his brief hours and weeks,*
> *But bears it out even to the edge of doom.*
> *If this be error and upon me prov'd,*
> *I never writ, nor no man ever lov'd."*

Erin was struck dumb; she had goosebumps from head to toe and sat in admiration, gazing at him like she had when they first met. It was a look of shock mixed with awe.

"Sonnet one hundred sixteen, I believe," he said with a smile.

"Yes, it's one of my favorites," she said softly. "That was extraordinary! The way you said it made me understand everything he was trying to get across. God, David!"

He shrugged and continued smiling at her. "Thank you, hen," he said humbly. "I've heard that before… in school. I reckon et's a talent—I dinnae ken; et's how I read it on the page."

Erin shook her head in disbelief and muttered, "Beautiful."

He leaned in close to her and kissed her cheek. "Aye, you are." He began kissing her neck. "*O my Luve is like a red, red rose… that's newly sprung in June; O my Luve is like the melody… that's sweetly played in tune.*" Gently, he advanced, in a modified crawl, so that she had to lay back on the sofa cushions. He kissed the top of her sternum,"*So fair art thou, my bonnie lass… so deep in luve am I; and I will luve thee still, my dear, till a' the seas gang dry.*"

He began unbuttoning her blouse, kissing the newly revealed flesh as it appeared."*Till a' the seas gang dry, my dear, and the rocks melt wi' the sun; I will love thee still, my dear, while the sands o' life shall run.*" He unfastened her slacks and pulled both them and her underwear off her, then he stood and undressed while she watched.

Erin sat silently, soaking in his delicious voice, speaking words from time gone by. She didn't know who had written what he was quoting to her, but she didn't care. In her mind he may as well be making it all up as he went, and she wasn't going to ruin it by saying something unimportant.

David knelt before her and helped her to sit upright. Then he pulled her forward by the knees, so her rear end was close to the edge. Wordlessly he entered her; the only sound being her gasp of pleasure and the fancy golden mantle clock ticking. He kissed her left breast and then her right one, flicking her nipples with the tip of his tongue.

She moaned as he thrust and leaned her head forward to kiss his lips, wrapping her legs around his waist as she did so. Her legs hugged him and pulled him deeper into her. They both gasped and panted, then Erin felt her body respond with a lovely orgasm.

He unexpectedly pulled out of her and took her hand to help her stand, then he led her to the bedroom and continued making love to her on the soft, comfortable bed. Neither of them spoke a word until David climaxed, and they were both worn out. Erin knew he would have to leave soon; he had to prepare for the meeting and get some sleep.

"And fare thee weel, my only luve! And fare thee weel awhile! And I will come again, my luve, though it were ten thousand mile," David whispered.

Sudden tears sprang to her eyes. She wanted to hide them, so she rolled away but then changed her mind and turned to face him again. "I love you," she cried as she wrapped her arm over his chest. It took her a while to regain control, and he didn't say anything until she did.

"I'm sorry I must leave tonight, my darling. It tears ma heart out tae see you cry, and I miss yeh every moment I'm away."

"That's not why I'm crying; at least that's not the major reason," she said with a soft laugh. "I'm just overwhelmed with hearing you recite poetry to me. No one has ever done that before, and I think I could get used to it. Who wrote the last one? It was beautiful and seemed fitting to the occasion. I thought maybe you made it up."

"Ach, then I'll try tae do et for yeh from now on. It was Robert Burns, no me; I'm no' a poet."

He stood, and she saw him check the floor for his clothing before remembering they were in the sitting room. She found her nightgown and slipped it on as he left the room, then she followed him and leaned on the door frame, watching him.

He looked up and smiled at her; then, he crossed the room to stand before her. *"And fare thee weel, my only luve! And fare thee weel awhile! And I will come again, my luve, though it were ten thousand mile,"* he said softly. "Sleep weel, ma bonnie lass. I'll see thee when it's morn..." Ach, I'll say it again—I'm no' a poet." He smiled, kissed her gently, and then left the suite.

Chapter Forty-Three

LONG DISTANCE

After David left, Erin remembered to call Lily. She waited while the call connected on the hotel's landline. It rang for a very long time and then finally went to voicemail. She figured, since Lily didn't recognize the phone number, she wouldn't answer, so she left a simple message saying she'd try back in a few minutes. She waited about five minutes, called again, and that time Lily answered right away. "Erin?" she said.

Erin laughed. "I knew you wouldn't answer. My cell phone isn't working right now; I guess I'll have to get a temporary one to use while I'm here."

"I was worried to death about you! You sounded completely beside yourself when you called on Friday. You sound so much better now."

"I *was* gutted when I called you. I had just left my house and said goodbye to Todd. Lily, I left my wedding ring next to the bed—on my nightstand," she said and heard a gasp.

"Oh, Erin, I'm so sorry! I don't know how you did it—Oh, umm, that reminds me—I have a confession to make," she said, sounding guilty.

"Is that so?" Erin said, smiling.

"Yeah, Nick invited Todd over for supper tonight. I wish he would have talked to me first, but I wanted to let you know about it."

Erin had a bunch of feelings well up inside her at hearing the news. First, she was shocked Nick would do something like that, but she knew it was a good thing. Then, she was jealous he'd get to be there and she wouldn't. Finally, she felt sad, knowing Todd probably wasn't taking care of himself and wishing she could make it all better. "It's okay, I'm—"

"I promise not to talk about when you and David were here... or anything about you two."

"I believe you, Lil, no worries."

"Where are you staying; is it nice?" Lily asked, and Erin chuckled.

"You could say that; he put me up at the Ritz! In the Trafalgar Suite!" she said and heard Lily squee. She knew her best friend would know exactly what she was referring to.

"Wait, he put *you* up? Don't you mean *us*? Isn't he staying with you?"

"There were things I didn't think of when I packed up and left everything I knew... and that was one of them," she said. "He can't stay here, Lil., he's got a wife and home... if he stays here, people will talk. It sucks ass, but that's how it is for now. He leaves late and comes back early every morning, though, so it's not too bad."

"Yuck! Well, at least you're in England! That's something, isn't it?"

"Yeah, it's a big something," she said. "Oh! Speaking of big somethings! I almost forgot! Lily! I'm ... pregnant!" She heard another squee and then silence. "Lily? Are you there?"

"But, Erin! Is it... David's baby or Todd's—or do you know?" she asked, sounding worried.

"To be honest, I don't know a hundred percent, but I'm pretty sure it's David's. I'd say there's less than a five percent chance it's not. I've already told Todd it's not his, so please don't mention it, okay? We'll get a DNA test when it's born and deal with it then."

"Okay, I won't say anything. I can't believe it! I'm so happy for you! Oh, and tell David congrats for me. Do you have a doctor yet, and... wait... doesn't he already have a bunch of kids?"

"Oh, crap! I didn't think about a doctor! I have no clue how that works here. I'll have to ask David tomorrow. Thanks for bringing it up; I would have forgotten all about it. And yes, he has four kids. I doubt I'll get to meet them right away, but I hope I will soon... and... I hope they like me."

"They will *love* you, Erin; I just know they will! What's not to love? I want to be you when I grow up!" she said and laughed. "Wow, pregnant *and* in England, that's so exciting. Make sure to send me a postcard!"

"Shoot! I left my address book at home. Let me get a pen," she said. She found a pad of stationery with the hotel's rampant lion and crown logo and 'The Ritz London' printed in blue at the top, and a gold pen, so she wrote down Lily's address on it. "I'll send you as many as I can! It will be like Harry Potter's acceptance letters; they will be coming out of every opening in your house." They both laughed at the thought, and Erin yawned suddenly. "Lily, I should probably get going now, it's getting late here and I'm still adjusting to this time zone. I'm glad I got to talk to you!" she said sincerely.

"Yeah, me too! I'm glad everything is going well there!" Lily said. "Say hi to David for me—God, what a crazy thing to say, isn't it? Oh, and please call me sometimes! I am always glad to talk to you! I love you lots!"

"I love you too, Lily! Hug Ariana! Bye!" she said and hung up the phone. Tired and melancholy, she took off her nightgown and crawled into bed, longing for sleep to make time go faster.

Chapter Forty-Four

MONDAY GO TO MEETING

David woke on Monday morning with mixed emotions; he was both excited and nervous about the meeting. He got out of bed and did his usual morning routine, but he needed to be with Erin. She'd be able to calm him down and get him in the proper mindset.

The meeting was meant to start at one in the afternoon, so he had plenty of time to get over to the Ritz and have breakfast with her. He hoped she would help him choose a tie, and then maybe he'd be able to make love to her. The thought of making love to her helped him relax a bit and took his mind off his doubts and fears.

Taking a deep breath, he chanced a trip to his bedroom. Susannah was nowhere in sight, so he went into his closet to choose one of his suits. Once dressed, he grabbed a few of his favorite ties, laid his suit coat over his arm, and made a beeline to his study, thankful he didn't meet anyone on his way there.

He lifted his rarely used briefcase out from the cupboard, set it on his desk, and opened it. It was empty, save a gold pen and pencil set Susannah had given him for Christmas a few years back. He rolled the neckties up neatly and placed them inside. After making sure he wasn't forgetting anything, he opened the top drawer of his desk and saw his alligator tooth keyring. He'd bought one each for him and Erin whilst they were in New Orleans only three weeks earlier. Smiling at the memory, he placed it in his pocket as a good luck charm.

He ordered a car and sat in his high-backed desk chair, waiting. If he kept out of sight, he might be able to leave quickly when the car arrived. As he closed the briefcase, he looked around the room. How many times had he sat at his desk or on his leather couch, avoiding Susannah? Too many times.

Tuesday, while she was away, he would bring Erin there. He wanted her to see his sanctuary, his retreat, created so he could hide from the turmoil he thought the rest of his life would revolve around. *Soon it will all be over and done with—as soon as I have time to apply for a divorce.*

Forty-seven minutes later, David was dropped off at the Ritz and walking through the lobby toward the lift. He touched the number three button, and just as the door was closing, a woman walked up to it. He reluctantly caught the door as it was sliding shut and returned her smile with an indifferent smirk.

She stood too close and asked him to push the number two button while she smiled and flirted, trying to get his attention. He acted as though he were too interested in his mobile to talk to her. *Again, the nose cast does nothing to keep these insane women away!*

The lift stopped at the second floor, and she hesitated. "Would you care to—" she began.

"No, I wouldn't," he said, and she finally stepped out.

He made it to the Trafalgar Suite and opened the door, hearing a noise coming from the water closet to his right. As he approached the small room, he saw Erin clutching the toilet and heaving into it. "Oh, my darling!" he said and dropped his briefcase to crouch down beside her.

She flushed the toilet and sat on the cool tile floor. "I don't like morning sickness!" she said and gave him a weak smile. "You look so good; that suit is perfect on you." He helped her up, and she hugged him.

"Thank you, it's one of my favorites."

"Let me brush my teeth, and I'll be right out."

"A'right, love. I've brought several ties with me—I was hoping you'd help me decide?" he said as he walked out of the room. Since she had her toothbrush in her mouth, what he heard as a reply was a 'Mmm hmmm' noise, and he smiled. He was waiting for her in the bedroom, sitting at the small writing desk with his briefcase open, ready for her inspection as she came back from the bathroom.

"I've got to get something in my belly before I die!" she said over-dramatically, pretending to swoon with her arm over her forehead.

"As you wish."

She started getting dressed, "I wish I could go to the dining room in my PJs and robe like at a budget hotel," she lamented, but the Ritz had a strict dress code.

"We could order room service if you'd like?" he said as if reading her thoughts.

Erin stopped and turned around. "That would be perfect!" She told David what she wanted, and he made the call from the sitting room. When he returned, she was examining each beautiful tie as she laid them out on the end of the bed. She picked up three of them and put them back into the briefcase. "I don't like these at all."

He removed them and laid them on the desk. "I won't need these in the meeting."

"This one is nice," she said, holding up a red silk tie, pleated to make a striped pattern. "But this one is beautiful. I had hoped you'd bring the Monet *Poppies* tie, but this one is what I'd pick for you to wear today." She lifted the luxurious blue silk with an intricate design of vines, flowers, and birds.

"A'right, then, the Turnbull & Asser it is then." He wrapped it around his neck, though he didn't tie it just then, not knowing how long he'd be in his clothing once they'd finished their breakfast. He watched Erin as she chose what she'd wear. "What are yer plans for the day... whilst I'm gone?" he asked.

———

"No clue. Maybe I'll go to the Victoria and Albert Museum; it's free to get in, right?" *Oh shit! I shouldn't have said that.*

"I believe it is, though I was plannin' tae leave a few quid anaway."

She bit her tongue; she wasn't going to have the same discussion every time he offered her something, though it didn't help her feel any less like a kept woman. "Thank you. I can use it for the taxi."

"You can ask the concierge tae order a car and charge it to the room."

"I know, but maybe I want the experience of using a London taxi."

Just then, there was a knock on the door. David opened it, and a young man brought in a cart with their breakfast and a newspaper. David thanked him and gave him a tip as he left the suite.

Erin started eating her eggs, not wanting them to get cold, and David opened the paper. "Is there an entertainment section? Something with a crossword puzzle or movie showtimes?" she asked. He pulled the requested section out of the publication and handed it to her. "Good night nurse!" she gasped. "We're on the cover!"

He stood behind her and looked over her shoulder. Right on the top of page one was a small photo of them at Harrods and one of them walking into the Savoy to meet Martin. The headline read:

**"*Future Explorations* Heartthrob David
Elliott, Seen Around Town with
Unidentified Woman and Nose Job."**

"A good reminder that we must be careful whilst we're in town. How did they know it was me with this thing on my nose?" he said and kissed her temple before resuming his seat. "Here are the film times; did yeh fancy going to the cinema tonight?" he asked.

"No, I don't want to go anywhere now."

"A'right, love. I'm not keen to go out either."

When breakfast was finished David placed the trolley outside of the room. When he came back, he found Erin looking in the mirror and frowning. "Ach, yeh look bonnie today, ma love," he said. She smiled at his reflection as he came up behind her and put his arms around her middle. "What's on yer mind that has you lookin' at yerself that way? Is it the newspaper photo? Because if it is, you shouldn't worry; they always choose the worse pictures tae print, trust me!"

She closed her eyes. "Yeah, I know," she said and put her head down.

"Ach, what is it, then. I can't read yer mind, yeh ken." She tried to turn around, but he held her in place, looking at her through the mirror. "Go on."

"I suppose it's partly that—I wasn't going to say anything, but I'm worried about gaining a bunch of weight during this pregnancy." He opened his mouth, but she put her hand up. "No, please don't tell me how bonnie I'll be or that you don't care about it; the point is I care. I don't want to be fat for the rest of my life, and if I get much fatter than this, I'll be very unhappy," she said earnestly.

"A'right ma love, we'll just have tae do somethin' about it then. Though you must promise ye'll no' get too thin. I just—"

She smiled and cut in. "I don't think you need to worry about that, but I promise. Thank you. One other thing… I need an Ob-Gyn."

He looked at her, not understanding. "An… Ob… what?"

"A… shoot, what do you call them here? Midwife, is it?"

"Ach, aye, we'll do that soon, though I dinnae reckon you need one until you're three months along," he said, then turned her around and kissed her. He wanted to make love to her and started to feel her breasts through her top. "I think yer pure braw, ma darling."

There was no throwing clothing around that time; David's suit needed to look nice and crisp, so they each undressed and knelt in the middle of the bed, facing each other. They kissed and touched, becoming more and more aroused until she laid on the mattress and he joined her.

David heard a notification bell sound on his mobile but ignored it as he made love to her, slowly and tenderly. He gently thrust into her and then pulled almost all the way out, only to do it again. She could feel his length keenly and enjoyed the slow, calculated rhythm. Each move was on purpose and brought them both to an orgasm at the same time.

"That was… lovely, David," she said breathlessly, "Thank you. It was perfect!"

He'd been thinking the same thing. "Aye. No complaints over here."

"Did you hear your phone make a noise?"

"Aye. Et can wait," he said and held her as they began to relax once more. Eventually, he rolled over and lifted his phone off the nightstand. "Ach! The meeting has been moved tae nine o'clock!" He looked at the time on his mobile. "That leaves an hour—" he began and trailed off.

———

Erin sat up to watch him as he started dressing again. *He's amazing! Look at him—every line is attractive! How did you end up here with him, Erin? Or are you in a very elaborate dream?* she thought to herself. *I don't think I'd have morning sickness if I were dreaming!* She smiled and then realized he was watching her.

"What're you thinkin', hen?" he asked as he buttoned his dress shirt.

"I was admirin' yeh, love. Ye're the one who's pure braw now!" she said, trying out his accent.

"I'm glad ye're here! Yeh make me happy," he said with a laugh. "I dinnae ken how long this meeting will last, so I'll message you when et's over, a'right?"

"That would be great, except my phone isn't working, remember?"

"I do now. We should've bought one yesterday, love. I reckon it'll be a nice surprise when I return then, aye?"

"The nicest. If I get a chance, I'll stop somewhere and get one. I'll send you a message if I do, so make sure your sound is off," she said.

"Ach! I must leave *now*," he said, looking nervous. "A few quid for the mobile phone and anathin' else you fancy today." He handed her a thick stack of folded pound notes. "Wish me luck, darling!" He kissed her and grabbed his briefcase off the desk.

"Good Luck! You'll be awesome, as always. I love you."

"I love you as well, hen," he said and hurried to the door.

She opened it for him and then watched him for a moment as he walked down the hall, looking so good; the suit really was fantastic! She closed the door and looked at the fold of bills in her hand. Her mouth dropped open when she realized it totaled *at least* five hundred pounds. *And that's a few quid?*

Chapter Forty-Five

A DAY OUT IN LONDON

An hour after David left for the meeting, Erin was dressed and ready for a day out in London. She headed to the lobby and was about to ask the concierge to order her a car, but then she changed her mind and decided to walk instead. The weather was beautiful as she stepped outside; the sun was out, and she needed some fresh air anyway.

She crossed Piccadilly and walked a few blocks to Clarges Street. Then, she went a few more blocks until she came to a Tesco and went inside. A new cell phone would have used up all her money, so she settled for a used Huawei, which was good enough for her. Half an hour later, the phone was working, and she sent a message to David, telling him her new mobile number.

With no particular direction in mind, she started walking and ended up on Carnaby Street, where she found some great shops. She bought a few things but didn't find much that fit her; UK sizes seemed to run small. She grabbed a sausage roll at a Greggs for lunch, and when she was tired of shopping, she hailed a taxi to take her back to the Ritz.

Halfway there, she received a message from David saying he was headed back to the room as well. She made it back before him and laid out all the things she'd bought on the bed. It was nice to go shopping without worrying, but she wouldn't ever enjoy paying the prices places like Harrods charged. She'd gotten some really nice things for a fraction of the price and was happy to say that even after buying a phone, she still had over a hundred quid in her pockets.

She laid the remaining money on the desk and heard David come into the suite. He looked tired but smiled brightly when he saw her. "Hello love, how was your day?" he asked as he took off his tie and made his way to her, then he took her into his arms and kissed her passionately.

She was so glad he was back as she returned his kisses. "It was nice! I got a phone at Tesco and wandered around for a bit, doing some shopping," She waved her arm in true '*Price is Right* girl' fashion, bringing his attention to the loot on the bed. "I'm tuckered out!"

"I wish I could've gone with you! The meeting was exciting, but some parts dragged on, and in the end, I'm puggled!"

"Puggled? That's a new one for me."

"Done in, knackered, cream-crackered, dead on ma feet, and so on," he said with a smile and then started taking off his suit, hanging it up as he went.

Erin removed her loot from the bed and pulled down the duvet. "I think we both need a nap; then we can have lunch, and you can tell me all the interesting stuff, okay?" she said as she began taking off her clothes and laying them neatly over the desk chair.

"Ach, that sounds lovely," he said. They finished undressing and climbed into bed, spooning until they both fell asleep.

———

David woke forty-five minutes later and lay watching Erin sleep until he could take it no longer. She was on her back, and he gently pulled the covers down, revealing her full, soft breasts. He cupped the one closest to him, taking it into his mouth, and used his tongue to harden her nipple.

When she started breathing heavily, he removed his hand from her breast and knelt beside her as he began exploring her body. She gasped as his hand made its way between her legs and moaned when he placed his first two fingers into her. "Oh, David! Make love to me!" she exclaimed.

"Don't yeh want more foreplay?" he asked.

"No! I want you to make love to me now!" she said desperately.

"A'right," he said, happy to oblige, and got on top of her. As he entered her, he was surprised to feel her climax almost immediately. He continued slowly, allowing her to get ready to do it again.

"I was dreaming we were making love at the Tesco," she said, "against the mobile phone counter. No one seemed to care, except this old man who was watching us and commenting like a sports announcer." She laughed at the memory. "I ignored him, but that's when you woke me—just as I was about to climax in the dream."

He liked the thought of her having sex dreams about him and started thrusting a bit faster. It didn't take long for them both to be taken over the edge, moaning and breathing hard, until all was still again.

"Holy Moses, David, that's so good! I can't tell you how thankful I am to have you!"

"You could try," he teased.

"I'm *SOOO* thankful. There ya go," she said with a laugh. They laid in the bed, relaxed and glad they had nowhere else to be. "So, tell me, how did it go, and when do you start filming?"

"Et went well. They were shocked tae see the nose splint, but I explained it would all be off this week. From then on, they ignored et. That reminds me, I've an appointment tae have it removed tomorrow mornin', which is perfect as I have somewhere tae show yeh at noon," he said.

"Well, good… about the splint, I mean. I imagine you're not gonna tell me where you'll be taking me?" she said. He shook his head and pretended to lock an imaginary padlock onto his lips. "I thought not. How about supper? Are you willing to discuss that?"

"I've heard good reviews for a restaurant that's meant tae be a lot of fun; I've wanted tae try et for quite some time, but it's not—I haven't had anaone tae join me… no one who would… enjoy it. Why don't we give it a go?"

"And you think I would be up for a lot of fun, do you?"

"Aye," he said and gave her his best smile.

"Since it's the last day you'll have your disguise… Okay, you talked me into it. Now tell me more about the meeting." They got out of bed and began getting dressed.

"Filmin' is set tae start sometime in September or early October and is expect tae run into July of next year. There will be wardrobe fittings and the like sometime in August, I imagine."

"Wow, that long?" she said. "Then I suppose it will all start back up again in September?"

"Aye, that would seem the way of et."

"Oh, I—well, we'd better go. I'll just check my hair, and—" she began haltingly and hurried to the bathroom.

"Erin?" he said with a soft tap on the door, a bit flummoxed at her sudden flight.

"I'll be out in a moment," she said brightly. A few minutes later she opened the door and picked up her purse. "Ready? All I had for lunch was a sau—"

"Are you… a'right? Yeh seem… upset and—"

"I don't want to talk about it now, David. Let's just have a lovely afternoon together," she said and kissed his cheek.

He knew something was bothering her but didn't want to upset her by needling, so he decided to let it go for the moment.

David and Erin walked along Piccadilly, past the old pale-stone buildings, acting as though they were a normal pair of tourists. They were careful not to stand too close or reveal their true relationship. As they progressed through Leicester Square, David tried to keep his head down and wore a pair of cheap sunglasses, attempting to blend in, hoping no one would recognize him.

The buildings became increasingly less grand, except when they came to the Covent Garden underground station. Across the street was a building covered in plants growing out of the walls. "That's amazing!" Erin said and talked David into taking a selfie in front of it.

Finally, they got to Drury Lane, and she squeed, which caught David off guard. "What was that about? Or do I want to know?" he asked.

"Well, do you?" she said cryptically.

"Do I… what, exactly?"

"Aw, come on! You know this, don't you?"

"I reckon I don't," he said with mock long-suffering.

"You're no fun. Fine—Do you know the muffin man who lives on Drury Lane?" She laughed as he rolled his eyes, then she started humming the tune of the old song.

"Ach, ye're a handful," he said and then pointed to the entrance to the restaurant. The sign read, *Sarastro Restaurant—the show after the show*, and had a scene painted on it that she thought looked like a naked woman with her hand between the legs of a naked man, though she couldn't be sure.

They walked into a magical place covered with art and tapestries that looked like the backstage or prop-room in a theater. The lights were low, and since it was both early and Monday night, it was quiet, except for the lovely music playing in the background. They were seated at a cozy, fabric-covered, private table, though they could still see most of the main floor.

"I need the little girls' room," Erin said, "I'll be right back." Five minutes later, she returned, wide-eyed. "Good night nurse, David! The bathroom walls are covered—painted with pornography! No subtlety, caricature, or innuendos—It's full-on, graphic sex, both oral and the usual kind!"

"Well, I think perhaps I should—" he began, but seeing her honest shock over what she'd witnessed, he stopped. "Was it that bad?"

"It wasn't exactly bad, just unexpected and shocking. There are things I can't unsee, you know?"

David took her hand and kissed it. "Mebbe you can describe it to me when we return to our room, eh?" he said with a wicked grin. "Oh, and I've taken the liberty tae order a pre-set menu; three courses, so I hope ye're hungry."

"Famished."

Chapter Forty-Six

FORGOTTEN LINES

David and Erin were about halfway through the main course, and the dining room was beginning to fill up when a man sat at the piano and began to play. Erin had just informed David that she was officially in love with the chicken dish when there was a commotion by the door. She gasped when she saw Barry (Baz) Thompson, the actor who had played Joe Whitehall in *Future Explorations*.

In stark contrast to how David tried entering a room, Baz and his husband, Vincent, who was a famous underwear model, made a grand entrance. He soaked up the limelight instead of shying away from it. She looked at David and smiled, "Can we… invite them to our table?"

He looked apprehensively at the crowd of potential onlookers, "I dinnae ken, Erin—" he began, but Baz had already spotted him.

He threw up his arms flamboyantly, like the father of the prodigal son welcoming him home. "Why, David! What a fantastic surprise to see you here!" he almost sang as he dodged the large center table and led Vincent toward them.

David stood and accepted the greeting of a kiss on both cheeks. "Baz! It is good to see you again. Please join us. My friend, Erin, is a fan of yours, aren't you?" he said to her.

She couldn't help but blush, "Oh, yes… uh… Mr.—I mean, Barry," she fumbled, presuming he also preferred his given name to his surname, as David did.

"What a lovely creature you are, too! I feel as though I've seen you somewhere before. Doesn't matter—We'll be fast friends before the night is through, I'm sure of it."

"I'm sure of it as well," David said. "Erin, as you already know, this is Baz Thompson."

"It's a real joy to meet you. Kind of ironic, isn't it?" Erin said and accepted a kiss on either cheek.

"Yes, that is just what it is, my dear. Oh, dear me, where are my manners? You simply must meet my eye candy… oh… that's not right, is it? What I meant to say is my trophy husband, Vincent."

Swept away by Barry's energy, she laughed as she received a kiss on both cheeks from Vincent, the tall, olive-skinned specimen of a man with a tousle of black, shiny ringlets, who was sliding onto the bench-seat next to her. However, before she could say anything, Baz was talking a mile per minute again.

"My dear man, whatever happened to that perfect nose of yours! If you have had it altered out of a deep-seated vanity which you've hidden from us all, I'll—I'll be terribly disappointed in you," he exclaimed passionately.

David couldn't help but laugh. "I've missed you, my friend. Unfortunately, I had a run-in with…" he leaned in and whispered, "…a jealous husband's fist."

Erin wasn't expecting him to say it like that and laughed a bit too loudly. She covered her mouth and opened her eyes wide, shocked at her reaction. "Oh, sorry, but that was funny."

"Yes, it was," Vincent said with a thick accent that sounded both French and Spanish to her.

"Ooh! Where are you from? Your accent is delicious!" she blurted out and then wished she hadn't since she figured it made her sound far too American. "I'm sorry… I—"

"Do not apologize, Erin. I am from Andorra," he said, his accent making her melt.

"Andorra? Good night nurse, I'm ignorant. I've never heard of it. What country is it in?

Baz laughed good-naturedly. "I'm afraid no one knows where it is, love. He's quite an exotic specimen, our Vincent. Go on, my darling, show her," he said and turned to David. "He has the most remarkable way of—Well, go on, then."

Vincent smiled at his partner and then held up his left hand with his fingers tucked down, palm facing them. "We are our own. This is France," he said. He then put his right hand, fingers down and palm facing away, off-center, just below his wrist. "This is *Espain*—Do you see?"

Honestly, she didn't know exactly what France or Spain looked like, but she nodded, smiling brightly. "Sure."

He wiggled the ring finger on his right hand. "*Aquí!*" he said, sounding proud of himself. "Not France, not *Espain*; Andorra."

"The next time I am near a map, I'll try to find it, I promise. You are not going to believe me, but that's just how I describe where I live," Erin said.

"Is this so?" he said and raised his eyebrows at Baz as if to say, 'I told you so.' "Then please show to me, where are you living? *Perdoni'm*; how do you say—"

"Please show me where you live; that's how you say it. I live in Wisconsin. She held her right hand out on its side, palm facing them, fingers together, and thumb up. "I usually don't have to show the whole country, but I'll try. This is America… sort-of. She showed him New York on her thumb and then moved toward the knuckle of her first finger. "This is where Wisconsin is in America." She then held up her left hand, upright, palm away, and thumb slightly out. "This is Wisconsin. I live in the crotch of the state," she said and pointed at the place where the base of her thumb met her hand. "It's called Green Bay."

It was David's turn to laugh out loud. "Aye, I reckon that about sums it up," he said, dropping the RP accent he had been using.

"Packers!" Baz said, and Erin's mouth hung open in surprise. "Don't know what it means, though I've heard the term before."

"American football. That's just amazing," she said to Barry and then looked back at Vincent, blushing and smiling.

He surprised her by grasping her face with his hands; he leaned in to kiss her on the lips, then kissed her forehead. Looking her in the eyes and still holding her face, he said, "*Moltes gràcies,* my dear friend!"

Erin was stunned, and her blush deepened. She was about to respond when they heard a chant rising from the tables surrounding them. It sounded like '*John Thomas Fife,*' though Erin thought she heard a few people saying, '*Joe Whitehall!*'

David and Baz looked at each other. "I've no clue what they want," David said.

"I have a guess," Baz said. Just then, a waiter approached the table. "We'll have the set menu; two courses—you choose whichever is the best tonight, and two dry martinis, one with olives and one with onions, please," he said over the crowd.

"Yes, sir," The waiter said and then leaned in close. "I've been asked— The people—Our patrons would like for you to reenact the scene in which you meet in *Future Explorations.* My staff and I have already told them—"

"Ah-ha! We'd love to!" Baz said, loudly, without asking David first.

"Woah! Wait one minute, Baz! I don't remember—That was over fifteen years ago—"

"Eighteen, since it was filmed, darling," Baz corrected him. "It'll all come back to you, don't fret!" he said and stood, expecting David to follow his lead. When he didn't, he took him by the arm and pulled.

David gave Erin a panicked look for a split second, and then replaced it with his beautiful smile. "I'll help you," she said quietly.

Baz whispered something into David's ear and pointed to a short set of stairs next to them that led to balcony seating. David pretended to be okay with the plan, though Erin knew he wasn't... at all. Barry leapt up the stairs, lithely, and waited for David to stand at the bottom with his hand shielding his eyes.

The people at the tables were going wild, whooping, shouting, and clapping in rhythm with their chant. Erin heard all kinds of comments, though most of them had to do with David's nose. As soon as David took his spot, they applauded, and then the room became perfectly quiet as he put his hand up to his forehead.

"Hello!" Baz began, and Erin smiled when he 'stumbled' down the steps and took hold of David's trouser leg. "My name is Joe Whitehall, and I'm from the future—" He looked around, and someone handed him a saltshaker which he held up and then gave to David. "This device will allow you to time travel; all you need do is touch it and think of being someplace else in time. You can't choose where or when you'll go, but there's always a task for you to fulfill when you get there."

David's eyes were wide; it was plain to see that he couldn't remember his lines. "Le' me help ye intae ma home," Erin whispered, and he repeated it. He reached down to help Baz up, but he shook his head and lay in repose against the first few steps, clutching his side.

"No, it's too late for me. What's your name?" he asked.

David stalled, crouching beside the actor whom he couldn't believe remembered all his lines. "Ma name's John Thomas—" It was gone; he couldn't remember any of it. Finally, after a few moments, the whole room began saying his lines for him.

"...of Fife. Ah dinnae understand what yer tellin' me!" they said collectively; even Erin joined in.

"Just do good and help people," Baz said, and then pretended to die.

David looked at the saltshaker in his hand, but the crowd didn't wait for him; they all said in unison, "Joe? Joe—What'm ah supposed tae do wi' thes?"

The room exploded with laughter, applause, and a few loud whistles. Baz stood and hugged David, then he took his hand and bowed grandly, pulling David along with him. "Thank you, everyone! What a joy to perform such a beloved scene for you this evening. Thank you for your applause; have a lovely night," he said and returned to their seat, where his drink and appetizers were waiting.

Erin noticed that David's face looked more pale than usual and noticed a few beads of sweat on his forehead when he set the saltshaker on the table. "That was amazing! I'll never forget it, as long as I live," she said, wishing she could hold his hand.

"Yes, Bazzy, you have made your husband proud tonight!" Vincent said with an adoring smile.

"Aye, *Bazzy*," David said mockingly, dabbing his face with his napkin, "*you* were brilliant, whereas I was most assuredly *not*! How is it you remembered every word?"

"I, my friend, have no shame and watch the blessed thing at least once per annum. I am not embarrassed to say that I have a party to celebrate it. I must say, David, that I'm rather put out you've not joined us, actually. Each year I send the invitation, and each year the RSVP comes back with your regrets. Are you ashamed of the very thing which has made us both a household name?"

"I'm sorry, Barry, but I was never made aware of the invitation. I'm afraid—I reckon ma wife wasn't keen to attend—" He trailed off and looked at his plate.

"It must be lots of fun," Erin said, trying to alleviate the mood. "Sounds like just the place I'd be dying to be invited to. I guess some people don't have any taste, do they, David?"

He lifted his head and smiled warmly at her. "Aye, ma love, I reckon they do not. In the future, please send an email to me and don't bother with the Royal Mail, a'right?"

"Oh, it is very much fun, Erin. I am believing that you would most definitely be loving it," Vincent said and took her hand in his. "You will be my very especial guest to honor this year. You will be a queen for me and my Bazzy, is this good? Are you understanding? *Perdoni'm* as my English is not so good; this is why I am not often speaking."

"There is nothing to pardon, Vincent. I wouldn't want you to speak any differently. I would be honored to be your especial guest of honor, but only if David comes with me; deal?" she said and smiled at David, looking for confirmation.

"Wouldn't miss et," he said as their dessert arrived at the table.

"Holy Moses! This looks so good, but I'm stuffed! I'll try to make room—"

"Take it with you, my dear. No need to make yourself sick, after all," Baz said and held his hand up to get the attention of the waiter.

They spent the evening laughing and lost all sense of time. David and Baz signed quite a few autographs, including one for the restaurant. They promised to keep in touch from that point forward and even exchanged mobile numbers with Erin.

As she stood to say her farewells to Vincent, Erin heard Baz say to David, "I've no clue where you've found her, mate, but I'd suggest you keep her. She seems the very thing you need to keep you… in the real world. I'm the last one to talk about staying there, I know. Just don't be a tosser and fuck it up, alright? Oh, and do rid yourself of *Susannnaahhhh,*" he said, exaggerating her name comically.

"That's the plan, mate," she heard David respond.

Chapter Forty-Seven

THE EYES HAVE IT

As they left the restaurant, Erin turned to David and smiled. "That was so much fun! I assume you can't do things like this very often, though, can you?"

"Et's doable now, barring a chance meeting with Barry Thompson, though I'm not sure what the future holds once *Doctor Who* airs," he said, and Erin laughed. "What?"

"Sorry… never mind," she said. He gave her a look, telling her to spit it out, so she rolled her eyes and blushed, "I'm sorry, you just said something about the future, and I went all fangirl about it."

"Ach, I see. I do use the word occasionally, just as everaone else does."

"I know, and I'm sorry. I feel stupid," she said.

"Et's a'right, I understand. Listen—I have an idea; follow me." He took his phone out of his slacks, and after a few moments typing and swiping, he started walking.

The buildings surrounding them were made from red bricks, and there were a lot of one-way streets. Out of nowhere, the buildings changed to a light-colored brick, and many of them had lovely storefronts made from painted wood. Each time they found themselves alone, he took her hand and even managed to kiss her twice.

On Wellington Street, the buildings changed again to grey stone façades. The Lyceum Theater was grand, looking like something transposed out of Rome, and Somerset House seemed unreal, sitting on the banks of the

Thames. "Oh, David! Look at that! There's the London Eye!" Erin said excitedly.

"Aye," David said, allowing her to fangirl over the city for a while.

They got off Waterloo Bridge and followed the river past a building with graffiti painted throughout the entire lower level, then walked under two bridges. "When I was here… before, I didn't see any of this. We were in Notting Hill, and I didn't get to see any real tourist spots. I bet there are things all around me that I'd recognize if only I… well, knew they were there," she said and laughed.

"I reckon you would," he said. "Scotland Yard and 10 Downing Street are just over the river, but I'll point everything out for you," he said as they approached the London Eye and bypassed the long line of people waiting to board. He showed his phone to the attendant in the fast-track booth, and after a few stops and starts of the giant Ferris Wheel, they were led to an empty car.

"Really?" Erin said in amazement.

"Really." The car began to move, and he pointed out landmarks, ignoring the fact that she was staring at him. "And there are the Houses of Parliament and… Westminster Abby—What is it?" he said, turning to her.

"You are simply amazing. Who else could touch a few buttons on his phone and manage something like this? If you're trying to impress me, it's working."

I wouldn't say it's to impress you as much as to entertain you, darling. Et's nice tae be with someone who enjoys the same things as I do, yeh ken? I've been keen tae do this for years, but et's no' as though I can just join the queue and hop on like everyone else. I'm countin' on this plaster for anonymity; this is as much for me as it is for you, now kiss me and let's enjoy the views before et's over, a'right?"

Half an hour later, they stepped off the car and almost forgot to keep their distance. A woman approached them asking for an autograph, and thankfully she seemed to ignore Erin. They only had to stop twice more for autographs and selfies as they walked to the road where David hailed a taxi to take them back to the Ritz.

When they got back to the room, Erin sat on the sofa, and David sat beside her. He lifted her blouse and placed his hand on her soft, smooth belly. "Have you sussed out your due date yet?" he asked.

"I think it'll be mid-March. I looked it up on a website that calculated it for me."

David gently rubbed her stomach. "Have you thought of any… names… yet?" he asked timidly. He didn't want to seem like he wanted to tell her what to name it, so he was treading lightly.

"Aye, I like how your children have simple, classic names. I was thinking Henry or Olivia, or something similarly British."

David looked at her and knit his brows. Then he nodded having figured it out. "Ach, I see, you've looked up my full profile online some—"

"What? No—" she said, sounding shocked. "Well, not in years, and the only thing I remember from it is your birthday for some strange reason. Why do you say that?"

"Ma father's brother's name was Henry, and ma mother's sister's name was Olivia; they were twins," he said, and Erin's eyes grew wide.

"Twins? Your mom is a twin? So… then, twins run in your family… oh crap! Charlie and Daniel are twins, aren't they? Good night nurse!"

David bit his lower lip. "Actually, ma mum… *and* da' were… both… twins. They married each other's brother and sister," he said tentatively, not wanting her to freak out, but she sat up.

"Are you kidding? That's just… well, it's really cool, and I'd love to hear the story someday, but… Holy Moses, David! What if we're having twins?" she said and laid back, staring at the ceiling.

"I dinnae think it works that way, darling, but dinnae fash, we can handle et!" he said, trying to reassure her.

She sat up again and looked at him, panicked. "We? You say that as if *you* will *also* be carrying two babies inside your body. I'm terrified of carrying one, but if it's two—" she said and stood. She started pacing and placed her hand over her heart.

"Ye're right, I'm sorry. I was thinkin' about after they're born," he said and then shook his head. "Wait, we dinnae ken that et's twins, so let's no' get worked up over it quite yet."

"True. It's just so scary, all of it!"

David came and stood beside her, kissing her head. "I'll be here for you; I'll help yeh all I can," he said softly.

"But how is this going to work? Am I gonna stay here the whole time? My due date is at least eight months away, and I'm only allowed to stay in the UK for *six* months with my passport. That means I'll have to go back at least once before then. Also, you'll be filming for some of the second trimester and all of the third, she said, sounding panicked.

"We'll stay in Cardiff, even if I have tae buy a house there. I'm sure Wales has some lovely midwives. Don't worry, love."

Erin smiled, "I'm sure they do, and I know you're right; it will be fine."

He put his hand on her belly again and kissed her.

At the end of the night, it was just as difficult to say goodbye as it had been every time. Erin tried not to think about him going home, where his beautiful wife was, but that was also getting harder to do each night.

Chapter Forty-Eight

DAVID'S HOUSE

In the morning, David was much later than usual. When he finally arrived, the splint was off, and Erin could see his handsome face again. "Oh, David! I'd forgotten how utterly beautiful you are under that thing! Come here," she said. He stepped up to her, and she gently touched his nose, sliding her pointer finger from the bridge to the tip. "I could just eat you up!" she said and kissed him, lightly biting his bottom lip, which made him laugh.

"It feels fantastic tae have the ruddy thing off finally. Are you ready tae go? We have only a short window of time," he said, and she narrowed her eyes at him.

"I could be ready in under ten minutes," she said. He stepped back from her and waved his hands to shoo her away.

"Go on then; tick-tock, tick-tock," he said, pointing to his wristwatch.

Ten minutes later, they stepped out the door of the hotel and into a hired car. David gave the address to the driver, and they were on their way through the crowded streets of London. After about thirty minutes, they were let out in front of some wide, very smart-looking townhomes. He waited until the driver turned the corner, then walked up the block, a few doors away.

"Here we are, home sweet home," he said, and Erin eyed him warily.

"You're sure there's no one home? I don't want to run into your wife."

"Dinnae fash; Susannah is at a women's luncheon. She's the secretary, so she'll no' miss et, and the staff will be out doing what they do when she's away," he said as he unlocked the door.

"Staff?" she said, feeling a bit overwhelmed. "You mean, like butlers and maids and all of that?"

David laughed as he turned the knob and the heavy wooden door swung open. "No, we have Kitty, who's the general housekeeper, and tends to be a bit flighty; then there's Francie, who looks after the kitchen, mainly."

They stepped in and Erin gasped audibly. The entrance hall was so grand; the wooden paneling had been painted white and made the room look much larger than it was. The furnishings were elegant, and there wasn't a speck of dust in the whole of it. "Good night nurse!" she said under her breath as she was led through the house and into a very clean and sparse kitchen which she privately thought was the ugliest room she may have ever seen.

"No muttering under yer breath for this room?" he said, and Erin blushed.

"It's… not my taste, I guess."

"Nor mine, love, but I wouldn't say that tae anaone but you," he said with a smile. He led her into a dining room that could seat at least fifty people easily. The tour of the first floor continued with the sitting room, sunroom, laundry room, and then back to the hallway where they came to a closed door. "This is what I've brought you here tae see," he said with suppressed excitement. He opened the door and allowed Erin to walk through first.

She instantly loved the room. It was so much like David, somehow capturing his personality perfectly. "Oh! This is lovely!" She walked to the wall that was covered from floor to ceiling with shelves and gently touched the things that caught her attention. There were huge conch shells, an old, twisted, rusty key, and framed photos of David with his kids and parents, as well as with a few actors she recognized. "This is the room where Daniel took the selfie, isn't it?" she asked, looking at the tan leather couch.

"Ach! I'd forgotten about that," he said as embarrassment colored his cheeks. "Again, I'm truly sorry about the whole thing," he said.

"It's alright, David. The photo is really nice," she said as she looked at all the interesting things on the shelves. She spotted his *Future Explorations* memorabilia and smiled; she recognized all the items, named them, and referred to when they were used in the show. Her eyes grew wide when she saw the time travel device and gawped at him.

"Go on, pick it up," he said. "We had five of those on set. I was given that one at the wrap party." She lifted it gingerly, and he laughed. "Ach, et's indestructible; no need for kid gloves, darling."

"This is so amazing! I can't believe I'm holding this in my hand, and I can't believe I get to hold you in my arms!" She put the time traveler down and went to stand in front of him. "I love this room!"

"So do I, and I'm glad ye've gotten to see it before et's gone," he said, sadly.

She looked at him, shocked. "What do you mean?"

"Right, well, we'll likely sell the house… in the divorce, now, won't we?" he said and quickly changed the subject. "Allow me tae show yeh somethin' else." He took her hand and led her out of the room, then up the stairs to the second floor like a small child, wanting to show his new friend how cool his room was. They stopped at a closed door, and he opened it; then he pulled her inside and closed the door behind them. The room was unremarkable, except for the expensive-looking furniture and drapes.

"Is this—"

"This is—"

They said in unison and laughed. "Aye. This is the room I've been relegated to since I came home with the news that I'd been tricked into signin' up for the Registry," he said. "This is where I've lain every night we've been apart, thinking about yeh and wishing so badly you were here." He stood in front of her, looking down at her face, and brushed a stray hair behind her ears.

"I have ached for you in this room, Erin. I've woken after dreams of you in ma arms, only tae realize, that in fact, I was alone, and it would still be a week or more until I'd see you again. I'm no' ashamed tae say I've wet the pillow with tears because of et. But here you are, hen, and I want—"

Erin didn't need to hear what he wanted; she already knew. She took off her sweater and lay it on a chair. "Take your clothes off," she said as she undressed herself. She pulled down the duvet and lay on the bed, waiting for him to join her.

He stood next to the bed looking at her. "Ma Losh, yeh look lovely in there," he said. "I'd like tae tie you up and make yeh stay." He smiled and then laughed at the look on her face. "I wasn't serious, but now et's out there—" He lifted one of her hands above her head and then added the other one, pinning her down as he climbed on top of her.

She decided to play along and acted as though she were struggling. "What are you doing?" she said, sounding utterly innocent. Wait… I don't think we should—" she said, interrupted by him putting a finger to her lips and then his hand over her mouth.

She squirmed and writhed, half-heartedly trying to get away, and each time she did, he advanced a little bit more, determined to take her. The next time she tried to protest, he simply kissed her at the same time he entered her, causing her to gasp and cry out, even with his mouth over hers.

He stopped and let her hands go. "Are yeh okay? That sounded like genuine pain; did I hurt you?" he asked.

She acted as though she were going to sit up, and he started to roll off her, but she took the opportunity to roll on top of him and laughed as she took hold of *his* hands and lifted them over *his* head. She sat on him, putting him back inside her. "If you don't struggle, things will go much more smoothly," she said, sounding calm and calculated. "Just relax, pet, and it will all be over before you know it." She leaned down and bit his shoulder, only to the point that he said 'ouch,' and then stopped. She put her hand on his belly and rocked back and forth until they were both moaning.

At the last second, he rolled her back over, mounting her once more. "Ach, yeh wee kelpie, ye'll no be takin' me like tha!" he said. Her body moved with his as he thrusted, dominating, and making her cry out as she climaxed. His arms broke out in goosebumps when he released inside of her, pulsing as he slid in and out a few more times. He kissed her as they lay together, breathing heavily with their eyes closed.

"Oh! That was so good, David!" she said after he rolled onto his back.

"Aye!" he said and then put his hand on his shoulder. "Wait! You bit me!" He looked down, and sure enough, there were little red welts in the shape of a set of teeth.

Erin laughed and kissed it. "Did it hurt?" she asked in a mock motherly tone.

"Aye, it hurt an awful lot!" he said pathetically.

They lay in each other's arms, enjoying the peace and sanctuary the room offered them. "We really should be going now; I don't know when people will be returning," David said. "This has been pure barry, Erin! Thank you."

Erin was drifting in and out of sleep. "Welcome," she whispered, and David laughed.

"Come now, love," he said and got out of bed.

She groaned and stretched out on the luxurious sheets which were so soft and comfortable she wanted to sleep. Nevertheless, she reluctantly rolled over and swung her legs off the edge of the mattress instead, knowing that would be too dangerous. They both got dressed and tried to make the bed look like it hadn't been used. Finally, David packed some clothes into a small travel bag, and they walked downstairs, hand in hand.

Erin's purse was in his office, so they went back in to retrieve it. "I really do love it in here," she said while he ordered a car on his mobile. She scanned the room, trying to memorize everything about it. "I hope you'll be able to find something like it when you move." She picked up her handbag from the desk, and they walked out to the entryway.

Just as they were about to open the front door, they heard a key in the lock, and then the doorknob turned. A sweet, rich soprano voice filled the room with a song Erin knew by heart. *Thinking Out Loud*, by Ed Sheeran. She smiled at David, figuring it wasn't Susannah. The door swung open, and a tall, slim woman of about thirty walked in.

She jumped, and her dark-brown eyes widened when she saw David and a strange woman standing in front of her. Her hand self-consciously went up to her short, brown hair to make sure it was tidy. "Bless me... Mister Elliott, sir! I forgot you said you'd be 'ere today! You sure gave me a fright!" She then looked at Erin and said, "'Ellow, ma'am."

Erin smiled, loving her accent, and took a liking to her instantly. "Hello, I'm—" She looked at David to see if she should give her name to the girl.

"Kitty, this is my friend, Erin. We were just on our way out, so we won't keep you," he said, using his posh RP accent.

Erin thought Kitty looked disappointed; it seemed like she would have liked to chat with her or something. "It's nice to meet you, Kitty," she said, meaning it wholeheartedly. "And by the way, you have the most beautiful singing voice! I *love* that song!"

Kitty was beaming as she smiled. "Thank you, ma'am. It's too bad we can't 'ave a chin wag, ain't it?" she said sweetly.

"It *is* too bad, Kitty; I think your accent is delicious. Maybe we'll get a chance someday," she said, also disappointed they couldn't sit and talk. She reached out and took hold of Kitty's hand, squeezing it, "I think we'd be fast friends."

Kitty squeezed Erin's hand in return. "I—I like yours as well, and I fink you're right, ma'am."

David stepped to the door, and Erin followed, sadly. "Bye, Kitty," she said.

"Goodbye," Kitty replied.

Once the door closed, Erin stared at him. "What?" he said, "Why are you glaring at me?"

"You said she was flighty. She didn't seem that way to me."

"Ach, well, yeh haven't known her verra long, have you? She becomes flustered and upset quite often. I feel for her, though; she may be out of a job soon," he said.

Erin froze, staring at him again. "Out of a job? You're not going to fire her, are you?" she asked, feeling shocked.

"I dinnae ken yet, love. I reckon it will depend on what happens in the divorce. She may wish tae stay on with Susannah, or perhaps remain with the new owners of the house if they're keen tae hire her."

Erin knit her brows together. "Couldn't you keep her... I mean... for wherever you move to?" she asked, trying to find a solution.

"Wherever *we* move, Erin. You speak as though I'm the only one makin' the decisions. You've a say in everathin' we do as well, yeh ken?"

"I—I guess so," she said. "I have a hard time thinking that way. I can't imagine living in a house with staff and... well, you. Okay then, if that's the case, I want to keep Kitty on, no matter where we end up living," she said boldly, "If it's okay with you," she added more gently, and David laughed.

"Aye, if that's what you want, ma dear, then you shall have et," he said. The car was waiting at the end of the block, so they got in. "I want tae take you somewhere tonight," he said as he typed something into his mobile.

"Ah, okay, where?" she asked, not actually expecting an answer though imagining it would be another interesting restaurant.

"Scotland," he said simply and smiled at her.

"Scotland! Tonight! Really? Ach aye, Ah'd love tae go tae Scotland wi' yeh, laddie!" she said and started laughing at her poor attempt to mimic a Scottish accent.

Chapter Forty-Nine

A TRIP TO SCOTLAND

Twenty minutes later, David and Erin were back in their hotel room at the Ritz, and Erin was packing. She was sad to leave the beautiful rooms and took out her new phone to take a few photos. "So, what are we going to do in Scotland?" she asked.

"There's… someone I want you tae meet," David said as they made their way to the lobby.

"And who might that be?"

"Ach, I… want you tae meet ma… mother." There was a chance his mum wouldn't approve of him bringing Erin to meet her, but he needed to know what she thought of her. His mum and Susannah had absolutely nothing in common, and it had been made perfectly clear to him, many times over, that she considered his wife too posh. Erin, however, was a completely different creature, and he thought his mum and her would get on well. For some reason, that meant a lot to him.

"Your mother?" she exclaimed in the elevators and then lowered her voice. "You think that's a good idea? I mean… technically, I'm your lover, and she might disapprove of me. First impressions are important, you know?"

The elevator door opened, and they walked through the elegant circular lobby, where Erin found a seat and David checked out, pulling her bags to the counter with him. He then approached the concierge, and the impeccably dressed man ordered him a car. They kept their distance while they waited in the lobby, and when the car arrived, the flawless man stepped up to him.

—

David stepped outside, and Erin stood, pretending to admire the nearest floral arrangement. When a few moments had passed, she took one more look around at the opulent luxury surrounding her and then left. The driver was holding the door as she slipped into the waiting car next to David.

"I reckon she'll—No, actually… I *know* she'll love you! Ye'll be thick as thieves before we leave," he said, continuing where they'd left the conversation since they were alone again. "I was thinkin' of stayin' for a night or two at her home, in Duddingston. We can visit ma old haunts and sleep in *my* childhood bedroom this time. Though you needn't worry, I'll make sure she doesn't get drunk and nearly walk in on us."

He laughed, and she groaned. "I would love to meet your mother, really; I only hope she's okay with me," she said as the car made its way through the heavy London traffic.

The hired car drove them to London City Airport, and they flew to Edinburgh in only one hour and twenty minutes. While they waited for Erin's luggage, she noticed David send a text. Then, as they stepped out of the terminal, a black SUV with tinted windows pulled up and stopped in front of them.

The driver got out and opened the back hatch. He looked to be about ten years older than Erin and had brown, slightly wavy hair, and a short, scruffy beard that was starting to go grey. "Mornin' David," he said.

"Good mornin', Roger, how're things with you?" David responded.

"Nothin' tae complain about," Roger replied.

"Go through town, will yeh?" David said when they were seated. Roger drove them through Edinburgh, past the back side of the castle.

Erin watched out the window as they passed places she remembered from her visit with Todd. "I just love Edinburgh!" she said and took David's hand. Roger's grey-green eyes peered at her through the rearview mirror, so she let go and moved away, not sure if David wanted him to know about them.

David turned to her, leaned closer, and took her hand back. "Et *is* a lovely town," he said and smiled at her.

"You grew up here? You lucky duck! That must've been exciting; to explore this amazing city as a kid would be magical! I can't wait to—"

Oh yeah, I forgot we can't be seen together, she thought and sighed.

David squeezed her hand. "What is et?" he asked.

She looked at him and smiled, trying to hide her disappointment. "It's nothing; I was thinking about how I'd love to explore it with you, but I know we can't."

"Dinnae worry, we'll have adventures whilst ye're here. I'll make sure of et."

They made their way around the Meadows and then around the Salisbury Crags, on the west side of Holyrood Park. Finally, they passed the Duddingston Loch and turned down a few small roads until they pulled up to a tall stone wall with an impressive wrought iron gate. Roger got out, opened the ornate black gate, got back in, and entered the property. He got back out, closed the gate, and then drove them up the horseshoe-shaped driveway, stopping at the stunning entrance.

"Welcome tae Owlgate; I grew up here," David said. Roger opened the door for Erin and then went to the back of the vehicle. David stood next to her while Roger fetched their bags and set them on the bottommost step on the stairs. He then got back into the SUV and drove it into the garage.

Erin watched for him to return, but when he didn't come back out, David explained. "Roger lives in the flat above the garage; he won't be back unless something needs doing, someone needs a ride, or until supper."

She was a bit overwhelmed; she had imagined his mother living in a modest, semi-detached home on a quiet street with a cat for company. So far, she'd only gotten the quiet street part right. "Why is it called Owlgate?" she asked.

David pointed to the heavy iron gate Roger had just closed. "If you look closely, ye'll see wee owls incorporated into the design. I'll show yeh later when we take a stroll." They walked to the bottom of the stairs that swept elegantly out on either side of them, and he picked up their luggage.

Erin was impressed and in awe of the stately house and lush landscaping. To say the entrance was grand would've been an understatement. The balustrades were carved sandstone, and ivy climbed the old stone walls surrounding the massive wooden door with its brass accents and hardware. She was nervous as she followed David up the nine steps to the landing, stunned by its beauty.

He smiled at her when they reached the top. "Ready?"

Not sure what she was in for, she said, "Uh, sure," and held her breath as he rang the doorbell. Immediately, a cacophony of barking dogs raised the alarm. She looked at him wide-eyed, and he laughed.

"She likes dogs."

"Evidently!" she said, smiling. A moment later, a stern-looking older woman answered the door. Shocked at how unfriendly his mother appeared, she smiled the best she could.

The grey-haired, older woman's eyes landed on Erin, and she sighed, apparently put out by the intrusion. She seemed ready to tell her to 'kindly leave' until the door opened fully, and she saw David, then she squealed like a young girl. "Davey!" she cried and put her hands up to her cheeks. "What're yeh doin' here? I wasnae told you were comin'! Come in, come in!"

"Et's good tae see you, Millie! Ye're a fine sight for sore eyes!" David said.

She wrapped her arms around him and then noticed Erin again. She looked suspiciously at her, like a protective mother hen, guarding David, her chick, from the wily fox, which was her, the stranger, of course.

"Millie, this is ma friend, Erin. I want you tae treat her like family whilst she's here; do you understand?" he said.

She eyed Erin up and down again. "Aye. A friend, yeh say? What sort of friend?" she asked as they were led into the grand foyer, as if unsure whether she would take heed of David's admonishment or not.

"Millie, that's none of yer business. Is Mum around?" he asked as the woman gave Erin a half-hearted smile.

Chapter Fifty

OWLGATE

As soon as she'd stepped through the door, Erin was in love with the grand old house. The foyer alone was breathtaking with its fireplace, stained glass windows, and beautiful inlaid hardwood floors. Below the crown molding was a foot-wide, coved border painted green, with white plaster garlands.

The elegant, coffered ceilings were twelve feet or more high, and the details of the stunning room enchanted her. She would've liked to stand there and soak it all in, but she followed David and Millie to the drawing room, where three small dogs were laying, quite calm by then, on padded beds by the large fireplace.

"Yer mother is in the garden; I'll fetch her," Millie said, and hurried out of the room.

"Oh, David," Erin whispered. She felt like she was in a library or a Holy place and didn't want to raise her voice. "It's all so beautiful! Your mother has such lovely taste!"

"Thank you, dear, I'm glad you fancy it," a dignified, older woman said. She was standing in the doorway, and David turned when he heard her voice. "Mother," he said as he went to her and kissed both her cheeks.

Her hair was short, straight, and well groomed, with fashionable, long bangs, styled perfectly in front. It was pure white except for a streak of brown on the right side of the part. Erin noticed that she had a lovely complexion and was probably only an inch or two taller than her.

Her cheeks were rosy from being outside, and having been complimented, her smile revealed perfectly straight teeth, though years of drinking tea had yellowed them slightly. She wasn't thin but not fat, either, and though her shoulders were slightly rounded, she carried herself with an air of dignity which made you take notice of her.

Even her gardening clothes are well put together and fit her perfectly, Erin thought, feeling drab and underdressed.

"I'd like for you tae meet ma friend, Erin March… née Wallace."

Née Wallace? Erin thought and looked up at him. "I'm so happy to meet you, Mrs. Elliott," she said, trying to be brave. His mother gave off an air of regality, so she felt as though she should curtsey.

"Ma name is Annis; however, you may call me Ann," she said with a slightly more refined accent than David's. "And how is it you've become friends with our David, then?"

Erin looked up at him; she wasn't expecting to be asked that question so soon and hadn't prepared a good answer yet. "Well—"

"We'll tell yeh all about it, Mother, though right now, I'd like tae get settled and show Erin around if you dinnae mind."

Erin was distracted by the exquisite details of the room, which made it difficult to pay attention to the conversation. She couldn't decide whether to look up at the magnificent ceilings and crown moldings or down at the intricate parquet flooring, gleaming in the sunlight that filled the room from the large picture window. The heavy drapery was gathered in perfect pleats on old brass hooks with finials that she wanted to examine. She was drawn to the pool of light, dappled by a few stray tendrils of ivy, wanting to curl up like a cat in its warm rays.

She heard something about the Sheep Heid, and the name Bran, which she didn't recognize, so her mind began to wander. "Isn't that right, Erin?" David said, but by then, she was studying the door pulls, which were enormous, engraved brass plates with intricately carved, short, round bars as doorknobs. They were truly extraordinary, and she didn't hear what he'd asked.

"Oh, I'm sorry! I'm drawn to so many things in your home, Mrs. ... Ann—It's difficult to stay focused. What was the question?" she asked, blushing furiously.

"I was tellin' ma mum that ye've been tae Duddingston before."

"Oh, yes, I was here four years ago with… well—I've eaten at the Sheep Heid and walked through Dr. Neil's Garden."

"Aye? And what did you think of it, then?" Annis asked.

"I loved it, all of it. The garden is lovely; I could live in it, and the Sheep Heid was nice as well—Oh, and not long after we got back home, I saw on Facebook that John Barrowman was there with his sister! That was fun… to see—"

God, Erin! Here you are with David Elliott, and you're telling him and his mother how thrilled you were about John Barrowman?

David laughed, and Annis smiled. "I mean—That was a stupid anecdote, I suppose… it's just… I forget who I'm with… sometimes." She looked down, wanting the exquisite floor to swallow her up.

"Nae, not stupid at all, dear," Annis said, smiling warmly at her.

Erin still felt ridiculous and needed to escape for a few minutes. "May I please use your water closet?" she asked, though she didn't really need to go. All she wanted to do was make a good first impression, but she sounded like an idiot.

"Aye, it's at the end of the hallway—across from the kitchen," Annis said.

Erin smiled sheepishly and left the room. She heard David laugh and his mother say, '*Well,*' but she didn't want to hear anything else and hurried away.

Erin washed her hands in the modern, slate-tiled bathroom, dreading the thought of returning to the drawing room. She took her time on the way back, studying the framed pictures and artwork hanging on the walls. Just outside the drawing room doors, she stopped and took a deep breath.

"So, ye're David's friend, are yeh?" Millie's critical voice said behind her.

Oh great! Not her, not now!

Erin smiled as warmly as she could fake. "Yes, I am."

"Is that so? And were yeh eavesdroppin, then?" the old, wrinkled, and unsmiling woman said.

She was stunned. "What? Eavesdropping? No! To be honest, I was trying to find the courage to go back in there. I don't think I'm making a very good first impression," she admitted, hoping the truth would win her a few points of favor.

Millie gave her a curt nod and gently led her by the shoulders into the room. "Lookie what I found loiterin' just outside the doorway," she said to Annis.

Erin blushed and quietly went to the sofa to sit next to David. She wanted to cry from frustration, embarrassment, and the feeling that no one in the household liked her. "I'm sorry I took so long. I was admiring the photographs and artwork hanging on the walls. I especially love the watercolors!" she said sincerely.

"Ach, David, your friend does have good taste," Annis said. "Thank you, ma dear. I painted them quite a number of years ago, now."

"Really? They're fabulous! I want to climb inside and see what's around the next turn or sit in one of the little boats and sail away," she said, which was, in fact, what she longed to do just then. Annis was beaming, though Erin could tell she was trying to be modest. Millie, who was standing behind her employer, seemed to be quite proud as well, which was interesting to see.

"And what do you do for a living then, Erin?" Annis asked.

"Oh, I… had to quit my job two years ago."

Annis looked confused. "You *had* to? Whatever for?"

"Um, well, I was born with the Fertilis Defect," she said, making both Annis and Millie gasp and cluck. "Until five years ago, I could predict when I'd have an episode so someone could take my route for me on those days. Then my symptoms started to go haywire, even more than normal. I began to have small, random episodes, or when I had a typical one, it would wipe me out for much longer than usual. It got to the point where it wasn't safe for the children anymore."

"Children? Were you in childcare, then?" Annis asked, sounding very interested.

"Oh! I didn't say, did I? I was a school bus driver, and I loved it. That's how I met Lily," she said to David.

"I can't believe I've never asked you about that. A school bus driver, hmm? I reckon you must've been verra good at et!" he said.

"I guess so; I loved all my kids. It felt like they were my own, not that I'd know how that really feels… but… I cared about them a lot."

"Do you not have children of your own, then?" Annis asked.

Erin blushed and shook her head. "Part of the curse of Fertilis, I guess," She wasn't about to volunteer the fact she was pregnant with David's baby just then. If he wanted them to know, he'd have to do the telling.

"Ach, you poor wee thing! Children are a gift from God!" Annis said.

"Aye, they are," Erin agreed. Annis and David smiled again. "I did it again, didn't I? Dang! I'm sorry. I don't mean to make fun or offend anyone; it's just that I love how you speak, and… I can't help myself." She was thoroughly annoyed at herself and knew she would start crying if she didn't leave the room soon, so she nudged David with her elbow. "I'm tired. Do you think it would be alright if I took a short nap?" Hot, stinging tears were building up, ready to fall at any second, so she stood, hoping he'd do the same.

"Right, of course. I'll take yeh tae ma bedroom," he said, then led her out of the sitting room and up the stairs.

About halfway up, the tears began to fall silently. *Dammit, Erin! Can't you just get one thing right while you're here?*

They reached the bend in the oval hallway that hugged the outer walls and was open in the center. Looking down, she could just make out the edge of the doorframe to the sitting room. She figured David's mother and Millie were 'discussing' the odd woman he'd brought with him. David opened a door and led her into a large bedroom painted pale yellow. It was just as elegant as the rest of the house, having crown moldings, coffered ceilings, and hardwood floors covered with large, soft area rugs.

The room was delightful; it had a bay window with a desk set into it and a fireplace at the end of the bed. She wanted to enjoy it and tell him just how lovely it was, but all she could do was stand there with tears rolling down her face. He closed the door, turned around, and Erin purposely turned her back to him, making it seem as though she was gazing out the window.

He stepped up and gently turned her to face him. "What is et, love?" At that, the dam broke, and she hugged him tightly, sobbing. "Whoa, Erin! What's wrong?" He held her and stroked her hair.

"I feel like a complete idiot! Nothing I said came out right… and Millie hates me! She's known me for less than an hour, and she can't stand me! What's wrong with me, David? I just want your mom to like me, and I've already messed it up!"

"What're yeh goin' on about? You were brilliant! Ma mother thinks ye're lovely, she said so herself!" he said, and Erin looked up at him.

"She did? But you were both laughing at me… not that I blame you. I sounded foolish with the stupid John Barrowman thing. John Barrowman? Seriously? What was I thinking?"

"That was endearing."

"What about Millie leading me into the headmaster's office, or at least that's how it felt, tattling on me, saying I was loitering in the hallway? I felt ridiculous and humiliated!"

"Ach, Erin, that was just her way of… I dinnae ken, makin' a joke, I reckon. I assure you it wasn't out of spite," he said, trying to make her understand.

"She doesn't like me, David. She's been giving me the stink eye from the moment she saw me! Why would she be like that—Oh, right, I get it! She likes Susannah, so she's suspicious of me!"

David laughed and shook his head. "Ach, no, ye're wrong there, love. No one in ma family particularly cares for Susannah. If Millie has an issue with you, et's most likely because of me. She was ma nanny and is suspicious of people she doesn't know, believin' everyone's after me because of the fame. Aye, she's a bit overprotective, I reckon, but et's nothin' tae do with you as a person."

Erin could see how that might be true, and she felt a bit better. "Okay, but—"

"Did yeh see ma mother beamin' when you mentioned her paintings? Yeh touched a soft spot with her! She'll no' take that lightly, especially as yeh didn't ken she'd painted them. Ye've won her good opinion, darling, to be sure."

"They *are* lovely! I'm sorry I had us bolt like that. I felt so foolish, and the tears were right there, so I—" she began but felt them welling up again and stopped.

"Dinnae fash. I wanted tae escape the questioning maself. As I'm sure you've already noticed, this is ma bedroom," he said, with a slight wave of his hand.

"I like it! It's so big!"

That's what she said! she thought.

"That's what she said!" he echoed her thoughts, and she laughed out loud.

"You won't believe me, but that's exactly what was going through my mind."

"Great minds think alike," he said, and led her to the bed, sitting her down.

She nearly fell over backward and swore. "Fuck!"

"Et's a Hästens bed," he said, laughing at her reaction. "Just wait till you lay in et; ye'll think ye've died and gone tae heaven!"

"I don't know what that means, but would you care to join me for a nap in heaven?" she asked, and he smiled at her.

"Aye! That would be nice," he said. They got undressed, got onto the bed, and held each other.

"This... is... perfect!" she said, barely able to keep her eyes open. He made a noise of agreement, and then they both fell asleep.

Chapter Fifty-One

A SCOTTISH SUPPER

Over an hour later, David and Erin woke to a knock on the door. "Supper will be served in twenty minutes," said Millie's disapproving voice.

"A'right Millie, we'll be down soon," David said.

Erin rolled over and snuggled up to him. "I don't want to get up! I'm far too comfortable!"

"Aye, but we dinnae want tae risk the wrath of Millie, though, do we?"

She moaned as she rolled to the side of the mattress and stood reluctantly. They got dressed and made it downstairs just in time for the meal to be served. As they walked through the doors that had been closed earlier, Erin gasped.

The room was grand and enormous; it had Art Nouveau-style wallpaper on the walls that looked like something out of Henry Higgins' home in *My Fair Lady.* The ceiling was painted blue and coffered with an intricate pattern, painted white. Around the crown molding was a wide coordinating floral border.

The floors were an impossible parquet masterpiece. A strip of wood stained darker than the rest ran around the perimeter of the room about a foot away from the beautiful floorboard moldings. There was an enormous inglenook fireplace as well, with hardwood paneling and leaded glass doors on curios that held books and knick-knacks.

In the center of the room was a stunning crystal chandelier that hung over a large wooden table with a linen tablecloth. Erin thought she could live entirely in that room and be content for the rest of her life. Millie was bustling into and out of the room, laying serving dishes on the table.

"Can I help you with anything, Millie?" Erin asked, trying to be helpful and get on her good side.

"Aye, you can help by stayin' out of ma way," she said, shortly.

Erin sat next to David, wanting to keep her head down, but Annis asked her to move closer so they could talk. Although she had no idea what to say to her, she moved, hoping for a chance to redeem herself a little bit. Roger was at the table, so she smiled and said, "Hello." He smiled back and gave her a slight nod of his head but didn't say anything. David was beaming when she looked at him, obviously thrilled to have her there, but she still didn't feel like things were going very well.

Annis said a quick prayer and then began pouring the wine, which Erin regretfully declined, opting for water instead. Finally, they started eating. They were served cock-a-leekie soup, lamb, roasted root vegetables seasoned with rosemary, and what seemed to be homemade bread, which was mouthwatering.

She had never tried lamb and was afraid she wouldn't like it, but it was delicious, and so was the soup. "Millie, did you cook this meal?" she asked. Millie blushed and nodded curtly. "It's so good. Truthfully, it's one of the best meals I've ever had. Thank you." There was silence at the table; everyone looked down as if she'd said something in bad taste.

"Did I say something wrong? I didn't mean to, honestly." She was confused and dropped her head, feeling ashamed, though she didn't know why.

Why do you keep opening your big, stupid mouth? she thought.

"Humph, ye're… welcome," Millie said, as though it were difficult. After that, Erin didn't say much; if someone asked her a direct question, she would answer quietly, with as few words as possible.

After dessert, Roger went back to the garage while the rest of them sat and waited for Millie to clear the table. Erin tried not to make eye contact with anyone, concentrating on the small weave of the linen tablecloth. When the table was empty, Millie didn't come back, and Erin was relieved.

"Let's move into the sitting room," Annis suggested, so they stood and made their way to the smaller, cozier, and more comfortable room adjacent to the drawing room. There was a cheerful fire in the fireplace, and Erin sat next to David, quiet and disheartened. Once everyone was seated, after-dinner drinks were offered, which Erin again had to decline, even though she would've liked nothing more at that moment.

"Would you mind telling me a bit more about your Fertilis Defect, Erin? I'd like tae know how it affects you and whether or not they've found a cure," Annis asked.

The last thing Erin wanted to do was speak, but it would be rude to refuse. She explained what her symptoms were and how they had been getting worse.

"Correct me if I'm wrong, dear, but your symptoms involve not being able tae breathe; for how long do they last, these episodes, as you call them?" Annis asked.

"The worst one so far... I wasn't able to inhale for over a minute, though I was unconscious by then, so I don't remember it," she said and looked at David. The memory of the ordeal was clearly visible on his face.

"Ach, that's terrible; whatever did you do? Were you alone?" Annis said, sounding truly concerned.

"No, I wasn't alone that time. I... was with David," Erin said and blushed.

"That's how I met Erin, Mother," David interjected.

Annis looked from Erin to David. "I don't understand... you met her because of the Fertilis Defect? Ach, I remember now; you did a charity telethon earlier this year. Was she also on the program, then?"

"No, it was all Martin's doing, actually," David said.

Millie had just returned with the drinks and heard Martin's name. Both women tisked and glanced at each other. "Help ma boab, Davey. I told yeh naught but trouble would come if you continued takin' up with that boy!" she said harshly.

"Aye, and I should have listened to yeh, except that in this case, his plan backfired," David said. "I think he did et in part tae sabotage ma marriage. He's been in love with Susannah since we met and has most likely convinced himself that if we separated, he'd manage tae sweep her off her feet. The problem is, she can't stand him, so the joke's on him. Plus, I've met Erin, so—"

"Wait, why would anathing having to do with the Fertilis Defect jeopardize your marriage?" Annis said, sounding confused.

"Well," he said and took a deep breath, telling her about the poker game and being tricked into signing up for the Registry. Then he told her what the Registry was and what the treatments involved. "In the end, Susannah told me I must do it to save face. She decided it would be better for 'us' if I registered quietly instead of havin' it end up all over the tabloids. So, that's what I did."

Both Annis and Millie sat wide-eyed, astounded at what they were hearing. He told them how they met in New Orleans, about the horrible episode she'd had there, and what he'd done to help her.

Erin sat, blushing, looking down at her lap, waiting for the judgment or harsh words, from Millie, at least.

"So, you didn't know whom you were meeting, then, Erin?" Annis asked her.

"Ah, no; no one told me anything. I was allowed to read some redacted data. His height, marital status, that he was employed, though not what he did, and that he lived in England. That's all I knew," she said.

"But did you know who he was... before you met?" she asked.

"Yes, I knew who David Elliott was," Erin said softly, and couldn't help but smile at the memory of their first encounter.

"Ach! That must have been a tremendous shock!" she said.

Both Erin and David laughed and smiled at each other. "You could say that! I literally fell on my ass—" Erin said and blushed for swearing in front of his mother. "He was sweet and sympathetic, and we hit it off right away, didn't we?" She looked at him and then laid her head on his arm.

David held her hand. "Aye, I was drawn tae her from the verra moment I took her hand tae help her up. We had an instant connection."

"Astounding! So, all this time—I mean, you're unmistakably meant to be together; it's apparent in evera way—But all this time, you were meant tae meet and... fall—I presume you're in love with each other—" Annis said, haltingly.

"Aye," David said simply and squeezed Erin's hand.

"But… does Susannah know? And… what about the children? Whatever will happen with them?" Annis said, sounding worried.

"Martin made sure Susannah knew by havin' us followed," David said. "I dinnae ken if he realized Erin was ma Registry match or no', but she knows I was with another woman whilst in New Orleans." There was more gasping from their captive audience. "As for the children, I dinnae ken, honestly. I imagine she'll petition for full custody, though they're old enough tae make up their own minds, or nearly so."

"And how do you feel about all this?" Annis asked Erin.

"All of what?"

"Of David's being married and having four children," she said.

Erin didn't know what to say and hesitated while she tried to think of something that didn't sound idiotic. "I… have so many feelings right now. I just left my husband of… fifteen years on Monday. I mean, obviously, I wish things were different; easier, but this is how things are now, and I'm just going to have to live every day on its own and take things as they come," she said.

David squeezed her hand again and kissed her hair. "I believe that will be the end of this interview, Mother. I'm goin' tae take Erin for a walk now," he said. "I dinnae ken when we'll be back, so please dinnae wait up for us." He stood and took Erin's hand to help her up.

Feeling like a bug under a microscope, she was relieved David ended it when he did. "I'm going upstairs to grab a sweater; would you like me to get anything for you while I'm up there?" Erin asked him as they stepped out of the sitting room.

"No, darling," he said and kissed her forehead.

She hurried up the stairs and headed to his room; the bed looked so inviting, but she was on a mission. She laid her large suitcase on the floor, unzipped the top, took a dark cardigan from it, and left it open as she ran back downstairs to join David.

They walked out the front door, down the nine stone steps, and down the driveway to the iron gate. David opened it and showed her the little owls which gave the home its name. "I love how people name houses here, it's so whimsical. I hope to have a named house someday," Erin said.

"This one will be ours someday. I see how much you fancy et, and I'm set to inherit—" David began to say, but she stopped him.

"Oh, let's not talk about that now! Your mom has quite a few more years on her yet!"

"Aye, she does, indeed. Did you hear what she said, love? She said it's obvious we were meant tae be together!" he said, and smiled one of his winning, glowing smiles at her.

"Yes, I did. Do you think she meant it? I mean, I've been a real numbskull all day, and—"

"What? Of course, she meant et. Ye've been lovely!" he said.

Erin looked at him as though he'd lost his mind or like he hadn't been in the room the whole time. "What was that at supper then? I gave a heartfelt compliment to Millie about the meal, and you'd think I'd just told them that I was the one who killed the family cat. And that's what we'd been eating the whole time," she said.

David couldn't help but laugh. "Aye, it *would* seem odd for someone new tae the family. Millie is no' one tae ask for compliments; in fact, she's rather averse to them, so we all know tae tuck in and no' say anathin' about it tae her. I should've warned yeh. I'm sorry, hen," he said.

"Aye, it might be nice if you'd fill me in on anything else you haven't told me about, okay?"

"I can't think of anathin' else now, but I'll be sure tae think ahead a wee bit more in future," he said and took hold of her hand since there was no one on the small street to see them.

They passed the Sheep Heid Inn, hearing the din of diners talking and people giving their drink orders at the bar. They walked around the block, along picturesque, cobbled streets, past ancient stone and brick houses, and then finally stepped through the gate into Dr. Neil's Garden.

They slowed their pace and strolled, hand in hand along the gravel paths, past flowers, hedges, both stone and brick walls, and the loch. Birds flew around a birdbath on one path, and they sat on a flat stone bench that jutted out from a stone wall and looked out onto the loch. It was so peaceful and quiet; they lost all track of time with the sun not setting until after ten o'clock.

"How're yeh feelin'?" David asked, out of the blue.

"What do you mean? I feel wonderful right now, sitting with you in this beautiful place," she said.

"I reckon it's been nearly a month since your last episode, and I'm just wondering if ye're doin' a'right?"

She hadn't even thought about it. "I don't think I've had any lead-up symptoms or anything; I feel fantastic—except for the morning sickness. I guess if it's not one thing, it's another!" She laughed and snuggled closer into his side.

"Aye, that's good. I was thinkin' it wouldn't be healthy for the bairn, perhaps, if you were tae have another one."

She knew he was probably right, but she hadn't felt so good in years, and she wasn't worried. However, she was glad he was thinking that way; it meant he really did care about her and the baby. "I'm not worried, and I promise to tell you if I even think I might possibly be having a symptom. Okay?"

"A'right," he said. "Let's keep movin'. I'm a wee bit cold." They walked around the garden a while longer and then made their way back to the house. Erin stared up at the huge, cream-colored stone bricks, the gabled roofline, and the grand entrance with its wide, stone stairs that led to a pillared stoop. The house was stately, and the yard was large and well-manicured.

"How did your parents manage to get this house? It's so... impressive and amazing."

"They inherited it from my grandfather, and his father built et. I've always loved this old place," he said.

"I can see why."

They walked in through the side door that time and went straight up the back stairs and into David's room. Erin was exhausted after such a full day and wanted to fall into bed, but there was a soft knock on the door, so she stopped getting undressed.

David opened the door. His mother asked to speak with him, so he stepped out into the hall. He came back a while later, looking a bit grim, but as soon as he saw her lying in his bed, he smiled and joined her.

321

Chapter Fifty-Two

A SMALL JOB

In the morning, Erin woke feeling great. She hadn't slept that well in a very long time, and snippets of dreams floated around in her memory. One of them involved David and a pack of dogs. She rolled over to find David gone, which wasn't like him, or at least not how he had been in the past.

She rolled out of bed and regretted it immediately, as the morning sickness suddenly hit her, and she had to run to the toilet. *This is getting old fast, and I really hope it ends soon!* She got dressed in some of her old, more comfortable clothes, brushed her teeth and hair, and headed downstairs.

The smell of bacon and toast made her stomach grumble loudly, and she hoped she hadn't missed breakfast. She walked into the kitchen to find David sitting at the kitchen counter on a high bench seat. He was fully dressed and finishing his cup of coffee. "Good morning!" he said when he saw her and patted the seat next to him. "I didn't want tae wake yeh."

"What's got you up so early?" she asked as she sat on the wooden bench, longing for a cup of tea.

"I received a message from my agent, Becky, with a last-minute job in London. I was about tae go up and tell yeh when you came down. Will yeh be a'right here for the night? I'll be back first thing in the mornin'." He must've seen the distress on her face because he put his hand on hers and squeezed it. "I'm sorry, love, but I'm contractually obliged tae do it. I tried to skive off et, believe me, but there's nothing for et, I'm afraid."

Honestly, she would rather have gone with him, but she wasn't going to say it in that company. "That's fine; I'll take the bus to Portobello and walk on the beach or go to a few charity shops. Maybe I'll go into the old city and do some window shopping—"

Damn! You just had to say that, didn't you? Why don't you think before you speak?

"You can ask Roger tae take yeh wherever you want tae go. No need for the bus. Oh, and I've left you a few quid on the desk."

"I didn't say that as a hint—I really didn't! But… thank you," she said quietly, not wanting to argue.

"Ach, Erin, I didn't mean tae make yeh uncomfortable. I just want tae provide for you. Please take it and have a good time, a'right?"

"I know you didn't. You're just so thoughtful, and I'm not used to being spoiled like you're able to do. Alright, I'll take it, but you know I don't need it to have a good time. I'm used to being… not wealthy, so I can do a lot on a little, but thank you again."

She kissed his cheek and thanked Millie for the hot tea, eggs, and bacon she'd set in front of her. "Millie, do you have some free time today? Would you like to come with me? Maybe show me around or take a walk on the beach? We could… have lunch or tea?"

Millie appeared scandalized, shocked she'd been invited on Erin's day out. She turned around to face the frying bacon, said, "I've too much tae do here," and that was the end of it.

Erin looked at David as if to say. 'I tried,' and he smiled at her. "Do you think your mother might like to come along?" she asked David. "I don't mind being alone, but I think it might be fun to make a day of it with her; get to know her a little bit—What do you think?"

Millie turned around. "Mrs. Elliott has her things tae do as well. She'll be havin' her hair done today, so it might be best for yeh tae go alone," she said, speaking for her employer.

"Oh, okay… I was just—Never mind," she said, feeling discouraged. David stood and took Erin's hand. She slipped off the bench and allowed him to lead her to the entryway. "She hates me! I can't say anything right to her. What will I do until you get back?"

"Ach, she doesn't hate yeh. She's just no' used tae people bein' overly nice tae her. Around here, she's considered the help and that's how she's used tae bein' treated by people outside of the family. I know et's old fashioned, and I'm sure in yer eyes, et's horrible, but that's how it often is here; et's what she's used to. Please keep cutting her slack; I see how ye're trying so hard tae get to know her, but maybe you should leave it for now," he said.

"Okay," she said, wishing they were in bed, nestled up to each other, and maybe even making love.

"I'm sorry, hen, but I must be off. I'll see yeh in the mornin', and then I'll take yeh someplace I know you'll love!" He kissed her and opened the door just as Roger pulled the car up.

He looked at her and flashed her his breathtaking smile. It made Erin's heart ache, knowing she'd be alone for so long. He got into the car, and she waved as they rolled down the drive. She watched as Roger closed the gate behind them, then went back into the kitchen to finish her toast and tea, but her breakfast had been cleared away.

Erin was tempted to go back to bed and feel sorry for herself the rest of the day. Instead, she returned to the bedroom and picked up the money he'd set out for her. It was a lot. The thought of counting it made her feel greedy for some reason, but it looked like much more than what he'd left her in London. She was grateful, but it didn't feel right, and she couldn't say why it bothered her so much.

After a shower, she did her hair and makeup and got dressed, feeling odd being alone in a strange house in a country a quarter of the way around the world. At first, she stashed all the money in her purse, along with the leftover pounds from the day before, then she changed her mind. She put some of it into her purse, and the rest she divvied out into her pockets; she didn't want to lose it all if her purse got snatched.

Memories of being mugged and assaulted in New Orleans flashed through her mind, and she shivered. The feeling of the thug's tight grip on her stomach and his large hand over her mouth was still too fresh in her memory. She shook her head, trying to clear away the thoughts, and left the room, closing the door behind her.

She didn't know how to go about asking Roger for a ride, so she went into the kitchen to find Millie or Annis to ask them. Taking the bus seemed like less of a hassle, but she didn't have any small change, so she headed out to the garage. Before she reached it, though, she saw Roger pull up to the gate, just back from delivering David to the airport.

She walked down the drive, trying to catch him before he pulled the car in. He seemed slightly confused, so she explained that she was trying to save him some trouble. He gave her a look that made her wonder if she'd grown another head, but he agreed to take her to the Old Town and gave her his mobile number so she could call or text when she wanted to return.

She watched out the window as they passed Arthur's Seat and Salisbury Craigs and as they snaked through the congested streets of the city. He let her out of the SUV at the Edinburgh Dungeons on Market Street, then drove away, leaving her alone.

Chapter Fifty-Three

OLD TOWN ALONE

Erin loved the Old Town with its cobbled streets and narrow alleys, called closes. As she walked up Cockburn Street, she admired the old stone buildings surrounding her. She followed the steep, winding hill to a small shop she'd been to before called Miss Katie Cupcake. They sold handmade soaps and unique things, like vintage-looking jewelry. She bought a pair of tiny ceramic teapot earrings and put them in right away; then, she made her way to the Royal Mile. As she walked toward the castle, she passed some of the places she and Todd had seen together. There were so many bittersweet memories all around her, and she was glad David wasn't with her so she could remember without having to hide her emotions.

She stepped into one of the tourist shops selling kilts and souvenirs. The walls were lined with pegs laden with hundreds of scarves and ties of seemingly every known tartan, listed alphabetically by surname. She searched for the Elliott tartan and found it easily enough. The pattern was medium blue, with a thick brown stripe and a narrow one in bright red. She asked what else they had in it, which wasn't much, and chose a cashmere scarf, which was an extravagance she would never have allowed herself to afford before.

Scattered clouds drifted high overhead as she stepped back out onto the old High Street, also called the Royal Mile. Street performers and buskers played their guitars, bagpipes, and artists created beautiful works of art while she watched. She walked through several tourist shops, looking at their bric-a-brac, consisting of mugs, magnets, and tins of shortbread.

Seeing a postcard with an adorable red highland cow, she bought it, plus a few others she liked and a sheet of stamps to send to Lily. Thinking of Lily made her a bit homesick, so she ordered a coffee at a cafe and sat outside writing her message on the back of the card.

Hi, Lily!

I miss you terribly and wish you were here with me! It would be more fun with you! David had to work today, so I'm shopping alone. I hope everyone is well. Please give Ariana a big hug for me!
Lots of love,
Erin

The rest of the postcards got a *'Wish you were here!'* then she found Lily's address in her purse and sent them all right then and there with a kiss. She needed a distraction, or she'd start crying, so she turned and walked down Upper Bow Street, taking the stairs down to the next level of the town. Victoria Street was one of her favorites; it was beautiful, with its multi-colored storefronts and bi-level walkway.

It had been one of J. K. Rowling's inspirations for Diagon Alley, so of course there was an enormous Harry Potter gift shop. She avoided it, only because she knew she'd buy up the whole store if she went in. There were all sorts of interesting shops and pubs that she window shopped, but near the top of the hill, she found one called John Kay's Bookshop and just had to go in.

Deep and narrow, the shop was jam-packed with amazing things. Hanging from the ceiling were vintage-looking hot air balloons, the planets of the solar system, chandeliers, and biplanes. There were tote bags, bronze figures, candlesticks, globes, and framed vintage artwork.

She saw a View-Master in the window, made with galvanized metal and wood, like an old stereoscope alongside a classic red plastic one. There were phrenology charts, astronomical gauges, and many other things that looked like they should be in Dumbledore's office. To top it all off, next to the cash register table, they had a wall of Pop Vinyl figures, as well as bits of merchandise from all her favorite shows.

She wasted well over an hour in that shop and got to know the young man behind the counter by his first name, Tim. He had a lovely thick accent and kind, gentle eyes. He asked her questions about America and told her how he'd love to go there someday.

She told him that everyone, at least where she was from, would love him for his accent alone and that she thought they'd continue to love him for his personality. They talked about *Future Explorations* when she looked through the View-Master and saw images from the show in it. She laughed as she clicked through the pictures of David and the other cast members.

Erin was determined to bring David to the shop; he needed to meet Tim, and she knew Tim would get a kick out of meeting David as well. She asked the young man if he had a business card with the name and address of the place and then asked him to write down the days he usually worked so it would be easier to find him again.

He was happy to do that for her and handed it to her with a big smile. She would've liked to stay all day, but she really wanted to get to Portobello with enough time to browse the charity shops. Sadly, she said goodbye and promised to come back again soon.

She thought about sending a message to Roger, asking him to pick her up, but it seemed silly to disturb him when she could take the bus. It wasn't far to Waverly Bridge, where the bus station was—right in front of Waverly Train Station. When she got there, she walked into the bright, clean Lothian Bus building.

After finding out which bus to take, she walked to the bus stop on Princes Street and took the No. 45. She rode in the front seat of the double-decker bus, on the upper level, enjoying the view of the New Town. Portobello was the last stop, so she got off at the edge of the village.

She walked down the street and entered the first charity shop she came to, but not seeing anything interesting, she left. She did that several more times then decided she needed a stroll on the beach. Following a side street toward the sound of gulls and crashing waves to the Portobello promenade, she sat on a bench, listening to the large white birds, and watched them soar while the water rolled up and down the sandy shore.

The beach was otherwise quiet; the only people she saw were an old, hunched-over man with a metal detector and a few men in casual business suits eating their lunch-hour sausage rolls on nearby benches. Far down the beach was a kid; his dog was running into and out of the water. All Erin could think of was how horrible the pup would smell when they got home.

She took a selfie with the ocean and beach in the background and then sent it to both David and Lily with a message attached to it, saying, *'Wish you were here on Portobello Beach!'* Lily replied right away, saying she would give almost anything to be there with her, but she didn't get a reply from David. *He must be working*, she figured.

There wasn't much else to do in Portobello. She had seen an arcade on the promenade, but groups of people and noise were the last thing she wanted. She was tired of shopping and walking around, so she stopped at a Greggs and sent a message to Roger, asking him to pick her up there. He sent a reply, saying he was on his way, so she bought a sandwich and an orange juice to eat while she waited.

Twenty minutes later, Roger pulled up in the black SUV. He got out and opened the door for her but didn't say anything. The only evidence to show he was a human and not a robot was a slight nod when she thanked him, though she figured even a robot could be taught to do that much. She was glad they were going to a place where she could rest and be alone with her thoughts.

Traffic was moving slow on the way back, so it took nearly thirty minutes, but the car was comfortable and quiet, and she was able to relax. She didn't bother trying to make small talk, afraid she'd make an even bigger fool of herself. Instead, she sat in silence, looking out the darkly tinted windows or on her phone, scrolling through Facebook.

They pulled up to Owlgate, and Erin thought Roger must be the most patient man in the world. Having to get out, open the gate and pull in, only to get out to close it again every time he went anywhere. She would've commented, but she figured he wouldn't take it well. He stopped at the entrance, and she thanked him again, not waiting for him to open the door for her, then walked up the nine steps to the enormous, black-painted door.

Not knowing if she should use the doorbell or not, she hesitated but decided that if she was a guest, she shouldn't have to. She walked under the transom window and onto the beautiful mosaic tile on the tiny entryway floor. Next, she opened the interior leaded-glass door and finally entered the foyer. It was quiet in the house, so she started upstairs with her bags.

She studied the photographs on the stairway walls; many of them were of David as a child. Quite a few looked like duplicates of him at the same age, except when she looked closer, there was something slightly different about some of them. However, staring at them didn't help her pinpoint what it was.

At the top of the stairs, she studied the many doors that lined the wide oval hallway, wondering whose rooms they were and what they looked like inside. *Are they all as grand as David's?* When she reached the bend in the hall she retreated into his room and shut the door. She noticed the bed had been made for them and felt guilty that she hadn't thought of at least pulling the covers up when she'd gotten out of bed that morning.

You'll just have to remember tomorrow! she thought to herself as she started changing into more comfortable clothes.

She took the things she'd bought out of their shopping bags and laid them out on the desk. It would be several hours before suppertime, and she was exhausted from the long day out on the town, so she got into David's bed and fell asleep almost instantly. It seemed like only a few minutes had passed when she heard a knock on the door telling her supper would be ready in twenty minutes. After acknowledging the warning, she crawled out of bed, thankful she'd been able to sleep instead of tossing and turning. She got dressed in one of her new outfits and went downstairs to eat.

Annis had gotten her hair cut a bit shorter than it had been before; it looked chic, and Erin complimented her on it when she sat at the table. David's mother thanked her, but Millie gave her what she thought was a disapproving look, so she didn't say much else. After an uncomfortably quiet supper, Roger went back to the garage, and Millie cleaned up while Annis and Erin went into the sitting room to watch the news. David replied to her photo from earlier, so Erin chatted with him.

D: *Oh Darling, I wish I were with you! How was your day? Mine was boring and monotonous! Mother is watching the news, I reckon? Can't be much fun for you, can it?*

E: *I had a good but exhausting day. The beach was nice! Sorry yours was boring. Yes, your mum is watching the news, lol I don't know how I'll be able to sleep tonight without you in the bed! Do you know when you'll be back?*

D: *I'll be back as early as I can manage it. Pack a small bag, I've somewhere special to take you tomorrow. Sleep well, my love! X*

E: *Special is nice! I miss you so much! See you in the morning! XOXO.*

She excused herself and went up to the bedroom to pack as David had said, which only took a few minutes. After her long nap, she wasn't tired, and it was still a bit early to go to bed anyway, so she decided to take a bath. She gathered towels and laid down a bathmat next to the large bathtub. On a table near the door, there were pretty jars of different colored bath salts, so she found one with a scent she liked and ran a nice warm bath to soak in for as long as it took to get tired.

Chapter Fifty-Four

A BRAN ENCOUNTER

After nearly an hour in the bath, all that happened was her fingers and toes became pruney and her rear end got sore from sitting so long. She tried going back to bed and laid there, looking at the high ceiling for a long time. She was tired; she just couldn't fall asleep all alone in that big room on David's bed. Sleep was nowhere in sight, so she threw on her pajama bottoms and an oversized, zip-up hoodie, then made her way downstairs to the kitchen for a glass of warm milk.

Although it was late, there was still enough daylight coming through the windows, so she didn't bother turning on the lights. She opened the tall, narrow refrigerator, pulled out the jug of milk, and set it on the counter behind her. Then, she found a glass in the third cupboard she opened, filled it about halfway, and returned the milk jug to the exact same place she had taken from, just in case moving it would bother Millie.

Her mind was preoccupied with thoughts of the housekeeper, so when she turned around, she was shocked to see a man, a naked man, walk from the dining room into the kitchen, no more than ten feet away from her. He was agitated and muttering something under his breath which Erin couldn't understand. Thankfully she was standing in a shadow, and he didn't see her.

She wanted to get out of there quickly, but she didn't want to bring attention to herself, so she backed up against the fridge, hardly breathing until he finally left the room. Glad she'd avoided that confrontation, she let out the breath she was holding and covered her face with her hand, trying to regulate her breathing. A moment later, she removed her hand and was about to pick up her glass of milk when he reappeared. The hairs on the back of her neck stood when he looked right at her.

Tall and thin, the man looked so much like David, it made her very uneasy. His messy, greasy hair was brown, flecked with grey as David's had been before he'd had to dye it grey for a part. The only thing that set the two men apart was this guy had a slight pooch to his belly and an enormous tattoo of a snake on his bare chest.

He didn't seem to care that he had nothing on and walked right up to her. She moved to the side, thinking he might want to get to the fridge, but instead, he looked her over. "And who do we have here, then?" he asked, his voice just like David's. "Are yeh one of Ann's friends? Yeh seem a wee bit young if I'm honest."

Erin felt cornered and tried to move away, but each time she moved, he followed, as though they were part of some intricate dance. "You look so much like—" she began to say out of sheer nervousness, and he raised his eyebrows.

"Like David Elliott? Aye, ah get that all the time, hen. Do yeh like the look of him, then?" he asked, interrupting her.

Erin did NOT like the way the conversation was heading and tried to leave, but he continued to block the way. Thinking she was in a house filled with women, she hadn't zipped her sweatshirt up all the way, and he was eyeing the skin he could see in the dim light.

"Now then, why are yeh here?" he asked again as he gradually, ever so slowly, backed her up against the cupboards in the corner.

She didn't want to look down because she had a horrible notion he was no longer flaccid. Pinned in the corner, she tried to think of ways to defend herself as he got closer to her. "I'm here with... with... David," she said.

The man's face changed from a cat playing with a toy mouse to a tiger stalking its prey, and he stopped advancing just as his cock-stand grazed her leg. She definitely felt something touching her leg through the thin material of her pajama bottoms and would've screamed if she hadn't been so afraid. "David's here, then?" he asked, sounding intrigued.

She didn't know what to say; if she said no, he'd know she wasn't protected, but if she said yes, he might learn the truth and know she'd lied to him. "Are you… related to David?" she asked, trying to sound casual and confident.

That was a stupid question, she thought, *of course he is!*

She was trying to buy some time so she could come up with something to do. He wasn't moving away, and she could still feel *him* against her leg, which was scaring the shit out of her. It wouldn't take much for him to pin her down, so she tried to stay as still and calm as she could.

"Aye, and who *are* yeh?" he asked once more, lifting his hand to brush a hair off her cheek. He then looked down at her chest and flipped her zipper pull with his first finger so that it landed upright, the cool metal touching her bare skin. "Ach, sorry about tha', hen," he said and went to put it right, but the kitchen light came on and Erin closed her eyes, breathing hard in fear.

The man backed away, and when she opened her eyes, she saw that, in fact, he was not flaccid. She also saw Annis standing next to the light switch in her housecoat, looking upset. Erin crossed the room to stand behind her as if the dignified older woman might protect her.

"Branock Dylan Elliott! What, in the name of Christ, are you doing, walking around ma house in naught but yer skin and scaring the devil out of ma poor guest. Now git yerself away before I come after you and skelp yer wee behind!" she said, dropping her RP accent for a moment.

He turned without a sound and left the room.

Erin didn't want the strong, bold woman to see the tears running down her cheek, so she pretended to have something in her eye. "Thank you," she whispered.

Annis turned and put her hand on Erin's shoulder, speaking to her kindly, "Ach, you've had a terrible scare, haven't you?" she said. "I couldn't sleep, so I came down tae get a glass of warm milk." She saw the glass on the counter and smiled "I reckon you had the same idea, then?"

"Yes. I had just poured it when I saw—a naked man walking through the house. I tried to stay out of the way, hoping he wouldn't see me, but—" Another tear escaped her eye, and she angrily wiped it away with the back of her hand.

"I don't believe he would have harmed you, dear; he has a way of trying tae intimidate people, especially women. I'm sorry you had to deal with it."

"Me too," Erin said quietly. She wanted David desperately and started to shake as the adrenaline began to wear off. It was just a slight tremor, but the keen woman noticed.

"Let us sit a spell. Perhaps a wee dram of sherry would be a good idea as well, dear."

"Thank you, Ann, you're so kind," Erin said.

Chapter Fifty-Five

ACCIDENTAL CONFESSION

nnis led the way through the grand dining room and the beautiful foyer to the sitting room. Erin sat on the comfortable sofa while Annis took out a small tray with a crystal decanter and six little matching glasses. She poured a generous portion in one of the glasses and pointed the decanter at the next one to ask if Erin wanted some. "I probably shouldn't since I'm—" She stopped and turned bright red. *Oh no! She doesn't know about the baby yet! Damn, David's not going to be happy about this.*

"Ye're what, ma dear?" she said as she turned to put the decanter down again. She suddenly straightened up and turned to look at Erin, who was very pale. "You're… with child? Is that it? With—I mean, is it—"

"It's David's, yes," she said miserably, dreading his mother's reaction and bracing herself for accusations of gold-digging or entrapment.

Instead, Annis smiled and sat down next to her, taking her hand in her knobbly, soft, wrinkled fingers. "Ach, Erin, how wonderful. David is beside himself, I reckon?" Annis said tenderly.

Erin was flabbergasted. "So, you're not upset? You're not going to accuse me of anything… sinister?"

Annis squeezed her hand. "Children are a blessing from God, ma dear, and to be frank, I like you. We are alike, I believe, and I know David loves you; I can see it in him. His whole demeanor changes when you're together. I haven't seen him this happy in a verra long time. You seem tae be well-matched; far better than that skinny-malinky-long-legs snob he married!

"Now, I shouldn't speak that way, but don't worry about being judged by me, ma dear. Millie may have a word or two tae say, but David's her pet, and she only wants him tae be happy. I think she'd agree with me that you are a far better match for our David than Susannah ever was. Ach, and I'll be a gran again! How lovely! Bairn are so dear and steal yer heart away, like that." She snapped her fingers, which set the dogs off; she then had to shush them for a good five minutes before they would calm down.

The two women laughed as they heard Millie thumping around upstairs and then clomping down the steps, muttering and swearing under her breath. She saw Erin and Annis sitting on the sofa and was about to turn around and go back to bed, apparently feeling left out, when Annis stopped her. "Millie, darling, would you care tae join us for a wee dram? We have good news."

Erin wasn't sure she wanted the housekeeper, who had been quite icy toward her, to know, but she wasn't going to stop David's mother from saying it.

"Help ma boab, she's what?" Millie said when Annis told her the news. Erin felt like a teenager, afraid to be thrown out of the house for getting herself in trouble. She wished more than ever that David was there to defend and shield her, but he wasn't, so she would have to take it all by herself until he got back. "And our Davey knows about this, does he?"

"Yes."

Annis gave Millie a look that was some sort of understanding between them, then Millie looked at Erin, smiling broadly, and took her hands. "Ach, I imagine our Davey is over the moon?" The old woman said sweetly, as though she hadn't been giving Erin the cold shoulder since the moment she'd opened the door the day before.

Erin looked at her in astonishment. It was the first time she had smiled at her since they had arrived. "But... you're not... upset? I thought for sure you would be angry or... something. I thought you didn't like me?" Erin's eyes filled with tears again, and again she wiped them away, not wanting to be a baby all the time. She was just so glad the woman who obviously cared very deeply about David was pleased about the baby.

"Aye, I imagine that is what yeh thought, dearie. I'm no' one tae be hasty in acceptin' new people, especially those as important as you are, into our Davey's life. I'm sorry yeh thought I didnae like yeh. A wee bairn! Oh my!" It was her turn to start the waterworks. She made a noise sounding something like wheezing and then burst into tears which made Erin start crying even harder.

Finally, Annis joined in, and all three women cried and laughed, then searched for the tissues which were across the room. Millie stood and brought the box over to them and then sat close to Annis, who took her hand, stroking the papery skin on the back of it.

"May I… ask a personal question?" Erin asked impulsively. She didn't want to ruin the moment, but she saw something between the two women that made her think of her and David. "Are… the two of you… in love?" She wished she could reel it back in and started backtracking "I mean, it just seems as though—You're just so lovely together, and—"

The two women exchanged another look, and then Annis spoke. "We've been found out, Millie. You are quite astute, ma dear. It's not something we talk about, but after David's father died, Millie was the one I leaned on. I learned that for me, it didn't matter that she wasn't a man, and I loved her just as much, and in some ways even more than I'd done Charles."

Erin smiled at the two of them. They were blushing like schoolgirls, and Erin felt a slight weight lift since they didn't have to keep the secret from her any longer. "Does David know? I won't mention it if he doesn't," Erin said.

Annis seemed to be unsure, but Millie spoke up. "We've no' said it tae him as such, but I think he must. We've slept in the same room for nigh on ten years now."

Erin's eyes grew wide. "Well, if he doesn't suspect, then he's blind on purpose. I imagine it might be hard for a man to think of his mother being in love with anyone other than his father, but for it to be his—Wait, what have you been to him, Millie?"

"I was hired as his nanny. Then, as he got older and no longer needed me, I stayed on as housekeeper, which was fine by me, as it meant I could stay with ma boy."

The tears were threatening to return, so Erin asked something she'd wanted to ask since Annis had saved her earlier. "Ann, who was the man in the kitchen? I don't remember David mentioning he had a brother, especially one who looks like his, well, less attractive twin." She shuddered at the memory of the encounter.

"Ye've not heard about Bran?" Annis said, sounding shocked. Erin shook her head. "Ach, dear, et's quite a long story." She exchanged glances with Millie, who resumed the disapproving air Erin had thought was her full-time look.

"Bran Elliott is my nephew. His mother, Olivia, was my twin sister, and his father, Henry, was Charles's twin brother. We both had sons, born only a month apart. The boys looked as though they were twins, not identical, as David's eyes are brown and Bran's are hazel, for example."

"That's it! I couldn't figure it out," Erin said.

"Aye, it was difficult tae tell them apart, especially when they were younger. It was quite entertaining then, but as they grew and their personalities began tae develop, the fun stopped."

"The boy's always been trouble," Millie added.

"Aye, he doesn't respond well to the word 'no' and has never been able to control his impulses. We came to realize it was best tae leave him alone, so we did. He was as stubborn as a mule and could become violent, so he was rarely disciplined by his parents, and when he was, they didn't follow through.

"They don't look as much alike as they once did because as he got older, he started drinking heavily and became hooked on street drugs, so his face broke out and became pasty and sunken in. He was also one tae start fights, so he usually had scars and bruises on his face.

"His parents lived in Glasgow, but he and David often had play dates here until misfortune struck. Both of his parents died suddenly in a train accident when he was ten, so he came to live with us."

"Aye, and it was no' an ideal situation, no' at all," Millie said.

"True; Bran was spoiled and ran wild most of the time. When David left for boarding school, Bran might ring from a payphone, pretending to be David with bad news, or when David was home on holiday, he would sometimes try to make us believe David had hurt himself whilst in the garden. Once, a neighbor came to the house after ringing for an ambulance, saying that David had been run over. It was actually Bran laying in the middle of the street in David's clothes, having poured ketchup and brown sauce all over himself and the road."

"No! That's crazy! Why would he do that—I mean go to all that trouble when it's obvious he'd be found out. It makes no sense," Erin said.

"Nothing he's ever done has made sense," Millie said.

"Aye, and et caught up with him. Soon after he left school at sixteen, he mouthed off to a police officer and found himself in court. He then proceeded tae insult the judge, which landed him in jail for three months. He has been in and out of jail often and is usually drunk or high when he's not. I believe he's also been known to ring David asking for money."

"Humph," Millie said.

"When he first came here, we tried all we knew tae get him under control," Annis said, sadly, "but he didn't want tae be good or control himself. Charles and I were at our wit's end on what tae do with him. He was dreadful wicked tae David. I'm sure there are things he's done tae him he's never told a soul about. He's not the type tae stand up for himself and takes a lot without a fuss. Anaway, when he quit school, he moved away, and tae our shame, we were glad he was gone. He comes back when he's nowhere left tae go, begs for money, eats us out of house and home, makes a mess, and leaves without so much as a thank you."

"Have you thought about... changing the locks or something?" Erin offered.

"Aye, he'd break in, and things would be worse. No, it's better tae allow the storm tae run its course and then leave, rather than trying tae stop it."

Erin had finished her milk and was starting to get drowsy. "I think I'll go upstairs now. Do you think he's still... walking around naked?" she said, nervous about the prospect of meeting him in a dark hallway.

"We'll walk you tae David's room, dear, don't worry."

Erin could smell bacon frying in the kitchen; she stretched out on her bed and lay her hand on the blue and white toile sheets next to her, but the spot was empty. She rolled over, sat up on the edge of the mattress, and took her morning vitamins. The clock read 7:24, and she could see the sun shining through the miniblinds, making narrow slashes of bright blue on the wall. The shadow of leaves flitting around played through the dust particles in the air, and she took a deep breath, looking forward to the crispy bacon and waffles or pancakes Todd was making for her.

Something was wrong. The slash of bright blue on the wall was now dark red, and instead of bacon, she smelled smoke. The room was suddenly hot, and her mind went to how she could escape from the second-story room. *My house doesn't have a second floor,* she thought and looked around her. The room was no longer her bedroom on Whistlers Way but was suddenly her bedroom at her parent's house.

Barkley, the sheepdog she'd had as a child, was barking like crazy, and then someone was at the window. She opened the sash and saw David on a ladder. He was smiling and offering to help her, *but what about Todd? Where is he?* she thought, frantically. David smiled at her and held out his hand, so she took it, and as soon as she did, she heard a noise that woke her up.

Chapter Fifty-Six

DAVID RETURNS

Erin heard someone enter the bedroom in the morning, despite how quiet they were trying to be. She rolled over, opened her eyes, and nearly jumped out of the bed when she saw the tall, dark-headed man walk into the room. She drew the covers up over her chest and backed away from him on the bed, shaking, until she hit the headboard and couldn't go any farther.

"You just stay away from me! Do you hear me?" she said and started crying hysterically.

"Erin? What in God's name is the matter?" She sat with her knees drawn up in front of her, terrified. "What—what's the matter, love?" he said a bit more gently and crawled onto the bed, shoes, and all.

She looked at him again and continued crying. "David? Is it... really... you? I—I thought you were... Bran. He... was here last night, and I had an... unpleasant encounter with him," she said, through sobs and hiccoughs.

"Bran was here?" He suddenly looked angry, "He didnae hurt yeh, or touch yeh, did he?"

He'd gotten close, but he hadn't *touched* her, exactly. "No... not really," she said quietly.

"No' really? What does that mean?"

She wrapped her arms around him, smelling his scent, drinking it in, and allowing it to calm her. She told him about not being able to sleep and going downstairs for a glass of warm milk. "Then I saw a man, who, now that I think of it... didn't look right in the head or was maybe he was drunk or high. That would explain walking around his aunt's house in the nude."

"He was naked? Walkin' around the house? The fucking bawbag! I'll kill him if he touched you!"

"He didn't exactly touch me, except—" She didn't want to say it; it just sounded so gross and disgusting. "His—I think his penis touched me, but only the slightest graze, 'cause it was... well, not... soft." Tears rolled down her face at the memory, and she shook her head, trying to get the image to go away. "Your mum saved me, actually. Apparently, she couldn't sleep either and came down, just like I did. She yelled at him, and he went away.

"I was so scared! I just wanted you to be here to hold me... but your mum and Millie calmed me down. We had a lovely talk, and I learned so much. But then you came in here, and your hair is dark again, and it... scared me. I thought maybe he'd woken up and come in here to—"

David was shaking with rage. "Et's just like him tae do somethin' like that! I mean being naked, not comin' in here... I doubt he'd be that stupid." He touched his hair and looked at her with compassion.

"Ach, ma darling, I'd forgotten about ma hair. I reckon it would give yeh a fright being used tae it grey. Et was dyed for the ad I did yesterday. I'll deal with Bran in a bit, but for now, I want tae hold you." He kicked off his shoes and leaned his back against the headboard, pulling Erin against him, and kissed her hair. "Dinnae fash, I'll no' be leavin' you again."

Erin started unbuttoning his dress shirt and unbuckling his belt. All she wanted was to be joined with him, to feel his warm body covering hers, to feel safe in his lovemaking. "Make love to me, please," she said quietly and lifted her head to kiss him.

He reached down and held her breast as he kissed her, then he got undressed and lay beside her, touching and kissing her body. There was a soft knock on the door, and Millie informed them breakfast would be ready in twenty minutes, just as she'd done the day before, though her voice was softer and much gentler this time.

David acknowledged her, and when they were sure she was far enough away from the door, he lifted himself on top of her and entered her. It felt so good to be with him, to be making love to him. She didn't want it to end, but she could feel the tension building inside of her. Before she knew it, she was reaching her climax, and he was shuddering as he finished too.

"I'm completely addicted to you, you know? I'll never be able to go without you ever again!" she said in his ear as he lay beside her in the aftermath of their excitement.

"Aye, I feel the same," he said and relaxed into her arms.

Reluctantly, they got up and dressed and held hands as they left the room. They had only gotten a few feet down the hallway before David stopped and told her he'd only be a few minutes. He walked around the circular hallway, wrapped by a banister, opened the door to his right, and stepped inside.

A moment later, Erin was startled when she heard struggling and a lot of cussing, though it was in such a thick accent, she couldn't make much of it out. She did hear Bran say, "Ach, yeh feckin' bawbag! Ah didnae ken she was with you, now did ah? Anaway, where's yer lil' wifey then, Mr. Beg shot? Mr. Better than me, beg shot, arsehole!"

The next thing she heard was David's voice, so low and menacing she couldn't and didn't want to know what he'd said. Apparently, Bran didn't have a comeback that time because she didn't hear anything more out of him.

David emerged from the room a few moments later with a red face and a slight smirk. "He won't be botherin' you, or anaone else for a long while!" he said.

"What did you do?" she asked, and then remembering the tone in his voice, changed her mind. "NO! Don't tell me! I don't want to know."

"Aye," was all he said, and then took her hand as they descended the stairs and stepped into the kitchen.

Millie was waiting for them in the kitchen and actually smiled when she saw them together. "Good mornin'!" she said brightly. I hope I didnae disturb yeh earlier!" Her face looked years younger, and she had a twinkle in her eye as she smiled warmly at them.

"A'right! What did I miss? Ye're actin' like yer in on a secret together! Now speak up!"

That's when Erin remembered that she'd accidentally given away their secret the night before. She blushed crimson, and Millie looked away, focusing on the egg timer as it ticked.

"Ach, so there *is* a secret! Let me in on it then!" he said.

Erin spoke first. "I didn't mean to tell them, but after the unpleasant encounter with Bran, your mum offered me a sherry. When I refused it, I—I let it slip. Well, not exactly, but she's smart and figured it out. I'm sorry."

At first, David looked confused, but then it seemed to dawn on him. "So, they know about the—" he said and looked at her stomach.

"The bairn," she finished for him. She didn't know what to expect, but his reaction threw her for a loop.

He laughed and then rubbed the back of his neck. "Ach, I'm glad you got it out, if I'm honest. Truthfully, I was rather dreadin' et."

"Dreading it?" she said, ready to get seriously angry.

"No… no' like that! I was afraid they'd be upset or—Ach, I dinnae ken, I just didn't know how tae bring it up."

Both Erin *and* Millie made the same 'humph' noise, but they smiled right away afterward. "Chicken!" Erin said, and he hugged her.

"Aye! Guilty as charged!"

They ate their breakfast with Millie hovering over them like a mother hen. When they finished eating, she whisked the plates away and even gave David a wee kiss on the temple, then she fixed an errant hair, tucking it behind his ear.

"I dinnae ken what tae think about Millie! She's either happier than she's ever been… or she's gone mad!" he said as they went into the sitting room.

"She's just really happy," Erin said.

He smiled at her. "I'm glad she is, love. Now, I've one more place tae show yeh whilst I have the freedom and time tae do so," he said when they were alone.

"Are you going to tell me where? Or is it another surprise?

"I'll tell you. I want tae take you to the cabin I bought quite a few years ago now, and et's a good time of year tae go. Et's one of ma favorite places, and I need tae share it with you. I reckon we can stay for a few nights and then come back here, seein' I've the magazine interview in London on Wednesday. Did you pack a bag?"

"I did, but before we go, could I ask one teensy-weensy favor of you?" she asked.

"You can always ask," he said and laughed. "What is et?"

"Yesterday, when I was in the Old Town, I went into an amazing store and met the sweetest boy. I just want to take you there and show you—" she said, and David narrowed his eyes.

"A boy, huh? I dinnae ken—" he said, feigning jealousy.

"Not only that," Erin said and nudged him, "they have something there I almost bought, but I wanted you to see it there first; it's just so perfect!" she said.

"A'right, I reckon we aren't in a hurry. We should probably get there earlier rather than later, though, as it might no' be as busy when they first open."

<h1 style="text-align:center">Chapter Fifty-Seven</h1>

DAVID MEETS SHOP BOY

Roger pulled up to the curb and let David and Erin out in front of John Kay's Bookshop just as Tim was unlocking the doors. He saw Erin and opened the door for her, smiling brightly, ignoring the person she'd walked in with. David didn't seem to mind and stepped over to a display that interested him. "Aw-right Erin? How yeh daen? It's so guid tae see yeh—" Tim said, excitedly, in his thick accent.

"Slow down," she said with a laugh. "You know I adore the way you speak, but it takes effort on my part to concentrate on it. I won't understand you without a playback button if you don't go a bit slower or bring it down to a primary school level. I'm sorry; I'm not trying to be rude, but I don't have a lot of time today."

"Ach, sorry; ah'm just thrilled tae see yeh back sae soon." He rushed over to a new display covered with TARDIS figurines and little figures of all the Doctors.

"That's cool, Tim, but I want you to—" Erin started to say.

"Here, these arrived yisterday afternoon—" Tim went over to a shelf by the window and pointed to a display of brand-new *Future Explorations* merchandise, including some new Pop Vinyl figures of David's character. They also had a resin model of the farmhouse John Thomas Fife had lived in when Joe Whitehall stumbled over the hill. "Ah thought of yeh soon as ah saw them."

She lost focus, and if David hadn't been standing right there, she would have bought it. "I had no idea they were still making new merch from the show! It's been years!" she said. David stepped up behind her and quietly cleared his throat, reminding her why they were there. She reluctantly looked away from the house. "Right, sorry. Tim—"

Tim had been looking at the shelf and commenting on which items he personally liked best and why, but when Erin said his name, he turned his head. "Fuck me!" He said and turned white as a ghost.

Erin laughed, completely thrilled she'd been able to get such a great reaction from him. "That's a fine way to greet someone, Tim!" she said, pretending to scold him on his manners. She smiled and turned, putting her hand on David's arm. "I'd like you to meet my good friend, David." Tim looked at her as though his brain had turned to scrambled eggs. "Come on, he doesn't bite; not hard anyway."

———

David laughed too; he was used to that reaction but having Erin there as comic relief made it much less awkward. "Hello, Tim, it's a pleasure to meet you," he said in the received pronunciation accent he used when he met fans. "Erin was telling me about you and was heart set on bringing me here."

———

Tim was still speechless, and Erin thought she saw his eyes getting wet, so she knew she needed to take action. "Okay, where's the toy I was looking at yesterday? Could you help me find it?" she said. He nodded slowly, clearly not wanting to walk away from David. "Don't worry; he won't leave until I do, so calm down." She put her arm around his shoulders and led him to the area where she'd seen the View-Master.

Once they were mostly out of earshot of David, she turned him around, put one hand on each of his shoulders, and looked him in the eye. "Now listen, Tim, I know you're excited, and you don't know what to say, but you're acting daft right now. Snap out of it, or we'll have to leave, and you'll feel like a right wanker! He's just like me, alright? He's nice, and he's funny, and just be yourself. Pretend you're talking to me and be cool!" she said, trying to bring him out of his slight mental breakdown. She nudged him, winked, and then picked up the small toy from off the shelf.

Tim smiled from ear to ear. "Aye, sorry. Yeh just caught me off guard! Ah'll be a'right," he said. "Well, I hope tae be." She then heard him say, '*belter,*' under his breath.

They walked back over to David, who had stepped up to the shelf of *Future Explorations* merchandise. He was holding the little farmhouse in his hand and shaking his head. "Erin, this is magnificent! I don't usually buy the merch, but I can't let this one go," he said, inspecting it the best he could with it inside the packaging.

She stood beside him and took it from his hand. It was in a lightweight cardboard box with a cellophane window to see it through. "Tim, could we open this?" she asked.

"Aye, on ye go," he said, and looked furtively at David, obviously trying not to stare.

She opened the end flap and pulled the cottage out of the box, which was about the size of a forty-bag box of Yorkshire tea. The farmhouse replica was so intricate you could see bits of the interior through its tiny windows. "Beautiful—No, stunning!" she said, holding it up and turning it around in her hands. "Makes you feel like you're there, doesn't it?" she handed it to David, who did the same thing she'd done. "And you'd know, wouldn't you?" she said to David and laughed.

"Uh, Mr.—Elliott?" Tim said nervously.

———

David turned around after smiling at Erin, knowing what would come next. "What can I do for you, Tim?" he asked and walked over to him, smiling his brilliant smile, and put one hand on his shoulder.

"Oh, God! Ah dinnae want tae be that guy, blatherin' on about bein' yer beggest fan and how ah love yer work, but… ah just dinnae ken how else tae say it. Ah think yer pure brilliant, a right beltah! Ah—ah cannae believe ah'm gettin' tae speak tae you," he said and blushed.

David let out a small laugh and decided to use his native accent from then on. "I can't say I've ever heard et said quite like that before! Thank you for yer kind words. I dinnae ken what yeh talked about yesterday, but Erin was buzzin' herself, tellin' me how I just had tae meet yeh," he said.

"David, you need to see this!" Erin said. She was standing at the window, holding the View-Master up to him.

He stepped over to her and took it from her hand, slightly uneasy at what he might see. He lifted it to his eyes, aimed it at the window, and rewarded her with a full belly laugh. "Ach, this is brilliant!" he said as he pulled down the lever to change the slide several times. "I can't believe this exists; I'd have thought you were takin' the piss if ye'd told me about et!"

"Are there more reels to go with it?" Erin asked Tim, and he pulled the box it had come in out from under the sales counter.

"Aye, here's the remainder of season one," he said, handing Erin the cardboard envelope with the rest of the reels for that season in it. "There's more; over here." He pointed to a rack with reels for all sorts of different shows and movies.

David and Erin looked them over, commenting on the ones that caught their attention. Tim stood back, watching them for a while, and then seemed much more relaxed when he approached them, as he would have any other customers.

About an hour after they got there, a customer came in, and they knew it was time to go. They'd been having so much fun, talking about *Future Explorations* and *Doctor Who*, that they'd lost track of time.

"I think et's time for us tae leave now, though I'm truly sorry tae say et," David said. "I've enjoyed maself immensely in here. Thank you, Erin, for insistin' I come. And, Tim, it was nice tae meet you. I now understand why Erin was so smitten with yeh." They bought the house and the View-Master with several extra reels. David waited until the customer left before asking, "Do you reckon anaone would mind if I signed this display?"

Tim handed David his change and then a felt-tipped pen. "Ah reckon the owner will want tae kiss me if yeh do!" Tim said. David was about to sign it but stopped and looked at him with his eyebrows raised. Tim laughed, "Ah dinnae think ah'd mind a kiss from her, yeh ken."

David smiled and signed the board.

"To Tim and the staff—
This shop is brilliant! Good luck on all your
FUTURE EXPLORATIONS.
~David Elliott."

Erin read it and laughed; then Tim read it and again looked like he might start to cry. "Ye've used ma name! That's just—" He ran out of words and turned around, acting like he was adjusting something on a shelf. After a moment, he seemed to gather his courage again. "Ah need tae ask; could ah get a selfie wi' you? Not tae share, like, only for maself… tae look at every now and then—Tae remind me that it happened." he said.

"Aye, I understand," David said.

Erin took the photo for them, and then got into a selfie with the three of them. "Do you mind if I take a copy of this one? I'll just—" she said and turned on the file transfer option, then they touched their phones together, so she had a copy of the file. "Thank you so much for this day, Tim. We really did have a great time! I knew he'd like it, and you!"

"Thank me? Are yeh daft? Ah'll never forget this day, Erin! Ye're awesome!" he said.

She smiled wickedly. "I am, aren't I?" she said playfully. "I'll try my best to come back again soon! Just don't quit or do anything stupid to get yourself fired! Okay?"

"Naw, I willnae dae that!" he said and laughed.

"Aye, I'd like tae come back as well," David said and then whispered something into Erin's ear.

"Okay. Tim, would you mind giving me your phone number, so I can text yeh… uh, you… to make sure you're still here, and to see if it's busy when we have time to return?"

The young man looked shocked. "Aye, that's fantastic. I look forward tae seein' you again!" he said and wrote it down for her.

Erin hugged him, and they both said goodbye as Roger pulled up and they left the store. She waved as Tim watched them get into the black SUV, and then they pulled away from the pavement.

Chapter Fifty-Eight

HIGHLAND BOUND

When Roger pulled into the drive and let them out at Owlgate, Erin overheard him tell David that something was ready for him, though she didn't hear what it was. David thanked him and then asked Erin to get ready for their trip and meet him in the garage with her luggage. She did as she was told, making sure to pack a jacket and sweater, it was Scotland after all, and she knew the weather could vary drastically day to day.

Erin made a quick stop to the kitchen for an apple and to tell Millie they were about to leave. She seemed to be prepared for it and handed her a hamper full of food and wine. "Dinnae fret, dear," Millie said, "Et's non-alcoholic wine. Wouldnae wannae harm the wee one, yeh ken."

"You're so sweet, Millie. Thank you!" she said and gave her a peck on the cheek, which made her face turn red.

The old woman shooed Erin away with her tea towel. "Have a nice time, dearie. Ach, and tell our Davey he'd better drive safely with you and the bairn aboard that machine!"

Erin laughed even though she had no idea what she was talking about. "Okay, I will. Bye," she said and went out the side door, which was closer to the garage. She took a deep breath, smelling all the green things and flowers surrounding her. She liked it there and hoped they'd be back often as she walked over to the open garage door and gasped audibly.

In the stall next to the sensible SUV that Roger drove was the most beautiful, sexy car she'd ever laid eyes on. It was sky blue and had curves which made you think hip and legs and bosoms. "Good Night Nurse! It should be illegal to be that beautiful!" she said, not caring if anyone heard her.

Both Roger and David stepped out of the shadows and laughed. "Aye, she is somethin', ain't she?" Roger said, "And I have tae look at her evera day of ma life!"

David nudged him and began, "She's a 1960 Triumph TR3A—"

"And he loves her," Roger broke in, making David laugh.

"Aye, and what's no' tae love? She was one of the first things I bought with my *Future Explorations* money," he said.

"Aye, and worth evera cent yeh paid for the bird as well!" Roger said. It was obvious *he* was the one in love with the car.

Erin smiled at him, glad and a bit surprised to see him open up. "I approve! Is this what we're taking on the trip?" she asked excitedly.

"Aye, I need a beauty tae transport ma beauty, now, don't I?" he said with a smile.

Erin raised her eyebrows. "You're blind as a bat if you think you can compare the two of us based on beauty," she said. She wheeled her small suitcase over to the car, and Roger placed it in the open trunk next to David's holdall.

The trunk lid closed with a smart *snap*. "Bags are in the boot; yer all set tae go," Roger said and opened the door for Erin.

David was already in the driver's seat, waiting to start it. "Are you ready, love?" he asked.

Erin wasn't sure what he meant, but she was ready for the trip, so she said, "Aye, tally ho!" He turned the key, starting the engine, and all three of them moaned at the leonine growl that came from the engine. "Holy Moses!" she said, feeling the rumble throughout her whole body and finally understood why guys got off on cars like that. "Take me now! Right here in the garage," she said. "Roger, if you'll please excuse us, I need to be made love to!" The two men roared with laughter, but Erin was only half kidding. That was the sexiest thing she had ever imagined coming from a car.

When they turned onto the road, Erin could feel the engine wanting to fly. Internally, she sensed the anxiousness of the tied-up animals inside the machine. The horses whinnied and the lioness growled in anticipation, but David was reigning them in. She wished he'd give it some gas and stop torturing the poor thing, though she knew he wasn't going to until they had some open, police-free motorways. As he drove through the busy, slow roads of Edinburgh, people in their cars honked, and those on the street shouted out their admiration. She understood why he wouldn't be able to drive a car like that one in London; he'd be recognized and followed. As it was, they heard his name shouted along with words like 'future' and 'explore' in most of the comments

She heard one woman shout out, "I love yeh John Thomas; will you marry me?" to which David honked the horn.

Erin laughed and said, "Careful; she might take that as a yes."

When they got onto the M9, he finally let her go a bit but not for very long. "Wouldn't want an actual working CCTV camera to spot us," he said.

Erin was in love, with David and with the car. "Does she have a name? The car, I mean," she asked.

"A name? Well, no, I hadn't thought of that. What name would you give her?"

"I don't know, but she needs a good one, something like Lucy, or Titania, or—or Betty," she said, and he laughed.

"Betty, huh?" he said, intrigued.

"Oooh! What about Neela? It's Hindi and means, 'Blue—the color of the sea.' I had a girl on my bus with that name, and I just had to look it up to see what it meant. It's pretty, isn't it?" she said excitedly.

"Say it again," he said.

"Neela," she said, and he repeated it a few times.

"Aye, et's a bonnie name for a pure, bonnie car. I dub thee Neela, Queen of the Road!" he said authoritatively. They laughed and laughed, acting immature and silly and not caring one bit.

Erin put her hand on his leg and suddenly felt the electricity pass between them. She had to catch her breath and slowly drew it away so he'd be able to concentrate on driving. He took hold of her hand and placed it back on his leg, a bit farther up than it had been previously. "David, you should be thinking about driving, not—" she began to say in protest, but he ignored her and pulled it farther up his leg until it covered the bulge in his trousers.

Traffic was light, so she unzipped his fly and carefully pulled his hard cock out of his trousers, making him gasp. "I can't think of anathin', only you," he said. She could feel her body pulsing with his energy and bent over his lap, taking his hard cock into her mouth. "Ach, Erin!" he said. "Don't stop!"

Finding and maintaining a good position in the tiny car was difficult as her knee was digging into the base of the gear shifter, so she sat up. That was all he would get just then; however, things would be different when they reached their destination.

"Ach, I want yeh sae badly, woman!"

She looked up ahead and saw a sign that read 'Stirling A90' and ignored him. "Does it say Stirling on the sign, up ahead?" she asked. Her breathing was rapid, and she felt her heart beating in her clitoris, which was extra sensitive.

He squinted, trying to see the sign. "Aye," he said breathlessly and then took the exit. He pulled into a lay-by and parked as far back from the petrol station as he could. He engaged the parking brake and put his hand on the back of her neck, trying to pull her back toward his hard-on.

"I'm afraid someone will see us, David," she said, trying to reason with him. There were cameras all over the place and she knew he would be sorry if someone happened to be watching and saw that he was receiving a blow job.

"I dinnae care, Erin," he tried pleading, but she laughed.

"Aye, yeh do care, laddie, and I'll nae ha' yeh gettin' a ticket fer indecent exposure wi' me en thes car! Do yeh want the tabloids tae have a headline handed tae them, love?" she said and then laughed harder at how silly it sounded.

He wasn't laughing as he tried to find a comfortable position and zipped up his fly. "Humph," he said under his breath.

"I'm sorry, David. I... didn't mean to cause you pain," she said when she saw his face. He looked like he was actually hurting and trying to hide it. She did feel bad, but what could she do? It was far too dangerous to be caught in the act in broad daylight. "I'm sorry," she whispered again.

Silently, he disengaged the brake, left the parking lot, and resumed their journey. After shifting to the highest gear, he took her hand. "No, I'm sorry, love. Dinnae fash," he said and kissed it, keeping his lips pressed against the back of her hand for a long time. "I shouldn't be so selfish."

They continued on the M9 and drove for what felt like forever until they came to a roundabout and took the A9, which had double warning signs saying speed cameras were used on the road and to average their speed. They got off the highway onto the A822, a small road winding through residential areas at forty miles per hour. Sadly, as soon as there was a place to speed up, friendly signs thanked them for driving safely.

The land was mostly flat, though Erin could see hills in the distance. Large rocks sat in an odd row on a mown field, appearing to have been strategically placed there and scattered randomly at the same time. Their purpose was a mystery to her. She imagined that perhaps they had once been ancient foundation stones but had lost all form by then.

The day was beautiful, warm, and sunny, with just enough intermittent cloud cover to keep it from being too hot. They passed a cemetery and wooded areas, as well as newer subdivisions. Much of the road was lined with beautiful stone walls, telling you they cared, at least in times past, about how things looked and functioned. She was happy to be in that part of the world, with David at her side.

She started to see what looked like mountains in the distance and was getting excited. They drove through a beautiful old town called Muthill, which she thought was the strangest name for a place. The buildings were old and made from enormous stone blocks, some red, others brown, and grey. After a loo break and a much-needed stretch, they got back on the road and soon passed a sign that read, 'Crieff Highland Games.' It was an open field that day, but Erin thought it would be fun to experience it someday.

The journey seemed to be taking forever, and she just wanted to get to their destination and relax. She thought they would never get there and would just keep driving forever. The land was becoming much more undulating as they drove up inclines and back down again, over and over, and she was getting impatient. Then, finally, David turned onto a tiny road, headed uphill into the woods.

Foothills, crags, and the beginnings of low mountains surrounded them. Then, the landscape gradually opened up, and the road became a narrow, one-lane path with no shoulders. The only way for two vehicles to pass were small, paved shoulders on the side of the road. Without them, someone would be stuck backing up for miles.

They were very much in the middle of nowhere. Erin had been very patient and not asked David if they were there yet, but she was tired of sitting and needed to stretch her legs. "David, my love, are we even close yet?" she asked, trying not to sound as restless as she felt. He replied by pointing to an even smaller road, and what she soon discovered was a driveway. He turned onto it, and she was relieved that the waiting was over and she could finally relax.

In the distance, she could see a loch, surrounded on three sides by the mountains, their peaks reaching, jagged and cold, into the sky. The air was crisp and clean, and Erin tried to imagine what it would be like to live there. Her thoughts were interrupted as they approached a thatched, stone cottage; it was idyllic, and she gasped. "Oh, David! It's lovely!" she said and couldn't wait to go inside.

He smiled and took her hand for a moment before he had to shift into a lower gear. "I'm glad yeh fancy et; I bought it nearly fifteen years ago now, though I rarely get a chance tae come here anamore. I used tae bring ma children during their summer holidays, but things have been busy, so we dinnae do it anamore," he said with a look of regret.

"At least you used to do that. I'm sure they have lots of good memories. Anyway, it's far more than many dads do with their kids."

"I love how you see the positive side, love. Yeh ken how tae keep me from beatin' maself up over things I can't change," he said and pulled up to the cottage. He set the parking brake and switched the engine off. All the rumbling and purring stopped, and it was quiet enough that Erin's ears still hummed with the memory of the noise.

Chapter Fifty-Nine

COTTAGE WITH A SURPRISE

"Good night nurse, it's quiet here!" Erin said softly.

"Aye, et takes a bit of getting used tae, but I love et," David said. "Let's wait tae bring our things inside; there's somethin' I'd like tae show yeh first."

They got out of the car, and he took her by the hand. She followed him to the back of the house then he headed toward the loch she'd seen on the way up the drive. They climbed a berm and then scaled a few small hillocks. The loch could be seen much better from the top of the third hill. "Oh! It's… just spectacular! It… makes my heart ache!" she said, holding her hand up to her chest.

"Aye, it does mine as well," he said. He'd never told anyone how the view from that very spot made him feel before, and for her to say those exact words shocked and thrilled him. They walked down a shallow valley, and then she saw it. The tiny, rustic farmhouse where John Thomas of Fife had lived in the first season of *Future Explorations* sat reposed, pristine in its idyllic setting.

Erin squeaked and stopped dead in her tracks. "Are you kidding me? Am I hallucinating! How on earth did you get it?"

He smiled and put his arm around her shoulders, feeling the goosebumps covering her skin. "The owner was a fan of the program and contacted me since I was the lead character. I noted ma interest in the property, bid verra high, and won et," he said. "Susannah was against it and called me a sentimental fool, but I knew I couldn't pass et up. Now, here I am with someone who… understands. It brings me so much joy that I'm able tae share it with you, ma love."

Erin turned and kissed him, then she ran down the hill and stopped at the front door. "Woah! That's exactly where Joe walked! Holy Moses! Can we… go inside?" she asked excitedly.

"Aye, although there's no' much in et," he said and joined her at the door, holding an old skeleton key. "A set was built for the interior shots." He thought she seemed like a little girl in front of Santa's *real* workshop. She was giddy, and the smile on her face gave him so much joy.

"Eee!" she squealed.

He laughed good-naturedly at her. "Ye're so childlike right now; et's bonnie," he said and didn't think he could love her any more than he did at that moment.

"I *feel* like a child. You know just how to make me young again," she said. He put the key into the lock, turned it, and it unlocked with a satisfying clunk. Then he turned the knob on the door, and it swung open easily, with a slight creaking noise.

To say the house was rustic would have been an understatement. It had obviously lived through at least a hundred, or more likely, three hundred years of coal fires by the dark grey soot covering everything from floor to ceiling, but it only added to the charm in Erin's mind. "Someone lived here a long time ago," she said. "I wonder who built this place and what they were like?"

"Aye, I reckon they stood here, as we are now," David said, imagining the transparent ghost images of people moving around them. Erin turned to find him right behind her and put her arms around his waist. "I reckon there was love and passionate kisses, leading tae wee bairns as a result." He kissed her tenderly, then she looked up into his face, smiling and blushing. "Ach, what's that about?" he said and touched her cheek.

The color in her cheeks deepened, and she laughed. "I don't want to tell you; you'll laugh at me."

He pointed at his chest, "Who me? No, I won't."

"I don't believe you."

He hugged her and repeated himself. "I won't."

She raised an eyebrow in disbelief but continued. "Alright, you've talked me into it… John Thomas," she said.

At that, he did laugh but played along, speaking exactly like his character would have. He even changed his demeanor so that Erin was slightly startled and more than a little turned on. "Ooch, wha' es a bonnie lass such as ye doin' oot here en thes wild country?" he asked her, sounding truly concerned for her safety.

She didn't know how to answer, so she said the first things that came to her mind. "I've come tae find yeh; I want tae be yer lass, and carry yer bairn, so you can see et suckle at ma breast. I wannae grow old wi' you, scratchin' a livin' oot of thes wild, barren land. Please, say ye'll have me," she said and was shocked to see his eyes well up with tears.

He turned away from her. "Nae, lass, ah dinnae deserve ye. Ye need a man wi' more than wha' ah've got tae gi'," he said sadly.

Erin stepped back, not knowing how to take what he'd just said to her. Was he still in character, or was this some confession of his? "More than what you've got to give, David? What are you trying to say?" He didn't turn around; he just stood, facing the cold, fieldstone fireplace. "What is it? Please speak to me," she said softly and placed her hand on his shoulder. He turned then, and she could see where tears had run down his face, with more threatening to fall from his wet, red eyes.

He wrapped his arms tightly around her, trying to get himself under control again. "That was lovely, what yeh just said. Et made me realize how unlike John Thomas Fife I truly am," he said. "He was strong and fearless and would know just how tae 'scratch a livin' from thes barren land.' I only ken how tae pretend tae be someone I'm not. I'd the most vivid image of everathin' yeh said, and it… broke ma heart tae ken just how inadequate I am… as a man."

Erin's heart ached for him. "Oh, my darling, that was nothing; I made it all up on the spot. I don't want to scratch a life out of the wilderness of Scotland. It's a nice fantasy while sitting in a warm living room watching the television set, but I'm not cut out for that. I love who you are! I love how you can tell me what you're feeling and that you aren't ashamed to cry in front of me," she said. "Those are the things that make you a good, strong, fearless man in my eyes. I want the life we'll build together, whatever it looks like, with our child, or children, 'it's unclear at this time,'" she quoted the fortune teller's words, and they both laughed.

"I love yeh, Erin March," he said.

"Née Wallace," she said and laughed. "By the way, what was that about anyway?"

"Ach, it was mad. I thought that if ma mum knew you were of Scottish descent, she might warm tae yeh right away. I wanted her tae like yeh so badly. I know, it was foolish."

"Maybe so, but it's okay; you are allowed to be foolish for good reasons like that." A strong gust of wind rose suddenly and hit the house, making soot fall from the chimney. A thick cloud of ancient coal dust bloomed out from the fireplace, filling the room. They coughed and covered their faces with their sleeves. "We should probably go now, don't you think?" she said as she headed for the door and fresh air.

"Aye," he said as they hurried out into the afternoon sunshine. "I'm sorry I ruined yer fantasy. It was a bonnie tale," he said.

"Ooch, et's a'right; I'll jest have tae make noo ones," she said, and they started walking toward the cottage. On top of the hillock, Erin turned. She took her phone out of her pocket and snapped a photo of the old house, then took a selfie with David and put it back into her pocket. She held David's hand, and they walked over the hills back to the house they'd pulled up to earlier.

Chapter Sixty

DREAMS AND DISCOVERIES

"I need to use the bathroom, so could you open the door before we get our bags—Please?" Erin said 'please' with extra sweetness.

"How can I refuse?" David said. He unlocked the door and gave her a quick kiss. "First door on yer right, love; I'll fetch the luggage."

Erin walked into the house and loved it instantly. The decor was shabby chic, and nothing truly matched. It was pretty and feminine with loads of flowers and stripes. She found the bathroom and heard David come into the house as she was washing her hands. "Who decorated this place?" she asked. "It's beautiful! I can't imagine it was Susannah."

David smiled at her as he walked out of the bedroom, where he'd taken the luggage. "No, it was partly the previous owner and partly ma mum, though ma Rosie and Charlie helped quite a lot. As you can see, they have a knack for et," he said.

"Perfectly my taste! I don't have that knack. I know what I like and what I don't, but I'm not good at putting things together so it looks right. I can't wait to meet Rosie and Charlie—Well, I think I can't wait—I mean—" she stammered, and David laughed.

"Ach, they'll love yeh. They may no' admit tae it at first, but ye'll be best mates eventually," he predicted.

"Holy Moses! I just remembered a dream I had with at least one of your kids in it," she said, feeling as though a jolt of electricity had just passed through her; not the exciting variety she and David shared, but the ominous sort.

"Ye've dreamed of ma children? Interesting; let's have a seat," he said, and she followed him to the couch.

"Yeah, I'm trying to remember how it went. I was... helping them get... dressed for an event. Assisting in choosing ties and shoes—that sort of thing. One of them was crying. I was holding them and saying it would be alright, though I didn't know what it was about.

"Next thing I know, I'm standing with the bride-to-be from Bourbon Street; I think Champagne was there, too. We were watching a parade; I thought we were at Mardi Gras, but everyone was in black, and they were crying. I looked around, and everyone had their faces painted like skulls for the Day of the Dead.

"There was a horse-drawn wagon, covered in black lace with a casket... topped with black and red flowers, along with more lace; people were moaning and crying as it passed by them. I then saw a dark bird like a raven or crow, and when I looked closer, I saw it was dark blue and black. As I watched, the bird landed on the casket and began... pecking, as if it was trying to get into it.

"I was trying to find you, but no one would tell me where you were. Finally, a lady said they saw someone who looked like you in a pub, so I went looking for you at St. Brendan's, but when I went in, it was cottage number two, in New Orleans. You were asleep on the couch, but when I tried to wake you, you rolled over, and... your face was painted like a skull, too.

"You were wearing a dark red t-shirt with a blackbird... wings spread out, kinda like one of the Aerosmith albums I have at home. You were drunk and started yelling at me for not being dressed in black or having my face painted," she said, feeling strange. "That's when I woke up."

"Wow!"

"I can't believe I remembered all that. It was obviously a nightmare, but I don't remember waking up scared or anything; I must have had another dream afterward. I also don't remember watching anything about the Day of the Dead or funeral processions in the last, oh, ten years, give or take. Do you think it means anything or was it just something I ate?" she asked, trying to lighten the mood.

"I cannae say, hen, but it did have a bird—Two, if yeh count the one on the shirt I was wearin'. We were warned about birds by the fortune teller, so— I hope not though; it seems I was a real prick."

Erin laughed and then became serious. "The thing was, I didn't think it was you… on the couch. The lady only said it was someone who looked like you, and I happen to know there *is* someone who fits that description."

David touched her goosebump covered arm. "When did yeh have this dream?"

"While I was staying at the Ritz... before I knew Bran existed." She was good and scared by then; she didn't want to be having crazy, prophetic dreams about death and people she hadn't met yet. "Hold me," she said, trembling. He held her and kissed her hair. "What kind of name is Bran, anyway? Is it short for something like Brandon?"

"I dinnae ken; I would imagine it is. Wait, I think it's short for Branok, now I think back on et."

Erin took out her phone to search for the meaning. "No signal."

"Ach, ma mobile's in the kitchen." He stood and grabbed his phone from off the counter. She watched him typing and then saw steady himself on the edge of the kitchen counter. His face went white, and goosebumps covered his arms. "What? Tell me!" she said. Her eyes were wide, and she suddenly wanted to cry, though she didn't know what for. "David?"

He read the result from his search aloud: "Bran is a Celtic name, meaning... crow. It can be a short form of Branwen or Branok, which mean the same."

Erin stood but shouldn't have; her head filled with buzzing, and she saw little dots as everything started going black. She woke up with David kneeling next to her. "Erin! Can yeh hear me?" he was saying as she came to. "Are yeh alright?"

"Crow? You're joking, right? This is a gag, and you're taking the piss, right?" she said, not knowing if she should be angry or frightened out of her mind, though he was still white as a ghost.

"I wouldn't do that," he said and helped her to sit on the sofa again.

"No, of course you wouldn't, but David, who—Oh, never mind."

"Who?" he repeated, but she didn't want to say it. "Ach, I ken—Who was in the casket, aye? The one ma children and all New Orleans were mournin'? I mean, where was I in yer dream? Is that what yer askin'?"

"I don't think it was you in the casket, David; I really don't," she said. "I was looking for you because I wanted to be sure you were okay. The person in the casket was someone you knew well, or loved, or had a relationship of some kind with. It wasn't you."

"Aye, I think we need tae change the subject. I dinnae want tae think about people I know dyin' or mournin'. Do yeh ken what's in the hamper?" he said.

Erin sat up; he was right; things were getting far too heavy. "No, Millie gave it to me, and I didn't open it or ask. She did mention it was non-alcoholic wine, so I reckon it must have wine in it, said Sherlock Holmes to Mr. Watson," she said with a smile.

He stood and went to the kitchen. Lifting the hamper lid, he lifted a note from inside it. Erin stood slowly, joined him, and read it along with him.

I figured you didn't think about food, so I've packed a few provisions for you. Put them in the fridge and then eat them! There are heating instructions on each dish.
Millie xx

"That was nice of her, and she was right," Erin said. They pulled out leftover stew, roast chicken, and a meat pie. There was also bread, cheese, a bit of fruit, and a few bottles of non-alcoholic wine. As Erin put the perishables into the fridge, David opened a bottle of mock Moscato and poured them each a glass.

"Would yeh like a tour of the house?" he asked when the hamper was empty.

"Aye, I'd love one, thanks," she said and took the glass of wine he was holding out for her. "Moscato is one of my favorites!"

David started the tour where they were standing. "This is the kitchen, and just over there is the dinin' room. Ye'll see the sittin' room just in front of you, and ye've already found the toilet." He stepped over to a short hallway and opened the only door to their left. He switched on the light, and Erin saw two single beds and a dresser. "This is the guest bedroom; if yeh weren't stayin' with me, ye'd be sleepin' in here tonight." He showed her the closet in the hall and the door leading outside to the back garden.

"That door leads to the cellar; et's no verra big, but et's where the coal is stored. The junction box is down there as well, so now yeh know, in case there's an outage or yeh get cold and need a fire tae warm yer toes."

"Nice, thanks!"

He turned around, invading Erin's personal space as he tried to pass her, acting like the hall was much narrower than it was, and pressed against her as he tried to get past. "Ever so sorry! Tight quarters, innit?" he said, pushing her up against the wall. "Here, ye'll find the master bedroom."

She walked in first, then he came in and closed the door behind him. At the sound of the lock, she spun around. He took the wine glass out of her hand and set it on the dresser. Her breath caught as he started unbuckling his belt. "Now, where were we earlier?" he said as he unfastened his trousers and let them drop. He did the same with his underpants and then took off his shirt.

Erin stepped up to him and ever so gently grabbed and caressed his cock, moving down to his balls every so often. He moaned as he unfastened her capris with one hand and then pulled them and her underwear down. "This time, we will both finish! None of this no' following through business, do yeh hear me?" he said.

"Yes, sir. Whatever you say, sir." She let go of him just long enough to take her top off and lie on the bed. He was rock hard, and she could hardly stand it; she felt like an earthquake would erupt if he didn't enter her soon. He laid on his back, and she straddled him, guiding him into her, then she arched her back as he reached her full depth. "Oh... God! Oh... yes!" she cried out.

He sat up, put his hand on her cheek, and kissed her. Then he moved his hand to her breast and kneaded it gently. "I've wanted yeh all day, hen. At the toy shop, when yeh took the boy aside and gave him a right tongue lashin' tae get him tae snap out of et; in the garage, when yeh told Roger we'd need a minute, seeing yeh needed tae be made love tae; when you named ma car; and especially on the motorway and lay-by. That was torture! Pure bloody torture! I wanted yeh the most in the old farmhouse; ye've been makin' me radge all bloody day."

They rocked back and forth together, keeping a steady rhythm. He put her nipple into his mouth, suckling it so that she felt it deep inside, in a place she couldn't name but which felt amazing. "Oh! Keep doing that!" she said as she felt an orgasm approaching. Suddenly, he stopped everything, just as she was about to climax, and then held her fast when she tried to move. "What are you—" she said, confusion and frustration evident in her voice.

She could feel the throbbing inside of her, wanting desperately to go on, to keep moving. "Are you... trying to make a point? You have, please—please," she begged. She could feel his erection pulsing inside of her, the blood surging into his engorged cock. "Please, David." Finally, he let her go, and their orgasms were so powerful. The anticipation made everything feel more, so much more.

"I didn't know anything like that was possible before you," she said, continuing to ride him until the last waves had subsided. "All my adult life, I have longed for something even close to this and could never find it. I could never get there, at least not in time... before everything was over with, but with you, I feel the best I've ever felt every single time! It's simply heaven." She dismounted and lay close to him, wanting to feel him near her. She lay on her side with her arm across his chest, her head nestled on his shoulder, twirling his chest hair around her finger. "This is nice."

"Aye. I'm glad ye're here with me." They lay like that for some time. The only sounds were their breathing, the refrigerator running, and the wind occasionally hitting the side of the house hard, making the windows whistle.

Erin sat up, listening intently. "I think I heard a car pull up to the house." David got up, threw on his clothes, and headed out to the front door. As she got dressed, she heard David open the door before the doorbell rang. He was talking to someone, and she overheard something about light bulbs. David thanked whoever he was talking to and then moved away from the door, telling them to come in as she entered the room.

Chapter Sixty-One

OLD JOHN'S BULBS

A man who looked to be between the ages of sixty and ninety, with pure white hair, bright green eyes, and about a million wrinkles stepped in. David shook his hand. "John Murray is the man who tends the place whilst I'm away," he explained to her. "I asked him tae check things over before we arrived. John, this is ma good friend from America, Erin March. She's never been this far north before now."

The man either believed him or didn't need a backstory. *Or maybe he's used to David bringing women up here for 'mini-breaks,'* she thought before she could stop herself.

"Pleasure tae meet yeh, miss," John said and then made his way through the cottage, replacing burned-out lightbulbs as he went. Once he was satisfied that their lighting needs were met, the man went up to David and said something Erin couldn't hear. David told him not to worry about it and thanked him. The old man nodded, walked to the door, and let himself out, leaving with a short wave over his shoulder.

"He didn't seem bothered by me being here with you," Erin said, partly for conversation and partly because she wanted to hear what reason he'd give.

"Old John keeps tae himself; that's why I hired him. Yeh dinnae want gossips workin' for yeh in my line of business."

Erin smiled, "I guess not; good thing you found him then." Her mind was trying to make her see things that weren't there again. Martin's words had affected her more than she'd thought and were coming back to haunt her.

"Aye, he's been minding this place for quite a long time. He knows it inside and out."

As well as all the women who've been inside and out of it, went through her mind, quick as lightning. She walked into the small living room and sat on the sofa. Her brain wouldn't shut up, no matter how much she wanted it to, so she started thinking about the things the fortune teller had said to them at the museum. Mainly about the birds pecking their eyes out, "…or was it just mine? I can't remember now," she said to herself.

"What was that, hen?" he said as he sat next to her.

"I was thinking about what the fortune teller said about the birds. We know there are at least two in your… I mean, our lives right now, Bran and Martin. Both seem to be bad news, so why would we trust them? What could they do that we're trusting them not to—Or what might they be capable of that we haven't thought about? Also, are there more than two? Who else might be part of it?" she asked.

"Well, with Bran, anathin' goes, really. He'll stop at nothin' when he needs a fix, so we need tae keep a wary eye on him, especially after I gave him that thumpin'."

"Oh, is that what you did then?"

"Somethin' like that," he said with a shrug of his shoulders.

She smiled and continued. "So that leaves Martin. He knows we're together, though it seems like he thinks I'm a temporary fixture in your life."

"Aye, I'm no' sure what he thinks or knows, but he doesn't know I've seen the pictures from New Orleans, so—"

"Wait! Pictures? What are you talking about?" she interrupted, with a look of sheer terror on her face.

"Didn't I tell you about them?" he said, furrowing his brow.

She closed her eyes, wanting to vomit. "Please, don't tell me there are photos out there of me… naked."

"Ach, Erin, I'm sorry! I thought I'd mentioned et!" He told her about what was on his bed when he'd returned home from New Orleans. "Most of them are nothin' to be upset about, though a few are—well, graphic. The worst of them were taken when we made love on the patio. Someone must've had a drone, I reckon. One is of you, laying on ma lap with yer robe open, and three of them... are of me... with you bent over on the table," he said timidly. "I should've been more careful."

"Yeah, I guess so," she said quietly.

"I'm so sorry—I reckon it was Martin who hired the photographer and then brought them tae Susannah," he said.

"Su—Susannah has seen them too? Of... course she has," she said, not believing what she was hearing and stood, thinking she might actually puke. Again, she felt the whooshing in her head, her ears filled with static, and then her eyes faded to black.

She woke to find herself on the carpeted floor of the sitting room with David hovering over her, trying to bring her back to consciousness. "Erin? Are you a'right? I'm so sorry. I should've been more delicate."

"No, I'm *not* alright," she said, sitting up with her back against the sofa. "So... Martin... has also seen me... naked? Oh, God! And he has pictures of us like that? If I'd known—I never would have gone along with the plan at the Savoy! He could... sell them... and—Oh—" She was breathing hard and fast, rubbing the back of her neck and shaking her head back and forth. "But—but if they're sold... and people see them—Oh no, Todd!"

"Christ, woman! Ye've left him! Why must yeh bring him up now?" David yelled and then covered his mouth with his hand. "Oh, ma God! I cannae believe I said that! I didn't mean et. I'm so sorry!" he said anxiously.

Erin's eyes expanded as disbelief flooded her features. She slowly got to her knees, leaning on the sofa, not saying anything. He opened his mouth to speak, but she put her hand up to tell him to be quiet. "My head is pounding." Her voice was low and steady. She started to get up, so he stood to help her, but she didn't accept it. "Please, leave me... alone. I need to lay down for a while." She said calmly but firmly and walked into the bedroom, closing the door behind her.

She pulled the covers back on the bed and got into it; her head was swimming and hurt horribly.

You *had a nice, normal, naked-photo-free life back home; what have you gotten yourself into?* The tears started when she closed her eyes, not helping the headache at all. David knocked on the door, but she ignored him, and he didn't do it again.

Not long after she lay down, she got up. It felt like a vacuum cleaner hose was attached to her ears trying to suck her brains out, and she needed a pain reliever. She quietly opened the door and didn't see David. The television was on in the sitting room. A woman was speaking French, which she couldn't understand, so she padded to the bathroom and found some Ibuprofen and paracetamol, which she took together.

She didn't want to talk to David yet; she needed air and decided a walk would calm her down. Back home, when she and Todd had big arguments, she'd walk around the block, and usually, by the time she returned, she'd be able to deal with whatever was wrong.

It was time to at least start thinking about supper, and she didn't know how long she'd be gone, so she slipped, noiselessly, into the kitchen, turned on the oven, and put the meat pie in, then set a timer. She hoped it would be nearly done when she got back. With that taken care of, she wrote a short note that said, 'Be back soon,' on the tablet near the fridge, then she got her shoes out of the bedroom, slipped them on, and left out the back door. She walked up the berm behind the house and took a deep breath.

After knocking on the bedroom door and getting no answer, David gave up and sat on the sofa. He figured he'd let her alone for a while. Maybe if she got some sleep, she'd come out, and they could talk about it, or he could at least apologize again.

He turned on the television and found an old French movie with subtitles, so he watched it, trying to follow along, but after a while, his eyelids grew heavy, and he fell asleep. He woke to an alarm and a horrible-smelling, black haze filling the room. He sprang up off the couch, ready to find Erin,

David woke outside in the front garden with an oxygen mask over his face, and the house, completely engulfed in flames. He tried to sit up, but an EMT was there to keep him still.

He lifted the mask, "Erin! There's a woman in there! She's in the bedroom!" he tried to yell, but his voice was raspy, and it came out as more of a croak.

The EMT looked shocked. "Are yeh sure? The entire hoose was examined thoroughly, already," the young man said. He rushed over to the chief fire officer and said something in his ear. David saw the middle-aged man shake his head and look over at him, then the two men came back and stood next to him.

"Ah'm afraid we've checked the whoole hoose, and we didnae find anaone," the chief fire officer said to him "Could she have left withoot yer knowledge?"

"No, I've been in the house the entire time! I'm sure she was inside. Please! Yeh must look again!" he implored.

The two men looked at each other, and the chief officer put his hand on David's shoulder. "Ah'm sorry lad, but we cannae doo tha'; the roof has collapsed. If she's stell in there, then... ah'm afraid et's too late," he said.

David sat there in shock. "NO! Et can't be! NO! I—I dinnae believe et! I need tae search for her! Please, allow me tae find her!" he begged and tried to get free of the EMT's hold, but the chief officer put his hand on his arm.

"Ah'm terribly sorry, Mr. Elliott, but there's nothin' can be doon right noo. We'll be goin' through et again once the fire's completely oot. If we find her body—"

"Her... body? Oh, ma God! No!" David cried out in horror.

The EMT put the oxygen mask back over David's face. "We need tae bring yeh to hospital; ye've inhaled quite a lot of smoke," he said.

"I—" David took the mask off again, "I dinnae want tae leave her!" he said, desperately trying to get free of the EMT's grasp. He was coughing hoarsely and tried to get up again, but the man held him down. Seeing the struggle, an assistant came to help, and David was taken to hospital anyway.

Chapter Sixty-Two

HERE I AM

Erin had just climbed a rather steep hill and was sitting in the grass at the top, looking out over the countryside. The air was crisp and fresh up there, and she finally felt like she could think. The old stone farmhouse was barely visible to her side, but she wasn't going there. She wanted to get to the loch, but it was farther away than she'd thought.

Hearing sirens, she turned around, amazed at how far she'd walked, and saw a large cloud of black smoke billowing from the direction she'd just come. Alarmed, she started back toward the house, *Holy Moses! David,* she thought, moving as fast as she could. On the way to where she was, she'd rambled over several small hills and then up the last, taller one, which was proving tricky to descend. She didn't want to fall and end up rolling, ass over feet to the bottom, as Joe Whitehall had done.

Managing to overcome that obstacle, she then had to traverse the rest. After the second one, she was panting, and her side pinched so terribly she had to stop and catch her breath. At the top of the next hill, she could see fire engine lights flashing close to the small stone house. *Oh, David! Please don't try to be a hero!*

She finally made it back, clutching her side and trying to catch her breath just as the roof caved in with a tremendous plume of smoke. Ashes flew everywhere, and flames licked the sky while the firefighters aimed their hoses at the blaze, though it didn't seem to be doing much. A few minutes later, an ambulance left the site with its lights on and sirens screaming for everyone to get out of the way, and she prayed David was safe.

When she eventually lurched her way to the house, several neighbors and curious onlookers were trying to see the show. She was pushed back several times before she got the attention of one of the firemen. She told him who she was and asked about David, so the man took her to the chief fire officer.

"I'm... Erin March," she panted, out of breath, and holding her side. "I am... the guest of David Elliott. What... happened? Is he alright?"

"Chief Officer MacDonald," he said as he shook her hand. "I'm sae glad tae see yeh, lass! I was worrit you were still inside, and we'd somehoow missed yeh. Mr. Elliott was beside himself weth fear. We dinnae ken what started the blaze, but it was a guid thing a neighbor was walkin' their dug and rang us at the first sign of smooke."

"Is he okay? Was he in the house?" she asked. The chief officer put his hand on her shoulder to calm her.

"Aye, he was in the house, though someone pulled him oot b'fore et was too late. He did breathe in a good deal of smooke, sae we've sent him tae hospital, but I dare say he'll be a'right."

Erin was relieved; her side ached, and she was still breathing heavily, but David was safe! "Thank God!" she said.

"If yeh dinnae mind me askin', where were yeh? Mr. Elliott said yeh were in the bedroom, but we searched, and yeh were-nae there."

Erin explained what had happened. "Which hospital was he taken to?" she asked, not sure how she'd get there.

"Ach, I'll take yeh there maself in a bit; there's little else we can dae here," he said. They both looked at the small house, which was now a heap of smoldering rubble.

Erin couldn't believe what she was seeing. An hour or two earlier, it was a beautiful house, and there it sat, a total loss. *Poor David! Thinking I was in there!* she thought sadly.

It took nearly an hour before C.O. MacDonald was free to take Erin to the hospital in his pickup truck. He walked her in and spoke to the nurses for her, explaining what had happened. They were shown to a room where David lay, with a nasal cannula supplying oxygen through tubes that sat under his nose and wrapped around his ears to keep it in place. He had an IV needle and tube taped to the top of his hand and soft restraints around his wrists and ankles. When Erin saw them, she gasped, "What on earth?" she said.

"He refused tae lie still; determined tae gee up and find yeh. We had tae restrain him for his health and safety. Even then, he wouldnae lie still; he fought tae gee up, sae we had tae gee him a mild sedative," the nurse explained, "He'll be comin' oot of it soon," she said.

"May I—" Erin said and pointed to him.

"Aye, on yeh go. I reckon he'll be glad tae see you!" the nurse said.

Erin was choked up as she looked at the nurse and C.O. MacDonald. "Thank you," she whispered and then went to David's side. She unfastened the restraints and took his hand in hers, kissing it as tears ran down her face. "I'm so sorry, David! Can you hear me? Oh, please wake up!" she said and sat, holding his hand with her head resting on the bed.

Erin was in and out of sleep, mentally and physically exhausted from everything that had happened that day. It took about an hour before David woke, groggy and worn out from fighting the EMTs and emergency room staff. He moved, which woke Erin. "David?" she said and kissed his hand.

"Erin? Oh, ma God! Ye're alive!" he said. His voice was hoarse and gravelly; it was painful to hear. He openly wept and pulled her to him, holding her for dear life. "I was afraid I'd lost yeh and the bairn!" He let her go for a moment, put his hand on her stomach, and then hugged her again. He was wheezing and coughing on and off the whole time.

"I wasn't in the house," she said as he held her tightly. "I—I'd slipped out the back door and went for a long walk to clear my head. I left a note, but you probably didn't see it. I'm so sorry! I was really far away when I heard the sirens and ran back as fast as I could, but... it wasn't very fast. I saw the ambulance leave, but I didn't know if you were in it. Chief Officer MacDonald brought me here, and... I'm sorry you thought I was in the house!"

David let her go and looked at her, tears running freely down his face. He pulled her to him again and kissed her, his eyes open. He tried to roll onto his side so she could lie next to him, but there wasn't enough room.

"I can't—" she said, and was interrupted by a very posh, received pronunciation accent.

"David?" Both of them looked up and saw a very thin, beautifully elegant woman in her late thirties, looking down on them distastefully, as if disgusted by their affectionate display.

"I'm a'right, Susannah, you dinnae need tae fuss, or stay, for that matter," he said after an aggravated sigh.

Susannah? Good night nurse! She's even more beautiful in person, Erin thought.

———

"I received a telephone call informing me you were in hospital, David. Am I not expected to come to you?" Susannah said. Not waiting for an answer, she continued, "And… whom, might I ask, is… this?" She looked Erin up and down with intense scrutiny, intent on making it clear that the woman did *not* measure up to someone worth speaking to civilly. She knew who Erin was from the photographs Martin had shown her, but she wanted David to have to explain himself to her.

"This is Erin, she's my—She's my match from the Registry, and—" David began.

"Your match? *Well, that explains a lot.* How… lovely it is to meet you, Ellen, was it? I'm Susannah Elliott, David's *wife,*" she said the word wife with venom in her voice.

"It's Erin, actually, and I know who you are. It's… uh, lovely to meet you… as well," Erin said.

They both put on fake smiles, and Erin started to back up so Susannah could get closer to David, but he held her hand tight. "Yeh dinnae need tae go anawhere, Erin," he said.

She put her hand over his affectionately. "I'm just going to sit over here," she said, and pointed to a chair by the door, so he let go of her hand.

Susannah approached David's bed and tried to kiss him, but he turned his head, making her furious, though she tried to hide it. "How are you, darling?" she asked him, her voice dripping with rotten honey.

"Why are yeh here, Susannah? I ken well enough yeh wouldn't come from London if yeh didn't want somethin'," he said, his voice hoarse and weary.

"Oh, David!" she hissed. "Must you speak that way? You know how I detest it!"

"Aye, I ken how yeh feel about it, but I'll not change the way I speak for yeh anamore. Ye'll have tae get used tae et."

Susannah saw him glance at Erin, who smiled, and her claws came out. "Oh, I see," she said, coiled up, ready to strike. "Trying to impress your whore, are you? Isn't that lovely? Poor, innocent David, standing up to the wicked wife. Do you know how pathetic you are?" Then she turned on Erin. "Go ahead with your fantasy, Esther, but eventually, he *will* grow tired of you and return to me. You may count on it! He *will* come to his senses, and if he does not—I'll take away *everything* he has, including his precious children. That will make him think twice, I should think." She slithered a bit closer to Erin, "Oh, and poor Enid! Whatever shall you do without your, how do you Americans say it? Your sugar daddy?" Condescension dripped from her fangs as she spoke.

Erin stood, and David sat up, which started him coughing in a way that startled both women. Erin rushed to his side while Susannah backed away, not knowing how to, or wanting to deal with a sick or injured person.

She watched as Erin got him to lay back and tried to get him to relax. "Shhh, Susannah was just leaving, weren't you?" she said, and Susannah looked incredulously at her.

"As a matter of fact, I wasn't," she said, trying to stand her ground, but a pain shot through her body, and she flinched. She covered it excellently, but she knew Erin had seen it.

"Leave, Susannah! Just… go!" David barked between coughing fits.

She looked at him as though she'd been slapped, watching as he and Erin held hands. Erin spoke soothingly to him, trying to get him to calm down. She knew she'd lost the battle, but the war for David Elliott had just begun.

"We'll speak when you return *home*," she said, and David waved his hand dismissively at her. She left the room, her head held high, and her £1000.00 heels, clicking on the terrazzo flooring.

———

"Oh, David! I love you so much!" Erin said and laid her head on his stomach.

"I didn't finish what I was gonna say; that ye're ma match and ma true love," he said, his voice cracking.

Erin stood and kissed him on the lips, but he started coughing again, so she had to stop. "Maybe she didn't let you say it, but I guarantee she knows it; she's not blind or stupid. She might have been in denial before she saw us together, but she'll have no doubt about how we feel for each other now," she said.

"Yeh awright, Mr. Elliott?" The nurse asked when she came back to check on him.

"Aye," he said, his face and eyes red from the smoke, coughing, and crying. Erin could see the tracks from the tears he'd shed on his face through the leftover soot that hadn't been entirely washed off. "When may I leave?"

"I think you should stay as long as you can, David," Erin said. "The oxygen will help you."

"This bed isn't comfortable. Is there a way I might get a more comfortable bed at least?" he asked.

The nurse came over to check his pulse and listen to his lungs. "I'll see what I can doo," she said crossly.

"Thank you," Erin said.

"Humph. Just keep 'im calm and gee 'im one of these if his throat hurts 'im," she said and handed Erin a small bag of yellow cough drops. "I'll fetch some water as well. Yeh need tae drink it—all of it—and continue drinkin' it until yeh float!" she said, practically yelling it at him, as if saying it loudly would make it sink in, somehow. David rolled his eyes at her and looked away.

"I'll make sure he does," Erin said and sat on the edge of the tiny bed as the nurse walked away.

"I know, I'm ill-tempered and petulant," he said hoarsely. "I'm sorry, I should be so grateful tae have you back that nothin' could get me riled, but Susannah has managed tae ruin the mood, as usual."

"What are we going to do now? The house and everything in it are—Oh no! My—My passport, and my driver's license—Were they in the house? Did you bring my purse in from the car?" she asked.

"Ach, I don't remember."

"Oh, David, why is this happening to us?"

Chapter Sixty-Three

PRIVATE ROOM & A KIND DEED

Erin was ready to move a chair next to David's hospital bed when the nurse returned with a wheelchair. "I've secured yeh a private room, but only because we are-nae full. If that changes, ye'll be asked tae leave," she said.

Erin was so thankful, she didn't think, and hugged her. "Thank you!" she said.

The nurse stood, stiff as a board until Erin let her go. "Humph. I'm meant tae bring yeh there noo. Are yeh ready?" she asked.

"Aye, thank you," David said, smiling at Erin.

The sturdy, no-nonsense woman unplugged his oxygen tube from the port on the wall and helped him get into the wheelchair. He was instructed to hold onto the IV stand as she pushed him out of the room and into a large elevator. She hit the third-floor button, and after a moment, he was wheeled into a hallway that led to a room with a normal-sized bed and a solid door that would close.

Erin helped him get into the bed, but not before he stood and held her. However, he soon started coughing again and reluctantly lay down. The nurse put the IV stand next to the bed and connected his oxygen tube to the wall. She listened to his breathing and felt his pulse. "Ye'll go for x-rays soon, sae ye'd best no' get too comfortable," she said and left the room without further ado.

"Please join me." He moved over and patted the empty spot next to him. "I need tae hold yeh."

She took her shoes off and climbed up onto the bed, lying next to him. She could feel his body relax as they lay side by side. Eventually, his breathing became deep and slow, and she knew he was asleep. She was exhausted herself, having rushed up and down all those hills, so she consciously relaxed her body and fell asleep as well.

Erin woke to the sound of people talking in hushed tones nearby. When she opened her eyes, she saw several nurses standing in the doorway to David's room, whispering and sighing. She didn't like being watched by strangers, so she made sure they knew she was awake, which made them scatter like cockroaches when the lights come on.

Oh, great! They're probably talking about David Elliott being here holding a fat woman who isn't his wife while he sleeps, she thought. She was embarrassed and ashamed of her size again and tried to sit up, but he was awake and held her tightly.

"I love yeh, and I dinnae care if they talk about us. We are together now, and it doesn't matter what anaone else on the planet thinks about it," he said, his voice harsh and dry-sounding.

"You saw them?" she said and relaxed again.

"Aye, they weren't judgin' us though, hen. I heard one of them say somethin' about et bein' sweet, and how lucky you were," he said and laughed, "though I ken et's the other way 'round." The laughter started him coughing again, so Erin fished in her pocket to get him a lozenge.

"If that's the case, then they're right," she said. "I am the luckiest woman ever. Well, except for the last few weeks; this has been a crazy month, hasn't it?" He nodded and lay his head back. She rolled over and lay her arm across his chest, with her head pillowed by his arm. He smelled like smoke and sweat, but she didn't care. "David, do you remember what happened? How did you get out of the house?" she asked.

"I dinnae ken. I remember hearin' an alarm and then standing, wantin' tae find you and get yeh out, but I stood into the smoke and couldn't breathe.

Next thing I knew, I was outside on the stretcher. Oh God, Erin—I was beside maself. You were gone; the firemen said they hadn't found yeh, and that the roof had collapsed. I couldn't imagine ma life without you! I dinnae want tae think of it, even now!" he said, shuddering.

"You could have died in that fire. I—I can't imagine life without you either," she said, and her tears started. As the shock and adrenalin wore off, the reality of what happened hit her like a speeding train. She touched his skin and smelled his scent, so thankful he was alive. There weren't enough senses to bring her close enough to him to truly realize he was safe and not lying in a charred heap inside the house.

"Shhh. I ken what yer feelin', love, but relax; I'm here, you're here, and we're both safe. Just keep holdin' me," he said.

The rotation of nurses, both male and female, standing in the doorway, whispering, and then leaving continued for about two hours, Erin guessed. She was in and out of sleep until her stomach began growling. That's when she remembered they hadn't eaten supper. "Why don't I run to the cafeteria and bring us back some food?" she asked.

"Did yeh no' hear the nurse earlier?" he said, and Erin looked up at him.

"No, what nurse?"

"The one who came in askin' what I want tae eat," he said and laughed.

Erin laughed too. "I guess I was asleep."

He held her tightly. "Aye, yeh were, and snorin' like a chainsaw!"

"Ha-ha funny. I don't suppose they'd bring *me* something?"

"I'm afraid no'. I did ask, but ye'll have tae go yourself. I'll wait right here for yeh, though."

"Alright, I'll be back as soon as I can, so don't go anywhere!" She got up and put her shoes back on, then she leaned over David and kissed him, running her hand across the stubble on his face. "I really *am* lucky!" she said and left the room.

Erin asked at the nurse's desk where the cafeteria was and noticed that the handful of people wearing scrubs were acting oddly. Feeling uncomfortable, she followed their vague directions and saw signs on the way. When she smelled food, she knew she was close. Not wanting to be away from David for very long, she grabbed a sandwich, a bag of crisps, and a drink from the refrigerated case and then went to the cashier to pay. As she drew near, the woman smiled strangely and then put her head down, not making eye contact.

It was somewhere around half past four in the morning, so there weren't many people there. However, she noticed that several of the cafeteria staff and nurses were watching her and whispering, though as soon as she'd look at them, they'd turn away. She was self-conscious, overwhelmed, and panicked, similar to how she'd felt on Bourbon Street.

Angry and flustered, she suddenly realized she had no money; her purse was still at the house, probably burned to a crisp. Close to tears, she looked at the cashier, wide-eyed. "My… purse is—It was in a—a fire. I have no money," she said, embarrassed and miserable.

The woman put her soft, warm hand on top of Erin's. "Dinnae worry, dear," she whispered. "I'll cover it for yeh. Now get yerself back up tae that man!"

Erin didn't know what to do and looked around her. All the people who had been whispering were now looking directly at her. Her face grew hot as one-by-one, they stepped up and put a few coins on her tray; ten pence here, fifty pence there, until it paid for her food and a piece of white cake someone brought over. Tears were flowing down her face as she watched them all. "I don't understand," she said to the cashier, "Who am I to them?"

"You and David Elliott have somethin' special. Dinnae ken what it is, love, but we all want it as well. We've heard what ye've been through, and we wannae help."

It was taking everything Erin had in her not to break down and bawl right there in front of them. She picked up her tray, "Thank you all," she said quietly and walked back through the hospital, taking the elevator up to David's room. When she got back, he wasn't in the bed. She was afraid they'd moved or discharged him while she was away since she had been gone for a long time.

She was about to go to the nurse's desk and ask but heard the shower running and breathed a sigh of relief. A prickle of excitement shot through her, so she set her tray of food on the small sofa. Assuming it would be locked, she walked up to the bathroom door, tried the handle, and it opened freely. She knocked, not wanting to startle him, and then stepped into the steamy room. He was standing in front of her, naked and wet, and her heart skipped a beat.

When he turned and saw her, he smiled, finished rinsing himself, and turned off the tap. She handed him the towel and watched as he stepped out onto a bathmat to dry off. He was absolutely the most beautifully crafted being she'd ever seen, and she stood in awe, staring, and trying to control her urge to touch him. Her breathing was getting deeper with each move he made, so she closed her eyes, trying to think of something other than kneeling to pleasure him orally.

When she opened her eyes, he was standing in front of her dry, though still naked. He took her hand in his and kissed it, placing it on his chest at his heart, then he kissed her. She moved her hand to his back, and he grabbed her ass, holding her tightly against his hard-on. He moved her backward, pinning her against the door, and then flipped the lock.

"Here? But—" she said, unsure of the wisdom of his plan. He put his finger up to her lips and looked around the room. Then, he stepped away from her, put the toilet seat down, and sat on it, motioning for her to disrobe. She reluctantly did so, and when she was naked, he pulled her to him and sat her on his lap, facing him. How she'd be able to do it without making noise, she didn't know, but there wasn't time to think about it. He reached down and parted her lips with his fingers, then took hold of his cock and slid it into her.

"Oh, yes!" she whispered into his ear. It felt so good, and she was already close to climaxing. He kissed her neck and grabbed her ass again, driving himself into her until she bucked and moaned as quietly as she could. Then he released, biting her earlobe to keep from making any noise. It surprised her that he had the strength and stamina to do it, though he was beginning to wheeze, so she stood right away so he could get himself back to the bed quickly. "I... can't believe we did this here!" she said breathlessly.

The exertion and heavy breathing caught up with him, and he started coughing, so she rushed to get herself dressed, figuring that at any moment, a nurse would come looking for him. She had just slipped out of the bathroom and sat on a chair when one of the nurses knocked on David's room door and stepped in.

"How yeh doon'?" she asked and seemed confused to see that he wasn't in the bed. Erin was about to explain when he walked out of the bathroom wearing a fresh hospital gown. "Ach, there yeh are! Yeh look a wee bit flushed, mebbe the shower wasnae a good idea," she said.

"I'm a'right; it's the coughin' that has me winded," he said with a smile.

Erin stifled a laugh into a sound resembling clearing her throat. Her cheeks were pink, and she tried to cover her knowing smile with her hand. "What are you gonna do about clothes? The ones you came here in must be ruined," she asked as the nurse helped him get into the bed and hooked him back up to the IV and oxygen.

"Ach, dinnae worry about tha'," the nurse said, "They've been sent tae be cleaned and will be here before yeh leave. I'll be takin' you for X-rays in a while, but I'll have yeh stay on the oxygen for a wee bit since ye seem a might oot of breath."

"Aye, thank you," he said.

"I'll be back soon," she said, giving them a warm, genuine smile and then left the room.

Another nurse came in soon afterward, and David was served his meal. Erin noticed that he was waiting for her to get her tray set up before he started eating, so she turned and saw her tray full of food. The scene in the cafeteria hit her once more. "Eat your food, yeh silly Scot," she said and turned her back on him to hide her tears as she opened her sandwich.

"What is it, Erin?" he said, concern unmistakable in his raspy voice.

"Nothing," she whispered, then sat on the small sofa and took a few bites of her food.

"What's the matter, hen?" he asked a second time.

"I'll tell you after we eat. I can't now," she managed to say quietly. He moved over on the bed and patted the spot next to him. She smiled as best she could and picked up her tray, setting it next to his on the rolling table the nurse had put over his lap. As soon as she crawled up next to him, she started sobbing.

Once she'd gotten herself mostly under control, she told him what had happened at the nurse's desk and the people whispering in the cafeteria. He interrupted her, saying he'd have to speak to the hospital director, but she put her finger up and continued the story. At the end of it, he sat with his mouth open in disbelief. "She said that? That... we have somethin' special, and they all wanted tae help yeh?" he asked.

"Aye," she said softly.

"What we have *is* unique. I just cannae believe they noticed it without even talkin' to us."

She lay her head on his chest. "That must be why people keep standing at the door and whispering."

"Aye, that would make sense, I reckon. There must be somethin' we can do tae thank them for what they've done for yeh," he said.

They ate their food and talked about what they might be able to do. "We could write notes to say thank you," Erin said. "It's simplistic, but sometimes that's the best way to show gratitude.

After they ate, Erin found a pad of paper and a pen in one of the drawers in the room, gave it to David, and he started writing. She watched him think for a moment, write something down, and then do it again, until he held it up, reread it, and smiled. "Aye, that's good," he said.

He handed Erin the pen, and she did the same thing. It was hard to put into words how she felt, but she managed something.

> *"To the staff members who helped me in*
> *the cafeteria, and to all those who have*
> *been wishing us well: I want to thank you*
> *from the bottom of my heart for your*
> *kindness. You didn't have to do what you*
> *did, and it means so much to us.*
> *Erin M."*

They exchanged notes; he read hers while Erin read his.

*"To those who stepped in and did such a
tremendous kindness for my friend, I am
truly   blessed.   You've   shown   true
compassion, far above common courtesy.
I won't forget your thoughtfulness.
Thank you,
David Elliott"*

They smiled at each other, then she took both of their notes, folded them together, and wrote on the front, *Hospital Staff.* She was about to find a place to hide them so they wouldn't be found until they left, but the nurse came back in with a wheelchair to take him for his X-rays.

Chapter Sixty-Four

X-RAYS, A LOUD NURSE, & THE DOCTOR

The nurse was young and pretty, and Erin felt the familiar twinge of fear and doubt in her mind. It was a relief when David didn't even look at her except to answer her questions. The slender woman unhooked his IV and oxygen tube, then helped him into the wheelchair. She told Erin they would be right back, but David interrupted her.

"Do yeh wannae come along?" he asked.

Erin looked at the pretty nurse, who bobbed her head to say it was okay, but she didn't feel right following him like a groupie. "I'll stay here," she said.

"Are yeh sure, hen? I'd like to stay near yeh, unless yeh really dinnae want tae," he said, sincerely.

Erin smiled; how could she refuse him? "Alright, if you put it that way." She braced herself for stares and whispers as they left the room, continued through the hallway to the elevators, and then headed down to the second floor. Thankfully, they didn't pass anyone on the way down, and she was glad for the seclusion of the empty waiting room. He smiled warmly at her, taking her hand in his as she sat awkwardly on an uncomfortable chair, waiting for his name to be called.

Finally, the X-ray technician called him in, and another nurse wheeled him into the room. Erin sat with the pretty nurse, waiting. The young woman obviously had something she wanted to say, but every time she opened her mouth to speak, she'd shake her head, and her cheeks would turn pink. "Is there something you want to say to me?" Erin asked after the third time.

The nurse's blush deepened, and she looked around to be sure no one could hear her, then she got up and sat next to Erin. "What's he really like? I mean, is he as sweet as this all the time?" she asked quietly.

Erin smiled at her; it was just what she would have wanted to know. "Yeah, he's wonderful," was all she said since she didn't want to sit and gossip about him like a silly schoolgirl.

"Aye, I thought so," the nurse said. "I'd like tae meet someone like him someday. Ye're so lucky."

"Yes, I am," she agreed and smiled at the woman. "I hope you do, as well."

A few minutes later, David was wheeled out to the waiting room, and the three of them went back up to his room. The nurse smiled at him as she helped him into the bed and hooked him back up to everything, then she smiled at Erin and then back at David. "The doctor will be in tae see yeh once he's viewed the X-rays," she said, then listened to his lungs, checked his pulse, and sighed as she left the room.

Erin laughed, and David looked confused. "What was that about?" he asked. "She was grinnin' like the Cheshire cat. Were yeh talkin' about me with her?"

Erin blushed, even though she knew she hadn't done anything wrong. "She kept starting to ask me something, over and over, so I decided to tell her to spit it out already. Okay, I didn't say it like that. She wanted to know if you are as nice as you seem to be," she said.

"Aye, and what did yeh tell her?"

"What do you think?" she said with a wicked grin, "I told her you were an asshole and that this was all an act so people wouldn't find out."

"Ach, good, so yeh told her the truth."

"I told her you were wonderful, and she said I was lucky. I agreed, of course. She said she hoped to find someone like you someday, so I told her I hoped she did too."

"Except there isn't anaone else like me, so she's out of luck. I reckon ye've snared a one of a kind."

"Aye, and he's modest to boot!" Erin sat on a chair, hoping to get a bit more sleep, but David patted the bed next to him. "One of a kind!" she parroted.

A few hours later, David woke to the sound of people standing at the door again. He was stiff from lying in one position for too long and stretched. Just as the groupies cleared out, a very noisy nurse came in to check on him and started talking to Erin. "Ach, yer tae gee yerself oop noow," she said in a very loud, thick accent while shooing her out of the bed. "We'll be needin' this room shortly, and ah've goot tae check his vi-tals."

Erin slipped off the edge of the bed and went to the small couch to lay back down. The nurse laid a neatly folded pile of David's clean clothes on the armchair and then approached the bed. "Ach and hoow're yeh this moornin', dear?" she asked. She was deafening, especially for the time of day.

"I dinnae ken; it's too early," he said softly, his voice sounding gravelly.

Laughing loudly, she went to work removing the IV needle and applied the gauze and plaster over it, then she gently took off the nasal cannula and draped it over the end of the bed. "The doctor will be in soon tae discuss yer reh-lease. Yeh may get dressed noow." She checked his pulse and pulled his gown down at the neck then she placed her stethoscope onto his bare skin.

He jumped and cried out. "Ach, that thing's ice cold!" he said, feeling aggravated.

She took it off him and laughed. "Ach, soo soorry, dear," she said, warmed it up in her hand for a few seconds, and then tried again.

"That's better, thank you," he said.

She had him breathe deeply, in and out, and then listened to his lungs through his back. "Soounds awright. Yer personal effects are in a bag on the table," she said and pointed to it, "Noow, gee yerself dressed."

I would if ye'd leave!" he thought but said, "Aye."

Finally, she took the nasal cannula and left the room. He stood and stretched; he'd be glad to be rid of the place! He went to the chair where she'd laid his clothes and removed them from the plastic bag they were in. The smell of smoke was nearly gone, and there were only a few burn marks and tears in them; nothing to make them unwearable at any rate. He put them on and watched Erin sleeping on the sofa. He would wait to wake her, at least until the doctor arrived.

Ten minutes later, an attractive, middle-aged man with grey and white hair and a clipboard came in, and David went to the couch to wake Erin. She stretched and groaned. "What time is it?" she asked. "I feel like I've been sleeping all day! Oh, and I ache all over!"

David waited to talk to her until she sat up. "The doctor is here tae discuss ma discharge from this place," he said. "I'd like for you tae listen, so at least one of us remembers what he says."

The doctor overheard him and laughed. "Aye, that's a good plan, although we do give yeh a few pages tae recap what I say," he said, kindly.

——

Erin stood and patted down her hair, which she guessed was all over the place, and then smiled at him. "Good morning," she said as brightly as she could.

"Good mornin' tae you, as well. I'm Doctor Gordon Wallace; nice tae meet yeh."

David and Erin smiled at each other. "My maiden name is Wallace," Erin said. "Small world, huh?"

The Doctor smiled at her, "Aye? I wish I had the time tae talk about that. I love genealogy, but I'm a bit swamped at the minute, so I'll assume ye're a cousin, a'right?" he said.

"Deal!" she said.

Dr. Wallace reviewed most of the things they'd already been told, adding that David needed to stay hydrated and get lots of rest. He was also to make sure to call his GP when he got back home to schedule a follow-up appointment in about two months. "Now, do yeh have any questions?" he asked.

"Can't think of anything, but I'll call if anything occurs to us," David said.

"A'right then. Again, it was nice tae meet yeh," he said, then shook David's hand and left the room.

She found the bag that the loud nurse had pointed to and emptied it onto the bed. Out tumbled his wallet, watch, mobile, a few coins, the keys to the cottage, and most importantly, the key for Neela. They looked at each other and then back at the key ring. "Thank God I'd thought tae put them in ma pocket," he said. "That would've been a right mess!"

"Yeah!" Erin agreed. "Oh! Where did those notes go?" she asked.

David put his wallet in his pocket, then walked over to the bedside table. He picked up the folded pieces of paper and handed them to Erin. She watched as he put his keys and coins into his pocket, placed his watch on his wrist and then check his mobile before turning it off. "A'right, love, let's go; I need some coffee," he said.

"Me too." She looked at him and smiled. Even in slightly singed and tattered clothes, he looked impeccable. They checked the room for anything they might have missed and then walked out into the hallway.

When they passed the nurse's desk, Erin handed the notes to a woman in blue scrubs. She smiled, read to whom they were addressed, placed them over her heart, and let out a sigh. Erin laughed, "It's just to thank you for being so kind. Please show it around or put it in a common room, please," she said.

"I will," she said, and they headed to the elevators. The door took a long time to open and then to close again, so they heard the nurse, who had been joined by at least one other. It sounded like a lot of noise, including some squealing and comments about it being David Elliott's signature!

When the door finally closed, Erin mimicked the nurse's squeals of excitement, which made David laugh. It also brought on a coughing fit, though it wasn't nearly as bad as the ones he'd had the night before. Erin waited until the coughing stopped and then kissed him on the cheek.

"I still can't believe I'm with you," she said. "Especially when I see the display people—especially women, make when in your presence; it just doesn't seem possible." She took his hand as the door opened, then remembered they had no transportation. They walked up to the information desk, and she asked the old man sitting there how to find a car to hire. He handed them a three-ring-binder and pointed to the courtesy phone on a small table nearby. David thanked him, while Erin found the correct page and made a call.

Chapter Sixty-Five

HIRE CAR

A black sedan pulled up to the hospital doors, and David told the woman who was driving the Uber the address of the cottage. "A'right," she said, then looked twice in the rearview mirror at David. Her gaze then went to Erin, but she didn't say anything else. She entered the address into her car's GPS and pulled away from the hospital.

David sighed audibly. "I'm glad tae be leavin'; I dinnae care for hospitals overly much," he said.

Erin was about to put her head on his shoulder and then changed her mind. She wasn't sure why the driver had looked at them the way she had when they got in and didn't want her talking to anyone about them later. "I'm just glad we're on our way back, alive and well," she said.

Twenty minutes later, they drove down the long driveway and got their first look at the ruined cottage. David and Erin both gasped. The stone walls were still standing, but every window was broken, and the roof was completely gone. Everything was dark black, and a thick layer of ashes covered Neela. Thankfully, he'd thought to put the top up and close the tiny windows when he'd brought in the luggage, so he hoped the inside wasn't too dirty.

They got out of the car, and David paid the woman. She thanked him for the tip and then slowly started back down the driveway. She didn't get far before she stopped, shut it off, and got out. "I'm sorry to intrude, but I want to make sure your car starts before I drive off, and you're stuck here," she said.

Erin looked at her in surprise. "You're an American? But you sounded Scottish when you spoke earlier," she said, and the woman smiled broadly.

"Most people around here doubt your driving skills if you sound like you're not from these parts, or at least from England, so I usually say as little as possible. Even then, I try to sound a bit more Scottish. Are you from Wisconsin, or maybe Michigan?" she asked.

"I'm from Wisconsin, and I'm guessing you're from Illinois or even southern Wisconsin?" Erin said.

She put her hands on her hips and laughed. "Damn, you're good, I was born in Illinois, and my parents moved to Wisconsin when I was ten, so you're right on both accounts," she said.

Erin wanted to hug her as though they were sisters, but she resisted the temptation. "Small world, huh?"

"Really small! My name is Liz, and I'm pretty handy with cars if yours won't start." David and Erin looked at each other, each one having vastly different memories of Erin's mother.

"My mom's name is Liz, so I'll remember it," Erin said. David took the keys out of his pocket and opened the door; they could see the black soot smear where he'd touched the handle, and they all grimaced. He gingerly sat in the driver's seat, put the key into the ignition, and turned it, but nothing happened. He tried it again, for good measure, but still nothing.

"Can you pop the hood, er... open the bonnet, I mean," Liz said as she walked to the front of the car and opened the hood, her hands smearing the soot as she did so. She looked at the engine and saw the problem right away. "The battery posts are corroded and just need to be cleaned off."

No one had anything to wipe them off with, so Liz went back to her car and opened the passenger door. She bent over and took something out of the glove box, holding up a thick stack of fast-food napkins as she walked back to them. Less than five minutes later, David tried the engine again, and that time it started right up.

"Thank you, Liz; I appreciate you stayin' tae help," David said.

"Eh, it's okay. Looks like you've had a rough time! I hope things look up for you after this. Oh, and I loved you in *Future Explorations*," she said and smiled at Erin. She walked over to her and whispered, "Do you know who I think he'd be great as?"

Erin looked at her and smiled. "Umm, anything?" Erin replied, and they both laughed. "Do tell."

"He'd make a fantastic Doctor, don't you think? We need a Doctor to fangirl over again, right?"

Erin smiled at her and then looked over at David, who was gazing up at the ruined house. "Yeah, he would be a dreamy Doctor!" she said. Erin had an idea then but needed to make sure David was okay with it. "Do you have a few minutes, and can you keep a secret?" she asked her.

"I don't have anything going on today unless I get another call, and I'm good with secrets; why?" she asked.

Erin held up her finger to ask her to wait and give her a minute. She went over to David and whispered something into his ear. He turned and looked at Liz, then whispered something into her ear. She smiled, and they both walked back over to Liz. "We'd like to show you something, as a little thank you for staying and helping us out. But you have to promise never to tell anyone about it, or there will be swarms of people ruining it. Can you promise us that?" Erin asked.

She looked at them skeptically, then shrugged. "Of course; I won't tell anyone. What is it?" she asked.

Erin smiled and took David's hand. "Follow us," she said. As they walked past the demolished house, the smell of wet ashes and melted plastic hung in the air. After going up and over a few small hills, the *Future Explorations* farmhouse came into view, and Liz gasped.

"Are you for real? No Way! Dude! I'm gonna tell all my friends about this place!" she said and then waited for their reaction. David looked a bit worried, but Erin just laughed. Finally, she smiled, "Just kidding. I don't have any friends anyway," she said with a shrug.

"What?" Erin said looking surprised.

"Nope, none. I have a few at home, but none here. It's okay, though. Scottish people can be so nosey." She looked at David, and her cheeks colored slightly. "No offense, but they can be, and I don't need that in my life, so I keep to myself."

"I'll be your friend if you'll have me?" Erin said, and Liz smiled.

"Okay, it's a deal," she said. They even shook hands, which made David shake his head.

"Are all American women as easy-going and friendly as you?" he asked.

The two women looked at each other. "Oh, no, we are few and far between; that's why when we find a kindred spirit, we become friends for life," Liz said, and Erin nodded emphatically.

"Can we get closer?" Liz asked.

"Aye," David said. They went down to the house and walked around it. The two women laughed as Liz quoted a line David's character had said in one of the episodes, standing by the farmhouse door. She said it exactly the same as he had done and with the same demeanor. She and Erin laughed so hard tears were running down their faces.

David watched them and smiled. "The two of you are incorrigible children. I wish we could stay, but we do need tae get going; we've still an hour and a half or more before we'll get tae Edinburgh," he said.

Erin and Liz walked to where David was standing, out of breath and laughing. "Thank you so much for showing this to me! It's one of the best things of my life," Liz said gratefully.

"I'm glad you've enjoyed yerself; I've enjoyed watching yeh act like school-girls," he said. "Thank you again for your help today."

They started walking toward the house again, and when they got back to the cars, the two women exchanged contact information. "If you're ever in Edinburgh, call me, and we'll have lunch. Oh, wait—I don't know how long I'll be in Edinburgh. I might be in London, or maybe even Green Bay, so— Umm, I guess, if you're in any of those places, call me, and we'll have lunch," Erin said and gave Liz her American phone number, just in case, then they said their goodbyes and Liz got into her car. She drove off while David and Erin looked at the wreckage of the house.

"It's so sad!" she said as they walked all the way around the building. It was totaled. "God, David, I'm so glad you got out of there. And I'm... so sorry! I feel like it's my fault! If I hadn't gotten mad and then turned on the oven while you were sleeping—"

He put his arm around her shoulders. "It's no' yer fault, darling. I'm no' bothered about the building, as it can be rebuilt. It's the memories and the meat pie we didn't get tae eat; that's the sad part! Millie makes an amazin' meat pie!" he said. He smiled at her and kissed her forehead. "We really do need tae go. We'll stop for a coffee on the way down."

Chapter Sixty-Six

SUSANNAH'S LAST STAND

David and Erin returned to Owlgate that afternoon, exhausted and longing for a nap. Erin went straight upstairs, while David went in search of his mother to tell her what had happened. Instead of finding her, though, he found Susannah on the sofa in the sitting room. She stood when she saw him in the doorway. "I told you tae go; I didn't mean for yeh tae come here," he said, not happy to see her. "Where's ma mother?"

"I'm sure I don't know," she said, turning her nose up at the state of his attire.

"How long have yeh been here, and why've you come?" he asked, his voice raspy. The thought of her being there without him to keep her from snooping through his room was not a comforting thought.

"I've been here since late this morning. I was instructed to wait in—" she began, but he didn't care to hear anymore.

"You need tae go. I'm exhausted, and I dinnae want tae talk tae yeh just now," he cut in.

"I'm not leaving until you—" she started to say and took a step toward him.

"Until I what, Susannah?" he said, his voice breaking as he spoke. "What do yeh want from me? I've never been good enough for yeh... the way I talk, the things I say... who I am as a person. Ye've changed every part of me, and I'm done with et. Our marriage is over, so ye'd better be gettin' used to it." He was on the verge of yelling but started coughing, so he took a lozenge out of his pocket and put it into his mouth.

Susannah went to him. "David darling, you're infatuated with that woman right now. It will wear off in time, and then where will you be, hmm?" she said, speaking with sickeningly sweet syrup dripping from her tongue.

David had heard her speak to their children that way, like Dolores Umbridge, condescending and rotten to the core. He wasn't going to allow her to patronize him like that, as well. "I will choose ma own path, whatever the consequences, and I will live with what becomes of et. Yeh willnae speak tae me as though I were a child anamore either," he said, hotly.

"You're acting like a child!" she yelled. "You have completely forgotten about us, your family, and are traipsing all over the country with that... woman as though it doesn't matter who sees you, but you know it does matter, and when a sordid tabloid tale breaks, you'll come crying to me to fix it—"

"I've never come cryin' tae yeh asking you tae fix anathin! Ye're so thoroughly conceited!" he snapped, losing his temper.

"What I am, is good at looking out for us. If there is no us, then I'll be looking out for myself. Remember, I still have those nasty pictures of you and her. I can and will sell them if I must. Do you fancy your children seeing them at the newsstands? Do you imagine they will look up to daddy when they see him screwing his fat, uneducated mistress from the Midwest?"

David opened his mouth to reply, but they heard his mother's voice from the hall instead. "You have some nerve, coming into ma home and speaking to my son in that manner. Also, I'll not tolerate you speaking ill of Erin, whom you know nothing about, so I suggest you get off yer high horse and leave now, Susannah!" Annis was in the doorway with her arms crossed.

Susannah stood, shocked and red in the face. "But, Mother, surely *you* see that this is an infatuation with someone of a lower class. Of course, she'll be more fun and... different, but that's because of her low upbringing. Surely *you* can see that he'll eventually get tired of the base, crudeness of her, can't you?" she postulated to her mother-in-law.

"What *I* see is that *you* should have appreciated David whilst you had him. You cannot come here now and try tae bully him into loving you and coming back; it doesn't work that way," Annis said.

"You do realize she got herself pregnant on purpose," Susannah turned on him and spat out. "You always have been naive and gullible."

David and Annis exchanged shocked looks. "What makes yeh think she's pregnant?" he said.

Susannah rolled her eyes. "I have ears and eyes, David," she said.

He had no idea when she could have heard anything about it, and Erin wasn't showing yet. "What are yeh on about?" he said.

"Ahhh was sae scarrred I'd lost yee and th' bairrrnnn!" she said with a terrible, mocking accent "That's what you said to her in hospital, I heard you. I then saw you place your hand on her enormous stomach; I can only imagine what she'll look like in nine months' time!" She puffed out her sunken cheeks to imitate being fat, but David had had enough.

"How was I so blind tae think there was anathin' good in yeh? You are just—" he said but started coughing again; it was rough and grating, and he flinched with pain at each one.

"Now, David, do save yer voice; she's not worth it. Allow me tae do it for you," Annis said and turned to her daughter-in-law. "Ye've been a terrible wife and mother from the start, and I'll no longer allow you tae insult the people whom I love and care about, not in my home. You'll leave now, and you are not welcome back."

Susannah flushed crimson and picked up her handbag. "You'll regret this," she said as David guided her toward the door.

"I'll be applying for a divorce on Monday," he replied coolly.

"Have it your way, but be prepared for a fight," she hissed while David stood in the entryway, holding the door. She stepped forward, and her face flinched, though an instant later, she resumed her air of dignity and pride. Erin was headed through the front hall, so Susannah put her hand on David's face and tried to kiss him.

"That's no' goin' tae work." He turned his head, backed away, and then smiled when he saw Erin walking toward them. "Susannah was just leaving, darling," he said sweetly to her. "Did you sleep well?" Two could play that game. Erin stood on her tiptoes, and he responded by taking her into his arms and kissing her.

"I haven't been to sleep yet; I was waiting for you to join me," she said, smiling up at him. He was still holding her when she looked over at Susannah and said, "Goodbye, Susannah." Then she added under her breath, "Don't let the door hit you on your way out."

David heard it and grinned. "My thoughts exactly," he said quietly.

Chapter Sixty-Seven

SUSANNAH DEPARTS

Erin noticed that Susannah seemed tired and withdrawn; the beautiful ex-model had enormous dark circles under her eyes and appeared to be sick. She saw tiny beads of sweat on her upper lip and thought her face had changed just before she turned to leave. "David," she said, as his wife walked out the door, "Do you think Susannah looks… ill?"

"Ill? I can't say I noticed; she's appeared unwell for a long time. Do yeh think she looks worse than usual?" he said with a slight frown.

"She seemed unwell to me, but you know her better," she said.

———

David went to the window and peered out at his wife of nearly eighteen years as she got into her hired car looking tired, yet she kept her back straight and her face as stony as ever. The car pulled away and turned out of the driveway.

Annis headed back upstairs, and Erin and David had just stepped into the sitting room to talk about what Susannah had said when they heard the doorbell ringing furiously. The dogs went wild, and David rushed to the door. He saw the driver of the hired car, pale and gaping at him. "There's somethin' wrong with Mrs. Elliott; ring for an ambulance," he said, panic-stricken.

Annis had come back down and hastened to dial 999. David ran out to the car and opened the door, *God, she weighs nothin'; she's all bones,* he thought as he lifted her out of the back seat. He carried her into the house and laid her on the hall floor in front of the fireplace.

"Susannah! Can you hear me? Susannah?" David said to her, over and over. He put his ear to her chest and gasped; she was literally a skeleton with skin stretched over it. He listened to her heart and checked for breathing, but he could feel and hear nothing. He started CPR, but his breathing wasn't good enough after being in the fire. Every time he'd take a breath in so he could breathe into her mouth, he'd start to cough. "Erin, I need yer help. Please do the breathing whilst I do the compressions," he bellowed, as panic started to take him over.

"I—I've never done CPR before; what do I do?" she asked, panicking herself. He quickly told her what to do, and before long, they were working together, trying to keep her heart beating until the ambulance got there. However, each time David would listen for her heartbeat, there was nothing.

"Susannah! God, just start breathin'! Yeh can't die! Susannah! Can you hear me?" he said again, looking at Erin and then at his mother. It wasn't working; she wasn't responding. He knew it was over long before the ambulance got there, but he kept doing the chest compressions while Erin breathed for her.

———

David was wearing out, and Erin could see tears falling onto his hands as he pushed on her tiny, emaciated chest, over and over.

The ambulance finally arrived, and the EMTs took over, though they stopped almost immediately. Everyone in the house stood still, as though they were suspended in a fog, unable to think or move. David and Erin were physically exhausted and in shock. Annis was standing with her hands on her cheeks, not believing what she'd just witnessed, and Millie was wringing her hands. She had come into the room after the ambulance arrived and got the dogs out of the way.

No one knew what to do once there was no more CPR or yelling anyone's name. The room was eerily quiet, even though the EMT's and care assistants were moving around and speaking with each other. The clock on the mantel sounded like drums, beating out a steady rhythm. When the Head Ambulance Technician came over to talk to David, he looked at her as though he couldn't understand what she was saying. After a moment, though, he seemed to wake up and respond, then he stood, and they walked outside.

Erin watched from the door as he answered her questions. Then he signed something on a clipboard and came back in to tell them he would be going to the hospital. He said he'd call Roger to pick him up when he needed to come back. She started toward him, but he had already turned and was heading toward the ambulance. By the time she got out the door, he was already in the back with an EMT and his dead wife.

She didn't know what to do and watched as the ambulance and her true love with it drove away. *What now? Should I go upstairs again or sit on the couch and watch Millie wringing her hands?* She could think of nothing. The memories of what had just happened flooded her mind; her lips pressed to Susannah's, David's tears splashing onto his hand, and her tiny, skeletal body laying limp under them as they fought to bring her back.

She had never witnessed anything so horrific before and certainly had never been involved in trying to save someone as she had done just then. Not only that, but Susannah had been so nasty to her and David, how was she supposed to feel about it?

What about my role in the middle of all this? Should I keep a wide berth or get involved so I can help David cope? Holy Moses; what about the children? The poor babies! She thought about what came next, and couldn't fathom the pain everyone would be in.

Next thing she knew, she turned around and found herself in Dr. Neil's Garden, not knowing how she got there. She wandered around until she found a secluded bench to sit on and cry, then wished for a box of tissues. The sound of footsteps on the gravel path nearby startled her; she didn't want to be seen but didn't have time to hide.

Chapter Sixty-Eight

HELP FROM THE HELP

"**A**re yeh alright, Ms. Erin?" she heard a man's voice say to her. It was Roger, and he had a box of tissues in his hand, so she moved over and took the box as he sat next to her. "Saw yeh wander off and thought yeh might be wantin' these, and... perhaps someone tae talk to, or just tae sit with," he said kindly.

"Thank you, Roger. I'm so confused; I've never experienced anything like that before." She shuddered and then thought about David going off as he had without so much as a look in her direction.

He seemed to read her mind. "Dinnae worry about David; he'll be feelin' conflicted just now. The guilt will try tae take him down, but if ye're strong, ye'll help him tae be so as well," he said. "That man loves yeh with a rare passion, so dinnae listen tae yer mind. Yer thoughts are no' yer friend now. They'll lie and tell yeh he doesnae love you anamore and that nothing will ever be the same between yeh, but they're wrong."

She gazed thoughtfully at him; he appeared to be around the age of fifty or so. He seemed strong and brave as he sat next to her, but she could sense there had been a time in his past when he'd been weak and afraid, just like she was. She wanted to ask him what had happened but didn't want to pry, and she also figured he'd tell her if she needed to know.

He stared at the swans floating on the loch and took a deep breath, as though he were about to jump in and swim with them. "Ma wife—We were newly wed, yeh ken, was killed in a freak accident twenty-three years ago," he said. Erin could tell he didn't like talking about it; he was rubbing his palms on his jeans, back and forth, from hips to knees, and shaking his head slowly. "We'd gone for a wee walk. It was the first bonnie day after a string of cold, dreich weather, so we found a wild lookin' place, with trees and bushes tae walk and do a bit of snoggin'." He smiled at the memory, his suntanned skin crinkling around his eyes.

"We came to an overgrown hedge and stopped in the shade. We'd just laid ourselves on the grass when… an arrow… came flyin' through the hedge… and pierced her neck at the carotid artery," he said quietly, and Erin gasped.

"An arrow? As in bow and arrow?" she asked.

"Aye. It wasnae verra big, in fact, it was a child's toy, but there was nothin' I could do except hold her and yell for someone tae ring for an ambulance. A laddie of about eight or nine ran 'round the hedge, and I dinnae remember much else, which is a small mercy, I reckon. The boy was after rabbits and squirrels and hadnae seen us on the other side of the hedge. He wasnae tryin' tae hurt anaone," he said, shaking his head as if he still couldn't believe it.

"Oh, Roger! That's horrible!" Erin said, not knowing what else she could say.

"Aye, et *was* horrible for me, but I reckon et was far worse for him, havin' tae live with somethin' sae dreadful from a wee child onward—for the rest of his life. It wasnae fair tae either of us."

"Good night nurse!" Erin exclaimed. "That's… just heartbreaking. Whatever happened to the boy? Do you know?" she asked.

"Aye, he rang me evera year on the anniversary of her death. I imagine his mum made him do it tae start, but as he got older, he would ring other times as well—I reckon we had a bond that sometimes follows a traumatic event. The poor lad has rung cryin' and beggin' me tae forgive him many times. The guilt tears him up, and I have tae remind him that there's no need. I mean, how could I hold it against him, a young boy with a toy—" he said, then he crossed his arms and leaned back on the bench.

"What a terrible thing to happen!" she said.

"What yeh must understand is that David may be feelin' a bit of what the boy experienced. He may convince himself it was his fault, and if he'd only done this or tha', it wouldnae happened as it did," he said. "He may also feel guilty about many other things, especially about you, though no' how yeh might think. He willnae want you tae see his grief, thinkin' it'll hurt yeh, and it may seem as though he's pushin' you away, but it's tae shield yeh from what he's feelin', so ye must be patient; allow him work it out and come tae you."

Erin knew what he was saying was right, but she selfishly wondered what *she* was supposed to do about her feelings in all of it.

"I reckon ye'll be having a fair number of feelings tae sort out as well," he said as if reading her mind again. "I reckon David will no' be able to deal with them, so if you need someone tae speak to, come tae me, I'll listen. And if yeh start feelin' as though you cannae be patient any longer, come tae me, and I'll remind you why yer waitin'. David is worth et, I think," he said.

Erin put her head on his shoulder. "Aye, I think so too," she said. "I can't believe all the crazy things that have happened since we met. It's like a bag of odd events has been opened up over our heads, and we have to pick up the pieces. I mean, just to start with, the Fertilis Registry and what we had to do… together. Then falling for each other right away, and my husband breaking David's nose. Next, the crazy fortune teller warning about the birds… and then my mom flipping out. Then, of course, I find out I'm pregnant and see Bran walking around the house, naked. What else—Oh… the cottage fire, where David could have died, and now this?" she said, putting up a finger for each thing. "Did I leave anything out? It's all just so much!"

"Aye, it does sound like a lot," he said and looked at her with a strange expression.

"What?" she said, not understanding.

"Ye're pregnant?"

Erin's eyes grew wide. "Oh, crap! Did I say that? I… I guess I did. Well, yes, I'm about a month and a half along."

"Congratulations!" he said with a genuine smile. "I reckon David's beside himself with joy?"

"That's just what Millie said." She returned his smile, feeling relieved by his response. "He is, and… don't tell him I told you this, but he talks to my belly. He lays his head on it, just waiting to feel it move, though he knows it's far too early for any of that."

Roger laughed heartily. "Aye."

"Oh, please don't tell him I told you! It would be… well, it might hurt him," she said, not knowing why on earth she'd told someone who was practically a stranger to her, something so private.

"Nae, hen, I willnae say anathin'. It's just that I can picture him doin' it, and I think it's lovely." His mobile started playing the theme song for *Future Explorations*, which made Erin laugh.

"Must be David; I use the same ringtone."

"Aye, et's catchy, ain't it?" he said with a grin.

"Yes, it is."

He looked at his mobile and read the message out loud.

D: *Would you please pick me up now?*
   Also, would you ask Erin to join you?

She raised her eyebrows and pointed to herself. "Me? He wants me to come along?"

"Aye, tha's what he said."

"Well, then, we'd better get going," she said and stood facing him. "Thanks for coming to find me. It means a lot."

"Ye're welcome. I wish I'd had someone tae help me with a few words of wisdom back then," he said with a shrug of his shoulders.

They walked back to the house together, then Roger drove them to the hospital. David was waiting outside in the shadow of a dark corner; it wasn't a good time for autographs and selfies. When he saw the SUV pull up, he nearly ran to the safety and privacy its tinted windows afforded him. As soon as the door was closed, he took hold of Erin, squeezing her so hard it nearly knocked the breath out of her. "Ach, Erin! I'm sae sorry! I can't believe I've treated yeh so poorly—No' even acknowledging you before I left the house earlier… and after what you did tae help—No' tae mention what you're most likely goin' through yerself. Please forgive me!" he said.

Erin and Roger exchanged the quickest of glances in the rearview mirror. Neither of them had expected what he was saying. "I understand, David, honestly I do. There was so much going on, and you needed to be her husband—just then. "Are *you* okay? That's what matters," she said.

He rested his forehead against hers. "No—darling, *you* are what matters. When I thought you were dead—after the fire, I made a vow tae God and tae myself, that if He brought yeh back tae me, I'd no' take you for granted— ever, and I dinnae intend tae do it now," he said, lifting his head and gazing intently into her eyes.

He looked anxious and worried as if she would be angry at him or feel slighted. "Oh, David, you've been through so much in the last few days; lay your head on my lap and rest. I love you, and I'm not upset. Dinnae fash, *mo ghràdh*," she said tenderly.

He did as he was told and then sat right back up. "Ach, Erin! I had tae ring the school! I'll have tae pick them up tomorrow. Ma Losh! And—please, dinnae be upset, but—I cannae have you—at ma mother's home—at least no' straightaway. I want you tae meet them more than anathin', but it's their mum and—"

"Shh—it's okay, I understand. I'll stay wherever you want me to. Will you have them come here, or will you go straight to London?" she asked calmly. He was working himself up, so she hoped to calm him with her demeanor.

"Her body is here, so I'll bring them tae Owlgate." He was quiet for a few moments as he stared out the window. "They told me... in hospital, that they see this sort of thing quite often with those suffering from anorexia and bulimia—Their hearts just can't handle the stress of et. It wasn't anathin' I did or her havin' any added strain that caused it. She was a tickin' time bomb," he said. He started coughing and allowed her to pull him down onto her lap again. "Erin, I need tae thank you again for what yeh did for her—and after everathin' she'd said tae you! You've a heart of gold, and someday ma children will know what yeh did—tryin' tae save the life of their mother."

Erin was embarrassed; it wasn't like she'd had much choice. David had asked her to do something, and she'd done it, simple as that. Heroics were not on her mind at the time. "You're making it bigger than it—"

He sat up and interrupted her, "No, Erin, it was enormous! Don't you agree, Roger?" he said.

"I—I dinnae ken what she did, actually, so I couldnae say truthfully," Roger sputtered.

David looked at him in the rearview mirror. "I thought you were standin' there the whole while," he said, shocked.

"Nae, I came inside after the ambulance arrived. What did she do, then?" he asked.

"She helped tae perform CPR. She breathed her own breath into Susannah's lungs when most people in her situation would have stood back and watched her die. She did as I asked and tried valiantly tae save her life," David said admiringly.

Roger switched his gaze to Erin and raised his eyebrows. "Tha's somethin', innit?" he said, "I dinnae ken another woman who would do the same!" He smiled at her and then fixed his eyes on the road ahead.

They wound their way past Craigmillar Castle, Duddingston Loch, Holy Rood High School, and the Kirk Hall. Within moments they were in front of the sturdy iron gates, waiting for Roger to perform his opening and closing ritual. Once they were inside the house, she made sure David went straight to bed, and he didn't fight her about it.

She helped him get undressed, his eyes drooping. He then allowed her to help him into his bed as though he were a child. She tucked him in and kissed him, "I'm going to tell your mum and Millie that we won't be down for supper. I'll be right back," she said and then realized he was already asleep.

Erin went downstairs and told them what had happened at the cottage and about his time in the hospital. She also mentioned how he didn't want her around once the children got there, which, of course, everyone understood. Roger said he wouldn't mind if she stayed with him in his flat for the time being. There was an extra bedroom with a door, plus a small bathroom and a tiny kitchenette they could share, so it was settled.

Chapter Sixty-Nine

DAVID RETRIEVES THE CHILDREN

avid woke in the morning dreading the day ahead of him, not knowing what to say to his kids. He rolled over, wondering how he'd ended up in his bed and spooned with Erin. She stretched and snuggled in against him, falling back asleep almost immediately. He had to leave early, so he kissed her shoulder, told her he loved her, and got out of bed.

He found the note his mother had left for him, explaining the decision about where Erin would stay, which took a load off his mind. Usually, Roger would pick the children up from school if they were staying at Owlgate or heading to London, and David would do it if they were staying at the cottage. However, it fell on David to do it that day, and he was long gone in the SUV by the time she and the rest of the house woke up.

Erin got up and took a relaxing, leisurely shower; she was going to have a long day, full of stress and a lot of unknowns to deal with and needed to be ready. She hadn't been able to shower for several days, and the hot water felt splendid on her stressed and aching body. An hour later, she came downstairs, nervous, and worried, though she tried hard to hide it. Millie and Annis were standing together, and Erin smiled at them. "Good morning, ladies," she said in an attempt to sound cheerful.

"Good morning, dear; how did you sleep?" Annis asked.

"I thought I might have trouble getting to sleep, so I took a sleeping pill before I went to bed. I was dead to the world and didn't even notice David leave." She realized too late what she'd said. "Oh! I'm so sorry; I didn't mean—"

"Dinnae worry, dear, we understand what yeh meant," Millie said and came around the island to put her hand on Erin's shoulder. "This isnae gonnae be an easy weekend for you; there will be a good deal of treadin' lightly. We'll do our best tae support yeh. If you need anathin' just ask us, a'right?" she said kindheartedly.

"Alright, and thank you; it's all just so surreal," she said. "I'm really nervous about meeting his kids. I know I need to be scarce, but I'm sure we'll be in contact at some point while they're here—I just don't know how to behave. I mean, they've just lost their mom, and here *I* am in the mix, it's crazy. I understand they'll feel all sorts of different things, and I'm sure accepting of me won't be one of them. I just hope David doesn't push them. I know he really wants us to meet and get along, but I'm afraid he'll try to make that happen this weekend, and now isn't the time."

Annis put a cup of tea on the counter in front of her. "Aye, he does want his children tae get on with you, but I reckon he'll be sensitive enough under the circumstances. Unless that is, they *ask* tae meet you, which, knowing them, they may just do, so be prepared," she said.

"You think they'd really do that?" Erin said with raised eyebrows.

"Aye," said Millie, "they're keen ones, they are, and verra curious, as well. I reckon they'd already begun tae see behaviors in their mum which were disturbin' tae them, and they may just surprise yeh with their ability tae accept you."

"I believe they'll be back within the hour, so perhaps you should begin moving your belongings now, dear," Annis said and glanced at the clock.

"Oh, right, thanks for the reminder," Erin said and drank down her tea. She grabbed a piece of toast from the rack, applied butter and raspberry jam, then went upstairs to pack.

It was just over an hour's drive on the M90 to the school, and David was all nerves, not knowing what to expect from the children. *Will they be inconsolable or numb?* He reckoned there would probably be a mixture of emotions on the way home. *Erin would know what to do; she's brilliant in every situation I've seen her in. I wish she were here!* he thought as he merged into the fast lane to overtake a lorry.

As he fought the hypnosis of endless white dashes, cat's eyes, hedges, and trees, he thought about all the things he'd be expected to do in the next few days, none of them pleasant. He'd have to put an obituary in all the newspapers and ring dozens of people whom he'd rather not speak with on a good day. Susannah didn't have any family, which was one silver lining. He'd have to go over her Will with their solicitor, plan the funeral, do a myriad more things he didn't yet know, and to top it all off, be a caring, available father to his children.

Then, there was Erin; his mind wandered to her lying beside him in the bed that morning, so warm and bonnie. His memory was filled with her smell and the softness of her skin. He realized quickly that he should stop thinking about her, as his trousers were becoming a bit tight.

He wondered how to tell them she was staying at their grandmother's house and reckoned telling them before they got to Owlgate would be the best course of action, in case she happened to be outside when they pulled up to the house. He had hoped Erin and his children would meet under better circumstances, and though he had no intention of forcing a meeting that weekend, they *would* be in the same vicinity and would, more than likely, encounter each other before returning to school.

He was thankful for the reassurance the doctors had given him that Susannah had been millimeters away from a heart attack for quite some time and there was literally nothing he could've done to save her. He marveled once again at what Erin had done to help him, though she was frightened and most likely conflicted. It revealed her character and selflessness to him anew.

He turned onto the school property and followed the long drive up to the main building. Carnoch Co-Educational Boarding School was constructed of large, dark grey stones—foreboding and strict in its lines and form. It brought back memories from his time as a student there, memories that weren't of his happiest days.

David pulled into the visitor's car park and turned off the engine, then took a deep breath to calm his nerves. The wide, stone steps that led to the school's offices were not at all welcoming as he scaled them. Not much had changed since he'd left; even the smell of the place was precisely the same twenty-six years later.

His heart skipped a beat as he approached the office doors and saw his children, seated in a row, oldest to youngest in their school uniforms. They were sat on hard wooden chairs with their heads down, looking at the floor. He opened the door, and Rosie, the youngest at nine years old and his only daughter, saw him first. She leapt off her chair and ran to him. He crouched down and hugged her tightly.

Peter, the eldest at sixteen, and Charlie and Daniel, who were fraternal twins, ages eleven, were more sedate as they stood and went to him. He knew Charlie would have done just what Rosie had if the office staff hadn't been there to see it. Reluctantly, he detached Rosie from his neck and kissed her cheek; she looked so much like her mother it was heartbreaking. "I must sign you out now so we can be off, alright?" he said.

"Okay, Daddy," she whispered and then backed away, standing with her brothers.

David stepped up to the secretary's desk, where she had the release papers ready for him to sign. He'd planned for the funeral to be held on Monday, though it was rushing things a bit. He wanted to get everything over and done with as soon as possible and get on with his life. He filled in that they would be back in school on Tuesday, signed the page, and was about to leave when the headmaster stepped out of his office.

Duncan Campbell, David's former headmaster and the man still in charge of the school, was an arrogant, condescending prig. He was one of those men who would live to be one hundred and twelve and only give up his position when he was forced out. "Hello, David," he said, which made David feel as though he were thirteen again; small, wiry, and terrified of the man. "So sorry to hear of your loss; your wife was a delightful woman! You'll let us know if you need anything, won't you?"

He shook the man's hand. "Of course I will, Headmaster, but we must be off, as we have a long drive ahead of us," he said without a hint of his Scottish accent.

"Yes, of course. Safe travels then," he said, and David made haste to get them out of there.

They walked silently to the car, not wanting to bring attention to themselves. Rosie sat in front, and the boys sat in the back. David started the engine and looked at them all, sitting so still; he wanted with all his heart to hold them. They would have time for that when they got back to his mum's, but it made his heart ache to see them so sad. "Is everyone alright? Does anyone need to say—anything?"

Daniel opened his mouth, but Peter nudged him. "We're fine, Dad," Peter said coolly, "We just want to get to Gran's house and away from here." They all nodded their agreement emphatically.

David's heart ached once more; he knew how dismal the school could be, and he'd wanted nothing more to do with it after he had graduated. It was Susannah who had insisted, when Peter was only a wean of eight, that he should be sent to a boarding school, so that's what had happened. "Alright, I understand," he said and pulled out of the car park heading back in the direction he'd come.

After about twenty minutes, he asked if they needed to use the facilities, though none of them did. It was quiet and dreary in the car. Nobody wanted to talk, or perhaps they did, although no one fancied being the first or to do it there. *This is going tae be harder than I thought.*

He'd been afraid he'd not be able to handle four weeping children, but four silent ones were far worse. He wanted to fill in the silence; to start them talking at least, but he also didn't want to push, so he sat, concentrating on his driving. It was a long drive, but they finally made it back to Edinburgh.

The very first thing he thought of when he pulled into the drive was Erin, where she was and what she was doing. That's when he remembered his plan to warn them about her before they arrived. "Before you leave, there's somethin' I need tae tell you," he said. They all looked at him expectantly. "Do you remember the lady—"

"Erin? Yeah, we remember," Daniel interrupted him.

"Well, she's here with me. She'll no' be stayin' in the main house whilst ye're here, so you won't have tae see her if yeh don't want tae, but I wanted you tae know about it."

Peter looked angry and made a noise in his throat.

"Does Gran like her?" Charlie asked quietly.

David was surprised by his question. "Aye, verra much."

Charlie had just the hint of a smile on his face, and David noticed that Rosie's did, as well. The smiles faded when Peter turned to glare at them, reminding them why they were there. "May we go now? I'm tired of sitting here," Peter said impatiently and put his hand on the door latch.

"Aye, that's all," he said. He put the car in park, and the doors unlocked. Peter opened his first and closed it hard as he walked away. Roger met the boy on his way outside, but Peter didn't look up or acknowledge him, so he didn't say anything. David was out of the SUV by then and exchanged a look with Roger.

Charlie waited for David to close the car door before wrapping his arms around him as Rosie had done at the school. "I love you, Dad," he said quite unexpectedly.

David was surprised; he had just looked up at the top floor of the garage where Erin was standing in the window looking down on them. He put his hand on Charlie's head, smoothing a cowlick, then crouched and put his hand on his son's shoulder. "Are yeh a'right Charlie? Do you need anathin'? Yeh know I'm here for you if you do?" he said.

"I'd like to be near you for a while if that's alright?" he said softly, and David smiled.

"Of course, it's a'right. I'll have some things tae do in a wee bit, such as telephone calls and the like, but you can stay with me.

Charlie seemed unsure about something and looked up at the window Erin was standing in, watching them. When he did, she saw him and moved quickly away from the window.

Chapter Seventy

I WANT TO MEET HER

"Dad, was that Erin?" Charlie asked, pointing at the window above the garage door and looked his father in the eyes.

"Aye, that was her," David said. "She was makin' sure we arrived safely and that everyone is a'right."

Charlie looked back at where Erin had been standing. He took a deep breath as if screwing up his courage. "I'd like to meet her, please," he said bravely, still looking up at the window as if hoping to get another look at her.

David wasn't sure what to do. He figured if the boy wanted to meet her, why should he stop him, but he also didn't want him to see her and let his sadness and rage over his mother's death out on her either. "Are you sure yeh dinnae wannae go into the house first? See your gran and Millie?"

Charlie shook his head resolutely. "No, Dad. I need to meet her. She's nice, right? I mean, she won't be cross that I want to see her, will she?" he asked him with a sudden look of fear which told David he was worried that maybe the woman wasn't who he hoped she'd be.

"No, she won't be cross at all; she'll be happy tae meet you. I just want tae be sure yeh know what yer doin'. I dinnae want yeh tae get upset or anathin'," David said.

"I'm sure, Dad."

David shrugged, and they headed in that direction. Rosie suddenly ran outside to them and took her brother's hand. "Charlie!" she said, "Where are you going?"

He looked at David and whispered, "I told Dad I wanted to meet Erin, so we're going to see her."

Rosie turned a bit pale and gasped. "Where is she?" she said anxiously.

"She's in Roger's flat." Charlie pointed to the window he'd seen her standing in moments before.

Rosie looked up at the window, then at Charlie, and then at her father. "I'd like to meet her as well, Daddy; may I come?" she asked.

David wasn't sure what to make of them. "Are you certain, Rosie? Ye've just arrived. Don't think yeh have tae meet her right away."

Rosie looked up at the window again. "No, Daddy, I want to meet her," she said, more boldly.

David was shocked and looked toward the house to see if anyone else would come out and demand to see his lover. When no one appeared, they set off again, and when they reached the stairs, he stopped them. "Now, I'll go up and prepare her; give her a wee warning that you'd like tae say hello, then I'll call you up when she's ready, a'right?" he said.

"A'right," they said together.

He suddenly felt butterflies in his stomach. *What if they don't like her, or she doesn't get on with them?* he thought as he climbed the stairs and knocked on the door.

Erin opened it and laughed. "You don't need to knock, silly," she said, but he must have had an odd expression on his face because she gave him a worried look. "David? What is it? Is everything alright? Are the kids okay?" she asked, starting to sound worried.

He smiled at her and took his chance to kiss her lightly. "No, love, nothin's wrong, but—ah, Charlie and Rosie are keen tae meet you. They're waitin' at the bottom of the stairs. I told them I'd warn you first," he said nervously.

Her eyes grew wide, and she mouthed, *'Really?'*

'Really,' he mouthed back.

"Okay, you know I'd love to meet them too," she said and smiled, then she raised her eyebrows at him and put her hand on her stomach. "I'm so nervous," she whispered, and he kissed her forehead.

"A'right, you may come up now," David called down to them, and Charlie came up straight away.

When Rosie didn't appear, David went to see what was wrong. He looked at his little girl, and she smiled sheepishly at him, so he went all the way down and sat on the third step from the bottom. "What is it, Rosie ma love?"

"She's a nice person, isn't she? I mean, she'll like me, right?" she asked nervously.

David was so touched; all those years of her mother's disapproval and overly high standards were revealing themselves. "Aye, she'll love yeh, darling. She's one of the nicest people I know, and I know a lot of people," he assured her.

Rosie took her daddy's hand and started slowly up the stairs as if she were afraid a dragon would be meeting her at the top.

Erin waited with Charlie while David and Rosie talked. It was a bit awkward, so she invited him inside. "Come in, Charlie, would you like something to drink? I think Roger has some Squash in the fridge. I'll get him some more later; I'm sure he won't mind," she said, stalling.

"No, thank you," he said politely.

She smiled at him and said, "Go ahead and have a seat if you want." She looked at the young man standing shyly in front of her and wondered how she could make the situation less uncomfortable for him. *Maybe getting down to his height might be better.* Something she'd noticed while being a school bus driver was that she sat at the children's height, not towering over them, which seemed to make her more approachable.

She had just sat down on the sofa when David came in with Rosie at his heels. She was a beautiful girl, very much like her mother, except tall, like David. Erin smiled at her. "Hello, Rosie, it's nice to meet you. Would you like something to drink?" Rosie shook her head and looked at her dad. "Why don't you come in and sit with me so we can get to know each other?"

David smiled at Erin, amazed at how she was with unfamiliar children she'd just met. She was easy and natural and didn't talk down at them. She was herself, only slightly simplified, and he fell in love with another side of her that day.

"So, your dad said you wanted to meet me. Was there something you wanted to know or maybe ask me? I'm an open book, and I won't get upset, even if it's difficult stuff to say," she said. There was silence as the children sat looking at her while twiddling their thumbs and being generally awkward. "Okay, I understand it's hard to start a conversation, so I'll begin. Do you mind if I ask *you* some things? They shook their heads, indicating they didn't mind.

"Let's see, what are some things I've wanted to ask you? Hmm, let me think. Think, think, think." She put her hand on her cheek and tapped her temple to show she was thinking, in Pooh bear fashion. David nearly laughed out loud at how childlike and funny it was, and both children smiled; the ice was beginning to crack.

"Charlie, you're ten, right?" He smiled and nodded. "Hmm, I'm trying to remember what ten-year-old boys are interested in—surely not girls yet?" He made a face, which made both David and Rosie laugh. "Now, now, you two," she said, smiling with mock correction, "We are trying to have a serious conversation here, do keep your sniggering to yourselves," she said in a perfect 'Eliza Doolittle at the Ascot races' accent. She resumed her normal accent with a smile and continued, "Do you like... sports?" He shook his head. "No, I didn't peg you for a sporty kind of guy. That only leaves deep-sea diving and furniture building—which is it?"

All three Elliotts laughed; the ice was now splintering rapidly. She looked at Rosie. "You're eight, correct, or are you nine now? Hmm, you're probably a bit too old for princesses, aren't you? Though, really a girl can never be too old for princesses! Yes, and we can't forget about Prince Charming, right?" Both girls looked at David and smiled, which made his life. "Who's your favorite princess, Rosie?"

She looked at her dad, and he nodded to say it was okay. "I'm nine, and I like Ariel the best," she said.

Erin was beaming. "Really? You won't believe me, but she's my favorite too. I wanted to be her when I was a teenager. I desired long, red hair flowing over my forehead. I wanted to sing like her and to meet my Prince Eric," she said whimsically.

Rosie smiled brightly. "Me too! I want to be able to swim underwater and have fishes for friends," she said and giggled.

"That would be so much fun! As long as you keep your eyes out for sharks!" she said and pretended she was going to tickle her, which made them both laugh.

"But you did, Erin, you did meet your Prince Eric, right?" she said, suddenly bold. "Except his name is Prince David."

Charlie rolled his eyes and groaned, while Rosie laughed and Erin looked at David, smiling. "Yes, Rosie, I did." She looked back at the young girl, leaned in, and whispered, pretending that she didn't want David to hear her, "Do you think he'd mind if I call him Eric every once in a while?" They looked up at him and he smiled.

———

Erin then turned to look at Charlie. "Now, don't think I've forgotten about you, young man. You didn't answer me, so I'm guessing it's not deep-sea diving or furniture making, then? Books? Do you like to read, or maybe write?" she asked, and Charlie perked up.

"I do like to read. I'm reading—" he began and then put his head down, apparently embarrassed at what it was.

"Go on, Charlie, I won't judge you," she said, and he looked up at her.

"*The Secret Garden,*" he said softly and then blushed deeply.

"*The Secret Garden!* I love that book! I haven't read it in years and years though, so I don't remember all the character's names, but it's a wonderful book! I remember Mary, and... I can't remember the names of the boys, but—"

"Colin and Dickon," Charlie interrupted her.

She smiled at him, remembering so many things from the pages of one of her favorite books. "Yes, that's it; Colin was the sick boy, who was afraid he was getting a hunched back, and I just loved Dickon! I bet you are a lot like him, aren't you, Charlie?"

"That's who I like the best as well," Charlie said. "I hope I *am* like him."

"Aye, you are, son," David said. It was the first time he had contributed to the conversation, and Charlie smiled at him.

"I'm gonna have to read it again soon! It really is one of my favorites," Erin said, delighted they had something in common.

"You may borrow my copy when I'm finished if you'd like," he said boldly at first and then became shy at the end.

Erin smiled and put her hand over his. "Thank you so much, Charlie, I'd love that!" she said warmly. He smiled broadly, and she could see that he had his father's smile.

"I like your accent, Erin," Rosie said out of the blue, and Charlie nodded.

"Well, thank you! I like yours too, but I especially love your dad's; he's been speaking with his Scottish accent more lately, and I just love it." They all looked at him, and he made a silly face that made them all laugh.

"So, Rosie, what else do you like? Oh, I know, ballet! I saw your dad's photograph of you posing. I don't know anything about ballet, but you looked beautiful in the photo. Rosie's face fell, and Erin noticed it. "Don't you like ballet?"

"Not especially; Mummy makes me—" she began, but then her eyes grew wide, and she put her hand over her mouth.

"Oh, sweety, I'm sorry," Erin said. The young girl looked at her dad, horrified, and Charlie put his head down. Erin wanted to hold her, to comfort her, but that was not likely to happen. She looked at David, who gave her a look to say it was okay and not to worry. He held out his arms, and Rosie went to him. He sat on Roger's easy chair, and she climbed onto his lap.

Erin thought about what to say now that the mood was broken. *What would you want an adult to say to you in this situation?*

"Do—either of you want to talk about how you're feeling, or… about anything, really?" Erin asked gently.

Charlie shook his head, but Rosie looked at her dad. "Why don't I feel sad? I should feel sad, shouldn't I? But I don't. Does that mean I didn't love Mummy?" Charlie looked up, obviously wanting to know the same thing.

Rosie seemed nervous to hear his answer—as if her worst fears were about to be confirmed.

David held her and kissed her hair. "It doesn't mean you didn't love yer mum, darling. It's hard tae say why you dinnae feel sad; everyone feels things differently. It's also hard tae truly grasp what's happened with it being so new tae us. Yeh might feel sad in a day or two or at the funeral, but you might no' feel sad for a verra long time. Yeh also might feel angry—at God, or me, or even at her—that's normal.

"You might also feel guilty, thinkin' that somethin' you did or said or thought made it happen tae her, but you need tae know yer mum was sick for a long time. The doctors told me it was just her time, and it was no one's fault. And yeh know what, yeh might no' feel anathin'—not for a long time, but that's normal, as well. You dinnae need tae worry about being sad; just be yourself, and if you need tae talk, I'm here, and so is yer Gran, and Millie, as well. You may also talk to Erin, if yeh feel like it, right?" he said, looking at her for confirmation.

"Yes, of course! I might not have an answer, but I will listen and not judge you," she assured them. The children smiled at her. Rosie got up and sat next to Erin on the sofa. "Now, is there anything you'd like to know about me?" Erin asked them. "I've asked you a lot of personal questions, so I think it's only fair for you to do the same."

They asked her what America was like, and about her job, and did she have any pets, or kids of her own, and her favorite foods. After a while, there was a knock on the door, and Roger poked his head inside.

"I've a pair of boys down here who are wonderin' where ye've gone to," he said.

"Aye, I reckon we've been up here a long while, haven't we," David said. "Send them up."

Roger made a face saying that wasn't what they wanted to do.

"A'right, then, I think we had better leave Erin alone now," David said and all four of them got to their feet.

Charlie went up to her and shook her hand, which was surprising but sweet. "I'm glad I asked Dad to... introduce us; it was nice to meet you," he said.

Erin smiled, completely in love with the sweet young man. "The pleasure was all mine, and that's the truth, Charlie," Erin replied.

Rosie looked sad to leave. She also stood before her, holding out her hand, but then changed her mind and hugged her. It was short, but it meant the world to Erin—and David for that matter. She looked at him and put her hand over her mouth, in awe of what had just happened. David smiled his best smile at her. "I hope we get to talk again very soon," Rosie said and then turned toward their father.

"Go downstairs and tell your brothers I'll be there shortly," David said.

They didn't close the door behind them as they left, so they heard Rosie say to Charlie, *"I like her—a lot."* Then Charlie whispered, *"Me too, though don't tell Peter."*

David went to Erin and held her, still shaking his head in disbelief. "Ye're magic; pure, bloody, brilliant! Do you know that?" he said. "I can't believe that happened!"

Erin felt the tears gathering in her eyes as she looked at him. "Me neither, I mean—how did I know to say those things? It all just came out of me. I guess all those years as a bus driver were training me for this moment," she said. One tear rolled down her face. "It was miraculous!" David wiped the tear away with the knuckle of his index finger and then kissed her. Erin stood on her tiptoes and ran her fingers through his hair.

Suddenly there was a noise behind them, and they broke away from each other. Rosie was standing there looking at them. "Prince David," she whispered, "I left my jumper." She grabbed her sweater from off the couch, and then just like that, she was gone. David and Erin stood there, not knowing how to emote; they wanted to laugh and cry and dance and shout all at the same time.

———

"Prince David," Erin echoed. "Truer words have never been spoken."

"I'm glad you think that way, love," he said.

They heard Peter yell up the stairs. "Oi, Dad! Are you coming or not?"

David wanted to say 'not,' but that wasn't really an option. "Oh, darling, I dinnae wannae leave you, but I must go tae London tae get her paperwork, register her death, plan the funeral, and put somethin' in the newspapers. I'm meant to leave at half past twelve, but I'll be back tonight. Will yeh be alright here or would you prefer tae come with me?" he asked, hoping she'd want to join him.

"Are you crazy? Come with you to London just after your wife dies? That would be a very bad idea! I'll be fine here, dinnae fash."

"I'll test the waters a bit and see how they all feel about havin' you tae supper. I'll also do all I can tae come up and say goodnight when I return. I'll miss yeh in ma bed, love!"

"Same here, darling. I hope I don't keep Roger up with my snoring!" she said, and David laughed.

"Why do you think he's been put up here? You'll make a lovely cacophony together, I'm sure."

"Go on, you need to be with them now. Go! Shoo, scat!"

Chapter Seventy-One

PETER'S DISTRESS

David reluctantly left the flat and joined his children. Charlie and Rosie looked back at the window, hoping to see Erin standing there. Daniel seemed oblivious to everything except tapping Charlie's shoulder and then scooting to his other side so he'd look over the wrong shoulder. After the first attempt, he figured it out and wasn't tricked again, but that didn't stop Daniel from trying over and over until Charlie turned. "Give it a rest!" he said and grabbed his brother's hand. Daniel started to whimper, so David had to tell Charlie to let go.

Head down, his hands in his trouser pockets and a scowl on his face, Peter walked a few feet behind them.

They walked into the house, and Millie greeted Charlie the way she had done the others earlier. "Ach! Ye've grown a meter since I've seen you last! Ye're Gran's in the garden; go say hello."

He and Rosie walked out to the back patio and hugged Annis. She took Rosie's hand and had her sit next to her. "So, what've you been up tae then?"

They looked at each other and then toward the door to make sure no one was listening to them. "We've met Erin," Rosie whispered.

Annis raised her eyebrows. "Did you, now? Ach, and what did yeh think of her, then?" she asked.

Again, they looked toward the door before they said anything. "I like her," Rosie answered first. "I don't think I'm supposed to, though; Peter would be cross if he knew."

"Yes, he would. I like her as well; she's easy to talk to and a lot of fun," Charlie said.

"She loves Ariel best, as well as the book Charlie is reading! I hope—" Rosie began, forgetting herself, then stopped as Peter and Daniel walked out to join them, and all talk of Erin stopped.

"Are you hungry? Et's a wee bit early, but we can start lunch if ye'd like?" Annis said. They all nodded, so she stood and went into the house to talk to Millie. The children stayed outside, and the atmosphere became quiet and awkward. None of them wanted to talk to Peter, as he was angry and sullen. They knew if they said anything he didn't like, he'd yell at them, and even Daniel didn't want that.

———

Peter couldn't stop looking up at the top floor of the garage and grimacing. *How dare he bring her here!* he thought bitterly. *She should go home now and leave us be! She's not part of our family.* He could feel stinging tears starting to form, so he shut his eyes tightly and dug his fingernails into his arms, which were crossed in front of his chest.

David came out to the patio while Peter was glaring at the garage. "Are you a'right?" he asked.

Peter shrugged; he wasn't going to talk to him, with his girlfriend there and his wife dead for only a few hours.

David told the others to go inside to see if Millie needed any help and then sat in front of Peter. "You know I'm here if yeh need tae talk, right?"

Peter was shaking mad; again, he felt the hot angry tears welling up, threatening to make him look weak. *He's the weak one, not being able to control himself with that woman.* "You want me to talk? Fine. You only care about *her* now, not about us—or Mum."

"That's no' true, Peter. I care about all of yeh—"

"God, Dad, why are you talking like that?" Peter interrupted him. "Is it to impress her? Did she tell you to talk that way? It's fine for Gran, Roger, and Millie, but it's not who you are! You speak like us, not like them; why are you acting this way? I hate it!" he yelled.

"This *is* who I am, Peter. I grew up here and spoke just the same as yer gran and the rest, but when I married yer mum, she didn't like it, so I stopped, and now I want tae be me again. I'm sorry yeh dinnae like it but this is who I really am."

Peter rolled his eyes and stormed away. He had never in his life spoken to his father like that; it shocked him, and he felt ashamed of himself for doing it. He had only ever wanted his dad to be proud of him and to show him what a good leader and eldest brother he could be, but there was just so much anger trapped inside of him. He nearly turned back to apologize, but he couldn't. Instead, he went to the small potting shed in the side garden to hide; he didn't want to talk to anybody ever again!

———

David sat on the back patio, wishing Erin had been there to help him. He didn't possess the skills to deal with or understand what was going on in Peter's mind, but he knew Erin probably did. Daniel scampered out with one of the dogs just then; the dog was barking it's head off, and Daniel was laughing, running after it. The boy saw his dad and stopped playing. His head went down, and the dog, not knowing what had happened, came and sat at the ready by the boy's feet.

"Sorry, Dad," he said, apparently ashamed of himself "I know I should be sad and quiet—"

David looked at his son and sighed. "Come here, Dan," he said, and the boy reluctantly went to him. David felt sure he thought he would be scolded, but instead, David took him and held him tightly. "You go on and play, Dan; it's alright."

Daniel wasn't one for emotions and squirmed free from his grasp, then looked at him disbelievingly. "Really, Dad? It won't upset you, or... the others?" he asked, but David smiled ruefully at his young son.

"No, Dan, it won't bother me or the others, and if it does, ask them tae come tae me."

Daniel walked away with the confused dog. A moment later, David heard him screeching while the dog chased him. He smiled and stood, gazing at the garage. *She cannae be expected tae stay up there for the entire weekend!* he thought and made a decision that would most likely not be popular, especially with Peter, but he wasn't going to keep his true love locked up in the tower to shield anyone anymore.

He had so much to do, but he walked over to the garage, climbed the stairs, and knocked gently on the door before opening it. Erin was sitting on the sofa in the dark room with an open book on her lap, though she was staring out the window at the passing clouds. There was a ray of sunlight bathing her in a gentle glow, and David almost gasped at how beautiful she looked.

When she turned her head and smiled warmly at him, he melted. "Ach, ye're bonnie!" he said as he stepped inside the small apartment and sat on the sofa next to her, then took her hand. "I've come tae fetch yeh and bring you tae the house with me. I've so many things tae do, but I want tae be with you," he said, then he pulled her to him and kissed her.

She returned his kiss and said, "I don't think that's a good idea. You don't want to push Peter and Daniel away."

"Ach, Peter has just now told me that I only care about you and no' about them. He's also angry that I'm speakin' with my native accent," he said. "Daniel is oblivious and just wants tae play, which is good, I reckon."

"Of course Peter is upset about me and your accent changing all of a sudden; I'm sure he correlates the two. I read somewhere that when something significant happens in a child's life, they need normality. I didn't think about it until now, but for you to change such a big thing as how you speak right now, at least in front of him, would be a difficult change for him," she said.

Suddenly, he moved over and laid on his side, putting his head in her lap. Not expecting it, she managed to move her book just in time. "Yeh ken so much about children and things such as this. I dinnae ken what I'm doin' most of the time with them, and neither did Susannah. I'm sure that's why she sent them away tae that school, so someone else would deal with them. I don't intend tae send them back next term unless, of course, they want tae go back; that place is no good." He started coughing and had to sit up to catch his breath, then laid down again.

Erin traced his earlobe with her finger and then stroked his sideburn. "Oh, sweetheart, you're run down. You should be resting after the fire and all the stress you've been under. I'm sorry you have to deal with this burden." She started rubbing his shoulder, and he rolled onto his chest so she could reach more of his back. "Is that a hint?" she asked with a laugh.

"Mebbe," he said and then relaxed his aching shoulders. "Ach, that feels fantastic. Dinnae stop, ever."

"Oh, David, it's already noon; you'd better go down and eat your lunch."

"A'right, but ye're comin' with me; I'll no' have you hidden away up here whilst we all eat together," he said, determined to have his way.

He knew she wanted to argue with him, but she stood when he did. "Alright, just don't be too hands-on, especially when you leave; it'll be too much."

———

They went down the stairs and into the house through the side door. Millie had her mobile out, ready to send David a message when they stepped into the kitchen. Everyone was already sitting around the table as they approached the dining room. David went in first, and Erin followed behind him. The family hadn't expected Erin at the table, so Millie quickly set out another place setting next to David.

Charlie and Rosie smiled but then resumed their gloomy faces when Peter shot them a glance from across the table. "Why is *she* here? Can't we just eat as a family?" he said fiercely.

"Peter!" Annis said sharply. "Apologize at once!"

Erin wanted to say it was alright and he didn't have to apologize, but it wasn't her place. She knew saying anything at all just then would only ostracize her, so she remained quiet. Peter ignored his grandmother, so Annis stood in order to enforce her command, but David made a small hand gesture saying she shouldn't bother that time.

"Humph," Millie said under her breath but didn't interfere.

"I must get things sorted in London, so I've decided to introduce Erin to you... formally, before I leave," David said.

"Are you taking *her* with you?" Peter said.

David scowled at him but then took a deep breath. "No, I'm not taking her with me," he said calmly, using his RP English accent. "That's why I've included her. I'll be back tonight, but I don't want her to be locked up in the garage for the rest of the day, like—"

"Rapunzel?" Rosie offered. Erin smiled at her, and she smiled back until she looked at Peter, whose face was red and frightening. "Sorry," Rosie said and put her head down.

David pulled out the chair for Erin and then sat next to her. "Yes Rosebud, like Rapunzel," he said, ignoring Peter.

"What time will you be leaving, Dad?" Charlie asked.

"I'll be leaving just after lunch, I'm afraid."

The three younger children groaned, but Peter sat sulking. They ate their lunch without much conversion; Annis and Millie made small talk with Erin, but the animosity coming from Peter was almost palpable. Each time anyone addressed her, it got worse.

"Peter, if you are going to behave this way, you may leave the table," David said, which made the boy explode in a growl of rage.

"I hate you!" he said and stormed out of the room, knocking his chair over and not bothering to pick it up. The other children looked at each other, presumably anticipating another outburst from their father, and breathed a sigh of relief when there wasn't.

———

Charlie and Rosie became animated once more and said 'Hi' to Erin in unison, which made everyone but Daniel smile. He was looking at her, not sure how to react.

Erin looked at him, smiling. "Hello, Daniel, it's nice to meet you," she said.

He looked around the table and saw everyone was relaxed, so he decided she was alright, for now. "Hi, call me Dan," he said matter-of-factly and then looked at his grandmother. "Can I have more gravy, please?"

"*May* I have more gravy," she corrected him.

He looked up at her, frowning. "You can have as much gravy as you want; why are you asking me?" he said, and the whole table laughed.

Peter was ashamed of himself, but looking at her made him angry, so did thinking of her. He heard them all laughing together and wished he knew what it was about. *They're probably laughing at me,* he thought bitterly. He just wanted to get everything over with, so he could go back to school, and everything could become normal again. He knew, deep down, nothing would be normal ever again; his mum was gone forever, and no one else in his family seemed to care.

He felt those bitter tears well up again, and this time he didn't stop them. He was determined not to bawl like a baby, but he could cry a few tears for his mum without being ashamed. He lay on his bed, listening to snippets of their conversations, growing more and more angry as his tears came down. He no longer cared about whether he looked like a baby or not and buried his face in his pillow, weeping with racking sobs.

He didn't hear his dad come to the door and was crying hard. He felt him sit on the edge of his bed, and all the pride and anger left him for the moment. Peter allowed his father to hold him as he sobbed.

———

David wisely didn't say anything; he just held him and let him get it all out. "I'm sorry, Dad! I didn't mean it," Peter bawled, and he shushed him.

"I know, son. I understand. I wish I could stay here so we could talk, but I must make this flight or I won't have things sorted by Monday. Can we talk when I return?" he asked.

"Yeah, Dad, but… I'm afraid if you leave, you won't come back—that *you* might have an accident as well," he said and started to cry again.

"Ach, Peter, no one knows when their time will come, but I don't reckon mine is here just yet. Don't worry, I'll be back tonight, and I'll be sure tae tuck you in—as I used to do when you were small," he said, and Peter smiled.

"I remember that. I wish you could still do it… I mean every day," Peter said, still holding tight to his father.

"You do?" David asked, surprised.

Peter looked at him seriously. "Yes, Dad, I miss you and… and… Mum a lot at school," he said.

David was choked up and didn't say anything for a minute. He looked at his son, nearly grown, wishing he could take back the years he wasn't able to do all the simple things like tucking them in. "I miss you as well." A tear escaped David's eye, and it was time to go. "I'm so sorry, Peter, I really must go now," he said and stood. "Peter?" The boy looked up at his dad. "Please try to be kind to Erin. I understand you're upset about the whole thing, but she's really nice, and—"

"Alright, Dad, I'll try… for you, but no promises," Peter interrupted.

David smiled and tousled his son's hair. "I'll see you tonight."

David went back downstairs smiling and saw Erin waiting for him. "Looks like you had a good talk," she said, and David held her tightly.

"Aye, and I dinnae think you'll have much trouble from him now."

She smiled and kissed him. "Good, he looks like such a sweet young man. He's just in a lot of pain right now. I can't wait to meet the happier side of Peter Elliott."

———

They didn't know Peter could hear them talking. *Maybe she's not THAT bad,* he thought to himself.

You also know the things Mum's said and done to us. She wasn't a good mum, and you know it!

What? Don't think that way about your poor mum, who's… dead!

Didn't you just wish her dead? Yes, only a fortnight ago when she completely ignored your birthday. At least Dad sent a card with twenty quid in it.

Yeah, the only piece of mail he's sent in nearly a year!

But at least he did that much.

His assistant sent it, I reckon, not him.

Shut up! Maybe Erin will be good to us—That's all I really want. I want a mum who loves us and to see Dad more often.

Oh, right, and you think that anything will change now that he has an American girlfriend? He'll be off to America all the time now, and he'll forget about us, stuck in that bloody school in the middle of nowhere!

Maybe… I mean, just maybe… Erin will convince him to take us out of Carnoch—

And why would she do that? Have you ever heard of a stepmother who wanted the kids? She's only after Dad because he's rich and famous! She won't care about us! You're dreaming, mate! You'll see, she won't like us; she's probably a self-serving minge who won't want to spend time with us! Test her!

Yeah, I'll prove it! Maybe we should spring a little garden party on her and see what happens!

She'll find some way out of it; just you wait!

He went to the washroom and splashed cool water on his face, then made his way slowly downstairs. He heard his gran and Millie speaking to each other and listened to them. They weren't talking about anything that interested him, but the way their speech sounded *was* pleasant to hear; he had to admit that much. *Perhaps it's not such a big deal for Dad to speak as they do. Mum hated it, but I rather like it, I reckon.*

Roger had already pulled the SUV up to the door and was waiting when David and Erin walked outside together. "Be safe, and I'll miss you," she said.

"Aye, you should, and I'll miss yeh just as much," he said and kissed her, thinking only Roger was watching.

Roger rolled his eyes and said, "A'right, lovebirds, ye're gonnae miss your flight if yeh dinnae break it up."

They looked at him and then at each other. "Fine, spoilsport! I love you, and I'll see you later," she said, and David got into the car. "I'll close the gate for you, Roger."

"I love you, as well. Goodbye," David said. He shut the door, and Roger drove off.

Erin walked down the driveway and pulled the heavy iron gate closed with a loud *clang.* When she turned around, the children were standing outside by the front door, waiting for her.

Chapter Seventy-Two

GARDEN PARTY

"Well, what's this about?" Erin asked when she got back to the bottom of the elegant entryway steps and smiled warmly at the four Elliott children. Peter's eyes were red, but he didn't look angry. In fact, she thought he'd given her the slightest hint of a smile, though it was fleeting and seemed to be infused with something akin to mischief.

Rosie came up to her and took her hand as naturally as if she'd known them for ages. "Would you like to walk with us to Dr. Neil's?" she asked.

Erin looked at Peter to make sure he approved of the idea. He shrugged and started down the drive. "That sounds lovely, Rosie; does your grandma know about it?"

"Yes, she knows," said Charlie.

Erin turned and looked through the windows; she could see Annis standing with Millie at her side, watching them. She smiled, giving them a small wave. Once Peter opened the side door in the tall brick wall, Daniel ran ahead of them.

"So, who's idea was this?" Erin asked, and Rosie pointed to Charlie. "Oh, right, I understand, good idea!" She thought of him reading the Secret Garden, and it made sense.

"It was Peter who suggested it to me, actually," he said softly, not wanting Peter to hear him.

Erin raised her eyebrows and cocked her head to the side slightly. *That's interesting,* she thought, recalling, uncomfortably, the plot of the movie *The Parent Trap.*

Rosie and Charlie stayed close to her as they walked the short distance to the public garden. Peter stayed about ten feet ahead, and Daniel arrived long before they did. They entered through the large, ornate gate and strolled along the path, past the cafe building, which was closed, then downward toward the loch. The day was perfect; the sun was out, and it was quite warm for June. In the shade of the many lush trees that surrounded them, they were as comfortable as they could ever be.

"I imagine one of you likes plants and gardening, right?" Erin asked, not letting on that David had already told her it was Peter's passion. Rosie shyly pointed to Peter, who was ahead of them a bit. Erin felt in her pocket and found some change, so she took out a coin and held it in the air. "Fifty P to the one who can identify and name the most plants in this garden!" she said, loud enough for all of them to hear her. She knew fifty pence was nothing to those kids. She hoped it would be the fun of the game that mattered to them.

Rosie ran to a rose bush and called out, "Rose!"

Erin laughed. "One for Rosie!"

"It's called Royal William, Hybrid Tea," Peter said quietly.

"One each for Rosie and Peter. Charlie and Dan, you're slackin'," she teased.

They spent the afternoon naming plants and running around the garden until Erin got tired and found a bench to sit on. She was almost six weeks pregnant and became tired sooner than she had since the Fertilis Defect was at its worst. She didn't know if it was normal to get exhausted so quickly that early in pregnancy or if maybe there were other reasons for the fatigue, but she just had to sit and rest sometimes.

Rosie and Charlie sat on either side of her arguing over who had won the fifty pence coin. When she decided the contest should be over, Erin began a countdown, and they both named as many plants as they could see. "...three ...two ...one," she said, and at the very last second, Rosie called out, 'grass,' which caused a tie between them.

"But that doesn't count!" Charlie was saying to Rosie.

"Why not?" Rosie asked him, "It's a plant!"

"Because—Because she'd already said one! Ha!" he said triumphantly, and Rosie crossed her arms in front of her. "What do you think, Erin? Did I win, or did Rosie?" Charlie asked her, using his father's smile and puppy dog eyes to try and sway her answer.

"Hmm, I don't know—Peter, what's your opinion?" she asked the unsuspecting young man.

He seemed a bit startled to be put on the spot but also secretly glad she'd asked him. Erin guessed he could've named nearly all the plants in the garden but thought that perhaps he didn't feel much like running around and was allowing the younger ones to win. "I reckon—I reckon Charlie won, but Rosie should have the fifty p," he said and looked at her as if hoping she would approve of his answer.

Erin looked at him, amazed at the problem-solving skills and wisdom of a boy his age. "That's a brilliant solution, Peter! Charlie, you get the satisfaction of having won, and Rosie gets the prize for sheer spunk. Does everyone agree?" she asked. The two siblings thought about it for a moment and then looked at Peter. He shrugged, and they agreed it was a good plan. Daniel had stopped playing as soon as he'd found a frog to put in Rosie's face and was off chasing a grass snake through the park.

"Alright, then Rosie gets the coin," she announced. She handed her the large, silver fifty pence piece and then turned to Charlie. She shook his hand with authority, "I hereby name thee: Charlie, King of the Garden… for a Day," she said. Rosie thought it was hilarious and giggled. Her laugh was so contagious that eventually, everyone started laughing, even Peter. "Who wants a group selfie to commemorate the occasion?"

Charlie and Rosie said, "I do" in unison. Daniel came out of nowhere saying he wanted in as well.

"Peter? Would you care to join us?" she asked. He smiled reluctantly and got up from the grass where he was sitting. He then knelt behind the bench where Dan was already standing. "Alright everyone, say… fungus!" They laughed, and she took several shots as they all smiled for the camera.

"All in favor of a silly face selfie, say aye." They all said 'aye,' so she held the camera up and took at least three more with everyone making a silly face, then she opened the photo gallery to look at what she'd taken. The children gathered around her and laughed at Daniel, who hadn't changed his smile at all.

"My face is already funny-looking with these freckles!" he said.

They rolled with laughter, and Erin was amazed at both his and the other's wit and sense of humor. It had been an impossible day, and she felt blessed, hardly able to keep her cool. She was itching to send the pictures to David but decided to wait for a better time.

"Are you going to send the photos to our dad?" Charlie asked as they walked back to Owlgate.

"I was planning on it; why? Don't you want me to?" she asked.

He smiled up at her. "No, I do; I'd just like to see his reply," he said and then continued softly, "That is if you don't mind at all?"

Erin tousled his hair. "Should I do it now, then?" she asked.

"Yes, please," he and Rosie said together, so she stopped on the road and opened her message app. She found her conversations with David and sent all the photos, even the blurry ones.

"Okay, it's done. Now, he might be in a meeting or something, but I'll gather you all once he replies, alright?" Her phone started playing the theme from *Future Explorations* right away. The children laughed, and she looked at them with her eyebrows raised. Her stomach had butterflies for reasons she couldn't explain. She opened the reply, smiled, and read it out to them.

> D: *God, Erin, you are magic, aren't you!*
> *I can't believe it. You surprise me*
> *every day. Looks as though you've had*
> *a fine time without me, and I'm*
> *jealous! I've just left the house to ... "*

"The rest of the message is about what he's doing now."

The kids smiled, then they became quiet and reflective as they continued. Erin was sorry that they were having to go through such a difficult time and hoped she could help them.

Having had a really good time, some physical activity, and lots of fresh air, everyone was tired and hungry as they got back and stepped through the gate.

They went in through the front door, and the dogs came to greet the children. Annis was standing in the doorway to the sitting room, and when Erin walked past, she quietly got her attention. "Hello, Ann, what's the matter?" Erin asked her.

Annis smiled warmly and said, "Absolutely nothing, dear. I want tae thank you for everything you're doing for them.

"Oh, it's nothing, really; we just—" Erin started to object.

"It's certainly not nothing; it's extraordinary. I've never seen anathing like it before. You, ma dear, are a natural."

Erin didn't know what to say. "Oh—" she began and then Millie called out that supper was nearly ready.

"I'm—not a verra sentimental woman, Erin, but I want you tae know I'm glad David's found you, and I'm glad he's brought you here," she said.

Erin turned back to face her and smiled. "Me too. I really like it here, and I think I'm going to fall madly in love David's kids. Thank you for accepting me so soon." She hugged the older woman and then walked away to clean up for supper.

Chapter Seventy-Three

SUPPER WITH THE KIDS

Erin went upstairs to wash her face and then headed to the dining room, where Charlie and Rosie were arguing. "But *I* want to sit there!" Rosie said, with a slight whine in her voice.

"I said it first!" said Charlie and crossed his arms over his chest. Peter was already sitting, and Daniel was reaching for something he'd dropped under the table. It looked and sounded like sheer chaos. Millie was starting to raise her voice in frustration, and when Erin walked in, it got even worse. Rosie and Charlie ran to her, both talking at once, so she put her hands up to halt them.

"Okay, okay, stop talking," she said and put her finger to her lips to drive the point home. "No one can understand you if you are talking over each other; now, what's the matter?" They both started talking again, but she put her finger up, and they stopped. "Charlie, tell me what's wrong?" she said.

He puffed up his chest at being called on first, and Rosie stuck the tip of her tongue out at him. "I said I wanted to sit next to you *first*, but Rosie—" he began, but Rosie butted in.

"But *I* want to as *well!*" she said, and Erin smiled at them.

"Oh, you two are so sweet!" The looks on everyone else's face in the room told a different story, though. "Don't I have two sides? Can't each of you sit next to me?" she asked.

"That's just what we said to Millie, but she said you should be able to sit next to an adult, especially after putting up with us all afternoon, so she's set you next to Gran," Charlie said.

"We can't go against Millie's wishes, now, can we? Personally, I don't mind sitting between the two of you, but Millie knows what she's doing, don't you think? And what about your gran? Do you think she'd rather talk to an adult or one of you two goofballs?" she asked.

They looked down at the floor. "An adult," Rosie said sadly.

"Now, don't look so sad; let me talk to Millie for a minute, and I'll see what I can do." They perked up at that, and Erin went into the kitchen, laughing.

"Oh, Millie, you've caused a real stir in there! I honestly don't mind sitting with one of them on either side of me, but I'm not going to go against your rules. Is it a big deal if I sit between them?" she asked, and Millie smiled, showing her small, straight teeth.

"No, not at all, dearie, only I didnae wannae force it on yeh. I wanted you tae be able tae choose, yeh ken?"

Erin went to her and put her arm around her shoulder. "You are a wise woman, Millie. I choose to sit between them. I'll let you be the hero and tell them you've changed your mind," she said, and Millie smiled again.

"I believe ye're the wise woman, ma dear." She put on her no-nonsense face and went back out to the dining room. "Now just houd her wheesht," she said, as the two siblings tried, at the same time, to change her mind, "D'ye think I'm buttoned up the back? I know what ye've been up tae, but it willnae work on me!"

They both said, "Awww," at the same time.

"You should thank yer lucky stars Ms. Erin is such an accommodatin' person! Now, Rosie, you sit next tae yer Gran, and Charlie, sit next tae Daniel," she said, sounding exasperated. "We're never gonnae eat at this rate!"

Erin sat betwixt the two children, and everything was peaceful again. They had a lovely meal of roasted chicken, sliced carrots, and jacket potatoes, which Erin called 'baked potatoes,' however, Dan was quick to correct her mistake. It was simple but perfectly satisfying.

The children were asked what they were learning in school, though none of them were keen to talk about it. "Won't you have your summer holiday soon? Erin asked them.

Peter volunteered to answer. "Yes, at the end of this month."

"And how long is your break?" she asked him.

"We return on the first Wednesday in September."

"Only two months? That's sad. In America, kids have off for three months, but you can leave school at sixteen, right?" she asked, and Peter smiled.

"Yes, unless you plan to attend university," he said.

"Ah, and I'm guessing you are—planning to attend university?"

"Yes, I'll be studying botany and horticulture," he said.

"Oh, so my contest was right up your alley! And yet you let your brother and sister win?" she said, and he looked at his plate.

"I—didn't feel much like playing."

The room got quiet.

"I see, that's completely understandable. I'm glad you came along though."

He looked up and smiled at her. "I am as well. I'm sorry about my behavior earlier."

Are these kids for real? she thought. "My goodness, Peter, you *are* very mature for your age! I accept your apology, and I'm glad we've cleared the air. You all are such great kids! I can't wait to get to know you all better this summer... that is... if I'm here. I mean, I might have to go back to America for a bit, but I hope we can spend some time together for those two months. That is... if you'd like that?"

They all smiled and said they would like it very much. She looked at Ann, who was beaming at her. "I can't wait for your dad to get home so we can do something together. Maybe we can go back to the garden tomorrow?"

The children all said, "Yeah," together.

Erin wished with all her heart that David had been there to witness it first-hand. She couldn't wrap her head around it. *It shouldn't be like this, should it?* She didn't know if it would last or if it would wear off eventually, but it felt really, really good!

After dinner, Annis went to the sitting room to watch television, and Millie went to the kitchen to do the washing-up. Erin followed her to see if she could help. Millie said no at first but then allowed her to dry the dishes and set them on the counter for her to put away.

"Millie? Are David's kids like this all the time?"

"Humph," she said. "Nae—Well, I take that back; they are when it's just David here with them." She lowered her voice and continued, "But if their mother was here, they were completely different. She was a verra hard person tae please, yeh ken, and tha's all the wee bairns wanted was please her."

"It must be hard to grow up like that," Erin said.

"Aye, but you'll be good for them if you don't mind my sayin' so. Ye're a verra kind-hearted woman, and they'll be needin' that."

"I'm so glad things have cooled off with Peter and that we are all getting along like we are, though it feels a little *Sound of Music* to me. Next, I'll be dressing them all alike in old curtains and teaching them folk songs!"

Millie couldn't help herself; she got the giggles. "The idea of the five of yous runnin' around Edinburgh and singin' atop Calton Hill! Ma Losh!" Her laugh was infectious, and before long, Erin was laughing along with her wiping tears from her eyes.

Later that evening, Erin was sitting on the sofa scrolling through Facebook. Rosie came into the room, saw her sitting there, and sat next to her. "Well, hello. What are you up to?" Erin asked. Rosie's eyes seemed to be drawn to her neck.

"May I see your necklace, please?" she asked. "I noticed it at supper."

"Sure." Erin took it off and handed it to her. "Your dad gave me that on the weekend we first met."

"What is it?" Rosie said as she watched the pointer move.

"This is a compass, a very tiny, beautiful compass. You know what a compass does, don't you?"

"Yes, but I'd like you to explain it, mostly because I like to hear you talk," she said and giggled. Erin acted as though she were going to tickle her but instead pulled her close. "A compass is a tool used for navigation. The pointer is magnetic and will always point north because the North Pole is also magnetic, and the two are attracted to each other.

"Just like you and Daddy?" she said innocently.

Erin smiled at her. It was nice to have a child to snuggle with. She thought of the little one inside of her, growing more and more each day, and she dreamed of sitting with it too, someday. "Yes, Rosie, just like your dad and me. When he gave it to me, he said, '*So we can always find our way back to each other.*' Isn't that sweet?"

Rosie smiled, gave her back the pendant, and wrapped her arms around her. "I hope—I hope my daddy marries you, and you become my new mummy."

"Oh, Rosie, I hope so too. I'd love to be your mum!"

"Mummy never allowed me to do this, and I like it a lot."

Erin kissed the top of her head, not understanding how a mother could be so distant with her children. "I do too, sweetheart." They sat together for a long time until Erin started to fall asleep, then she looked down at Rosie, who was fast asleep. *Poor, sweet baby,* she thought and woke her with a little nudge.

"Let me take you to bed, and I'll tuck you in, okay?"

Rosie nodded drowsily and stood. They walked up the stairs together very tired and ready for sleep. Rosie put on her pajamas, and Erin pulled back the light blanket on the bed. After Rosie climbed in, Erin covered her up and kissed her forehead. "Sweet dreams, Rosie," she said, and the young girl smiled.

"Night, Erin," she replied.

Erin went back downstairs smiling and feeling very happy. She met Annis on her way down, said goodnight, and then walked out to the garage. It had been a full day, and she wouldn't have traded it for the world.

Chapter Seventy-Four

AND THERE HE KEPT HER

That night Erin woke to David and Roger entering the flat. She listened to their conversation as she waited for David to come to her. She had nearly fallen back to sleep when she heard, "Yes, she's bonnie, but I won't have the time for her now. I dinnae ken if I should take her tae London or leave her here? If I take her tae London, people will gossip and talk, sayin' I'm havin' a midlife crisis, and I can't verra well keep her at the house! I could put her up somewhere, but that's no different than leavin' her here, but if I leave her here, it may end up bein' years—"

"Ach, yeh ken I'm fond of her. I reckon you should keep her here; I mean, she hardly takes up any room. Plus, mebbe, if she gets tae lookin' forlorn, I couldn't take her out for you every now and then?" Roger hinted.

"Aye, if I were gonnae trust anaone with her, it'd be with you. I'm so torn, I'll have tae think on it a while longer," David said with a laugh.

Erin heard the bedroom door open and then shut gently. She heard David taking off his clothes, then he got into the small bed with her, spooning her and holding her tightly.

"Ach, Erin, I missed you today!"

Erin missed him too and had longed for him to be holding her like he was then, but what he said frightened her, and she couldn't keep from trembling.

"What's the matter, love? Ye're shaking! Bran wasn't here again—"

"No, I haven't seen him since that night," she whispered and pulled his arm even tighter around her. "Just hold me." *Is he really thinking about leaving me here, and does he really think he won't have time for me anymore? Am I losing him?* "I missed you too!" She hid the silent tears that fell on her pillow.

"Please, make love tae me before I have tae return to the house." He moved his hand down to her thigh and pulled her leg up over his. She moaned as he put his fingers between her lips and found her clitoris. As she felt him getting more and more hard against her backside, she started breathing heavily. All her cares melted away for the moment while he touched her and kissed her neck and shoulder. She took his hand and guided it to form perfect circles at the ideal speed until she gasped.

David could feel the pulsing of her climax and lay on top of her, needing to be in her; he couldn't wait. He pressed his head against her folds and felt the pressure around him as he slid easily inside. He had longed for her all day, and now that he was there, he wasn't disappointed; he never was. After a few strokes, she arched her back. Once again, he felt her spasms pushing against him, and he could hold it no longer. "God, Erin, I love you!" he said in her ear as he felt his own spasms fill her.

Erin was confused; was he only saying that in the heat of the moment? If not, then what was all that about letting Roger take her out and not wanting her in London with him? Was it only the sex he loved? She managed to hold her emotions together, although she didn't know whether to be scared or furious. She chose scared just then so she could hold him. He rolled onto his back, and she lay beside him, holding him as tightly as she could, not wanting him to leave her side.

"Erin, darling, what is it?"

All she could do was whisper, "I just missed you, that's all," she lied. She ran her hands over his chest hair and then put her hand on his face, feeling the end of the day stubble on his chin. *What if he's done with me? What if he leaves me? I can't live with that!*

"I'm sorry, hen, but I must go. I promised Peter I'd tuck him in.

Erin smiled at the thought of David tucking in his eldest son. "Okay. I had an amazing day today. Your kids are above average; believe me, I know! Being a bus driver, you get to know the good ones from the ones who haven't been taught to give a shit. Yours are the cream of the crop, David."

"Aye, I can't argue, though there's somethin' special about you, as well. Yeh ken how tae read children before you even know them. How do you do it?"

"You have to in my line of work. There are a lot of tells, but we can talk about that another time. Sweet dreams."

"Sweet dreams, darling. I'll see you in the mornin'. I love you!"

"I love you too, David!"

In the morning, Erin was trepidatious; she didn't want to be angry, but the things David had said to Roger were so horrible. She presumed he didn't know where to keep her while he was filming Doctor Who, but he'd already told her he wanted her with him. Had he changed his mind, and if so, why? She heard Roger filling the kettle for tea and wished she could talk to him, though she figured he probably wouldn't discuss it without David's knowledge. *What on earth could have happened to make him change his mind so abruptly?*

Oh, you know, Erin! Don't be so dense! He must have seen one of the other women Martin told you about and remembered how much he liked her. You don't matter as much anymore, and you're the one on the backburner now.

"SHUT UP!" she yelled at herself.

The noises in the kitchenette stopped. "Sorry," Roger said.

Holy Moses, you're an idiot, Erin. She got up, put on some loose-fitting clothes, and went out to talk to him. "Roger? Where are you?"

He stepped out of his room, looking a bit sheepish. "Sorry, Erin, I didn't think I was bein' that loud—"

"No, Roger, I wasn't yelling at you; I was yelling at me," she said miserably.

"Ach, pretty hard on yourself, eh?" He looked relieved that she wasn't upset with him.

"Oh… my mind is trying to convince me of… bad things," she said timidly, not wanting to admit to essentially eavesdropping on their conversation.

"Bad things? Can I help?" He leaned against the small bit of countertop, crossing his arms and his ankles, waiting for her to tell him what the 'bad things' were.

"I don't think so; it has to do with something I overheard last night."

"What did you hear?" he asked.

"Well—" She felt tears sting her eyes, and did NOT want to cry *again*, so she turned and faced away from him. "David said he was thinking of leaving me here and not bringing me to London… and you said how I hardly take up any room, and that if I get lonely… you'd take me out every now and then." She knew it sounded ridiculous, but that's what she'd heard.

Roger didn't say anything right away, but then he chuckled lightly. "Aye, we did say those things, but it's no' what ye're thinkin'. I'll ask him to explain it to yeh."

"I don't know what there is to explain; I heard what he said." The hot tears were back, so she returned to her room to get dressed.

"Will yeh be wantin' any tea?" he asked sympathetically.

"No, thank you." She got dressed and did her makeup, afraid maybe she'd gotten too lazy and should try a bit harder. She followed Roger to the house for breakfast, feeling confused and unsure. They entered the kitchen, and before Erin could say 'boo,' Roger had David by the arm and was leading him out of the room.

A few minutes later, David returned, and it was his turn to take Erin by the arm and lead her away. She tried to talk to him while he pulled her up the beautiful staircase, but he wasn't listening. He opened the door to his bedroom, drew her inside, and shut the door. "David, I—"

He kissed her passionately, not allowing her to finish, then he gazed into her eyes. "Erin, ma darling—How could you think—No, wait, I ken how yeh might; I'm sure it sounded bloody awful! We weren't talkin' about you."

Erin took a step back. "Not me? Well then who *were* you talking about?" she said, wondering who the other woman was. He laughed, though she couldn't imagine what might be funny.

"Neela." That's all he said, allowing it to sink in before he continued. "We were talkin' about the car, Erin! I'm torn on what tae do with *her*."

Erin turned red and took a deep, shaky breath, ready to say something, but then changed her mind. She turned around, facing away from him, not wanting him to see the tears of relief pouring in rivers down her face.

He stepped up to her, holding her to him from behind, and rocked her gently to some silent music only he was hearing. "I would never leave you like tha'. I'm no thinkin' of ways tae get rid of you if that's what ye're thinkin'? And, although I'm certain Roger would love tae take you out on the town, ma love, I'll not allow him tae do et. Ye're mine, and I'll be the one takin' yeh out." He let go of her and she turned around.

She looked him in the eyes and smiled, but she didn't know what to say, so she just hugged him tightly. Her makeup would be ruined, but she held him, pressing her face against his chest, crying, and laughing at how stupid she'd been. "I'm sorry. I shouldn't have thought twice about it, but my mind was poisoned by Martin's lies. Your love is everything I own in the world right now, and I don't know what I'd do without it. I was so scared you were— Well, it doesn't matter now."

"Please, promise ye'll always come to me when I say things that confuse you. There will most likely be a perfectly good explanation. I'm just glad you opened up tae Roger, or today would've been miserable for you and probably for me as well... wonderin' what was wrong all day! Jinks, it's every man's worst nightmare!" he said.

"Okay, I will. Let's go back downstairs; I'm hungry," she said and then checked her makeup, hoping it wasn't all over her face, though it was. She wiped it off, and they returned to the kitchen hand in hand.

"Good mornin'," David said brightly to his family as they entered the dining room.

Rosie and Charlie ran up to him, speaking over each other, so he put his finger up and they stopped. He pointed to Rosie, and she said, "We want to go to Dr. Neil's with you and Erin today; may we... please?"

David smiled at her and then at Erin. "That would be nice, but first, we must sort out the proper clothing for tomorrow."

The children's faces fell, and the room became very quiet and still. Peter had watched his dad walk in holding Erin's hand and felt the anger rise in himself again. She was fine on her own, but he didn't like seeing them together like that. She was great with the younger ones, and he really liked her, but everything in him was torn and confused. He knew his mum was not the nicest person, so he was afraid he'd end up liking Erin better than her, which made him feel horrible. Taking a furtive glance at her, he noticed that Erin was sat at the dining room table next to his gran with a cup of tea. His thoughts were interrupted by his dad.

"I searched the house and found some clothing, but I don't know how much of it will still fit. We may need tae go shopping," he said.

His grandmother had the newspaper in front of her, and when she found what she was looking for, she interrupted him and read it out.

> ***Susannah Jane Sutcliffe Elliott***, *36, of London, passed away at her mother-in-law, Annis Elliott's home in Edinburgh on the 14th June this year of a heart attack. She was known worldwide for her modeling career and social activities, through which she helped raise millions of pounds for various charities. She was also a loving mother and wife. She is survived by her husband, David, her children: Peter, Charlie, Daniel, and Rosie Elliott, and her mother-in-law, Annis Lamont Elliott.*

"The rest are funeral details," Annis said. Everyone listened to her, each person having their own thoughts on who Susannah Sutcliffe Elliott had been. "That was verra nice, David; did you write it?"

His cheeks grew pink as he said, "No, I asked Tina tae write it for me and then added a thing or two before it was submitted.

Chapter Seventy-Five

STORY

"Darn! I... left my phone in the flat. I'll run out and get it before breakfast," Erin said, really not wanting to hear any more about Susannah Elliott just then. She walked out the front door and noticed what looked like a camera lens aimed through the iron filigree work on the side door, next to one of the gates. Startled, she rushed up to the flat and sent a message to David, telling him what she'd seen.

A moment later, she saw Roger walk down the drive and approach the door in the wall. He spoke with someone for a minute and then headed back to the house, shaking his head. Erin texted David again, asking him if she should stay in the flat or come back to the house? He responded that she should come back to the house through the back door.

When she was safely inside, David met her in the hallway, away from the children. "It's a reporter covering 'the suspicious circumstances of Susannah's death,'" he said, using air quotes. "Roger tried the diplomatic approach, askin' him tae kindly shove off, but the tosser said he had every right to be sat there on the street."

"But I don't understand," Erin said, "Why would they say it was suspicious?"

"I reckon it's because she was so young, and few people know heart attack is one of the risks of Anorexia."

"So now we're prisoners in here?" Erin said, not liking the feeling.

"I expect he'll follow us into town—"

"How awful!" She furrowed her brows and hugged him.

"That's how it is sometimes. Perhaps, once he goes, you should bring yer things back tae the house. That way you'll no' need tae leave again, and ye'll be with me, which is much preferred, anaway."

"So much for going to the garden with the children later; they'll be so disappointed."

The mood was not cheerful as the family sat around the table to eat breakfast. None of them wanted to be stuck in the house on such a beautiful day, and neither did they want to go to some stuffy clothier to find mourning clothes.

"Ach, yeh may as well go on and get it over with! No use moping around here," Annis said. "Perhaps you should consider leaving after breakfast, David. Then you'll have plenty of time for an activity when you return."

David sighed and Erin sensed his apprehension, presuming that he didn't fancy a trip to buy clothing for his children any more than they wanted to go. She knew he wouldn't think to ask his mum for help, so she decided to take action. "Ann, could I have a quick word with you?" she said while the kids were getting ready to leave.

Annis turned to her and smiled. "Aye, dear?"

Erin made sure David wouldn't overhear her and then asked, "How can I say this delicately? David isn't about to admit it, but I believe he's afraid he'll buy the wrong things or make some mistake with the clothing. I wanted to— to ask if you wouldn't mind tagging along to help him out?"

The older woman's eyes softened, and she smiled at Erin. "You certainly are astute. I agree; he'll need someone with experience in these things tae help him."

Erin kissed her cheek. "Thank you. I'll stall him until you're ready to leave," she said, then Annis hurried up the stairs, and she went to find David.

He was standing on the back patio. "Come now, Dan, yeh must go; you don't have a choice," David was saying as she opened the back door.

"What's the matter?" she said and then saw Daniel on the ground, laying on his belly with his arms crossed under his chin. It seemed the boy was bound and determined he wasn't going clothes shopping, and that was that. "Oh, I see." Erin sat cross-legged, or as close to it as she could manage, on the ground next to him. "What's the matter, Dan; why won't you get up for your dad?"

He turned his head away from her. "I don't want to go clothes shopping. I hate that," he whined.

"I don't blame you one bit; I hate it too, but you don't want to show up tomorrow wearing something too small, being uncomfortable all day, and looking silly, do you?" she asked.

"I don't care!"

"Oh, I bet you do care. Now, what's really the matter?" The boy shrugged. "Okay, then, since you don't want to go shopping, what would you rather be doing?"

Dan put his chin on his arms, looking at her, then smiled, so that his dimples showed. "I'd rather go to the arcade and eat candy floss," he said.

Erin laughed, "That does sound like a lot of fun, doesn't it, David?"

"Aye," he said and watched her.

"I'm sure your father would much rather do that with you than buy stupid clothes, but he has to do it, and so do you. How about we plan a day, though it might not be until you're on summer holiday, where we all go to the arcade, eat pizza and candy floss, and drink nasty fizzy drinks until we are too tired to stand up? There's an arcade on Portobello beach—Oh! We can dip our feet in the ocean, too! I love doing that. You know, where I'm from, we don't have an ocean anywhere nearby. We have a lake, but it's not the same."

Daniel looked at her, weighing his options. He could lay there having a temper tantrum, or he could get the clothes and come back with a promised reward. He could also ask Erin all about what Wisconsin is like. He looked at his dad, rolled over, sat up, and allowed him to give him a hand to get to his feet. "Alright," he said and then helped his dad pull Erin up.

Dan ran off, and David hugged her tightly. "I marvel at your way with children. It's as if yer weavin' a magic spell and they cannae resist yer charm. How do you do et?"

"No clue," she said with a shrug, "I guess I try to put myself in their place and take it from there."

By then, Annis was ready and came to find them. "I thought I might join you, that is if you'd like my help," she said, wisely.

David's face brightened. "Aye, that would be lovely, Mum," he said.

"All I ask in return is to make a quick stop at Marks and Spencer for a few bits and bobs."

As everyone made their way to the garage to get into the SUV, David walked Erin back into the house and kissed her. "I have a feelin' ye've done a wee bit of orchestration today. I've never gone clothes shopping for the children before and I was quite anxious about the ordeal. Ye're a fine woman, and I appreciate you more than yeh know!"

"I'm glad I could help. Are you sure you don't want Roger to take you?" she said, worried he wasn't getting enough rest.

"No, we may have tae go to several places, and I dinnae want him tae sit around all day waiting. He told me he was plannin' tae work on cleanin' up poor Neela," he said.

"Okay then, have as good of a time as you can under the circumstances and be patient with the wee things. I love you, now go," she said.

He kissed her forehead and walked out the door. As soon as the SUV was out of the driveway, the car with the cameraman followed. Roger closed the gate after them, and the inhabitants of Owlgate were free once more.

Erin met Roger on her way to the garage flat, and he offered to help her bring her things back to the house. "I'll miss havin' a flatmate, even though it was just one night," Roger said.

Erin smiled at him and put her hand on his arm. "You're just a big ole softie, aren't you?" she said.

"Who're yeh callin' old?" he asked.

Erin packed her suitcase again and Roger carried it down the stairs, into the house, and back up the stairs to David's room. "I really hope I don't need to do that again for a while," she said.

"Me too!" Roger said and sat in the desk chair, a bit out of breath. They both laughed, and Roger stood to leave.

"Wait," Erin said as he started toward the door. "Do you have something pressing to do, or could you keep me company for a little while?"

He stopped and returned to the chair. "I can sit for a spell if ye'd like. I'm plannin' tae clean the Triumph today, but it can wait."

"Thanks," she said and smiled at him. "So, how is it you started working for the Elliott family, and how long have you worked here?" Erin asked him as she unpacked her things. She didn't much care for the nomadic lifestyle and hoped they would soon find a more permanent place to live.

"Ach, I reckon it's been about twenty-three years now. After ma wife died, I stopped workin'; stopped doin' anathin', really. Eventually, I couldnae pay ma rent or buy food, but I didn't care; there was always a soup kitchen when I was desperate. I wandered the streets and... sometimes begged. I'm no' proud of it, but I saw no point tae life anamore."

Erin sat on the edge of the bed and looked at him with compassion. "Oh, Roger, that's so sad," she said, with feeling.

"Aye. I reckon it was, but I wasnae thinkin' about it like that. One day, I ended up at Dr. Neil's and noticed this house; it was old and needed repair. I'd been a carpenter and did some handy work before I'd become homeless, and for some reason, only the fates know, I walked up tae the front door and spoke with David's father, Charles, about fixin' the place up for room and board.

"Now, I kent I looked and most likely smelt rough, but he brought me in and sat me on his beautiful, clean sofa. He heard me out and asked, gently enough, how I'd found maself in the state I was in. He gave me a payin' job with a room in the flat and food for every meal. He trusted me, and no' many are willin' tae do that when ye're homeless. He was a verra good man; I owe him and his family so verra much."

"Sounds like David's dad was someone I would've liked. I doubt things like that happen very often now; nobody trusts anyone anymore. Hmm, twenty-three years ago, David was what? Twenty-two?" Erin smiled as she continued putting away her things.

"Aye. And you want tae know what he was like then, do yeh?" he asked.

Erin laughed and shrugged as her cheeks colored. "Aye, I can't get anything past you!" she said.

"He was a lot like he is now that he's met you. Quick-witted and funny; kind, friendly, and happy. And always those looks! The girls were constantly comin' 'round, asking for David, but he never seemed interested in them. He had several girls he was friendly with, who I know were head over heels for him, but he never seemed tae look twice at them.

"This went on for upwards of four or five years, and honestly... between you and I... for a while, I thought perhaps he didnae fancy girls at all, yeh ken? Then he started actin', acquiring parts in ads and the like, and met Susannah at a party." He rolled his eyes when he said her name. "No' verra long afterward, perhaps two months later, he had us all, even me, sat on the sofa, tellin' us he was in love, and he was gonnae get married.

"Really? That quickly," she said as she took several hangers out of the closet and started putting her tops on them.

"Aye, as soon as they were married, he began behavin' differently. He was suddenly posh and started usin' an RP English accent, even at home. We rarely saw him, and when we did, he was dressed in verra fine things, and Susannah began tae look down upon Millie and me as 'the help' and only spoke tae us when she needed somethin'.

"No one but David saw anathin' good about her, and I reckon we all hoped he'd realize she was usin' him and leave her. Then she became pregnant with Peter, and we knew, by the way that David carried on, he would never leave, no' with her havin' his bairn."

Erin finished unpacking and set her suitcase beside the bed. "How is it someone can come in and take control of someone's life like that? Changing and molding them into who they think they should be? And the idea that the person lets them! I don't understand that," she said and sat on the edge of the bed again.

"Aye, David wasnae himself anamore; he was much more quiet, afraid he'd say somethin' she wouldnae fancy. Then, when wee Peter was born, he wasnae allowed tae hold him for longer than a minute or two before she'd rip the bairn out of his arms, sayin' he needed tae be fed or changed. She wasnae right in the heid, that woman. He wasnae happy at all anamore, but I reckon he thought it would improve eventually. That's why I'm so verra glad he's found you, Erin. Ye've brought our David back tae us!" he said, and she smiled at him.

"Thank you for saying that. I can't imagine my life without him now." She stood, and Roger put her suitcase into the closet for her. They walked downstairs together, and then Roger went his way and Erin went into the sitting room to check her Facebook messages.

Chapter Seventy-Six

FAMILY TIME IN THE GARDEN

David, Annis, and the children returned from their errand tired and ready for lunch. Millie didn't disappoint, serving a pot roast that melted in the mouth. The food was like manna, and everyone was in high spirits when the table was finally cleared. They hadn't thought they'd get to go to the garden because of the reporter, but once again, Erin had a plan.

She spoke with Roger before he returned to the garage and asked him for a favor, then she told David and the children what she'd come up with. Everyone thought it was brilliant, and they made ready for an afternoon at Dr. Neil's. Millie prepared a hamper with biscuits, tea, and a nice big blanket to sit on, and once everyone had changed into clothes they could get dirty, her plan was set in motion.

The reporter had done as David thought and followed them into town earlier. Erin figured he would do the same if he thought David was leaving again, so she asked Roger to go for a drive and lure him away. Then, they would be free to walk to the garden. Annis thought David and Erin walking together wouldn't be wise, as the neighbors might see them, so Erin and the children would walk there together first, then David would follow, ten minutes later.

Being a Sunday, it would be more populated than on a weekday, so David wore what they called his nerd glasses and a baseball cap. If he didn't smile, he was a bit less recognizable, anyway. They also decided that if anyone were so bold as to ask, they would be told that Erin was their new nanny from America.

Her scheme worked perfectly, and they all ended up at the garden together walking the paths and watching the swans on the loch. Peter was in a good mood, and as long as his dad and Erin didn't act all lovey-dovey, he was fine. He regaled them with the scientific names of many of the plants and trees they passed, and David beamed at his son's knowledge. Rosie made ringlets of daisies and dandelions, crowning them Prince David and Princess Erin.

When they got hungry, they had a picnic of homemade Jammie Dodgers, chocolate digestives, Custard Creams, and Jaffa Cakes, as well as tea, served from a large silver thermos. The day was lovely, although it did sprinkle once, and they all ran to take shelter under some trees. David made sure to stand as near to Erin as he could manage, using the short canopy of the tree they were under as an excuse to be close to her. The rain didn't last but a minute and made everything look clean and fresh once the sun came out again.

After several hours they grew tired and wanted to go back, though Erin thought returning to Owlgate would be slightly more difficult than leaving it. She didn't think the wild goose chase would work a second time, so when David messaged Roger to decide what to do, he was surprised to learn the cameraman's car was gone and it was clear for them to walk back. David went first, and then five minutes later, Erin and the kids joined him.

Millie ran baths for the children, and Peter took a shower. David and Erin went to their room and took a much-needed nap before supper. An hour later, everyone was well-rested and the children were clean, although Daniel nearly gave Millie a nervous breakdown when he ran into the back garden with the dogs and managed to find every tiny bit of mud from the short rain shower earlier. After spot cleaning him and forbidding him from leaving the house, everyone was called into the dining room for supper.

The children recounted their trip to the garden for Annis and Millie while David bragged about Peter's plant knowledge, which made Peter beam and blush. Erin revealed her and David's new titles of Prince and Princess, which of course, made Annis the Queen. Everyone called her Queen Ann for the rest of the evening, which she seemed to enjoy.

After supper, Millie cleared the table, as usual, and Queen Ann retired to the sitting room for her news and television programs. The children were allowed to play outside with a stern warning to Daniel to keep clean, while David and Erin sat on the patio, enjoying the warmth of the summer evening. Roger took a break from what he'd been doing to Neela and joined them, commenting on how unusually warm it had been the last few days.

At eight o'clock the children were sent to bed. David and Erin tucked them all in; Rosie, Daniel, and Charlie were read a story, even though the boys were really too old for that, and Peter was just kissed on the forehead and told to have sweet dreams. By nine, the lights were out, and the adults went about their own business.

Erin and David retired to his room to sort out what he'd wear the next day. He chose a black suit he'd brought from London, a white dress shirt, and a black silk tie with tiny swans on it. He laid everything out and groaned. "I want it all tae be over and done with already. I want tae take you tae London and start makin' our home together. Poor Kitty and Francie are beside themselves without anathin' tae do at the house."

Erin was sitting at the end of the bed, looking through a magazine. He knelt in front of her and gently took the magazine away, then he smiled at her and eyed her belly. He lifted her top, and she pushed down her pants so he could kiss it and run his hand over the tiny, invisible life dwelling inside of it.

"Hello, ma darling bairn, it's yer daddy. How're yeh doin' inside of there?" He put his ear against her stomach and listened. "Ach, I can't hear yeh yet. Stay well, ma love." He kissed her belly again and then pulled her top off her. He unfastened her bra, pulled it off, and pushed her back onto the bed so he could remove her bottoms. Then he parted her legs and used his tongue to part her lips.

"Oh, David, I love it when you do that!" she said.

He didn't need any more encouragement, continuing to explore her with his mouth and fingers. She rocked her hips and panted as he brought her closer and closer to orgasm. His tongue made large circles, round and round, slow and steady, building the sensations up until he felt her clenching and heard her moan and sigh as she reached her first orgasm.

He took off his clothing and pulled her further onto the bed, running his hand over her body, feeling her soft skin. Her dark nipples rose as he touched her breasts, and she got goosebumps as he ran his fingers lightly over her arms. He put his hand on her cheek and neck, running his thumb over her lips. Her eyes were closed, enjoying the sensation of his touch on her body, and he kissed her eyelids, which made her smile.

He kissed the tip of her nose and then her mouth as he entered her. Her lips parted as she gasped, and he plunged the tongue that had given her so much pleasure moments earlier into her soft, wet mouth. She kissed him back intensely, matching his speed and movements. Finally, they broke away as they each reached their climax, shuddering and holding their breath, enjoying that ultimate moment of release.

After a nice long snuggle, Erin got up, went to the bathroom, and put on her pajamas, then David did the same. After a long, busy day, they finally got back into bed and fell asleep.

Erin and David were fast asleep when Rosie knocked on the door. It was a good thing they had both worn pajamas because when they didn't hear it, the door opened, and she entered the room. "Daddy," she said quietly and touched his shoulder. David startled, "Daddy, I've had a bad dream. May I please sleep in here, with you?"

The light-blocking shades were down, so there was nearly no light, so David turned on the bedside lamp, and Erin rolled over. "What is it, David?" she asked, and Rosie gasped.

"I—I didn't know… I'm sorry," she stammered, clearly not expecting anyone else to be in bed with her father.

"Rosie's had a bad dream and would like to sleep in here," David explained.

"Oh, you poor thing! It's fine with me; climb in sweety," she said tenderly.

"Really?" Rosie said, sounding truly shocked.

"Aye, Rosebud, up you come," David said as he lifted her and set her on the mattress between the two of them.

"Do you want to tell us the dream?" Erin asked as she pulled the covers up over the young girl.

"Not tonight; it's too scary," she said.

"A'right, now go back tae sleep, and dinnae worry," David said, then he kissed her on the forehead. He looked up at Erin, and they smiled at each other before he rolled over and switched off the lamp.

Erin woke in the morning feeling a bit chilly and found that Rosie had kicked all the blankets off them in the night. She got out of bed and went to the bathroom, as usual, to be sick, and left the light on so she could find her way back. When she returned, Rosie had rolled over and was now in her spot. David made a quiet *psst* sound, moved to the middle of the bed, and Erin took his place.

He held her tightly as she lay next to him. "Thank you for allowin' wee Rosie tae stay; it means a lot. Her mother was no' one tae allow the children in the bed, so for you tae do that was special," he whispered in her ear.

"I've slept with my parents because of bad dreams plenty of times. There have also been times when I was nearly grown and newly on my own when I wished I could. I think this goes without saying, but I love your family, David, so if one of them needs to be held or to sleep with us, I'm going to be there for them."

"Ye're a marvelous woman, Erin; I love you more and more each day," he said, smelling her hair and holding her.

Chapter Seventy-Seven

A DREAM REMEMBERED

David, Erin, and the children woke first thing in the morning. He had chosen in the end to have the funeral in London, since all of Susannah's friends were there. It was planned for early in the day, so they'd make it back in time for the children to head to school that evening. They quickly ate breakfast, then started getting ready.

In the younger children's bedroom, Erin stood behind Rosie, brushing out her long strawberry-blond hair. The young girl was wearing a black dress with black flats and had a large black bow she was meant to wear in her hair. Erin felt so sad for her. *She should be playing outside, not stuck in here, preparing for her mother's funeral.*

Charlie and Daniel walked in, each holding a tie and asking for help. Erin turned around and nearly fell to her knees. As it was, she dropped the brush and had to sit on the end of the bed. Rosie was at her side almost immediately. "Erin? What's wrong? Are you alright? You're not going to… die, are you?" she asked, sounding terrified.

Erin looked up at her beautiful face. "No, love, I'm not going to die. I'm alright, but please get your father for me."

Before the sentence was entirely out of her mouth, Charlie ran out of the room. A few moments later, David came rushing in and knelt before her. Her eyes were wide, her cheeks flushed, and she had tiny beads of sweat on her forehead. "What is it, darling?" he said, sounding terrified.

She looked at him with fear in her eyes. "Do you remember the dream I told you... in the cottage? The one about the children, the Day of the Dead, and the crow?"

David sat on the floor. "Ma Losh, I do."

"The boys came in with ties in their hands... it was exactly as it was in my dream... before I'd even met them," she said, trembling. "I don't remember what happened at the end—Wait, a bird landed on the casket, and at the end of the dream, I thought it was you who was drunk and yelling at me, but it was Bran. I think the bird was Martin, and Bran was pretending to be you or something."

"Will Uncle Martin *and* Cousin Bran be there today?" Daniel piped up.

Erin and David looked at him. "I don't know, Dan. I'm sure Martin will be, but I don't know about Bran," David replied. "Alright, children, please ask your Gran and Millie for help with your ties and things." They reluctantly left the room, and Erin took a long, staggered breath.

"That scared me more than I think I've ever been in my life. It was so vivid! I think you should pay close attention to what Martin and Bran are doing if they show up. I think something bad might happen."

Everyone was dressed and ready to go with time to spare. Erin kissed David and the children goodbye, and Roger drove them to the airport. Erin didn't know what she'd do with her day; they wouldn't be back until supper, so there was a lot of time to fill. Annis suggested a game of Cribbage, so they played a few hands and Annis won both games.

"Well, there's an hour gone, now what?" Erin said as she put the pegs back into the small compartment in the back of the cribbage board.

"Don't you have some friends in America you could write a letter to? I've some lovely stationery you may use," Annis offered.

"Oh, what a great idea!"

Annis went to her desk and returned a few minutes later with a very nice fountain pen, a stack of stationery that looked to be made of linen and had a deep blue 'E' in raised calligraphy at the top, along with matching envelopes with the same 'E' on the back flap. "There you are, dear."

"These are too lovely for me to use, Ann! They're so luxurious! Are you sure?"

"Aye, I don't write letters as often as I once did, so they're goin' tae waste. Not only that, but it's also perfect for you. Obviously, the 'E' is for Elliott, but for you, it will stand for Erin." She smiled and patted Erin's hand.

"Oh, thank you," Erin said and headed upstairs to David's room. She sat at the desk in front of the bay window and started writing to her parents:

Dear Mom and Dad,   *June 17*

> *Hello from Edinburgh! David and I are staying with his mother (who is allowing me to use her beautiful stationery—Yes, the "E" is for Elliott!). Annis Elliott is a lovely woman, and I hope you'll get to meet her someday. Her home is named Owlgate, and it's amazing! I've also met David's kids! They are so sweet, and I know you'll love them! Maybe we will visit later this summer. I really want you to meet my new family.*
>
> *In case you didn't know, I left Todd—I just can't make it work. I told him to call you, Dad, if he needed help. Please don't gossip about David and me; it won't do him any good.*
> *I hope to see you soon! I love you!*
> *Erin*

She folded the beautiful stationery in half and put it into the envelope, then she addressed it, sealed it, and set it aside while she started one for Lily. She filled her best friend in on all the crazy things that had happened since she talked to her on the phone at the Ritz. By the time she decided to end the letter, it was five pages long—both sides. She folded the thick stack of heavy paper and put it into the envelope, knowing it would need extra postage, then she sealed it and found Lily's address in her phone.

It felt like a real accomplishment, though her hand ached, not being used to writing so much at one time. She rubbed her wrist and palm, then took the envelopes and headed downstairs to ask Annis to mail them for her. She found her new friend sitting on the back patio and joined her. They ended up chatting and laughing, enjoying each other's company for most of the morning.

Chapter Seventy-Eight

DEARLY DEPARTED

David and the children entered the funeral home together. He overheard Rosie say in a whisper to Charlie, "I wish Erin were here; she makes me feel less nervous."

"Me too," he said.

They were the first to arrive, and the funeral director greeted them warmly. He then led them to the room where Susannah lay in an ornate coffin. The long narrow box was black with gold rails and decorations. Under her body, the black velvet lining and pillow were draped with black lace.

In front of the whole thing was an enormous arrangement of red roses intermixed with black foliage that David couldn't remember choosing, and it gave him an ominous feeling. The Sutcliffe family had an elaborate mausoleum in which she would be interred. Nearly all the funeral and burial arrangements had been planned many years before, including a horse-drawn carriage ride to the cemetery, which wasn't far from where they were.

All four children hesitated at the door, not wanting to see their mum in that state. Rosie held onto David's arm, and Peter was biting his fingernails. Charlie stood behind him, and Daniel, who was usually carefree, stayed close to Peter, too. "Alright now, we must all be brave," David said, trying to be so himself. "I understand you're afraid, but it will all be over soon, so chins up."

Martin entered the building just then and swept past their huddle, looking severely at David, though he didn't say anything. He went straight to the casket and gazed longingly down at Susannah's lifeless body. He took the liberty of touching her hands and whispered something to her as he bent over to kiss her cheek, or at least David presumed it was her cheek. He stood for a long time, beholding her and muttering under his breath.

Finally, David asked the children to sit in the back row of chairs and approached him. "Hello, Martin," he said calmly.

Martin glared at him with a red face. "This is your fault!" he spat, so low that David had to strain to hear him. "Whilst you were off fucking that big girl, she was sat at home, pining away!" David didn't want to start a fight right there or then, but Martin seemed determined to make one happen. "You should have seen her face when I showed her the pictures of you and your whore."

"If a fight is what you want, Martin, it'll have tae wait for another time," David said, managing to keep calm.

"If you'd been home more often, you'd have seen her torturing herself," he said venomously, continuing his attack.

David lowered his voice, not wanting anyone to hear the row ensuing in front of his dead wife's remains. "It was your idea for me tae join the Fertilis Defect Registry, so if you want tae blame anaone for her most recent decline, you may blame yourself. Also, it was you who hired someone tae have me followed in New Orleans, and you were the one who showed the resulting photos to her. You are the one who fucked up, no' I. Now, please take yer seat; I've people tae greet."

Martin was shaking with rage. "You once were a man of your word, for example, where's the money you promised? You betrayed me and her! You never loved her—not as I did!" he said too loudly as David walked away.

David had had enough and got right up in his old mate's face, "Maybe no', but she hated you." He knew he shouldn't have said it, but the man wouldn't let up.

People were starting to arrive, so David turned on his heels and left Martin fuming in front of the coffin. He shook hands with and hugged too many people to keep count. He watched as people clucked and fussed over his children, drowning them with pity and overwhelming them with platitudes and clichés. *'You poor dears!'* they'd say, and *'She's in a better place now.'* Or *'Your mummy was such a sweet, wonderful woman, I hope you remember that about her.'*

The children said, 'Thank you,' so many times the words stopped making sense. Poor Rosie had it the worst, though; she heard, '*Oh my, you look just like your mummy! How beautiful you are!*' ad nauseam, until David rescued her, saying he needed her help with something.

The rest of the day was a blur for everyone; David stood to give the eulogy but couldn't remember what he'd said afterward. Martin hovered, whispering in the ears of all who would listen. Most people politely brushed him off, but some were seen looking sideways at David as though he'd murdered her or something.

He managed to ignore it until the crowds were finally leaving and a beautiful, well-dressed woman approached him. "Is it true you've had a mistress the entire time your wife was declining in her health? Is that why you've expedited the funeral?" She didn't let him reply. "I have it on good authority you were seen with another woman in America recently. I've been told there is photographic evidence proving you were—intimate with her."

David was furious. "This is not the place for these questions. I will have to ask you to leave," he said, trying to keep his cool. She smiled, held up a small envelope, and then turned around, walking away. David went after her. "What've you got there?" he asked, already guessing the answer. She continued walking toward the exit, and he followed her outside. He was about to ask her to show him what was in the envelope when she turned abruptly, managed to wrap her arms around his neck, and kissed him. He had no way to push her away except by the waist, and he did so immediately.

"What in… the bloody hell—Get away from me you bitch!" he yelled fiercely, "How dare you do something like that here—ma children are in the building! Now get the fuck out of here!" He knew it was a set-up, and he'd fallen for it. *FUCK! Can this day just be over with now?* He thought as he stormed back into the funeral home.

He went straight to the water closet and looked in the mirror; there was lipstick all over his mouth, and he felt sick about the whole thing. There were going to be photos and he could already envision the headlines:

**"David Elliott Seen Kissing Beautiful
Woman at Wife's Funeral"**

And what about Erin? How will I explain it to her and to ma kids? Et'll be everawhere come morning. Her dream is comin' true; the only silver lining is that Bran isn't here.

It had been a very early morning, so by ten o'clock, Erin was tired. She knew Millie did her housekeeping at that time every day, so she decided to take a nap in the spare room in Roger's flat. Roger was weeding the borders along the driveway, so she knew it would be quiet in there for at least an hour. She climbed the stairs, entered the apartment, and finding it empty and peaceful, she knew it would be perfect.

She pulled on the end of the window shade, but something caught on it, so she couldn't get it to go all the way down. It was dark enough, and she didn't want to fight with it, so she closed the door, took off her clothes, and slipped under the light summer covers. It only took a minute for her to fall into a very deep sleep.

Chapter Seventy-Nine

NIGHTMARE OF BRAN

Bran knew very few people would be home because of the funeral, *except Millie and possibly Roger—Ach… and most likely that woman David has here.* He had been awake and high on cocaine and speed for the past seventy-two hours, and now that he was back in Edinburgh, he needed a place to crash. He thought he'd sneak into the room above the garage, which he'd done many times before, and no one would be the wiser.

Managing to get past Roger by coming into the grounds through the side door that joined the public garden, he silently stole into the garage, crept up the stairs, and into the flat. The place was outdated and smelled faintly of motor oil, but he didn't care. He slipped into the spare bedroom, closed the door, and took his clothes off, ready for a good twenty-four hours of much-needed sleep. As he slid under the blanket, he was thankful for the darkness which enveloped him.

Something moved next to him, and he nearly jumped out of the bed. Then, much to his shock and amazement, he felt a soft, warm arm stretch across his chest. A plump leg then crossed over his hips and grazed his cock, which woke up immediately.

"Woah!" he began but then started to enjoy the attention and hesitated. She nestled herself up to him, and it felt so comfortable that in his sleep-deprived, drug-addled mind, he thought it wouldn't hurt to lay there for a while. Suddenly, and yet so tenderly, she grabbed his cock and began stroking it. He got a whiff of her hair; it smelled so delicate and feminine; her touch was too intoxicating for him to resist, so he reached over and touched her breast, which made her moan.

Somewhere, deep in his conscience, he knew it was wrong; she obviously thought he was David, but he was all in it now. He wasn't going to stop for fear of *David*, and he was long past any sentiment of integrity or honor stopping him. *If she's too thick tae take heed of who's in her bed before seducing him, then it's her fault, not mine.*

Her touch became more urgent, and he knew what the next step would be; he chose to do it, damn the consequences. He rolled on top of her, and she spread her legs, welcoming him. As he entered her, she gasped and moaned, but then she froze. "You're not… David! Wait! Get off me!" she yelled, rage saturating her voice. "How dare you! Get off—"

"Oi, bitch, I'm no' the one feelin' up a stranger's cock the way you were doin' just now! What do you expect me tae do? I'm no saint, yeh ken?"

"Get off me right now!" she shrieked, but he wasn't moving.

All of her thrashing about was feeling quite good to him and seeing there wasn't anything she could do about it he was going to stay right where he was. She started to scream, but he backhanded her hard across the face, then she cried out in pain, so he hit her again in the same place, for good measure.

Once she'd caught her breath, she tried a different approach, "Please, Bran, please stop. I was asleep and I thought you were David—"

"Shut up, cunt. I havnae had a good shag in a long time, and this is feelin' far too good tae stop!"

———

He started to thrust; Erin could feel him inside her and felt sick. She didn't know what to do, but then she heard a noise in the kitchenette and took her chance. "Help—Roger!" she screamed as loudly as she could, praying he would hear her.

Bran raised his hand to strike her again, but the door opened, and light streamed into the room. A strong male arm reached out and grabbed Bran by his arm and greasy hair, lifting him off her. She scrambled to cover herself with the blanket and sat against the wall, trembling.

Roger hurled Bran out of the bedroom, naked, his arms and legs flailing. "Ring 999," he growled.

Erin knew she couldn't do that; she didn't have her passport or ID anymore. She feared she'd get deported or something awful, plus it would bring even more attention to David in the media. She quickly got dressed and ran out of the room. Roger had just thrown Bran down the stairs, and she could hear him moaning at the bottom.

"Roger, I—I can't call 999. I don't have my passport... it was lost in the fire, and—and I don't want more reporters camped outside of Ann's house."

"Aye, I'll think of somethin' tae do with him until Ann gets home," Roger said and descended the stairs before Bran could run.

Erin didn't want to know what he might do, so she went back to the room and sat on the floor against the wall, crying, not sure how she'd tell David.

Annis had not gone to the funeral because she had a charity luncheon to attend. When she returned home, Millie was waiting for her at the door, looking cross, Erin was on the sofa in the sitting room, hugging herself protectively, and Roger was standing behind Bran, who was now clothed and sitting on one of the dining chairs that had been brought into the room. Bran's eyes were both black and blue, as were his arms and legs from falling down the hard wooden garage stairs.

She entered the room and sat calmly on the sofa next to Erin, who looked traumatized; her eye was also beginning to turn black and blue. The mature woman took hold of her hand. "What happened, dear," she asked kindly.

"It was all my fault—I took a nap in the flat above the garage. I—I didn't want to disturb Millie... and—I must've thought it was David... and—I... well, I invited him to make love to me, but—I thought it was David, I swear!" Erin said desperately. She covered her face with her hands and started to cry, great sobs that made it hard for her to breathe.

"There! It's her fault, she said it herself! She grabbed hold of ma cock—What was I supposed tae do—Roll over and ignore her?" Bran spat. Roger grabbed a chunk of his hair and pulled hard, warning him to shut up.

"Go on, dear," Annis said, once Erin had calmed down enough to speak.

———

Erin was blushing with shame and wished she could go back in time. "When I realized it wasn't David, I told him to get off me, but he wouldn't. I—I tried to yell, but he hit me—twice. Then I heard Roger and yelled for help."

"So, Bran had intercourse with you, knowin' you thought he was David?" Annis said, so calm and controlled it sent shivers up Erin's spine.

"I said it to him… that I'd thought he was David… while I was trying to get him to stop, but he wouldn't stop," Erin whispered, feeling like every word she said was somehow amplified.

"And why is it you did not call the police, dear?"

"My passport and ID were lost in the fire… and—I didn't want to get deported. Also, with the reporter already sitting outside of your home, I didn't want to make it worse. And I—I did invite him… until I realized who he was."

"Aye! She invited me, the clatty cunt! Better David finds out now," Bran hissed.

"Dinnae be callin' names, yeh bastard!" Roger said and thumped him hard across the top of his head.

"She's naught but a hackit slut and a whore!" Bran spat. Roger turned red with fury and boxed his ears, which shut him up.

"Aye, perhaps you did invite him, but he knows tae stop when he's meant to. Branock Elliott, ye'll be the death of me yet!" she said, shaking her head.

"Please, don't say that, Ann!" Erin cried out, "I know it's an expression, but… just—just don't say it."

Annis smiled at her. "Aye, perhaps you're right, dear," she said and turned to her nephew. "What am I going do with you? If David sees yeh after this, he'll kill you, not that I'd blame him."

"And then David will be the one in prison, instead of—him," Erin said.

"You leave me no choice, Bran. I don't want tae do this, but it may be the only thing for et. I happen tae know someone who may be able tae help deal with him," she said to Erin. She stood and took out her mobile phone. Erin could see her searching her contact list until she found the name she'd been looking for. She dialed the number, and everyone waited in silence as she started speaking.

"Hello, Oscar?"

At that name, Bran lost it; his eyes grew large, and he tried to stand, but Roger took hold of his earlobe. He twisted it until he cried out and sat still.

"Aye, this is Annis Elliott…yes dear. No…No, but I have a situation I'm hopin' you can help me with. Aye, it's tae do with the hospital…Aye, I see. Yes. Aye, the situation has occurred at ma home, and…Aye, that would be grand. I thank yeh. A'right, I'll see you soon." She brought her mobile with her as she returned to her seat next to Erin.

Bran was dark red with fury and fear. "Ah won't go! Yeh cannae force me tae go tae a place like that! Ah—have rights!"

Annis stood and walked right up to him. "You lost your rights when you chose tae rape our Erin. Now, ye'll sit and not say a word. Also, *IF* you make it out of there alive, ye'll not be welcome back here, do yeh hear me, boy?"

Bran spat at her. "Fine way tae treat ye're only sister's child, and with her deid all these years," he said, trying the guilt trip route.

Annis took the handkerchief Roger handed her and wiped the spittle off her face, then she bent down so they were eye to eye. "Ye've been nothing but a trial tae yer uncle and me. Ye've done naught but vex us and managed evera way in yer power tae do all manner of evil things tae us and to David. Do not speak tae me of my poor deid sister, God rest her soul," she said, sending ice through Erin's blood.

"I won't—" Bran began.

"Please find some strong tape tae cover his gob, Roger! I don't want to hear him anamore."

Roger gave her a quick nod and left the room. Bran looked as though he would bolt, but Millie took Roger's place, so he didn't bother trying. Roger came back a few minutes later with something that looked like duct tape. He ripped off a good length and applied it firmly across Bran's mouth, making sure to press it into his two-day stubble.

Erin thought the whole thing was bizarre. Bran just sat there while everyone pretty much went about their business, waiting for the mysterious Oscar to arrive. Millie even made a pot of tea.

Finally, there was a knock at the door, which set the dogs off, though Millie managed to get them to calm down quickly enough. Erin didn't know what to expect, but an aging Keanu Reeves with long grey and sandy-blonde hair, standing at about six foot five, was not anything close to her vague imaginations.

Oscar was welcomed into the house, and Erin got a good look at him. He was at least sixty, maybe older, and obviously spent time lifting weights—NOT someone you wanted to cross. Everything about him was intimidating, including his interesting choice of apparel, which included tall leather boots and cut-off leather gloves.

She had to stop herself from staring, open-mouthed, at the man, who was actually really hot but who was also scary as shit. She felt a little bit sorry for Bran, who was unmistakably terrified; trembling, sweating, and staring at his aunt in disbelief. Annis introduced him to Erin and then explained what had happened.

Oscar's face plainly showed pity and compassion for Erin as they all listened to Annis's account of what had happened. Then they watched Bran literally shake with fear when Oscar's attention turned to him and they saw the flash of disgust and righteous anger on his formidable face.

Bran was hauled, unceremoniously, away after Oscar kissed Erin's hand and wished her the best of future luck. It all happened so quickly her head was swimming. She theorized that for a sizable donation, a nuisance of a human being could be admitted to a 'hospital' and would be 'taken care of' in a manner befitting the person.

All she wanted to do was wash Bran's smell, touch, and—memory off her. She excused herself and took a long, hot shower, scrubbing her skin and crying, as she knew it wasn't working. His rancid breath was still hot on her face and the memory of his hard cock inside her was far too vivid.

She could feel his weight pressing her down onto the mattress, as well as the prickly feeling of what she assumed was the energy a match might have. His wasn't strong, like David's, and it wasn't pleasant. It was like being jabbed by a thousand needles—or what a limb feels like when it's fallen asleep, and the blood starts to flow back into it again. She felt suffocated and took deep breaths in the steamy room, trying to escape the feeling.

Later that night, Erin's face was bruised where Bran had backhanded her. Annis went upstairs with her to help her cover it up with concealer and lots of foundation, and in the end, it was hard to see unless you were looking for it. As the household began planning for David's return, they made the decision not to say anything to him about what had happened until the children were back at school to save them hearing about it somehow.

Chapter Eighty

A SOLEMN HOMECOMING

David and the children returned from London just before supper time, emotionally and physically worn out. Rosie and Charlie ran in to greet Erin right away, and Daniel ran off to play with the dogs before it was time to eat. Peter walked in last with his head down and went straight to his room.

Erin and David watched him trudge up the steps, looking angry and miserable. "What happened with him?" Erin whispered to David.

"I've no clue. He was fine one minute and sullen the next. He wouldn't say boo tae me the whole trip back, and I haven't pushed it."

"That's strange. I imagine he'll say something sooner or later," Erin said, very self-conscious about him seeing the bruise on her face and somehow being able to smell Bran on her. She was afraid his scent was still lingering, maybe coming out of her pores, since she could still smell it in her memory. She could've kicked herself for not putting on some perfume or something, even though she'd scrubbed herself until it hurt.

"A'right, yeh wee beasties, go on upstairs now and change yer clothes for supper!" Millie said, "And Charlie—find yer brother and tell him the same."

"Yes ma'am," Charlie said as they left the sitting room.

"How'd it go, David?" Millie asked him once the children were gone.

"Ach, we made it through. Martin was the first one there—"

"Humph," Millie said at the mention of Martin's name.

"He made a scene, wantin' me tae fight him! Can you believe it?" He looked at Erin, "Yer dream and the fortune-teller were no off in the slightest," he said, wearily. Erin's face started to burn, so she busied herself helping Millie set the table, and he didn't notice it.

Once the table was set, Millie called everyone to come and eat. Roger walked in just then as well, so they all sat at the table. Peter was late and didn't explain himself; he sat, not making eye contact. Erin caught him staring at David with a look of hatred, but he looked away when David turned in his direction. *What would make him act this way?* she thought.

Millie had made Cranachan, a traditional Scottish dessert made with fresh raspberries, toasted oats, and whipped cream as the pudding for the adults. She made Eaton Mess for the children and Erin, as Cranachan has whiskey in it. However, she did take a taste of David's and said, "Holy Moses! That is fantastic! As soon as—" She stopped suddenly, remembering just in time they hadn't told the children about the baby yet. All the adult's eyes had grown wide, and the children looked at them like they were mental or something.

"As soon as what, Erin?" Charlie asked.

"As—soon as—your dad looks away, I'm going to eat the rest of his pudding up!" she said, which made the younger kids laugh.

David played along and covered his dish with his hand, holding his spoon as if it were a weapon. "I'll fight yeh first!" he said, which Erin realized was a quote from *Future Explorations*.

No one else caught it, but Erin laughed until her side ached as they used their spoons to duel. *This is so nice! Why can't things like this last?* she thought, dreading having to tell him about Bran.

"I've made a decision," David said after dessert. "I don't feel like drivin' all the way tae your school tonight, so we'll do it in the mornin' if that's agreeable with everaone involved?" The children were happy with the plan, and all but Peter ran off to play when they were excused from the table. Peter stood and went outside, looking miserable.

Erin was feeling pretty miserable, as well; her face hurt, and she felt guilty for not telling David what had happened right away. That was one more thing she was worried about; how would he react to learn everyone but him and the kids knew about it the whole evening and didn't say anything?

That night, David and Erin tucked the younger children into bed, as they had the night before, but when they went into Peter's room, he was already sleeping or was acting as though he were, so they left without saying anything.

When they got to David's room, she said she was tired and looking forward to a good night's sleep. She didn't want him to look closely at her face, so she quickly put on her pajamas and crawled into bed, facing away from him. She knew he wanted to make love to her when he got into bed and lay behind her; she could feel him press himself against her.

She wanted him to make love to her so badly. She wanted him to replace the feeling of Bran inside her with himself, but she was unsure how he would feel the next day after learning about what happened. He might feel dirty afterward, polluted as she was, and maybe he wouldn't ever want to make love to her again. She had no way of knowing what he'd think, knowing men often think differently than women, so she was worried.

He ran his hand down her hip to her thigh, and she couldn't help but respond to his touch. She could feel his erection growing against her tailbone and let him pull her pajamas off. He drew her leg back over him and she allowed him to take her from behind while they spooned. When he entered her, she could feel the pleasant, powerful energy they shared pulsing through her. It hadn't felt the same when Bran entered her; that's how she'd known it wasn't David.

It felt good, and she was able to relax in that position, but then he pulled out. "Doggy style?" he whispered, so she got onto her hands and knees, and he entered her again. He took hold of her hips and thrust deep inside her, making her cry out, though she was able to smother the noise with a pillow. He placed his hand on her back and ran it up to her shoulder, pulling her up so that she was partly sitting on his lap.

He rocked her back and forth, covering her mouth with his hand to keep her cries of pleasure from being heard throughout the house. "Roll over," he said, and before she could protest, he'd pulled out and was trying to help her roll onto her back. The only light was in the bathroom, and she didn't think he'd be able to see her black eye with so little illumination, so she did it. He entered her once more and thrust hard, pinning her to the mattress.

An intensely vivid flashback of Bran, who was the same in nearly every way to David, hit her hard, and she let out a slight sob, though she hid it as a moan of pleasure. All she wanted was for him to get done and to get off her, though she hated herself for thinking it.

She couldn't continue in that position, not without the flashbacks torturing her, so she stopped him. "Please, let's change positions; I'm not comfortable like this," she half lied.

"Alright, hen, are you okay? Did I hurt yeh?"

"No, I just liked it the other way better," she said hoping he wouldn't hear the distress in her voice. She got out of bed and bent over the side of it, with her chest on the mattress, ass up in the air. He stood behind her and playfully slapped her rear end, making her flinch. The hard slaps Bran had given her were still fresh in her mind, and it startled her. "What the fuck!" she snapped, without meaning to.

"I'm—sorry. I was... just playing," he said, surprised by her reaction.

"No, it's okay... it just... startled me."

The mood had shifted; it had become the mechanics of lovemaking and no longer felt good. Erin didn't think she'd be able to reach orgasm, and David also seemed to be having a difficult time of it. It was the first time since they'd met that things weren't working.

"I... think we should stop now. I'm sorry, but I'm just not—I don't know, feeling it... anymore," she said and hung her head as he pulled out for the last time. "I'm sorry." She laid on her side, facing away from him, curled up in a ball. "It's my fault, not yours. Please don't be upset; I'll help you out if you want me to."

He lay beside her. "Erin, what's wrong? I can tell somethin's botherin' you. Was it the slap on your rear? Why don't you tell me? Ye'll feel better."

Her face was throbbing, and even though it was all in fun, the place where he'd smacked her was tingling as well. "I just want to sleep now; I'm sorry, David, truly I am," she said as she sobbed in silence.

That night she dreamed she was sitting in her school bus at the elementary school. She was in line with the other buses, waiting for school to be let out, and she heard a noise at the door. A tall, thin man was standing there, staring at her. He wanted her to open the door, but she was too scared to do it, so he started banging on the window and yelling something she couldn't understand. She looked at the bus to her left, then turned back, and he was gone.

At first, she was relieved, but then she heard the emergency door in the back open, and her blood ran cold. She couldn't escape because the bus was trapped between two others, and leaving the bus seemed like a bad idea. She began honking the horn and turned on every flashing light she could find until another driver, who looked like Oscar, came, and dragged the man, who now looked like Bran away. She woke up sweating and shaking but didn't wake David.

Chapter Eighty-One

BACK TO SCHOOL TIME

It was daylight even though it was only five am as they piled, once more, into the SUV. Erin was persuaded to join them and got into the front seat. Peter hadn't said anything more than 'yes' or 'no' since the funeral was over and sat staring out the window, brooding. The rest of the kids got in tired, but happy Erin was coming.

Annis and Millie said their goodbyes as Roger put the children's things into the back, and then it was his turn to say farewell. It would only be two weeks until they were off for their summer holiday, so no one was overly sad. Once everyone was ready, they rolled down the drive and waved to Roger as he stood, waiting to close the gate behind them.

"Erin, please tell us about America," Dan said once they got out of town and onto the motorway.

"Goodness, there is so much to tell, let me think. In America, we drive on the other side of the road, and our cars are built opposite to yours. The driver's seat is where I'm sitting. I was terrified the first time I drove a car here. Though once I did it a few times, I found that I like it better, probably because it's different.

"Oh, and in Wisconsin, we have tons of roundabouts; more than anywhere else in the country, I think. I'm guessing some guy, way high up in the state's government came here, saw how awesome they are, and went back home saying, 'We need roundabouts in Wisconsin!'" She said it with a funny 'official man's' voice that made the young kids laugh and even made the corners of Peter's lips move in an upward direction. "Then every year afterward, he must've said, 'More roundabouts!' until he got his way.

"Let me see, our money looks different, but you've probably already seen that. We don't have nearly as many different candy bars and sweets as you do here! We don't have Squash, but we have Tang, which is similar. I'm afraid I can't think of anything more off the top of my head. Do you have any specific questions?"

The children asked some really good questions, and a few just silly ones to get a laugh. Rosie asked, "Do people know who my daddy is in America?"

Erin smiled. "Well, I did. I would say some do and some don't. He's not as well-known there as he is here but loads of people love *Future Explorations*. Actually, we met a girl about your age when we were there, Rosie. She asked your dad to sign a book that was part of a series about the show. She was sweet, wasn't she?"

"Aye, and so was her older sister—" he said, and Peter made a disgruntled noise.

Erin and David exchanged looks. "Peter, please tell us what's wrong," Erin said. "You're obviously upset about something. Did I do or say something to make you angry?"

Peter looked at her, wide-eyed. "No, it wasn't you," he said quietly and then glared at the back of David's head.

"Well, good, I'm relieved to hear it. So, it's obviously something your dad did or said. Why don't you tell him, so we can clear the air and have a nice trip back? We're nearly halfway there already."

"Aye son—" David began, but Peter didn't let him finish.

"Why don't you ask him?" he yelled "He was the one covered with lipstick right after the funeral! I saw it when he came in from the car park!"

Rosie gasped, and Erin was stunned; she looked at David, and his face was bright red, but not with lipstick. "I didn't know you'd seen that, Peter. I was going to explain before we got to the school. It's a long story, but—"

Erin was now red in the face and felt her breakfast coming up, so she told David to pull over, but he hesitated. "Pull over!" she yelled and nearly flew out of the car when it stopped, to be sick. She stood for a few moments to make sure she was finished, then got back in and put her seatbelt on. She didn't look at David; she just stared out the window as he merged back into traffic.

"A woman approached me once most of the people had left, asking questions about how I'd been seen with Erin in New Orleans. I told her it wasn't the time or place for those questions, but then she held up an envelope—You see Martin had me followed whilst I was there, and pictures were taken of the two of us together. I knew that's what was in the envelope, so, when she walked away, I foolishly followed her out to the car park, where she turned and… kissed me.

"I had no time to react; you must believe me. I'm sure it was a set-up, and I would hazard a guess there's a photo of her and me in every tabloid in Great Britain this morning. I'm gutted about it, but I didn't know how to bring it up. That's why I had lipstick on my face, Peter. I'm so sorry yeh… you had tae see that. I went to wash it off right away. I reckon Martin was behind it, what with the way he was behaving when he got there."

"Is that the truth, Dad?" Peter asked quietly.

David looked at him in the rearview mirror. "Aye, it is."

"I'm sorry," Peter said. "I thought—Well, I thought you were kissing someone behind Erin's back and at Mum's funeral. I just got mad instead of thinking it through and asking you first."

"I understand, Peter," David said.

"I'm sorry, Erin," David said, "I should have told you right away, but we were having such a nice time together—I didn't want it to be ruined. It was foolish, and I reckon it makes me look guilty as well."

Erin knew she had no right to be upset; there was plenty she was going to have to confess, though it still felt like a knife in the heart. "I… believe you. If you say it was a set-up, and you didn't want to… kiss her, well then… I believe you." The car was silent.

"I was going to tell you, children, so if the kids at school started in on you about it, you'd know the truth. That way you wouldn't be taken by surprise and perhaps… believe them.

"Alright, Dad," Peter said contritely. "I really am sorry—"

"Ach, dinnae—I mean, don't think on it anymore. You had every right to be upset at what you thought ye'd seen. Let's not talk about it anymore."

David turned onto a narrow, hedge-lined road and passed a sign informing them that they were only three miles away from the school. Erin tried to put on a brave, happy face, but it took all she had to do it, dreading the conversation she was going to have on the way back.

They pulled into the car park, and everyone except Erin got out. David opened the back, and they each unloaded their bags, then they went to the passenger side door to say goodbye to Erin. The door was open, but she didn't get out; the fewer people to see her, the better. Rosie and Charlie hugged her and looked as though they were going to cry.

"Now, now, I'll see you in two weeks, don't be upset," she said, then hugged and kissed them both again. "I'm going to miss you like crazy, though!" she added. Next, Daniel made his appearance. He gave her half a hug and said, 'Bye,' before running off toward the main building.

Peter stopped in front of her and crouched with his head down. "Erin, I'm truly sorry for what I said; please don't be angry with my dad."

Erin nearly broke down into sobs at his sincere apology. She placed her hand on his arm and lifted his chin with her other hand. "Peter, you are so dear! Thank you, and all's forgiven, alright? I think I'm going to miss you the most."

He gave her an honest-to-goodness, full-on bear hug and smiled at her. "I'll miss you as well," he said and then joined his siblings, who were standing with their father near the front of the SUV. They walked away from her, and she watched as they crossed the parking lot, then headed up the stairs to the large, formal building.

Her heart ached; it was too much! The drama and unimaginable events were happening far too close together to be believed. *When will things… or will things ever be 'normal' for us, or will we continue to live in a soap opera forever?* The dread of what she had to tell him nearly suffocated her as she watched him walking back to the SUV, and she wasn't entirely sure she'd be able to do it.

He got into the driver's seat and reached out for her hand. She gave it to him but didn't say anything. "Are we a'right, Erin?" he asked.

She couldn't speak without crying, and she was so sick of crying, so she nodded instead.

"So… you believe me?"

Again, she nodded; her heart was in her throat, and her stomach was right behind it. She nearly told him everything right then, but something stopped her.

You can't tell him now! Are you crazy? He won't be able to drive you back after hearing it! You'll end up in a mangled pile of steel and fiberglass on the side of the road! No, you need to wait until you're in the safety of his mother's house.

She knew she had to pull herself together, at least long enough to get to Owlgate, so taking a deep breath, she put on a smile and looked at him. *Oh, God, he's going to hate me! He's never going to get over it!* she thought miserably. "I believe you, David," was all she could say before the tears began to fall down her face.

Fearing her makeup would run and he'd see her bruise, she reached into her purse and took out several tissues. She managed to look away just in time, so he didn't see her tears, though he must've guessed there was something wrong. "Are you… sure ye're alright, hen? If you believe me, then what's troublin' you?" He kissed her hand and looked at her.

She had to change the subject; that was the only way to get past the emotions; once she did, she could move on and not start bawling again! "Are you still going to do the interview tomorrow?" she asked, and he furrowed his brow.

"No, Tina has rescheduled it for next month. I dinnae ken why ye're changin' the subject, Erin."

It worked, at least for the moment, and she was able to focus on something besides Bran. "Never mind; I'll tell you when we get back. For now, let's just have a nice trip." She managed a weak though genuine smile, and he headed out of the car park. "Have you heard anything about the cottage?" she asked him.

"Ach, I have. I've learned the oven is what caused the fire. There was a bad fuse or faulty wiring which started the fire in the cellar. The coal stores were why it was so acrid and why it knocked me out straight away. I also learned it was Old John who pulled me out of the house. He'd been one light bulb short when he'd come earlier that day and came back. If he hadn't been, or if he'd not bothered to come back—I'd—Well, let's no' think on it."

"Oh, David! Then it *is* my fault!" Erin exclaimed as a sense of guilt washed over her already frazzled nerves. "I turned it on, thinking we could eat the meat pie when I returned from my walk. I can't believe I almost killed you!"

"Dinnae fash, darling; there's no way you could've known it would happen. Besides, et turned out a'right in the end, didn't it?" he said.

About halfway back, Erin needed to use the bathroom, so they stopped at a petrol station, and she ran in. On her way back out, she happened to glance at the newspaper racks and nearly fell over. On the front page of several tabloids was an enormous picture of David with his hands on the waist of a tall, slender woman, their lips pressed together firmly.

Erin's heart jumped up into her throat, and she nearly gagged on it. She didn't know what to do. Should she buy one to show him? She decided against it; she didn't want to pay for that trash.

She got back into the car, and David did a doubletake. "What happened?" he asked. "You look as if ye're about tae pass out?"

"The kiss—The woman—It's… a huge… photo—" was all she could manage to say.

He got out of the car and walked right into the building, obviously not caring that someone might recognize him. He came back out pale and looking ill as well. "Ach, it looks worse than I'd imagined it would," he said. "It looks like I was—Erin, please believe me, please. Et's no' what it appears tae be," he pleaded with her.

"I said I believe you," she said calmly. "Now, let's go. I don't want to think about it." She did believe him, but seeing his lips on hers and his hands on her hips was just so disgusting. It was one more thing she couldn't unsee, and all she wanted to do was escape the memory of it.

Why isn't he going? she thought since he hadn't moved the SUV yet. She didn't want to be seen with him at a petrol station, fighting.

Boy, wouldn't that be a great photo op; not only was he 'caught' kissing a woman at his wife's funeral, but he was also seen having a row with a mystery woman at a random petrol station in Scotland.

"Just go!" she snapped.

He pulled away from the station and merged back onto the motorway. They were both silent for a few minutes. "I'm sorry I snapped at you. I'm— I'm so stressed out. I... didn't mean to—" she said miserably, but he interrupted her.

"Shh, it's a'right, so am I," he said tenderly. "I want things tae go back tae some form of normal. I keep thinkin' that mebbe after this event, things will be a'right, but then somethin' else happens... then somethin' more. I cannae imagine what more could possibly go wrong!"

I do! she thought bitterly. "When we get back, we need to go straight to your room. I have to tell you something, and I can't do it here. I'm afraid normal isn't going to happen again for a long time," she said.

He looked at her questioningly but didn't ask. "A'right, but whatever it is, I love yeh, and nothin' is gonna change that."

When they finally arrived at Owlgate, they were shocked to see several cars parked outside the house. "Fuck!" David said. "I'm sure et's tae do with the photo." He drove past the house and parked at Dr. Neil's Garden.

"What happens now?" Erin asked.

David crossed his arms over the steering wheel and put his head down on them. "I dinnae ken. I do ken that I wouldn't blame you if yeh wanted out of this mess. I'm sorry you have tae deal with it, it's no' fair tae you," he said miserably.

Erin looked at the nearly defeated man sitting next to her. How could she add the final blow by telling him what Bran had done? She put her hand on his back and rubbed it, hoping to give him a tiny bit of relief before the knock-out punch. "I don't want out, my love. I want nothing more than to be by your side, and I'm going to do everything in my power to stay here, even if it kills me," she said. "Now, how are we gonna get into the house?"

"I'll call Roger and have him open the gate—" he began, but Erin interrupted him with an idea.

"What if I walk to the house from here and knock on the front door as though I'm a friend of your mum's; then you can drive up into the garage. That way, we aren't seen together," she suggested.

David smiled and kissed her forehead. "Ye're a verra clever girl; I'll let Roger know the plan. When you get inside, send a message, and I'll leave here." He took out his mobile and started typing, then a few moments later he received a reply, and the plan was set.

Erin got out of the car after kissing him and started walking, really hoping it would work. As she approached the house, three reporters, sitting in their cars watched her. When they saw that she was about to enter the door in the gated wall, they rushed out of their vehicles and began hurling questions at her. She made it into the yard and closed the heavy door just in time.

"Oi! Do you know anything about the photograph in the papers today?" one of them said through the open ironwork gate.

"Do you know who the woman is?" another one said.

"Why was David Elliott kissing someone at his wife's funeral? Was he cheating on his poor, sick wife?" the third one shouted, then they started over.

"How do you know the Elliott family?"

"You look familiar; what's your name?"

Erin ignored them and walked up the slight incline of the driveway, trying to look dignified and calm. When she got to the door, shaking from head to foot, she rang the doorbell. The dogs threw a fit, and a moment later, Millie answered it.

"Ach, do come in, dearie; Annis is waitin' for you," she said, hoping they'd hear her. She looked out at the crowd and yelled, "Yeh ought tae be ashamed of yerselves, harassin' a poor, innocent girl, come tae visit a friend! Be off with yeh, now!" Once the door was closed, Erin leaned her back against it, and Millie placed her hand on her shoulder. "Are you a'right?" she asked.

Erin was breathing hard and still shaking; she took out her phone and sent David a message, though she didn't realize it said, 'Inn inn' instead of 'I'm in' until she'd already sent it.

Roger's mobile sounded the *Future Explorations* theme song, so he left out the side door. Erin watched through one of the clear panes in the stained-glass windows by the front door as he walked down to the gate, ignoring the questions hurled at him. She saw the black SUV pull up and honk at one of the idiots who was standing in his way. He pulled in, and Roger quickly closed the gate.

493

Chapter Eighty-Two

WHAT HAPPENED WITH BRAN

David pulled into the garage, and Roger walked in behind him, closing the door. Erin breathed a sigh of relief and then remembered she still had to tell him about Bran. She ran to warn Annis and Millie that she planned to do it when he got in; she didn't want them to get upset if they heard him yelling or something. "I just couldn't do it in the car; he might have crashed or something," she said, wanting to crawl into a hole and hide.

"Alright dear, we're here for you," Annis said and hugged her. "Ach, ye're trembling like, I dinnae ken what! Do you want a wee nip of sherry or… whisky tae steady you?"

"No, thank you," she said, then her eyes grew wild as she heard David and Roger come in. "Oh, God, what should I say? He's going to—"

"Ma Losh!" David said when he entered the room. He kissed his mother on the cheek and then turned to Erin. "Now, you said you had somethin' tae tell me?"

She'd hoped maybe he'd forgotten about it. "Yes, come upstairs with me," she said, feeling sick.

Millie covered her mouth, and Annis put her hand on Erin's shoulder for reassurance.

David watched their display and started to worry. Erin led him up to his bedroom and closed the door. "Now, what's all the fuss—" he began, but she put up her trembling hand for him to stop. "Ma Losh, yer white as a ghost—"

"Please, sit and try to let me get it all out." She closed her eyes and started rubbing the palm of her left hand with the thumb of her right until she was wringing her hands. Her breathing was thin and jittery as she paced back and forth at the end of the bed. "Yesterday... we were up so early—I wanted to take a nap… but I didn't want to be in Millie's way, so… I decided to use the room above the garage. I was asleep, you see, and when I rolled over—I—I thought it was you… next to me, and—"

David stood to his feet, not liking where the conversation was heading. "Erin?"

She started to breathe heavily, fear covering her with goosebumps as it washed over her. "I… thought it was you! I swear to God I did! You have to believe me, David!" she pleaded. "I was asleep... and wasn't thinking about it being too early for you to be home yet—"

David's eyes grew wide. "What are you sayin', Erin?" he said, his voice already sounding angry.

"I… invited you to make love to me—" she said and put her head down.

David inhaled deeply and turned away. "Bran! Oh… ma God! You—" *She invited that bawbag tae—No!*

"But then I realized it wasn't you, and I tried to get him to stop, but—I tried to scream, but… he hit me hard, twice. I tried begging him, but… he wouldn't stop. Finally, I heard Roger come up and yelled for his help. He came in and pulled him off me—"

David clutched his chest at his heart and put his hand on the desktop, leaning hard against it, still facing away from her. *He's no' gonna get away with this!* "I… just don't—" he began and then stopped. *It's no' enough tae ruin ma childhood; now he's at it again? Can't he just stay away—Wait—Why was he with her at all?* He felt completely blindsided; his reasoning was impaired, and he couldn't think straight. "Didn't yeh fight him? Didn't yeh try tae get away?"

"What? I told you... I thought—" The room was silent for a long time. "Please... believe me... I swear... I didn't know that it wasn't—"

His whole torso moved up and down with his heavy breathing; in and out, in and out. *She's just admitted that she didn't fight him! Did she—Was she—* Finally he spoke, his words soft but menacing. "You were too deeply asleep tae ken it wasn't me until… until when, exactly? When he entered you? After yeh opened yer legs for him?"

It was Erin's turn to gasp. "What? Are you saying that… you think I—"

"And when we were makin' love… last night… you were thinkin' about him? Ach! It all makes sense now! That's why—Where is he now? I'm gonna kill him!" He wanted to vomit, but more than that, he wanted to wrap his hands around his cousin's neck. *That's et! I'm finished with that miserable—*

———

Erin was trembling; nowhere, in any of the scenarios she'd dreamed up of how he might react, did he say or do anything like that. He turned, and she could see his face; it was red, and a blue vein was bulging out on his forehead. His eyes were wild, and he wouldn't look at her as he stumbled to the door. "He's been… taken care of," was all she said.

David's head snapped around, and he looked her straight in the eyes. "What does that mean, Erin?"

She was now utterly terrified of the look on his face. He started toward her, and she screamed as she backed away.

"What does that *mean*? Tell me where he is!" he demanded.

She was shrinking back against the desk, ready to raise her arm to block him if he hit her. "Your mom called someone named Oscar—" she said, quivering.

When David heard the name Oscar, he stopped and looked as though someone had punched him. "Oscar? She didn't!" he yelled. He turned and saw Roger standing at the door, but he pushed him out of the way and staggered down the hall. He flew down the stairs, tripping and stumbling to the sitting room, Roger and Erin following close behind. "Mother, yeh didn't call Oscar without me knowin' first? How could you?" he roared.

"I knew that if you found out beforehand, ye'd kill him, but your woman and your bairns need you here, no' in prison, David," she said, trying to reason with him.

Erin stood in the doorway, terror-stricken. She had never imagined he could ever look so frightening, and she wanted to hide or wake up from the nightmare she was in.

He turned his fury once again onto her, staring her down. "And you—yeh told *them* before you bothered tae tell me?" he growled and then turned, pointing around the room. "Ach, and you all knew… the whole night? You knew, and none of you said anathin'?"

"David… she… we didn't want the children tae learn about et—like this, yeh ken?" Annis said and put her hand on his arm, but he pushed it off.

He looked at Erin with what appeared to be disgust and loathing, then he stepped toward her, but Roger stood between them. "*I* told them, no' her," he said. "She didnae want tae ring the police since her identification was destroyed, and tae save you havin' more reporters sittin' outside the doors. On the other hand, you made a fine show of yerself, kissin' that lady, eh? I think yeh ought tae look in the mirror before you go accusin' our Erin!"

David turned his anger toward Roger. "Ach, so now she's *yer* Erin as well? Do yeh also want tae fuck her? Just wait till she's asleep, and she'll open her legs right up for yeh!" he hissed.

Roger punched him hard, hitting his chin and giving him a bloody lip. "How dare you! Ye've some nerve, coming in here and no' believin' her, when I'm positive she believed yer story about the beautiful lady. Aye, I saw the papers today, David, and yer in no position tae be harsh with her!" he raged back at him. "*You* weren't there; I was! She didnae want that bastard on her any more than you wanted that bitch kissin' you. Her poor wee eye is black and blue from his blows, but did yeh notice? Aye, et's covered with makeup, but you can still see it if you're no' too busy bein' full of yerself! You bloody hypocrite!"

David looked at her tear-streaked face and gasped.

———

Erin turned, dazed, and feeling utterly rejected as she lurched away from him. She was reeling as she climbed the stairs and reached his bedroom. Her heartbeat was making her ears ring as she stepped into the bathroom and stared at her ugly face in the mirror. Her mind was racing, and she couldn't think straight. *How could he... be so... horrible!* The memory of his face. The look of hatred and distrust was vivid in her mind. *He hates me! What am I going to do? I thought he loved me, but that wasn't love!*

He never loved you! He just liked the sex and... it's just like Susannah said— He was obsessed with you, and now he's tired of your base... commonness, or whatever she said.

She saw her bottle of sleeping pills sitting on the counter and wondered how many of them it would take to make the pain of his words go away. *"Just wait till she's asleep, and she'll open her legs right up for yeh!"* She had never once thought seriously about killing herself before, yet she picked up the bottle and looked at it. *There must be over twenty pills in there, she thought, and then whispered to herself,* "Surely that would be enough."

Her hand gripped the top, ready to open it, but another hand covered hers and then gently took the bottle away. She looked up and saw Annis's face, lined with pain and sorrow at what she'd just witnessed of her only son's agony and from what she must've known Erin was contemplating.

"Ach, ma dear girl, don't think of doing it; he's already calmed down quite a bit," she said soothingly.

"Ann! How could he say that? I... mean—" she said, feeling defeated, as though she'd just lost her best friend, but only after finding out they weren't really such good friends after all. Annis wrapped her arms around her and let her weep; great, deep, mournful sobs, coming in waves that made it hard to breathe. Erin had never been hurt so badly in all her life, and she didn't know what to do.

She had nowhere to go, no place of her own to return to; she didn't have a Passport and had no money or way to get back to the states. She'd have to go back, she presumed; what was there for her in Great Britain anymore? *"Just wait till she's asleep, and she'll open her legs right up for yeh!"* kept running through her mind, and the look on his face haunted her—as though she'd known and for some reason *wanted* to sleep with Bran.

David and Roger sat on the sofa, listening to Erin's sobs fill the house. David was beside himself, knowing he'd gone too far. He'd said the very worst thing he could ever have said her, the one person he couldn't live without. After Roger punched him and he'd seen her black eye, he'd wanted to take it all back, but she was gone by then. He wanted to escape, to run out to Neela—*Fuck that is the perfect name!* and drive away, but the reporters kept him from doing that. It was most likely the best thing, seeing he probably would have ended up killing himself or in jail for some random act of violence.

"I ken it's too little too late, but thank you for rescuing her as you did," he said quietly.

———

Roger gave David a curt nod but didn't say anything. Another sob broke the silence and his heart. He stood, flexing his fingers in agitation as he began pacing and then turned, giving David a fearful look. "Do yeh ken what yer problem is? I'll tell you, whether you care tae hear et or no'! Ye've a victim mentality; everathin' is someone else's fault, never yers. You saunter around with yer head high in the clouds thinkin' everathin's gonnae go yer way." David sat silent as Roger criticized him.

"You get yerself intae scrapes and promises you believe you can just charm yer way out of, but when et all goes pear-shaped, we hear about it. Poor David—his lovely, enchanting woman was *RAPED* by the only person she might mistake for himself, and all he can entertain in his bloody mind is *HIS* wounded pride! I'll no' tolerate it, so I'm warnin' you, David—If—you dinnae mend things with that beautiful soul up there—I'll lose all respect for yeh and I'll no' be speakin' to yeh again, do you hear me?" he said with such emotion, that he hoped it put fear into David's heart.

David swallowed hard and whispered, "Aye."

Roger wanted to go upstairs to try and help her somehow. Her broken heart was too much to bear. Instead, he walked out the side door, ignored the reporters scrambling out of their cars, and entered the garage where he had been working on cleaning David's car after the fire. He sat in the passenger's seat, having to move the seat back to fit, and closed the door. Thoughts of his lovely wife, all those years ago, flooded his mind, and he cried.

When he was ready to leave, he opened the door and saw something in the footwell. He reached down and picked it up. "Ma Losh!" he said and went quickly back into the house.

Erin ended up on the floor, utterly exhausted and lying curled up, clutching her belly, holding the one thing that would forever link her with David Elliott. Her throat hurt from wailing, and she felt embarrassed at having done so. "I'm sorry, Ann—" she whispered.

"Nae, you had every right tae mourn and wail as you have. David was wrong to speak tae you as he did. Just rest now. Shall I help you to bed?" she asked.

"I—I can't stay in here. I—" she began, and Annis looked at her warmly.

"I reckon you'd not be keen tae stay in the flat now, either?" she said, and Erin shook her head. "Aye, I'll speak tae Millie; she doesn't use her room anamore, I'm sure she'll allow you to use it."

Erin's eyes filled with tears again. "I don't want to put anyone out or be a nuisance—" she said as Annis took her by the hand and helped her to stand.

"You'll never be a nuisance tae me, nor tae Millie, dear; we both think of you as our kin. I'll ask her straight away." She left the room, taking the bottle of sleeping pills with her.

Erin took her large, empty suitcase out of the closet, exhausted as she was, and lay it on the bed. Once again, she filled it, though she didn't have the strength to move it once it was full. All she wanted was to sleep, so she sat on the side of the bed, leaned over, and the soft feather tick cradled her.

She woke with David looking down on her with a tear-streaked, anxious face. She sprang up and went to the end of the bed. "What do you want? Go away," she yelled. *"Just wait till she's asleep, and she'll open her legs right up for yeh!"*

"I—I was so wrong—" he was saying as she looked for an escape. "I can't imagine what ye've been through, and for me tae—"

"Where's your mother? Ann!" she bellowed.

He took a step back. "A'right… I'll go. I'm sorry."

Annis returned, and seeing David standing there, scolded him. "Just what do you think yer doin' in here? Ye've done enough damage today. I would suggest you leave her alone now."

Erin's heart ached again; she loved him so much and wanted nothing more than to have him hold her, but he'd been so cruel that she also didn't want to look at him. He gazed at her with so much sadness and fear filling his eyes as he backed out of the room, then he was gone.

"Alright, dear, Millie has agreed tae your using her room; now, let's get you settled." Annis pulled the suitcase off the bed and rolled it to Millie's room, which was smaller than David's but very nice. It was painted light blue, and on the ceiling, there was a coffered pattern painted white. It was striking, and Erin loved it.

"Oh, that's so pretty!" she couldn't help but comment.

"I'm glad you like it! This was my room when I was a wee girl. I used tae trace the pattern with ma eyes in order tae help me fall asleep; worked a trick every time."

Out of nowhere, Erin thought about the date. "What is today's date?" she asked.

Startled, Annis replied, "It's the eighteenth of June, dear; why?"

Erin's face fell again. "Yesterday was my fifteenth anniversary… with my…husband, Todd. He was so good to me—He didn't deserve this," she said.

"Ach, yeh poor thing, if it's not one thing it's another for you. Why don't you take a wee kip, and I'll come for you at suppertime?" she said softly.

Erin didn't think she'd be hungry, but she agreed, and Annis left the room. She took her phone out of her pocket and found the last thing she'd sent to Todd. Through her tears, she slowly typed a message to the man she had once thought was the love of her life.

E: *I'm sorry. Please forgive me. You deserved so much better than me. Thank you for giving me all those years of love.*

Chapter Eighty-Three

SUPPER WITHOUT DAVID

Eight hours later, Erin woke from a knock on her door. She sat up, not knowing where she was at first. She wondered where David was, and then all the memories of the last twenty-four hours hit her like a punch in the gut. "Come in," she said as she swung her feet off the end of the bed.

Millie opened the door and stepped in. "Time for you tae come take yer supper," she said sweetly. "How're yeh feelin', love?"

Erin took a quick assessment of how she actually felt. "I feel like someone punched me in the guts, then slapped me, and then ran me over with a truck; other than that, I'm alright. Oh, thank you for allowing me to use your room!" she said gratefully.

"Yeh poor thing, dinnae think of et! Now come down and get yeh somethin' inte yer wame. I tried tae wake you for lunch, but you weren't havin' it," she said.

"Thanks for letting me sleep. I'll be right down; I need to brush my teeth and wash my face."

"A'right," Millie said and left the room, closing the door behind her.

Erin heard her phone notify her she'd gotten a reply from Todd. She'd forgotten that she sent him a message earlier and hesitated to look at it.

> T: *I need to know where to send the*
> *paperwork for the divorce. I think we*

should just do it and get it over with
so we can have a clean slate.

She hadn't expected that, and it hit her hard. Her eyes pricked with sudden and unwelcome tears. *No,* she thought, *you wanted a divorce, now don't get all weepy about it!*

> E: *I'll get it for you. I may be back for two weeks at the start of July, so do you want to send them now, and I'll bring them back, or just wait until I get there? Also, if you want to set up the court date for when I'll be there, that would be ok. I don't intend to take half of anything…I mean, you can have the house and your pension, etc. I would just like to get my things eventually. If you'd be ok with storing them until I have a permanent place to live, I would appreciate it very much.*

Ten minutes later, she descended the stairs and walked cautiously into the dining room. Roger stood and walked around the table to pull out her chair as she was seated in front of him. Annis was to her left and Millie was sat on her right. There were no other place settings at the table, and Annis saw her looking for David's seat. "David will not be joining us tonight; he will be eating in his room," she said.

Erin was torn; she desperately wanted both to and not to see him at the same time. "That's not necessary—I mean, if anyone should be eating in their room, it should be me! I'm the one who caused all of this in the first place," she said and put her head down.

The table erupted with noise, everyone disagreeing with her. "NO! Tha's no' how it is!" Roger said passionately.

"Dinnae think that way!" Millie said.

Annis took her hand. "Erin, ma dear, you are not at fault; dinnae fret," she said.

A tear ran down Erin's face. Her makeup had been washed off, and she knew her black eye was dark and purple, pooling at her cheekbone. "I—I just miss him. I know it's ridiculous, but—No, you're right! I need to give it some space," she said, trying to sound confident. Then her shoulders slumped, and she looked miserable. She tried to put on a brave face and eat her supper; she was starving, but it was difficult, and she couldn't eat much. Her mouth was dry, and everything stuck, not wanting to go down her throat when she tried to swallow.

"Ach, Erin, I found something of yers in the Triumph today," Roger said.

"You did?" she said distractedly.

"Aye. Yer handbag was caught under the seat—"

"Oh, Roger!" Erin's eyes smarted once again with hot tears. "That means I still have my passport and driver's license!" She let out a long sigh of relief and gave him a thankful smile.

"You were asleep, so I set it on the sideboard in the hallway below the stairs."

"Thank you."

When it was time for dessert, her heart skipped a beat when she saw David go into the kitchen and put his tray on the counter. He looked right at her, and she melted like butter on top of a toaster oven. She wanted to run to him, but the thought of what he'd said came back to her, and she looked away. When she was brave enough to look back up, he was gone.

After supper, Erin couldn't imagine sitting in the house, knowing David was just in the other room. She'd heard about Arthur's Seat the last time she was in Edinburgh, with Todd, but never had a chance to climb it. When she asked how difficult it would be to get there, Roger offered to take her.

She grabbed her purse and went upstairs to change into something comfortable to walk in. As she left Millie's room, she looked at the closed door to David's room. Her heart hurt so badly; it literally felt like someone was holding onto it, squeezing with all their might. She placed her palm on her chest, looked away, then descended the stairs.

When she entered the kitchen, she smiled up at Roger, who was carrying two vintage-looking walking sticks; one of them folded out into a little seat, which Erin thought was brilliant. They didn't need to worry about it being late; the sun didn't set until nearly ten, and Erin had just taken an eight-hour nap.

As they passed the kitchen, Millie handed her a satchel and thermos, "Hot tea, dear, and a wee bag of biscuits in case you need et," she said.

Roger led the way as they walked out the front door and down the driveway to the gate. As soon as they were seen, the reporters were roused, though, when they saw it wasn't David, they went back to their cars. The two friends walked past the Sheep Heid inn and restaurant, then turned, following an old path up to Queen's Drive.

They came to a beautiful loch backed by a tall, dark crag rising to the sky, which Roger told her was Dunsapie Loch. Then they turned onto a meadow-like path that led right up to Arthur's seat. It was steep, but they took their time and paced themselves. The path was smooth and grassy at first, and sometimes it was covered in carefully laid rocks as though a road had once been paved to the top. Occasionally, rocks jutted out, ready to trip you if you weren't watching your step, or loose gravel, that could make you slip.

When they were out of breath, they stopped to look out over the breathtaking city. As they climbed, Roger told her how David had thanked him for rescuing her, "I don't think he truly believed what he said to be true. I reckon he was just beside himself with anger and pain, knowing he couldnae do anathin' about et. Doesn't excuse him for sayin' et, but yeh may want tae keep it in mind," he said.

It was hard going as the path got steeper; Erin was glad for the walking stick and Roger's strong arm to help her up sometimes. Several times that evening, she caught herself wishing David were there, sharing the experience with her, although walking with Roger was much better than sitting in the house brooding. "This is a workout!" she said breathlessly at the halfway point, "I might just have to do this every day now that I know my way."

After about an hour or so of starting and stopping, they made it to the top, sweating and panting. However, once the heat of their exertion wore off, it was windy, and the evening air was quite chilly. Roger saw her shivering and offered her his long-sleeved flannel shirt. "Thank you," she said and put it on, surprised it fit her. "Oh, Roger! It's magnificent up here! You can see forever! I wish David—Well, I'm sure he's seen it already."

With Roger's help, Erin sat on the top of one of the two concrete plinth-like markers on the mountain's peak, looking out on the whole expanse of Edinburgh. She gazed across the Firth of Forth to the Kingdom of Fife, which made her think of John Thomas and then of David again. She suddenly felt weary and longed for home, a long bath, and for David to be the one giving it to her.

Roger opened the thermos, and they shared a cuppa, toasting 'King Arthur and his grand seat!' He told her how he'd brought his wife there before they'd gotten married and how she'd sat in the same spot Erin was when he'd proposed.

"I feel utterly exhausted now; I think we should go back," she said after a moment of silence, sorry to leave but too tired and sad to enjoy it like she wanted to.

It was faster on the way back, although descending the hill was hard on her feet, and there were many places she had to take hold of Roger's hand for stability. She was exhausted when she finally got to the nice, warm house and froze when she saw David coming down the stairs as they walked in. He saw her wearing Roger's shirt, and his face grew red.

She quickly took it off and handed it to Roger, who had also seen the look on David's face. "Et was cold at the peak; no need tae overreact, man!" he said. David looked at her black eye, closed his eyes, and turned around, stepping slowly back up the stairs without a word.

Aching from head to foot, she longed for things to be okay again. They didn't have much time before the children would be home from school for the summer, then he'd be filming in Wales, and then they'd have a newborn baby to take up all their time. "Thank you, Roger, it was so sweet of you to go with me. I need a nice long bath now; I'll see you tomorrow," she said with a weary smile, then gave him a hug and a peck on the cheek.

———

Roger took the walking stick and turned toward the kitchen to return the bag and thermos to Millie. He looked back at Erin as she climbed the stairs. *He'd better do right by her, or I swear I'll take her for ma own—if she'll have me,* he thought.

Yeh old fool; she'll no' have you, are yeh daft? Ye'd better get that notion out of yer heid, right now!"

When she got to the top of the stairs, Erin noticed that David's door wasn't closed all the way. She stood for too long, watching it, hoping to see him pass by the opening, or even better, come out, take her into his arms, and beg her to forgive him. She saw nothing, so she stepped into Millie's room and left the door open a crack as well. With a heavy sigh, she continued into the bathroom to draw a hot bath.

She took her clothes off, put some bath salts into the steaming water, and slowly eased herself into it. She remembered not to make it too hot; she didn't want to cook the baby, but after the cold wind outside, the water felt extra hot. She longed for David to appear at the door, to hear his voice saying her name, but the only thing she heard in her memory was, *"Just wait till she's asleep, and she'll open her legs right up for yeh!"* She lay there alone, soaking and crying softly.

A knock on the bedroom door startled her awake; she couldn't believe she'd allowed herself to fall asleep in the tub. "Erin?" she heard very softly coming from the bedroom, near the door to the bathroom. "Erin, please dinnae be afraid. I'll no' come in," David said. "I... was a coward and... a hypocrite today, and—Well, I am that, often, I reckon. I know you won't be forgivin' me for a long while, but I want yeh tae ken just how gutted I am over what I said."

She could hear him pacing and wanted to tell him to come in, to come and hold her, but she wasn't going to do that, not yet. It was one of the hardest things she'd ever make herself do, and it made her ache inside, but she couldn't let what he'd said become nothing. If she gave in too soon, it would be forgotten and made into something small instead of the enormous thing it was.

"I… didn't mean et, Erin; I don't believe that ye'd—Ye're no' to blame, he is! Oh, God, it's rippin' me tae shreds! How could he do that to you? And after I'd just told you… the first time ye'd run into him, that I'd no' leave yeh alone—Perhaps I'm tae blame—I should've taken yeh with me. You could've stayed at the house, where ye'd have been safe, no' here, alone and… and raped by that… worthless—"

Erin could hear him crying. Her heart was pounding in her ears, and her resolve was wearing thin, but she didn't say anything.

"I love you, Erin. Please, even if yeh can't forgive me, you have tae believe I love you," he said and then was silent for a few moments. "I'll go now—" he said, at last.

She wanted to jump out of the tub and take him into her arms.

"I'll wait for yeh tae decide how you feel—Whether you can go on with me… or not."

She waited a long time for him to say something more, but he didn't. She cried as she let the water out of the tub. *Why is this so hard? Why can't I let him be—To stew on things for a week or two?* She knew other people could, but it hadn't even been twelve hours since he'd been so cruel, and here she was, wanting to give in and make everything all better.

As she got out of the tub and reached for the towel, she saw him standing in the bedroom, watching her. She looked into his sad, bloodshot eyes, willing herself to be strong. Using every ounce of determination she had in her, she walked over and closed the bathroom door, trembling and shaking as sobs racked her body once again.

Stop bawling! You can't live the rest of your life going from pure joy to the depths of despair, she chided herself.

After a long time, and once the sobs had died down, she dried off the parts of her that hadn't already air-dried, then looked at herself in the full-length mirror behind the door. Her body had already changed a little bit since she'd met David. It made sense; she was eating differently, and walking much more, instead of sitting around the house, too tired to do anything.

What she could see of her body looked better than it had even two or three weeks earlier. *If I keep this up, I'll feel and look better than I have in a long time.* The last thing she wanted was to get huge with her pregnancy. Noticing a bathroom scale, she stepped onto it, and the dial stopped at 13. She looked closer and saw that it measured in stones. *What the—Now what does that mean? Is thirteen stones good or bad? How much does a stone weigh? I'll ask Ann in the morning.*

She closed the door, turned off the light, and decided to get into bed, not worrying about pajamas. She thought about David, laying in his bed, naked, as she crawled under the clean white sheets and ran her hand over her belly. It didn't feel any different; just two days before, David had kissed it and spoken to it with so much love and tenderness. As she thought about it, her heart started to melt, and she found herself longing desperately to pad over to his bedroom and climb into bed with him.

No! Not yet!

Longing for sleep to take her out of her torture, she closed her eyes. Suddenly, she felt the weight of Bran on top of her, smothering her; the smell of him, stale cigarettes, cheap booze, and body odor filled her nostrils.

She sat up, not able to take it any longer. She had to get away, or she would give in, and it would become meaningless and forgotten. *I'll go to Green Bay and get things finalized with the divorce. Maybe I can also pack up some of my things and ship them here,* she thought.

Chapter Eighty-Four

PACKING ... AGAIN

Erin got out of bed and pulled her suitcase out from under it so she could start packing some of her clothes. She wouldn't need her beautiful new outfits in Green Bay unless they met with a judge or something, so she only packed one. *Oh no! I can't leave; I don't have any money!* she thought, feeling utterly defeated.

"Dammit!" she said out loud and then sat hard on the bed. Almost immediately, she heard a light tap on her door, "Who is it?" she asked, hoping she hadn't woken anyone since it was very late.

"It's Annis, dear," she heard on the other side of the door.

Shit! Now I'm gonna have to tell her, she thought miserably. "One minute," she said and quickly put on her pajamas. "Come in." Annis was in her dressing gown and had a towel over her hair, turban-style. "I'm sorry if I woke you up."

The older woman smiled at her kindly. "You didn't wake me—I heard you say somethin' in frustration and thought to ask if I can help."

"Thanks, but I'm—I was just thinking of flying back home for a bit... to settle things with my... husband and get away from David for a few days, but I can't," she said.

Annis seemed confused. "I don't want you tae leave us, but why not? If it's a matter of money, I'll help you," she said.

"Well, I don't want to—" Erin said, choked up by her kindness.

"Well, ma dear, I know that David will help you if it would be easier to ask him. He also received a parcel from Crieff today; perhaps you might ask him what was in it… as a way to break the ice, so to speak?"

Erin's eyes grew wide; the last thing she wanted to do was talk to David. However, if it were about something practical, maybe she could do it. "I—"

"I can ask him for you if—" Annis began.

"No, I'll do it," Erin interrupted, "I'm a grown woman for Christ's sake. Oh! I'm sorry, I—"

Annis waved her hand. "Don't you worry, dear. Just talk to him." She turned away and then stuck her head back in, "His door is still open a wee bit."

Erin smiled at her. "Thanks," she said, wanting to call the amazing woman 'mum,' but she wouldn't until they were married.

What if we don't get married? What if this breaks us up? I can't think about that—

You always do this! You become dependent on someone, and when they hurt you, you break down and run back into their arms, only to have the same thing happen all over again! NO! This time I'm going to be strong, or I never will be.

She walked to her door with purpose and peered down the hall. David's door was still open a few inches, and the bedside lamp was on. *Just do it, Erin. Go on!* she thought and stepped into the hallway.

"Just wait till she's asleep, and she'll open her legs right up for yeh!" filled her mind once again.

Erin! Be a fucking adult!

She tiptoed to his door and stood there for a few seconds screwing up her courage. Her hand was raised, ready to knock, but then she heard a soft noise that sounded like talking and maybe even quiet sobs in between some of the words. She nearly walked away but knew if she didn't do it right away, she'd change her mind.

She knocked lightly on the door and then pushed it open a bit further. "It's me," she said, "I need to ask you about something." She heard him sniffle and pull a tissue from the box next to the bed.

"Come in," he said excitedly, so she stepped into the room. He was off the bed in a heartbeat, holding her in his arms and weeping. She didn't hug him back, so he loosened his hold. "Erin? What's the matter? Are you alright? I thought maybe ye'd—"

Erin braced herself, he was only wearing his boxers, and feeling his arms around her felt so good, so right, but she had a task to fulfill. "Your mum told me you got a box from Crieff today. I was wondering if—if it was from the cottage, and... if anything of mine was... salvaged?" she managed to ask calmly, and he stepped back.

"Aye, I wanted tae tell yeh, but—They found several items from your travel case." He turned on the room light and went to the desk where the box was sitting.

He looked so good standing before her, nearly naked. She had to fight to keep from breaking down, kissing him, and forgetting all about going back to Wisconsin. She noticed his eyes were red and bloodshot when he handed her the neat stack of her slightly charred possessions. "Thank you. Roger found my purse in Neela, so I have my Passport. I was—I'd like to go back to—"

"Are you... considering leavin' me? Of going back tae—tae Todd?" he said, his eyebrows knit together and his voice shaking with fear.

"What? Back to Todd? No. I—I just need to get away from here for a few days to get some things settled and—I don't know what. Get my head around what's happened here and maybe—" she said, haltingly.

He gently but firmly put his hands on her arms. "Please, Erin... don't leave me. I—I ken what I said was loathsome, but we can sort it out... can't we? Have I ruined everathin'?" he asked, beside himself with panic.

"I'm not leaving you, David. I'm upset, and I'm not ready to let it go just yet, but I'm not going to leave you—Not unless you want me to, and then— Then I still won't, because I love you. I just need some space."

David nodded, though he didn't seem fully convinced. "Please dinnae leave, not now. We can go together once—If you leave now... whilst yer upset—I'm afraid ye'll no' come back. Please, stay here with me—What can I do tae change yer mind?" he said and knelt before her, begging.

"I'll only be gone for a few days, but I need to leave here. I'm utterly dependent on you, and it scares me."

"Ach, I ken you'll leave meanin' tae return, but what if, when ye're with Todd again, you remember how you loved him and then… then chose him?" he said as tears rolled down his beautiful face.

Erin was hardly able to stand his torment. "That won't happen! I swear to you I'll come—"

"Please, ma love, please stay," he interrupted, wild-eyed and panicking as he took hold of her hand.

Erin wanted to hold him and tell him she would, but she couldn't do that. "Will you please help me?" she asked, trying to keep her cool. "I'll leave tomorrow and be back by Friday or Saturday. Also, would it be alright if I had some of my things sent here?"

———

"Yeh ken I'll help you, but—" he began but stopped, knowing that no amount of pleading would change her mind. "No, send yer things tae London. I'll give you the address as well as Tina's contact information. Have the bills sent to her," he said, governing his heart and ending his pleas for the time being. He stood, not three feet from her, and yet a thousand miles away.

He could hear his watch ticking on the bedside table and the sound of her breathing. It was torture for him not to reach over and pull her to him as he'd done when she'd first come in, but he knew she wouldn't respond. "Erin," he said as she turned to leave. "Please… please dinnae leave whilst ye're so angry at me. Can we at least make peace before you go?"

———

Erin turned around and gave him a quick hug. "I love you, but I need some time to… heal," she said, and then hurried back to Millie's room, shutting the door behind her, feeling utterly sick.

Holy Moses! What are you doing? Do you really think a man like him will wait around for you? You had better go right back in there and beg him to keep loving you! one side of her mind told her in fear.

If we can't be apart for a few nights, then this isn't real love anyway. Just relax and don't panic; if it's meant to be, it will all be fine… I hope.

Erin didn't want to leave, but she had to, if only to prove to herself that she could if she needed to. She wanted nothing more than to be in David's bed, being held and loved, but it would continue a pattern of dependency she was afraid of. She could still hear his voice pleading for her to stay, but what would that solve? How would that make anything better?

Honestly, she didn't know how leaving would solve anything either. So many things had happened to her in such a short amount of time, including almost being raped by Todd, learning she was pregnant, learning there were naked photos of her out there, having to give life-support to David's dying wife, being raped by Bran, and then, to top it all off, David blaming her for opening her legs for him. The thought of it all was so overwhelming; she needed to escape and process everything. She just hoped their relationship was strong enough to take it.

Do you really believe he'll be thinking of all those things while you're gone? More likely, his pride will be bruised, so he'll find someone else who won't leave the love of their life like an idiot!

She finished packing her suitcase, wishing she still had her carry-on and then thought maybe the extra room would come in handy on the way back. She thought it would be a good idea to let Todd know her plans, so she sent him a message.

> E: *My plans have changed. I'm coming to get things settled and send some of my stuff back here. I'll leave here tomorrow, so do you think the paperwork could be ready by then or early Friday at the latest? Sorry it's last minute.*

> T: *Are you ok? I'm sure the paperwork can be ready by then. Where will you be flying into? Should I pick you up?*

Where will you stay? You can stay here if you want to.

E: *I'm fine. I just want to get things settled, that's all. I don't have any information about the flight or where I'm staying, but it won't be there. I'm coming back here on Saturday, so it's a short trip. Do you still have those boxes in the garage rafters?*

T: *I'm glad you're ok. I think the boxes are still up there. I'll check on it and bring them down. Let me know if you need a ride or anything.*

E: *Thanks. I'll take a taxi to the house. Can I use my car while I'm there? That would help a lot.*

T: *Of course, you can. Let me know the details of when you'll arrive.*

Then she sent a message to Lily:

E: *Hi there! Sorry for the last-minute notice, but would you mind if I stayed with you tomorrow and Thurs night? I'll be in town to get the divorce worked out and to pack a few things.*

L: *Oh, I'd love for you to stay, but we're going up north... leaving in the morning. I'm so sorry we'll miss you!*

E: *Me too! I'll just stay at a hotel then, no big deal. I just thought I'd ask you first. I'll be alone this time.*

L: *Oh no! Is everything ok with you and David?*

E: *Yeah, everything's fine, just getting some things settled. Have fun up north!*

L: *Will do! Safe travels to you too! Xoxo*

Great, one more thing to ask David for. She *could* ask her group of girlfriends for a place to stay, but either they lived too far away to be practical, or they'd want to talk about her match, and even though they had no idea who he was, she really didn't want to talk about him. There was nothing she could do about it just then, so she put her suitcase on the floor and took her nightgown off.

She went into the bathroom and found her bottle of pills; it had two or three of everything, Ibuprofen, Acetaminophen, anti-diarrhea, and a few sleeping pills. She took out one sleeping pill, snapped it in half, and took it with a handful of tap water. It was bitter on her tongue, so she downed another handful of water to get the taste out. She needed to sleep, not lay there in bed feeling smothered by the ghost of Bran. After climbing into bed, she stared at the ceiling, thinking about Annis tracing the pattern of the moldings to fall asleep, and was out in only a few minutes.

Chapter Eighty-Five

FAREWELL FOR NOW

Erin woke up with a headache *and* morning sickness, which wasn't a pleasant combination. She brushed her teeth and fixed her hair, putting the toothbrush and comb Annis had given her into her small makeup bag. Thankfully, she'd left it there when she and David had gone to the cottage. She used concealer and foundation to cover the bruise the best she could, then she put the bag in her suitcase and got dressed, not looking forward to the day ahead.

She didn't want to make Millie come get her, so she opened the bedroom door and stepped out, seeing the last fleeting image of David's head descending the stairs. She knew it might be awkward, but she wasn't about to go back to her room just because he was also on his way downstairs. He had just sat in his usual spot at the table when she walked in. He began to stand, but she put her hand up. "Stay there; it's just breakfast. You shouldn't be forced to eat in your room just because we had a fight."

"Are yeh sure? I can go if it would make you more comfortable. I wasn't thinkin' when I sat here," he said anxiously.

"Stay. It's fine." She pulled the chair out and sat in her usual place, next to him.

"A'right, thank you," he said soberly. "Good mornin'."

"Good morning," she replied.

———

Annis and Millie were quiet when they arrived at the table. The day before had been so chaotic they were glad for the respite. They were waiting for Roger to come in, and as he approached the door, he only saw Erin. "Ach, Erin, how're yeh feelin' after yer climb last night?" he asked cheerfully.

He hadn't noticed the subtle awkwardness in the room, so when he walked in and saw David sitting next to her, he stopped and did a doubletake. He looked first at Ann, then Millie, and finally at Erin to understand what was happening. Annis and Millie gave him tiny shrugs, and Erin smiled.

"I feel good, a bit sore, though. I had a really good time, so it's worth it. No pain, no gain, right? Thanks again, Roger," she said. She took a sip of her tea and reached for a triangle of toast.

David sat eating his food without saying anything and without looking up.

"My… pleasure," Roger replied, a bit awkwardly. "Did you plan on goin' back today, as you said yeh might?"

She swallowed the bite of toast and jelly she'd just bitten off. "No, I won't be able to; I'm taking a flight back to America sometime today. I was going to ask if you wouldn't mind taking me to the airport? I'm not sure of the time yet," she said calmly.

Roger's mouth hung open; he blinked several times and looked around the table in complete shock. "Aye, of course, I will, but you cannae be leavin' us, Erin. Can't you… and David sort things out?" He knew it wasn't his place to comment on their relationship, but it was such a shock, he couldn't help himself.

"I'm not leaving for good, Roger; I'll be back in a few days. I need to get some things settled back home, and… let things cool off a bit here."

David still hadn't looked up or said anything.

"Aren't you gonnae try tae stop her?" Roger said to him, utterly dismayed that he was sitting there with his head down, allowing her to get away… allowing her to leave with no guarantee she'd return.

David closed his eyes but didn't look up. "I tried, mate," he whispered.

"David," Erin said, casually. At hearing her say his name, he startled and looked at her. "I don't suppose you've messaged Tina yet, have you?"

"Aye, she's workin' on it now," he said quietly.

"Could you please ask her to add a hotel room? I'll use my old car while I'm there. Todd—" At that name, David tensed. "…said I could," she finished softly.

"Aye," was all he said, then he stood and took his plate and coffee cup into the kitchen. Erin closed her eyes as they all heard him put his dishes on the counter and then go up the stairs.

"Todd is yer husband then?" Millie said gently.

"Aye. David thinks I'm going to run back into his arms and not come back."

"And are you?" Annis asked.

Erin flinched and looked at the woman in disbelief. "No! No, I'm not! I… can't believe you just asked me that," she said defensively.

"Now, don't get upset, dear. I didn't mean tae imply anathing, I just… wanted tae hear it from you, that's all," she said.

———

Erin's phone started to play the theme from *Future Explorations*, so she knew it was a message from David. "I am not going to leave him for Todd. I'll be back, I promise. Please, excuse me." She stood and read it.

> D: *Tina has it all sorted. I'll forward her
> message. Also, would you please come
> up? I need to give you something.*

She scanned the forwarded message from Tina and saw the whole itinerary mapped out. "Roger, we need to get going right away! I wonder if David might let you use Neela?" she said, drinking down the remainder of her tea.

"Neela? What's that?" he asked, appearing confused.

"It's his car's name; I'll explain it on the way. Oh, and I'll bring my suitcase down with me."

"No, I'll fetch it for yeh. Et's in Millie's room then?" he said, still looking sad and unsure of the whole plan.

"Aye." She ran up the stairs, though when she saw the door to David's room, she slowed her pace. When she knocked, he opened the door, allowing her to come in. "What is it? I've really got to get going," she said.

———

David studied her face; she was wearing makeup, but he could still see the bruise, which was already turning yellow and green, and it made him feel horrible. "I have some money for you—There are pounds and dollars in there," he said and pointed to a white, letter-sized envelope lying on the desktop. "Ye'll need cash whilst ye're—There's a credit card for you tae use, as well; I've cleared it with the card company. Use it tae send yer things back, or... anathin' you need. The address to ma home in London is in there as well. Erin—"

He took hold of her arms and kissed her, praying she'd miraculously change her mind, but she didn't respond, so he let her go. "I love you, Erin. Please dinnae forget—" He had a sudden flashback to the greeting card he'd read after he'd folded the clothes in her suitcase in New Orleans. Todd had written, '*Please don't forget about us.*' David felt a pang of pity for how he must have felt when the woman he loved more than anything walked out the door to meet a stranger in order to have sex with him.

"I love you too, and don't worry; I won't forget. I'll be back in a few days."

She hadn't planned on falling in love with her match. She most likely said the same thing to Todd. 'Don't worry, I'll be back in a few days—I love you,' and look how it turned out for him? David thought, still afraid she'd leave and be gone for good.

———

She took the envelope off the desk, "Thank you for helping me with this," she said, and stood on her tiptoes to kiss his cheek, then she turned to leave. "Oh, one more thing—would you mind if Roger used Neela to take me to the airport? She really should be used."

"Aye, I'll let him know," he said without emotion.

"Thank you, David." She wanted to go back to hug him, but she heard, *"Just wait till she's asleep..."* and walked out the door. She quickly looked over her room to make sure she hadn't forgotten anything she might need and then remembered her US cellphone. She heard David leave his room and go down the stairs, so she slipped into his room again, took her old phone from the nightstand drawer, and left.

Roger had Neela out of the garage and purring away in the driveway as Erin hugged and kissed Annis and Millie. She felt so sad, yet it was what she needed to do. Roger was holding the car door open for her, so she got in and buckled up. He slipped into the driver's seat, and they slowly rolled down the driveway. The reporters sat with their mouths open, watching the sexy classic car leave the drive and turn away from them.

They didn't have time for the opening and closing of the gate, so for once, Roger left it open. Erin wanted to look back, though she knew David wouldn't be outside, not with reporters sitting there, so she smiled at Roger, who looked like a kid using his friend's toy and trying to be extra careful with it.

"Are yeh truly alright, Erin?" Roger asked as they drove through the streets of Edinburgh. "And ye'll be comin' back? I don't think David will be able tae live without you."

"Aye, I'll be back. I'm having my things sent to his house in London. I just—I need to prove to myself that I can do it," she said and closed her eyes.

"Erin—" he said and then hesitated. He wanted to say she could count on him. That he would take care of her if she needed him to, and well, none of that mattered. He couldn't say those things; it would ruin their friendship. Instead, he said, "He's worth comin' back for, remember?"

"Aye."

"We'll miss yeh."

Erin smiled and put her hand on his shoulder. He looked at her and saw that she was smiling, though tears were falling down her face. "I'll miss you too," she whispered.

They arrived at the terminal, and he drove into the departures drop-off area, which looked like a parking garage, then he took her suitcase out of the small trunk. She hugged him, holding on for longer than usual. He felt her shaking and held her until she'd gotten herself under control once more. It took all his self-control not to pet her hair and then kiss her as she stepped away from him. "Dinnae worry, I'll see yeh in a few days' time, eh?" he said.

She smiled sadly, nodded, and then walked away into the terminal. He watched her, wanting to keep her from leaving, doubting that she would really come back, even though she thought she would then. When he could no longer see her, he got back into Neela and pulled away from the pavement. He headed back to Owlgate, sad and not enjoying his one chance to drive her.

DISCLAIMER

Striking of the Match is a work of fiction. The drug, Fertilis, the disease, the Fertilis Defect, and all treatment methods, and 'science' behind it are a work of fiction and have come from the author's imagination. Any resemblance to real diseases or drugs is coincidental, and no offense is intended on its portrayal or treatment.

ACKNOWLEDGEMENT

Special thanks to my mom, Christy, for being a really great mom and to my dad, Ron, for teaching me so many things I didn't know I'd need to know.

To my daughter, Elizabeth, for reading everything until you just couldn't anymore, and for helping me so very much! I love you!

To Pragya for her fantastic medical and scientific knowledge! You've helped to make my story believable! I owe you so much!

Thanks to my buddy, Marshal Dillon, who's helped me so much with this book!

To Becky, who's always ready to help, encourage, and give me the courage I need to make hard decisions!

Thanks to Marni MacRae, for editing this monster and for all the good advice (even if I sometimes chose to go another way)!

Thanks to my cover designer, Rehman, you are so great to work with, and I'm thankful that I found you!

Thanks to Linda and Tori for beta reading for me!

To the sisterhood of the heart for being amazing and for the crazy weekends!

Again, thanks to Chris and Sue Graham for their wonderful hospitality! Next stop, ROME!

Thanks to everyone who read my first book, Meet Your Match, and then begged me for the next one!

www.ingramcontent.com/pod-product-compliance
Lightning Source LLC
Chambersburg PA
CBHW050842210726
48290CB00004B/1049